PROOF EVIDENT

A SUSPENSE OF MIND CONTROL, DECEIT
AND HIGH STAKES LAWYERING.

JOHN DICKE, PSY.D., J.D.

PROOF EVIDENT
PUBLISHED BY SYNERGY BOOKS
2100 Kramer Lane, Suite 300
Austin, Texas 78758

For more information about our books, please write to us, call 512.478.2028, or visit our website as www.bookpros.com.

All characters in Proof Evident are entirely fictional. Any resemblance to any person now living is entirely COINCIDENTAL.

ISBN-13: 978-0-9764981-5-5
ISBN-10: 0-9764981-5-4

Publisher's Cataloging-in-Publication
(Provided by Quality Books, Inc.)

Dicke, John.
    Proof evident / by John Dicke.
    p. cm.
    LCCN 2005926621
    ISBN 0-9764981-5-4

    1. United States. Central Intelligence Agency—
Fiction.   2. Insanity—Jurisprudence—Fiction.
3. Brainwashing—Fiction.   4. Ohio—Fiction.   5. Legal
stories.   I. Title.

    PS3604.I283P76 2006   813'.6
                                QBI05-600061

10 9 8 7 6 5 4 3 2 1

To Cari

PROLOGUE

Although frigid outside this early January morning, the bedroom was cozy. Thick comforters and lush pillows protected and supported the two naked bodies. Despite being middle-aged, they had taken good care of themselves and one another in the seventeen years they had been married; they still had flat bellies and toned bodies. Their passion and love for one another had not waned.

That morning, their talk had been with their bodies. When that was complete, Betty broke their trance. "Tough day today, honey?" she asked in just slightly more than a whisper.

"The only thing I have to do," replied Gene, "is speak before the Downtown Rotary Club, just a little half-hour thing. The rest of the day is going to be the normal hassle."

"Maybe you'll have the energy to take me out for dinner tonight? We haven't done much of that lately."

"It's a deal," he said apologetically. "I'm sorry. I'm still really tired. Remind me not to run for office again, at least not for another four years." Gene had been elected county sheriff by a thin margin in the November general elections. The race had been brutal. "This very moment is the best I've felt in months," he added, knowing that would end quickly once he left his wife's arms and walked into the frigid morning air, and then to the hurly-burly rat race of his office. "What about you?"

5

"I have some stuff to do around the house, and then there's a meeting at school with the principal. This PTA stuff is extremely time-consuming, and I really doubt it's very productive," Betty sighed. "The usual problems—the teachers and school administrators put their needs ahead of the kids while pretending selflessness. You know, we've talked about it."

"Just like all bureaucracies, and mine is no different. If I ever get to the place where it's more important for me to get my ass kissed than to do my job, I want you to promise to tell me so I can move on."

"Maybe you need to talk about that in your speech today at Rotary."

"What? Getting my ass kissed? I'm sure the Rotarians would be interested in that," Gene said playfully. "Of course, that's what they do to one another at Rotary meetings—kiss each other's ass." He chuckled. "I know. I had to do enough of it when I was running for this office. It's what the whole world does. Anyway, after I get done kissing the Rotarians' collective asses, and they get done kissing mine, I'll go back and start to untangle the mess in the department."

Betty adroitly rolled on top of him, looked straight into his eyes, and thought what a wonderful man she had married. He was thinking the same thing about her as he looked into her eyes.

They reached for each other's lips—then tongues. "It's wonderful we can still share this," Gene whispered into Betty's ear. "Maybe we can share more of it tonight."

Monday—8:00 A.M.
Sinclair University, Dayton, Ohio

The students filed into the classroom ready to begin their Evidence class; their cheeks were red from the morning cold. Most of them were just beginning to appreciate the importance of this course. They had started the term believing that restraining, arresting, shooting, fighting and self-defense were all that were important in becoming cops. They were just now beginning to understand that it didn't make any difference how much butt they kicked on the street— if they didn't know how to present the evidence, all their thumping was meaningless. If they blew their testimony in court, the defendant could get on the elevator with them and walk out of the courthouse, call them punks and pigs and get away with it.

Their professor had already covered competency, relevancy and foundation in the class. That was easy; it was this hearsay stuff that was a big problem—it was so abstract. It didn't have the exactness of guns, bullets and handcuffs. It just seemed way too early on this frigid morning to be talking about hearsay, but it wasn't like they had a choice; that was what the professor, Avery Jackson, was teaching today.

Jackson, a slight, middle-aged, black man with salt and pepper hair, began by asking, "What's hearsay?" He looked around for responses; nearly everyone was frozen with fear until one female recruit with piercing dark eyes raised her hand: Marvella Dixon. She always seemed to have the answers. Professor Jackson acknowledged her with a nod of his head. "Marvella?"

She spoke haltingly. "It's just like on television. It's when a person hears something from someone else, and they're trying to use it in court as evidence—what that person heard—to prove something."

Jackson smiled. He had always believed the hearsay rule was the most difficult concept in law to master next to the Rule Against Perpetuities, an arcane property rule about the vesting of land. "That's not bad, but it is more than that. If I came into class, still freezing, and yelled, 'God, it's cold today!' and you were later called as a witness in a case where today's weather was relevant, could my statement be used to prove that it *was* cold today?"

Blank stares everywhere.

"Shit," somebody mumbled.

Marvella answered again, this time even more haltingly. "No—because the statement would be considered hearsay?"

"Good," Jackson complimented her. "Okay then, what if in the same trial the statement were presented to prove that I was exasperated when I came into class—I was unsettled emotionally because I yelled loudly, 'God, it's cold today!?'"

"Of course, that would be hearsay, too," Marvella said.

"No, that's not hearsay," Jackson said.

The recruits who could follow what was going on were flabbergasted.

"Why? What's the difference between the two statements?" Marvella asked, deflated.

"Because in the first example, the statement 'God, it's cold' was offered to prove the truth of the matter asserted in the statement: namely, that it is cold. In the second example, the statement was not being offered to prove the truth of the statement, but rather to prove that I was exasperated when I came into the room."

"I don't get it," Marvella sighed.

"I know a lot of lawyers and judges who don't get it either, so it's important that you learn it; you'll have a leg up on all of them. These are the things we'll be talking about in here for the next few weeks, and I expect you to be able to understand and apply the hearsay rule to statements you get from criminal defendants and other witnesses in criminal cases. If you ever rise to detective level, you'll need to know these fundamental principles. Read the chapter on Hearsay for tomorrow. Expect to be completely confused for awhile."

The class looked defeated.

"Don't worry about it," Jackson assured them. "You'll get it eventually." An hour later, he called out, "You're done here today. Don't freeze."

Avery Jackson felt a tinge of loneliness as the class got up, put on their coats, gloves and earmuffs and started filing out of the room. Usually, a bunch of students swarmed him after class. Not today; only Marvella had the courage to ask questions about hearsay without fear of making a fool of herself.

"I hope you're going to *really* explain this stuff to us," she implored him.

"Of course, I will. It's just a very tricky concept, Marvella. By the way, I admired your courage today. You had the guts to take risks on a very difficult topic."

Marvella blushed. It wasn't often one got a compliment from a professor and ex-judge.

Avery responded to her blush with another encouraging, "Don't worry, we'll spend lots of time on it. You'll get it in a very short time. Okay?"

Marvella nodded but felt unsure. She left the room along with the last of her classmates.

Jackson loved the hearsay rule. He was no longer a judge applying it, though, because he had lost the last election in the midst of an avalanche of bad publicity after sentencing a two-time rapist to probation. The press had eaten him up. There'd been one blistering editorial after another at election time, and he was toast with the voters. Women's groups were ready to castrate him. Law enforcement organized against him. Secretly, the crudest of the male lawyers and cops called him "Easy Pussy," and snickered at him. He'd ultimately been beaten in a landslide by a Republican in a Democratic county.

Judge Jackson's career on the bench was over. The question was, where could he go and still make a living in the law? Big firms wouldn't want him; he would've been bad for their image. He couldn't go to the district attorney's office; they'd appear "light on crime" by associating with him. He'd already been unsuccessful as a public defender. Academia was his only refuge. He fell back on his political connections, who pulled strings to get him this position as an associate professor at Sinclair University.

Avery loved teaching but felt underemployed. He knew he wasn't using his law degree or his experience to its fullest. And he didn't know how he was going to be able to keep his two kids in college and support a wife on forty-five thousand dollars a year, a huge comedown from the one hundred three thousand a year he'd made as a judge. Maybe a cup of coffee would help soothe his worries; he could smell its aroma coming down the hall from the snack bar. He would head down there for coffee and the morning paper as soon as all his students had left the classroom.

CHAPTER 1

Monday, January 15—12 noon
Renaissance Hotel, Dayton, Ohio

Dayton is a city in the Ohio Valley with a population of roughly a half million people. Just up I-75 from Cincinnati, it is intersected by I-70, making it a major mid-western, commercial hub. Its culture appeals to basic human nature or, perhaps more accurately, is a product of it. While Cincinnati is relatively highbrow, Dayton is more lowbrow. Larry Flynt of *Hustler* fame got his start in Dayton when he opened the Hustler Bar, a strip joint, where he indulged his prodigious, sexual appetite with his dancers before sexual harassment became a concept. The Hustler did so well in Dayton that several other Flynt strip joints successfully joined it.

Dayton is the home of the Wright Brothers and Jonathan Winters. It has Wright-Patterson Air Force Base. It used to have National Cash Register when the big, mechanical cash registers were used. High-tech industry has taken its place there, just as it has changed the fabric of much of America.

Dayton has the Great Miami River. It is a muddy brown and meanders from the rich farmland in the north to the Ohio River in the south. It has been ruined by pollution from the many industries that have abused it over the years. It's making a comeback, though. Along the Miami are huge oak and maple trees that add lushness to the countryside and the city where the river runs close to the Dayton Art Institute, Sinclair University and the downtown Justice Center. The county jail and state and federal courts are all just two blocks from the river.

Like many mid-American cities, Dayton has rich people, a big middle-class and a lot of poor people. The rich people and the people with status, like doctors, lawyers and judges, live in the southern areas like Oakwood, Kettering and Centerville. Poor African-Americans—simply called niggers—live north; poor whites—called briars—live east. The middle and upper classes look at both groups with disdain. According to them, the less-privileged are both the cause and source of all the city's crime and rowdy behavior.

The Montgomery County Jail and courts experience a steady flow of poor whites and blacks, with a sprinkling of middle-class whites and blacks, some Hispanics and an occasional Jew who may have been involved in some white-collar crime. The tension between the poor blacks and poor whites is considerable. It is contained, however, as long as these groups stay in their own part of town, steal from their own, fight in their own bars and don't screw each other's women.

Dayton has lots of needles and drugs, which leads to burglaries and thefts—got to support the habit. With those burglaries and thefts come lawyers. The lawyers typically defend thieves with a SODDI defense (Some Other Dude Done It). Then there are lots of bar fights and killings. These defendants are defended with a DDI defense (Dude Deserved It). Like everywhere else in the country, there are many domestic-violence cases. These are defended with a BDI defense (Bitch Deserved It). If the truth be known, Dayton is an all-American city in spite of what the politicians and media tell us about justice in America, it all runs pretty much like Dayton.

* * *

It was bitterly cold on this day. Steam wafted from the partially-frozen Miami into the frigid air. The gray, overcast sky sat like a shroud covering the city. Gene Hardacre, the newly-elected, Republican sheriff of Montgomery County, was preparing to give a thirty-minute speech in the ballroom of the Renaissance Hotel before the Rotary Club of Downtown Dayton.

The Renaissance was located in the heart of the city, just a block from the Justice Center. It was the ideal meeting place for the many downtown merchants, doctors, lawyers and accountants who wanted to get out of the office, do a little networking and have a nice lunch. It was noon and a hundred and fifty Rotarians filled fifteen tables in the large room. Gold and white filigree mirrors covered the walls. Crystal chandeliers hung high above an intricately-designed parquet floor. White linens and red napkins adorned each table. Red, yellow and white roses were centered on the white-linen tablecloths. The tables were clustered toward the front of the room, where the head table was reserved for officers of the club and the speaker. A wooden podium with the Renaissance logo divided the head table in half. Channels Two and Four were videotaping the sheriff's speech for the evening news.

District Attorney Alec Hunter normally attended these Rotary Club functions and encouraged his deputies to also attend. He knew it was good politics for him to be involved in the city's affairs and have relationships with community leaders other than just the lawyers. His sixteen years in office and four successful re-elections proved his political and legal acumen.

Today, though, other people occupied the table where he and his senior staff normally sat. Hunter and his entire staff had an in-service program on jury selection and would not be coming to the Rotary meeting. In attendance at Rotary were a number of judges, including the Presiding Judge Karl Kessler, Appellate Court Judge Wulf, and Municipal Court Judge Duncan. They were all Democrats. Hunter was a Republican.

"Wonder where Hunter is today?" Kessler asked his colleagues. "He never misses a chance to endear himself to the electorate."

Wulf, a legal scholar, replied, "I wonder. Maybe he couldn't get all of his Armani suits back from the cleaners on time."

The three men laughed, but while they made fun of Hunter, they also envied him. None of them could argue with Alec Hunter's success with the voters. In many ways he'd been far more successful and popular than any of them had been.

The defense bar, a group of iconoclasts by nature, was predictably missing.

One thing about the Rotary Club is that it always starts on time. Aubrey Shell, the president, was standing at the podium fidgeting with his tie. He gazed at his audience and the room. Nearly every seat was taken. Members were just finishing their salad and were settling in for the main course as they listened to Aubrey. Waitresses and waiters hovered over the tables with pitchers of steaming coffee, iced tea and cold water.

"Welcome back, fellow Rotarians, from the trials and tribulations of the holidays," he started. He was never at a loss for trite phrases. "I, for one, am glad to be back and hope we can approach this year with the same vigor as we did last year. We raised ten grand for our scholarship fund. This year we need at least another ten grand to meet our projected goal; we're attempting to fund the same number of students as last year. Be thinking of projects or donors who can help us meet this goal. You all need to be congratulated because the annual Christmas party and dance were a success. We made a profit of twenty-two hundred dollars from the event. So, we all need to give ourselves a round of applause."

A few Rotarians clapped their hands, but most were more interested in their food and making idle chit-chat with their friends. Aubrey, sensing he could lose his audience, decided to move on to the next topic. He fiddled with his tie nervously. "Let's move right along to the meat of today's program. I think that would be fitting since we had no meat with lunch." Again, there were a few chuckles from the audience in the farm belt that lives and dies with beef, pork and poultry. Back to the tie.

"Today, we have as our special guest the newly-elected, Republican sheriff of Montgomery County, Gene Hardacre. This is a man who had the power and wherewithal to defeat the incumbent and long-time sheriff of Montgomery County in a sometimes bitter and hotly-contested election. I'm standing here looking at his vitae, and I see that he is a native of Montgomery County who went to high school here and college at Sinclair just a few blocks from here. He graduated from the police academy twenty-two years ago. This is a man who has paid his dues, having worked as a Dayton police officer for years. Then he got the political bug and decided to run for office. He has numerous decorations for bravery in the line of duty and has earned the respect of the entire law enforcement community. He is a husband and the father of two children, both of whom are in high school here in Dayton. Let me introduce you to Sheriff Gene Hardacre."

Aubrey joined in the applause with the other Rotarians. The audience was interested in hearing from Sheriff Hardacre. They had seen his political advertisements on television and heard his spots on radio. He had run on a "stamp out corruption and crime" platform against incumbent Hugh Lane and won, but only by one percent.

Hugh Lane had been a popular figure in the area for twenty years. He had won five successive elections and was a Vietnam War hero, having been decorated with a Silver Star and Purple Heart. He parlayed his war record, tough-guy attitude, John Wayne good-looks and swagger into an election victory just five years after returning from the war, when he had no real law-enforcement experience at all. The Rotarians had come to see Gene Hardacre, the man who had defeated Lane.

Sheriff Hardacre got up slowly from his seat. As he rose, he took his red napkin, placed it next to his plate of half-eaten pasta and approached the podium. The television videocams began to roll. They captured the nervous smile of a man obviously appreciative of the applause but nervous about speaking in front of such a large crowd. Sure, he was a politician and had done this many times during the election, but it still scared him. He pulled a piece of paper out of his breast pocket. He felt as if he still needed votes. He put the paper on the podium and looked at his audience.

Aubrey Shell sat down at his place at the table to the right of the podium.

Sheriff Hardacre began to speak, "Thank you for the kind introduction, Aubrey. I'm not good with jokes so I'll just jump right in. This is my first public appearance since being sworn in and taking office on January second. I'm proud to have been elected to carry out a mandate to clean up this city. We have a daunting task here in Dayton. During the past twenty years, crime has escalated almost geometrically. Two months ago, it wasn't safe for me to admit that this was not *all* the fault of my predecessor." A few chuckles. "The growth of our city, and its location in the heartland of America and on two great thoroughfares, has contributed not only to the strength of, but also to the blight on this city. Gambling, prostitution, drug use and sales have prospered here in Dayton for years. Our homes have not been safe because addicts have to become thieves to support their habits. People have always killed over drugs, women and alcohol. They just seem to do it more in Dayton."

Was this just another politician who defines a problem and then gives no meaningful way to solve it? Waiters and waitresses were pouring coffee and filling-up water and tea glasses while at the same time picking up dessert plates full of half-eaten cheesecake. Few people noticed the small, slightly-built, black man who entered the room all bundled up with his hands in the pockets of his overcoat. Why would they? He was a long-time Rotarian and former judge. He looked normal enough. It was a frigid day, so of course he had on an overcoat. Everyone did. Except for the fact he was black, he looked like many of the Rotarians. He began circling to the right of the ballroom, acknowledging no one, his eyes fixed on Sheriff Hardacre.

As he approached the dais, Aubrey recognized him as Professor Avery Jackson, a long-term Daytonian and Rotarian. Probably just late for the meeting, Aubrey thought.

Sheriff Hardacre began moving into the heart of his speech. The videocams continued to run. "You might ask how we in law enforcement can create a better Dayton. It is my opinion that police officers must become part of the community. Over the years, police officers have become increasingly isolated; they operate from their cars; they no longer walk beats; they no longer know the members of their community, except for the criminals. I intend to change that."

Professor Jackson had almost reached the podium. He was certain to be taking off his coat and seating himself at the judges' table along with Kessler, Duncan and Wulf. After all, they had at one time all occupied the bench together, were from the same party and there was an open seat at the table.

But instead of sitting, he withdrew a .38-caliber handgun from his overcoat pocket as Hardacre was saying, "Beginning immediately, we will be opening satellite offices. I—Avery—? Judge?"

Jackson purposefully raised the gun and pointed it directly at Hardacre, who raised his left hand to protect his head while reaching beneath the lapel of his sport coat for his own gun.

It was too late.

A bullet exploded. The sound was sharp and clear and echoed throughout the room.

The slug passed through the webbing of Sheriff Hardacre's outstretched hand and entered his left frontal lobe just above his eye. The hollow-point bullet exited the right parietal lobe taking off the back half of Hardacre's head. Fragments of his skull flew backward, and part of his brain now covered the front of Aubrey Shell's shirt. Blood was everywhere.

The shooter looked dazed. He dropped the gun and just stood there watching as Hardacre fell to the floor, the blood draining from his body into a dark-red pool that was soaking him as he lay in it, dead. Professor Avery Jackson turned to face the transfixed audience.

Time stopped. No one moved. Both the witnesses and Avery Jackson, the shooter, were frozen.

Then time started up again in fast-forward. Rotarians more removed from the violence ran from the room while punching 9-1-1 on their cell phones. The judges and Aubrey Shell were but a few feet from the now unarmed, former judge. They all stared at him, trying to determine whether it was safe to rush the man they all knew and had once trusted. Shell saw the gun on the floor. He leaped over the head table onto Jackson's back. As Shell landed on the professor, Judge Duncan lunged forward and subdued him while his colleagues and other Rotarians jumped on top of him. Jackson put up no resistance under this football pileup. In the midst of all the confusion, Judge Kessler spotted the .38 on the floor and secured it by taking a knife off his table, running its small end under the trigger guard and putting it on the table.

The videocams continued to run.

Deputies from the sheriff's department and Dayton Police force arrived within minutes. Not knowing if there were more shooters, they came into the room with guns drawn, yelling, "GET DOWN, GET DOWN!!" They stormed the ballroom and quickly took over for Shell and the judges, slamming handcuffs on Avery Jackson, a man whose court they had testified in and brought their prisoners to.

Everyone looked at Sheriff Hardacre; his body was perfectly still. Rage simmered among the police. If there had not been so many witnesses, the deputies would have imposed a sentence of death and executed it immediately.

Third Street, just outside the Renaissance, was chaos: police cars, ambulances and the SWAT team, sirens screaming, flashing yellow lights, a cacophony of police radios. A cadre of emergency medical technicians emerged from the hotel lobby to the portico and hurriedly placed the gurney carrying Sheriff Hardacre's body into the ambulance. An oxygen mask was on his face and an IV was in his arm, heroic gestures to deny the reality and finality of the event.

Third Street is one-way, running east to west. Six police cars had already been parked crosswise on it, east of the hotel, to bar traffic that was already backed up for blocks from entering the street. Steamy exhaust billowed from each tailpipe. Despite the bitter cold, drivers and passengers emerged from their cars in an effort to find out what was happening. The ambulance whirled around, righted itself and sped west from the portico, its siren going full blast and its bubble-top spinning. The emergency room was only blocks away; its function this day would be to validate what everyone close to the horror suspected.

With hundreds of people now milling around the barricade of police cars, six officers emerged from the Renaissance holding a handcuffed, black man tightly. The spectators had only seconds to see his face before he was whisked into the police car. The cruiser whirled about, wheels screeching, sirens blaring, heading just two blocks to the county jail to be booked and interrogated.

"Everyone knew he was having some problems with the DiSalvo rape case. I heard he was drinking, but to fall this far? Unbelievable," one black officer whispered to another.

"Scumbag, oughta fry," one white cop said.

"Avery Jackson is no scumbag," the black cop retorted.

"He should fry just like anyone else who commits murder," the white officer declared. The two cops approached each other with fists clenched and hatred in their eyes.

"Break it up. Break it up. Hold on there," the cooler-headed cops implored these incipient gladiators. The two separated, still seething contempt for one another, each symbolizing what the other abhorred. Other officers just shook their heads not knowing what to think. Their shock, and the shock of the community, would continue for months.

Monday—12:51 P.M.
Montgomery County Public Defender's Office

On the opposite side of Third Street from the Renaissance Hotel is the Montgomery County Public Defender's Office. Established in 1972 with federal money, it has grown from a five-man office to thirty trial lawyers and an appellate division, and is now funded by Montgomery County. The trial lawyers' offices are on the lower floor of the two-story building, and the appellate lawyers are upstairs close to the law library. Unlike the big-money mills down the street that represent corporations and specialize in tax law and estate planning, the public defender's office has no rich-cherry paneling, marble floors or thick, white carpet. Its walls are textured sheetrock with off-white paint. If a lawyer wants to fix up his walls, he or she can hang diplomas.

Public defenders look at corporate and civil lawyers as pansies because they rarely venture as gladiators into the ring of the courtroom. It is not unusual for a deputy public defender to try two jury trials a week. While a jury is deliberating the fate of one defendant, a public defender is most likely picking a jury for his or her second trial of the week. Some of their cases are well investigated and some aren't. What the public defenders sometime lack in terms of investigation and case preparation, they make up for with superior trial experience, knowledge of criminal law and procedure, sheer guts and survival instincts. While some clients believe that their public defenders are not "real" lawyers, most of them are in fact very good lawyers. Some great trial-lawyers and judges have been public defenders. A lousy lawyer in the public defender system does not survive because his colleagues ostracize him or her.

Burt Porter, one of the charter lawyers from 1972, runs the Montgomery County office. Everyone else that started with him has long since gone into private practice or become a judge. Now fifty-five years old, Porter has tried hundreds of cases, walked clients he had no business walking and lost cases he should have won. He is tough, knowledgeable and he cares. If he ever feels one of his deputies has sold out a client, no matter how despicable the person or his crime, that deputy is history. Porter is both revered and feared by his deputies, especially those who have not been with the office long. He is an icon not only in the office, but in the Dayton legal community as well.

This January day, Porter could hear the screams of sirens and screeching tires. He wandered outside and saw one of his deputies, Yolanda Crone, running across Third Street to the office. A young, black, attractive woman just out of law school, she was bundled in a long, charcoal-color, wool coat with a black, felt collar and scarf, with steam blowing from her mouth. She'd been coming back from a morning in municipal court when she'd seen and heard the commotion that drew her to the front of the Renaissance.

"What the hell is going on?" Burt asked.

Yolanda could feel her throat tighten; this was unexpectedly one of her first conversations with Burt since he had hired her. She'd just passed the Ohio Bar, was still uncertain of herself, but was certainly in awe of Burt Porter.

"You'll never believe this, Mr. Porter, but someone just shot the new sheriff. I can't remember his name," Yolanda said, finding it difficult to catch her breath.

"It's Hardacre, and don't call me Mr. Porter. It's Burt," he insisted, never missing a chance to make himself open to a deputy and concurrently establish his dominance—especially with a woman deputy. "Do the cops know who did it?"

"Yes, they just took somebody away in a squad car."

"A client of ours?"

"I don't think so. One of the sheriff deputies said it was an ex-judge."

"Who?"

"One of the deputies said a guy by the name of Jackson." Judge Jackson had left the bench before Yolanda had graduated from law school. She knew nothing of Avery Jackson, except that he had been run off the bench because he'd given probation to a rapist.

"White dude or black dude?" Porter asked while thinking of any former judges named Jackson. There had been two—one white, one black.

"Looked black to me when they were taking him away."

Porter's face reddened. There had only been one black Judge Jackson. He had worked for a brief time in this very office as a public defender before leaving to take the bench. "Are you sure?"

"I'm not really sure of anything, but the man they took away was black, well-dressed and looked like he was in shock," Yolanda said.

"He's gonna be in some real shock after they get done with him. Let's go," Porter said.

"Where?"

"To the jail. This will be good experience for you."

"Maybe you should take someone who's more experienced."

"When you're asked to do something in this office, woman, you do it. When you get a chance like this, you don't stall around, you take it. Everyone else is at lunch and you're it. Got it?"

Yolanda said nothing. She simply nodded. All she could feel was her heart about to explode as they walked the three blocks to the jail.

Although Burt was out of shape from too much drinking, chain-smoking and too little exercise over his fifty-five years, he and Yolanda walked, then ran, the three blocks to the county jail in just minutes. He knew Jackson would be taken there for interrogation before being booked, fingerprinted and locked up. Time was of the essence. Porter knew only too well that cases were won or lost as the result of defendants opening their mouths to the police. Jackson probably wasn't indigent and wouldn't qualify for a free lawyer, but that hardly worried Burt at the moment. "Here to see Avery Jackson," he said to an officer at the front desk whose name tag read "Brady."

Brady was a man who looked like he'd worked out three times a week for years. No stranger to the bench press, he had huge shoulders and arms that bulged against his tight, short-sleeved shirt. "Who?"

"Avery Jackson—formerly Judge Jackson—he was just taken into custody."

Brady looked at Yolanda, as if asking her if Burt were crazy. She said nothing. "He's unavailable," Brady said.

"What do you mean, he's unavailable?" Burt asked. "We know he's available because he was just brought over a few minutes ago. We followed the car that brought him here."

"He's unavailable because he's in custody," Brady said.

"That's okay, Officer Brady," Burt said as he glanced at the cop's name badge. "I'm the director of the public defender's office and I see people who're in custody all the time; this is no different. If a detective is questioning Mr. Jackson at this point, I'm insisting that it stop."

Brady picked up the phone and dialed a number, waited a few moments and said, "I got two public defenders over here who want to see Jackson. . . . okay, I'll tell them." He looked at Porter. "My commander will be right out to talk to you. Have a seat."

Neither Burt nor Yolanda sat. Burt knew what was happening. The longer the police could stall, the more time they had to get a confession from Jackson. The sheriff's office was not about to let Burt Porter interfere with a murder investigation involving one of its own.

"I want you to write down everything that's been said to this point and from here on," Burt ordered Yolanda. "And note the time is now one-twelve p.m. These guys are creating an *Escobedo* problem for themselves if they get a confession or statement while we're outside waiting to see him." Burt was referring to the famous Supreme Court decision that held that statements taken from a defendant after counsel has asked to see the defendant and requested the cessation of interrogation are inadmissible as evidence against the defendant.

Porter wrote down 1:12 p.m. and took it over to Deputy Brady. "Could you initial this paper so we can have a record of the time we were here?"

"No way. That's up to my commander," said a now irritated Brady.

"Where is your commander? I thought you said he'd be right out."

"Please have a seat," Brady said.

"I'm not having a seat until I see your superior," Burt answered.

Brady picked up the phone again. "We have a problem out here with the PDs." He hung up.

Yolanda was watching her boss at work. She admired his guts and wondered if she had the wherewithal to assert herself like he did. She noticed a logbook for all visitors to sign that was placed on a table by the entrance to the jail behind Brady. She immediately signed her name to it with the time one-twelve p.m. and wrote Avery Jackson in the space marked PERSON VISITED.

It wasn't twenty seconds before two men appeared, one with a brace of bars on his uniform and a nameplate that said Ellison on it. He was older than Brady, maybe fifty-five, with thinning hair and the body of a middle-aged man who had gone through the Academy and then let himself go. Burt didn't know him. Next to him was Deputy Ronnie Elias, a black, amateur bodybuilder, more muscle-bound than Brady. Both were armed.

"We're here to see our client, Avery Jackson," Burt stated forcefully.

"Get serious, Counselor. He's with Detectives Solano and Guteman now and they're not to be disturbed. Besides, you can't make me believe you're his attorney. He's a former judge. Why would he want a public defender to represent him? He'd want a *real* lawyer, so don't pull that bullshit on me," Ellison retorted.

"I am his lawyer at this time," Porter stated, raising his voice an octave. "I demand you tell him his lawyer is here."

"Counselor, let's get this straight—you don't demand anything of me. This is my jail. While I'm on duty, I run this place. You take orders from me. I don't take orders from you. Got it? Now get the hell of out my jail," Ellison yelled. "When Jackson calls for a lawyer, we'll be glad to let that lawyer in here."

"You might like to know you're creating an *Escobedo* problem for yourself," Burt said firmly.

"And who the hell is Escobedo?" Ellison asked. "Is he like that asshole, Miranda? Fuck both of them low-life scumbags. They all need to be locked up. You know what, Counselor? Your low-life, murdering, scumbag client ain't gonna see you now. That's final."

"Ellison, you see this woman here?" Burt asked calmly. "Her name is Yolanda Crone. She's writing down every word you're saying, aren't you, Ms. Crone?"

"Yes, Mr. Porter, I am," Yolanda said, trying to act calm and in control while trembling inside as she scribbled down words on her spiral notebook. *Jesus, they didn't teach us this sort of thing in law school,* she thought.

This was no longer about the law for Ellison. This was about testosterone. Ellison could not back down in front of his deputies, not to mention a woman. This was the law of the jungle and it was Ellison's jungle. "That's it, Counselor, you're under arrest, and if Ms. Crone says one word, she's under arrest, too. Slap the cuffs on him, Deputy Elias. The charges are Disorderly Conduct and Interference With a Police Officer. If he gives you just one little bit of trouble, add a charge of Resisting Arrest."

Burt hadn't been arrested since college when he got caught up in an anti-war demonstration. He hated it.

Brady came around to help Elias; he grabbed Burt's left arm and Elias grabbed his right. It took only a second until both cuffs were in place with a whirring click. As he was being led to the door to the jail's booking section, Burt regained his composure and said to Yolanda, "Find Jack Maine and tell him what happened. Have him get a writ from Judge Grice, who's in federal court, over here right away."

Brady went back behind his desk and pressed the button that opens the lock on the jail door. It buzzed loudly. Elias pulled the door open, then escorted Porter down the hall to booking.

Yolanda left before the deputies could confiscate her notes or lock her up, too. She hit the cold air just seconds after the jail door slammed shut behind Porter. "If this is what it's like to be a public defender, I don't know if my heart can stand it," she muttered to herself as she broke into a dead run. She was like a Green Beret thrown into her first battle. The adrenaline rush was intoxicating; she could feel the juices flow into her blood and her body took over. If only she could control her mind. She was trying to recall a Writ of Habeas Corpus from her criminal procedure class, but her thoughts jumbled. She had never gotten a writ. Hopefully, Jack Maine had.

Monday—1:15 P.M.
Montgomery County Jail

Detectives Dave Guteman and Orlando Solano escorted Avery Jackson into an interrogation room fifty feet from where Burt Porter was being fingerprinted. Burt could see Jackson as he was led into the room, still in handcuffs. Porter acknowledged him with a hand gesture and a smile. Jackson stared back at him blankly. Porter put his finger over his lips to signal Jackson's need to remain silent, but Solano blocked Johnson's line of sight. Avery Jackson had been a judge and had advised prisoners of their rights thousands of times. The problem was that lawyers, when in trouble themselves, generally break every rule they'd preached to defendants.

The maxim was true: lawyers representing themselves have fools for clients.

It was up to Guteman and Solano to get a confession from Jackson. This was a cop killing, and not just any cop killing. This was a death penalty case and everyone knew it. The only question was whether Avery Jackson's execution would be carried out before or after his trial. Certainly a deputy could set up Jackson's demise in his cell and no one would be the wiser. It could be made to look like suicide.

Guteman and Solano had worked as a team on numerous homicides. They were a hybrid of Mutt and Jeff and the Odd Couple. Guteman was a short, forty-four-year-old man, well-dressed and neatly groomed. He was smart, tough and incisive. He was reputed to be the best interrogator in the department. He was known for meticulous, marathon inquisitions where he wore down his prey until they folded. He had been involved in many criminal cases in which defense attorneys attempted to get the confessions he'd gotten from prisoners thrown out because of coercion. No one had been successful in doing so, but the scuttlebutt was fairly strong that he used dirty and unethical means to achieve his ends. He used a psychological, rubber hose.

Solano was a hulk of a man. He was six foot two and weighed two hundred fifty pounds. Burdened by a large belly that hung over his belt, he moved and dressed sloppily. However, he was soft and gentle in his interrogations, the voice of empathy. Defendants really believed he cared for them. Solano and Guteman were equally cunning; Guteman was the hammer, and Solano was the velvet.

Solano began slowly with Jackson, his ham-like forearms resting comfortably on the table before him. A videocam had been activated on the other side of the one-way mirror. "Mr. Jackson—Judge Jackson. How do you want us to refer to you?"

"Avery would be all right," Jackson said, his eyes still on the table in front of him, dazed. He was still in his shirt, tie and sport coat, but he had undone the top button and loosened his tie.

Solano went on. "I have here a form advising you of your rights. I'm going to read them to you. When I'm done, I'll ask you to check the boxes next to the rights and sign this form. Do you understand?" Jackson stared at Solano. "Okay, then. You have the right to remain silent and refuse to answer questions. Anything you do say may be used against you in a court of law. You have the right to consult an attorney before speaking to the police and to have an attorney present during questioning now or in the future. If you cannot afford an attorney, one will be appointed for you before any questioning if you wish. If you decide to answer questions now without an attorney present you will still have the right to stop answering at any time until you talk to an attorney." When Solano finished, he said, "Would you please sign here?"

Jackson perfunctorily glanced at the form and carelessly signed it. There were two other blanks for date and time. "What is the date?"

"January fifteenth, and it's 1:20 p.m.," Solano told him.

Jackson filled in the time and date, then suddenly, his face changed. He went from stupor to relative awareness in a blink. "I know my rights. I've read those rights to hundreds of people over the years. Why are you reading them to me?" he asked. "Have I done something against the law? Why am I here?"

Guteman and Solano successfully suppressed nearly irresistible impulses to either laugh or beat Jackson to pulp. They'd interviewed hundreds of prisoners over the years who had denied wrongdoing. But this was different. Never had they interviewed a prisoner who denied a crime when there were a hundred and fifty eyewitnesses *and* a videotape of it.

"What am I charged with?" Avery asked.

Dave Guteman took over. "You've got some balls, Avery, coming in here and pretending like you don't know what you did."

"I'm a bit miffed about this inconvenience," Avery said, almost succeeding in surprising his interrogators. "Has anyone called my wife to tell her I'm here? Has anyone called the dean over at the university to tell them I won't be able to teach my afternoon classes?"

"We haven't done that as yet," Solano said, "but we'll allow you to do that after we're done here."

"Let's not be long here then, because I have a two o'clock Criminal Procedure class. Can you assure me that I'll make it? That's only thirty minutes from now. I need to be out of here in twenty minutes."

Guteman and Solano stared at one another.

"Listen, Avery, you son-of-a-bitch, you aren't going anywhere. You just killed a man and that man happened to be the sheriff of this county," Guteman said.

Avery looked at Solano and Guteman. He stood up as if to leave and said, "Oh, yeah, sure I did, and I'm also Martin Luther King and John F. Kennedy rolled into one—just kind of a mulatto version."

Solano, who was sitting between Avery and the door, also stood, making clear to Avery Jackson who was in control. "You might as well sit down, Judge, because we have a lot to talk about." Jackson sat his five foot six inch, one hundred forty-five pound frame back down.

"Apparently then, I'm under arrest. Would that be a correct statement?"

"Hell, yes, you're under arrest," Guteman yelled.

"Well, then, I'll need a lawyer."

"Judge, of course you know your rights, and you can have a lawyer," Solano said. "We don't want to ask you about the shooting. We just want to know some background stuff," he reassured the man, though actually trying to squeeze in through the back door.

"There was a shooting?" Jackson asked.

"Yes, there was a shooting, and you were the shooter," Solano said. "But we don't need to talk about that. We just want some background information."

Jackson's whole body tightened, his mouth went dry and his heart began to beat faster. His sympathetic nervous system had taken over; the adrenaline was flowing; he knew he was in danger. "Like what kind of background stuff?"

"Like, how did you get to the Renaissance Hotel? "Guteman asked.

"The Renaissance? I haven't been at the Renaissance."

"You were arrested at the Renaissance," Solano said.

"I must have driven," Avery mused.

"What do you mean you must have driven? You either drove or you didn't," Guteman said.

"I must have driven," Jackson muttered.

"Where is your car?" Guteman asked.

"I don't remember off hand. It's probably over at the university in the parking lot."

"Bullshit," Guteman said.

"Look, Detective, I don't have to talk to you at all," Jackson said.

"Of course you don't, but if you could answer just a few more questions, we'll be done, okay?" Solano said. Jackson said nothing. "Do you own a gun?"

Jackson thought about the .38 he had owned. "No, not anymore. I used to."

"Not anymore? Does that mean that you did once own a gun?" Solano asked.

"I think I need a lawyer right now. I'm being accused of a crime I didn't commit. You're talking about a gun I no longer have."

"If we could just get that information, we could stop the interview," Solano said.

"I think I gave the gun to a friend and haven't seen it since."

"Who's the friend?" Solano asked.

"I'm not talking to you about any of my friends or about me anymore."

Solano said, "We hear you've been having a problem with drinking and cocaine after you were run off the bench."

"I'm not going there with you guys," Jackson said, red-faced.

"We hear that you're separated from your wife and that she's having an affair. Is that the cause of the drinking and drugging?" Solano asked.

"Gentlemen, this interview is over," Jackson stated, banging his fist on the table. "I want a lawyer right now. What's my bond?"

"If you'd talk to us about this case maybe we could arrange some bond," Guteman offered, knowing very well that the district attorney would never agree to any sort of bond in a case of this magnitude.

"What kind of questions?" Avery snapped out.

Motive and intent were important, and Solano and Guteman needed some evidence to establish it. This would likely be their only opportunity to do so. They realized they were on very thin ice having been told three times by Avery that the interview was terminated.

23

"Did you know Sheriff Hardacre?" Solano asked.

"Of course I knew Sheriff Hardacre. He appeared in my court many times, and I knew him in the community. Lots of people know Hardacre. How do you think he got elected?"

"Did you have a personal relationship with him or were you mad at him at all?"

"No."

"Oh, bullshit, do you expect us to believe that?" Guteman shouted. "You just killed the man, and you're trying to tell us you weren't mad at him?"

"I didn't kill anyone. The only thing I have against the sheriff is that he's a Republican. Other than that, he seems like a good guy to me. Now what is my bond? Certainly there must be a bond if the charge is manslaughter or murder in the second."

Solano and Guteman looked at each other. Only an idiot would think this crime was going to be booked as anything less than murder in the first degree. And this guy was a judge and a criminal justice professor.

"Just one more question," Solano said. "Have you had any mental problems we should know about?"

"Nothing more than the usual problems associated with living and growing to middle age."

"What does that mean?" Guteman asked.

"The interview is over," Jackson stated again. "What is my bond? I need to make the necessary calls to make bond."

Guteman wanted the final word. "Listen, Jackson, it'll be forty below in hell before you'll be given a bond. There is no bond for murdering the county sheriff. We will recommend to Alec Hunter that you be held without bond. You're free to call the college to cancel your afternoon classes, call your wife, or an attorney, or whoever the hell you want, but you're going to need somebody smarter and more powerful than God to get you out of this one with the bullshit story you're telling us. You could make it easier on yourself by fessing up and telling us what really happened and why you did it. If you get a sudden burst of memory, get in touch with us."

Avery had no reply, trying to act in control and unfazed by what was happening; fortunately, the cops couldn't see the knot in his stomach. Hopefully they couldn't tell how disoriented he felt. He looked at his hands; they seemed as if they weren't part of his body; he couldn't feel himself existing; he felt suspended above the room. He needed to find something, or somebody, to ground him.

His wife kept going through his mind. They'd been trying to repair their relationship and now this. His two children, Aaron and Rebecca, away at college, popped into his head. How could they possibly understand this?

He couldn't remember where his car was. He couldn't remember being at the Renaissance Hotel that day. All was a blur. Fatigue engulfed him. "I don't want to call anyone. I need to lie down. I'm not feeling well."

Detectives Guteman and Solano obliged.

"I'm sure you'll be feeling much worse soon," Guteman said as they led Jackson to his isolation cell.

Monday—2:00 P.M.
The King's Table/Federal Court

The most logical place for Yolanda to find Jack Maine at lunchtime was the King's Table Restaurant next to the public defender's office. It had good food and drink at a reasonable price, and half the lawyers in Dayton fed and watered themselves there. She went in, scanned the booths, then looked to the bar. She recognized his back. He had light brown, almost-blond hair that was cut fairly short and parted on the left. His broad shoulders stood out in his brown-corduroy sport coat and tan pants. He was having a beer and a hamburger. Most people in the office were in awe of him because he was such a talented lawyer. She just hoped she didn't say something that made her sound stupid.

She approached him nervously. "Jack," she said, still out of breath, "Burt sent me to get you."

"What? I'm sorry," Jack said, "I've seen you in the staff meetings, but we've never talked. I'm Jack Maine." He extended his hand and shook hers.

"*Uh*, yeah, Yolanda Crone."

"Where is Burt?"

"He's in jail and wants you to get him out on a Writ of Habeas Corpus," Yolanda said in a rush.

The Latin term, *habeas corpus*, meaning "deliver the body," was created in 1679 by the English Parliament in response to the abusive detention of its citizens. Petitions for writs brought unjust detentions to the attention of justices or barons, who then had the discretion to continue a prisoner's detention, release the prisoner on his own recognizance or on bond. This important right was built into the United States Constitution. Writs of *Habeas Corpus* are rarely used nowadays but have always been an important part of American jurisprudence. Burt Porter's arrest was an ideal occasion for its use.

Jack's smile quickly disappeared; something outrageous must have happened. "Okay, let's go," Jack said as he took a large bite out of his burger and left the rest. "You can explain it to me on the way to the office. Does this have something to do with Avery Jackson?"

"Definitely. Burt tried to get in to see Judge Jackson, and the cops threw him in jail."

They ran back to the office and pulled the necessary forms out of his filing cabinet. He had a secretary fill in the blanks. Yolanda swore in front of a notary that the facts concerning Burt's arrest were true. Then they were off into the frigid air for the three block walk to federal court. They entered Judge Wilber Grice's court at two o'clock, red-faced from the biting cold and breathing heavily.

Judge Grice had been a deputy district attorney before he'd become a state district court judge, then a federal judge. President Clinton appointed him to the federal bench, and he'd been confirmed by a Republican Senate without resistance. His brilliance, fairness and toughness earned him the respect of prosecutors and defense attorneys alike. Now fifty years of age, his jet-black hair had turned mostly gray. His broad shoulders easily filled his black robe. When appearing in front of him, an attorney could not help but feel the power and sharpness of his intellect. He punished criminals and the government equally for misdeeds. His was truly a court where an individual citizen stood on level ground with the government. He was the rare judge who put the law and Constitution ahead of his own political self-interest. Now that he had a lifetime appointment to the federal bench, he was immune from the political process and free to attack the shenanigans of government personnel or anyone who abused his or her power. He was unimpressed by titles, including his own.

Burt Porter was putting his hope in the notion that jailing a defense attorney attempting to represent a criminal defendant, no matter how infamous his crime, would irk Judge Grice.

Judge Grice's court was grand, with beautiful oak paneling, thick silver-and-blue carpeting and large counsel tables. One can always tell the difference between a state courtroom and federal courtroom—the former is functional, sometimes even attractive, but rarely grand. The latter is opulent and exudes power.

It was the first time Yolanda had been in federal court. Her heartbeat went back to normal as she watched Judge Grice sentence a bank robber by the name of James McGhee to fifteen years in federal prison. A heroin addict who had done time in the state system for burglary and theft, McGhee graduated to bigger and better things when he stuck up a bank for ten thousand five hundred dollars. The moneybag the teller gave him had exploded ink just outside the bank. When the police arrested McGhee, he was running away from the scene, black ink dripping from his nostrils and chin and soaking his shirt. There would be no SODDI defense—as is usually the case; some other dude *hadn't* done it. The U.S. Marshall took him into custody and led him away in handcuffs.

Grice looked up from his bench and saw Jack Maine and Yolanda Crone standing at the back of his courtroom. Judge Grice had always thought Jack Maine was a way-above-average lawyer. He had tried cases in front of the judge when he was on the state court bench. "Do you have a matter before the court, Mr. Maine?"

"Yes, Your Honor. I have filed a petition for a Writ of Habeas Corpus with your clerk asking the sheriff of Montgomery County to deliver the body of Attorney Burt Porter to this court. Mr. Porter was jailed this afternoon attempting to visit a criminal defendant in connection with a crime for which he was being interrogated. Mr. Porter's arrest was solely for the purpose of preventing him from representing his client while the sheriffs were trying to extract a confession from him." Grice smiled. He had known Porter for years and respected him for the work he had done for the indigent. Like Jack, Grice was mildly amused that Burt Porter had been arrested; Porter was a tough guy—a man's man and would be furious at his treatment. On the other hand, keeping an attorney from his client was a serious matter. "Who is the defendant and what is the crime?"

"Former District Court Judge Avery Jackson. The crime is murder."

Judge Grice's smile turned to a deadly-serious glare. Word of Hardacre's murder and Jackson's arrest had already traveled through the grapevine to Grice. "Do you have any witnesses to call, or do you wish me to rule on the basis of the affidavit signed by . . . let's see here, Ms. Yolanda Crone?"

"Ms. Crone is here to testify, Your Honor, if the court so desires."

Yolanda's pulse went from seventy to one hundred twenty in two seconds. The thought of testifying in federal court terrified her. Four years ago she was teaching learning-disabled kids. Her first thought was of her ex-husband, who was committed to keeping her in her place. "If he could see me now," she muttered.

"Let me get this straight, Counsel," Judge Grice said, "you wish me to release Mr. Porter from the custody of the sheriff's office when his client has just killed—excuse me, allegedly killed—the new sheriff?"

"Yes, Your Honor."

"Call your witness, Counsel," Grice ordered. "I would like some testimony on the record for this one."

Jack called Yolanda. She was sworn in. When she entered the witness box, her heart was pounding. She'd survive, of course; this was an *ex parte* hearing—there was no opposing counsel to cross-examine her—and her testimony only consisted of a recapitulation of the events, but still, it was unnerving

"Had Mr. Jackson requested Mr. Porter's services? In other words, was there an attorney-client relationship in place?" Grice asked her.

"Not a formal one that I'm aware of, Your Honor. However, Mr. Porter and

Mr. Jackson were friends and colleagues. I have the feeling Mr. Porter and Mr. Jackson had sort of an understanding as friends that they'd help each other should either one ever get in trouble. Burt, *uh*, Mr. Porter, said something like that while we were running to the jail."

"I'll grant the petition, Counsel, on an *ex parte* basis. Not that I need to tell you this, but the right to counsel, especially in cases as serious as this one, is so fundamental to our system that it cannot be fettered. It's the duty of the public defender, or any attorney, even the district attorney, to make sure that the rights of the defendants are protected. I find that Mr. Porter is the public defender of this county and has a right and duty to be there. I find that he acted appropriately when insisting on seeing Mr. Jackson. I'm ordering the Montgomery County jailer to release Mr. Porter immediately. If they wish to pursue their charges against him, that's up to them. If they refuse to release him, I will consider them to be in contempt of this court and will dispatch the U.S. Marshall to the Montgomery County Jail immediately to bring the jailer to me so I can lock him up. I'm signing the writ now, Counsel, and I leave it up to you to execute it. Is there anything else?"

"No, Your Honor," Jack said.

"There's no need for this sort of nonsense over there. I don't care how serious the crime. The man has a right to counsel," added Grice. "Court is in recess."

Judge Grice left the bench. Yolanda got up from the witness chair relieved that this was over. Jack could only think that the fireworks on this case had just begun. He doubted he would be part of it. This case would be Burt's baby; Jack had already given his notice to leave the public defender's office and go into private practice after months of deliberation between himself and his wife, Marci.

Jack and Yolanda left the courtroom with the signed writ in Jack's briefcase. As they made their way to the elevators and out the side door to the frigid, gray day, Jack gave a thought to how much he enjoyed these small victories. "That was fun," he said to Yolanda.

"I never thought I'd be doing that, ever," Yolanda replied.

"It's good for the system; it has a cleansing effect. I hope I get the chance to do this kind of thing in private practice. You've got to savor these small victories when you get them because there aren't many of them for a defense lawyer."

"Private practice? Are you leaving the office?"

"Yeah," Jack said. "You didn't know? I only have a few days left. This may have been my last official act as a public defender."

"What are you going to do?"

"Put out a shingle. I've been with the office ten years, way too long to be a public defender. I don't want to end up like Burt."

"What does that mean?" Yolanda had only been with the office two weeks and had heard little gossip. Now she was privy to information from the top.

"You haven't been around long enough to know when a defense attorney is really burned out."

"Tell me what the signs are so I'll know them when I see them in myself."

"You start drinking too much, or using coke, because you're depressed. You might screw up your marriage or your relationship. You can't stand seeing another broke, hopeless human being in a jail cell with his breath reeking of cigarettes and skin turning to a sickly pallor. You'll know the smell. It's a combination of underarm body odor, dirty underwear and reeking cigarette-breath."

"I know that smell already."

"When you get to the time when you can't tolerate it any longer, then you know you're in trouble. The smell gets all mixed up with the anger and hopelessness you feel when you've been lied to for the thousandth time. Your client doesn't know that lying to you will get him destroyed in court. The client hates your guts anyway because you're not a 'real lawyer' they paid a bunch of money to. You're just a public defender. For me, it's a combination of the stink and the feelings that accompany the stink."

"I was asked if I was a real lawyer for the first time last week. I almost laughed, then I thought maybe I ought to be mad."

"Keep your sense of humor because that reaction will become routine," Jack said. "You can handle their cases better than most lawyers can, but they'll still think they got screwed because you weren't paid a lot of money. They think if a lawyer gets a big retainer, they can pay someone off, keep a bunch of money for themselves and get their client a better deal. The system doesn't work that way." Jack thought about his opinion of the system for a moment. "It's based on concepts of honesty, integrity and fairness. Many of our clients are people who are emotionally, morally, spiritually and economically bankrupt. They don't understand honesty and fairness 'cause they've never experienced it in their lives. They come from broken homes, were abandoned as kids, have been beaten and abused, you name it. Many have no hope, but you do the best for them you can because it's their right and the system demands it. You try to be more than just a blanket that warms up their body before it goes to the penitentiary. Usually, you've given them everything they deserve from their lawyer. And, though I understand all that, I'm tired of trying to fill their tank because it's empty. It's like peeing in the ocean."

"You're burned out?"

"I am. When you feel like this, you know it's time to get out. Burt is much more burned out than I am, but he stays. He owes it to himself and the clients to move on."

Yolanda was surprised by Jack's openness—she was just a greenhorn, female lawyer with no status. She hung on every word. "Feeling that way seems so far in the future, I can't imagine it. Your reputation is so good around the office and the courts, I'm surprised you feel that way."

"That and seventy-five cents will get me a ride on the bus."

"Do you think our office will be handling Jackson's case?"

"I doubt it. He's probably got some money, or at least can get some money. But I don't know, a case like his will cost a ton. I don't know if he has the kind of money it takes to afford private counsel."

"Maybe Jackson will hire you to represent him."

"I don't want it. From what you told me, it's a dead-bang loser. Representing him could put me out of business before I even opened my doors. Avery is a nice guy, a smart guy. He was something of a disorganized lawyer and made some politically incorrect decisions as a judge, but I surely wouldn't have thought he'd be a murderer. I've known dozens of them."

Monday—3:30 P.M.
Montgomery County Jail

Avery lay in a suicide cell without clothes, belt or bedding. His inflammable mattress was bolted to the bed. A camera monitored his every move. A lightbulb shined within its protective, metal cage on the twelve-foot ceiling above him. There was an aluminum toilet and sink in the room within camera sight. There were no square corners anywhere that he could use to hang or cut himself with.

He couldn't believe his life had come to this. He closed his eyes and fell asleep and then the dreams came—the goddamn dreams: a faceless man lying prone on a gurney; white all around; the hand with the hypodermic needle...no arm or body connected to the hand; only black, horn-rimmed glasses. The body lying on the gurney stiffened with terror.

Avery jerked awake, but only for a few seconds until he was drawn back into sleep. Then came the next dream. He hated this one, and it always nauseated him.

"Sometimes I think you're just a worthless nigger who'll never change!" exclaimed the tired-looking, misshapen, wretched, black woman.

"If I'm so worthless, why'd you marry my black ass? Come over here, bitch, and let me give you summa this," yelled the black man with horns and a tail, holding his crotch. The man had leprosy that caused grossly-malformed body parts. His hands had knots on them, and his lips were distorted with swollen nodules. His penis hung out of his pants and dangled down to his knees. Flaccid, it was distorted with lumps.

"You'll never get any of me again, you bastard."

"Okay, bitch, if you don't want this," the leper slurred, all liquored up and holding his crotch, "I'll give you summa this." The man held up his fist.

"You better never touch me again or I'll call—*owwww!*" she screamed as he slapped her grotesque face. She then began sucking feverishly on his dick until *she* came with a shuddering orgasm.

Avery woke for just seconds. He felt nauseated. Sleep again sucked him into its painful vortex. In utter darkness, a deep voice, sounding as if it were coming from the bottom of a well, bellowed, "The moon is full. The moon is full. The moon is full." And a sliver of a moon grew slowly, one width at a time, until the darkness was filled with a bright, full moon. It was when the moon was full that he could hear the penetrating report of a gunshot, which was also when the green fluid began running. It ran across a tile floor, down a spout and into a barrel. Then the red fluid started to run. It ran across the tile floor, down the spout and into the barrel.

Avery awakened in a cold sweat, terrified, hyperventilating. He hated these dreams; they had no meaning to him, yet punished him relentlessly and unmercifully. He hated his life; it was an enigma to him. Its pieces did not cohere neatly together. Instead, he felt as if his life consisted of shattered parts, emptiness, blackness and numbing anxiety, the source of which was somehow lost to him. And *now,* they were saying he was a murderer.

Although it had only been three hours since he'd apparently put a bullet through the head of Sheriff Hardacre, he realized that his life as he knew it—though he didn't necessarily like it—was over. Maybe that was a good thing. If he was in prison for the rest of his life, he might get relief from the dreams and anxiety. There, he could just allow himself to be taken care of. Or better yet, he could be put to death—Ohio was a death-penalty state.

Sure, that would be good. He'd thought about suicide hundreds of times, but he hadn't had the courage to do it. Killing the county sheriff in front of hundreds of witnesses was tantamount to suicide by a cop, wasn't it? Sure, *that's* why he had done this, he reasoned, to get done what he had not had the courage to do himself. Or maybe he hadn't killed himself earlier because he had two children in college who still needed him.

He couldn't be sure about Gloria, his wife. She'd had it with his nightmares, his disorganization, his fall from grace. As far as she was concerned, it was just his laziness and stupidity that had cost him his judgeship and her social position. She could not understand the alcohol and reefer he occasionally used to calm himself . . . but neither could he. Come to think of it, when he thought of her, the ledger demanding suicide got really full.

The scraping of his metal cell door as it opened interrupted Avery's tortured reverie. The metal-on-metal made him grind his teeth and irritated him to the roots of his fingernails. Its slam, when fully opened or closed, had a finality about it. He was just now realizing he'd better get used to, for he was going to be locked up for a long time—maybe eternity. He wondered if this was what hell was like.

A deputy sheriff stood in the doorway. "You have a professional visit, Jackson."

So much for professor or judge, Avery thought.

Getting out of his cot and to his feet was an unbelievable chore. Bringing himself from his horrible dreams, through morbid thoughts of suicide, to being presentable to professionals in a matter of minutes, required just too much acumen. "Probably the two detectives again, wanting to ask more questions," Avery muttered. "I'm fucked."

But it was Jack Maine and Burt Porter who were sitting in the visitor's room. The boulder that had been weighing down his stomach lightened when he saw their familiar faces. Although not close social friends with Avery, both Burt and Jack had the kind of relationship with him where they would see him in the courthouse coffee shop, enjoy a latte and a Danish, and talk about legal gossip, interesting cases and sometimes, a bit about who was sleeping with whom, who was buying what, who was being promoted, that kind of thing.

Avery had been a public defender only briefly before being appointed to the bench—not an especially good PD, but one whose heart was in the right place. No one doubted his intelligence, but he occasionally had difficulty keeping things straight; more than once he'd forgotten important dates on which motions and briefs were due. When he was appointed as the first black district court judge, Burt was relieved. He, as well as everyone else, liked Avery and respected his intelligence, but a guy like him was hard on malpractice premiums when he was late filing a motion or appeal. Burt saw Jackson's appointment to the bench as a win-win situation. It was good for Avery and good for the office. Avery could be very helpful as a political ally on the bench, and Burt no longer needed to worry about his idiosyncrasies and absentmindedness in the PD's office.

As Avery came into the visitation room, Jack was telling Burt about the just-concluded hearing in front of Judge Grice. He'd sent Yolanda back to the office but agreed to stay with Burt for the initial conversation with Avery.

Avery tried to say hi, but was only able to mouth the words. He was embarrassed to the point of speechlessness that his friends and colleagues would see him like this.

Burt and Jack rose to shake his hand. Their grips were firm; his was weak, wet and clammy. Avery had difficulty looking them in the eye. All three of them sat back down on plastic chairs at a round table. Fluorescent lights created a glare that reflected off the white, semi-gloss, cement blocks. They stared at one another.

"Who's representing you?" Burt finally asked. "I don't know," Avery said.

"Do you know any good lawyers?" Both Jack and Burt smiled. "I have no lawyer in mind and I don't have much money."

"In that case, it looks like you're stuck with us," Burt said.

"I don't know if I'm broke enough to qualify for representation by a public defender—though, God knows, I seem to be broke enough for everything else. Anyway, I have my state retirement and a house with a little equity and two kids in college, but I don't know if I can afford a 'real' lawyer."

"You need to tell us if we're your lawyers right now so you have the benefit of attorney-client privilege," Burt said. "We don't want the district attorney claiming this is a social visit and trying to use your conversations with us as evidence. If you scratch up the money for a private attorney, that's fine; we'll just give him whatever we've got later, but right now, claim us."

"Of course, you're my lawyers now," Avery said. "I'm so happy to see you guys I can't tell you."

"What happened?" Jack asked.

"I guess I shot Sheriff Hardacre," Avery said.

"You *guess* you shot Sheriff Hardacre!" Burt exclaimed. "No shit. You did shoot him all right—it's all over the TV."

"Look, I have a splitting headache and feel terrible. Take it easy because I already did round one with Guteman and Solano."

"Avery," Jack said, "you have to help us understand what happened here. They've got you on videotape shooting Hardacre with three judges and a hundred and fifty Rotarians watching."

"Avery," Burt tag-teamed, "you need to know what you're up against. It wouldn't surprise me a bit if this was the number one, national story. When you say you *guess* you shot Hardacre, what do you mean?"

"Just what I said. I guess. I guess. I guess. I really don't know."

"Are you saying we're going to be claiming that some other dude done it? This is not a two-bit burglary where we can claim misidentification. The ID is positive. What I heard is that half the judges in Dayton jumped you right after you blew Hardacre's brains all over the dais. Is that true?" Burt asked.

"I guess so. I don't really remember anything until they started taking me away. All I know is that a whole bunch of guys were on me, kicking and hitting me, and that a bunch of sheriff's deputies took me to a patrol car, and someone was calling me a nigger."

"You're leaving a bunch of stuff out, aren't you?" Jack asked.

"Like what?"

"Like how you got there, what you did prior to getting there, where you got the gun, and the little unimportant part about walking up to the podium and putting a bullet right through the sheriff's head," Burt said.

"I can't tell you anything about that. I don't remember."

33

The two PDs felt all balled up inside, but didn't show it.

"Okay, what's the last thing you remember?" Jack asked.

"Teaching my Evidence class this morning over at the university. We were going over hearsay. I had a discussion with a student after class about the difficulty of the hearsay rule, and then I started feeling really bad about DiSalvo, the probation thing, and my marriage. I felt like having a cup of coffee."

"Did you have the coffee?" Burt asked.

"I must have, but I don't remember," Avery said, looking up to his left, trying to recreate his life from thoughts and images given him by the left side of his brain.

Burt and Jack looked at one another and said simultaneously, "I hope—"

Burt finished the sentence, "You haven't told the cops anything."

"I didn't tell them anything. I just kept asking for a lawyer."

"What time were they with you?" Jack asked.

"Between one and one-thirty."

"That's right when we were trying to get in to talk to you. You sure you said nothing to them?" Burt asked.

"The only thing I told them was that I used to have a gun and didn't know where it was. I guess I also told them that I had no history of mental illness," Avery said, knowing he had committed the cardinal sin that all lawyers should know not to commit—never give a statement to the police if you're a suspect.

"I probably don't need to tell you this, but don't talk to them about anything else," Burt said. "You've probably already created a problem for yourself with your statement about your gun. You may also have made a mental status defense more difficult by saying that you have no mental health history. And what about the gun? Where is it?"

Avery's eyes again rolled up and to the left. He looked down at Burt, embarrassed by his failure to pull a rabbit out of his hat. There was no rabbit there—only darkness. "I don't know," he whispered. "It just seems to me that I gave it to someone. I don't know when, or to whom, or for what reason."

Burt and Jack looked at one another and each simultaneously asked, "Avery, do you—" Burt trumped Jack and asked, "Do you have a mental-health history?"

"None. Well, I did see a psychiatrist a few times in the service. That's all."

"Why'd you see the psychiatrist in the service?" Jack asked.

"I have no idea. I was ordered to see one."

"Did you get hit in the head as a kid or something?" Burt asked, trying to figure out why an army shrink would've wanted to see him.

"No, but I got whipped by my dad. He was a drunk, though, so it's not too hard to figure out why he took it out on me."

"If you expect us, or any lawyers, to have an easy time believing what you're saying, then you're full of shit," Burt said. "Let's do a reality check on what we've heard so far. Let's see, you just killed the county sheriff in front of a hundred and fifty Rotarians, it was filmed on videotape, you don't remember doing it, you don't remember how you got to the Renaissance Hotel, and you don't remember who has your gun, or where you got it. Now, if you were a judge on a case and someone brought a bullshit story like that into your court, what would you think?"

Avery looked at the two of them. He then started slowly. "Sounds like bullshit, doesn't it?" He paused for a few minutes, then looked at them. "I'm telling you the truth. Look, you guys, I don't know what happened. I just know that this is the second time today that I've been told that *I* killed the sheriff. I must be nuts, because I don't think I did, but I can't be sure. If you think I need to see a psychiatrist, I will."

"Count on it," Burt said.

"Are you telling us the truth—that you've never been in psychotherapy for depression, panic attacks, drinking?" Jack asked. "Right now, it would be a help. This is no time to be proud."

"No, brothers," Avery said, assuming the role, "Niggers don't do therapy. It ain't cool, man. We just run faster, jump higher, fight the white man's wars and get high-blood pressure and die."

"I'm feeling better all of the time," Burt said. "Not only are you guilty as hell, but you're also telling us that we have no insanity defense."

Avery just looked at Burt and Jack. "Burt," he said, "if I didn't know you so well, I'd tell you to get your white ass out of here and get me a lawyer who believes in me. Now, can you help me or not?"

"Hey, brother, I want to help you, but I'd like to be more than just someone who keeps you company before they strap you to a gurney and put a needle in your arm. The only reason I believe in you is because your story is so bad, it couldn't possibly be a lie."

"I agree, Avery," Jack said.

The hint of their belief in him diffused Avery's anger.

"Did you have any history with Gene Hardacre?" Burt asked.

"Hell, no! I knew the man well enough to say hello to him. That's it."

"Did you hate him?" Burt asked.

"I hardly know the man. He'd come into my court with cases when I was on the bench. He testified before me a number of times. I know him well enough to say "hi" on the elevator."

"Did you vote for him in the November election?" Jack asked.

"No, but not because I have anything against him. It's just— I've known Hugh Lane for a long time; I couldn't *not* vote for Hugh. But I have nothing against Hardacre."

"You're talking about Hardacre in the present tense. Don't you mean you *had* nothing against Hardacre?" Jack asked.

"I still think he's alive. I don't think of him as dead just because you say I killed him—I don't think I killed him," Avery said emphatically.

"Either you're the cleverest liar I've ever heard, or you're genuinely crazy," Burt commented.

"That diagnosis doesn't leave me much room, does it, Burt?" Avery sighed. "Can you think of a third alternative?"

"No. I can just tell you that I'm not deceiving you guys. As far as I know, Gene Hardacre is alive."

"We're with you," Jack agreed.

Burt realized they had done all the work they could for the day. Avery had been pushed to his limit. Although burned out to the point that almost nothing in the law interested him anymore, Burt could feel his blood flowing now. For the first time in years, he had a case that stimulated him.

"It's four-thirty now," Jack said. "The news will be coming on soon. You probably don't have access to a television, so you can't see the video, but I can assure you that it'll show you shooting Gene Hardacre to death."

"I'm in a suicide cell. They'd be afraid of me electrocuting myself with a TV cord, or cutting myself with the glass. Can you tape it for me?"

"I don't think that'll be necessary. It'll be the first piece of evidence provided to us by the district attorney. It'll be the substance of their case," Jack said.

"Let's talk about bond," Burt said. "You'll appear in county court tomorrow for advisement. We'll ask that a bond be set. It would be helpful if your wife and kids could be there. Do the kids still go to Miami?"

Jack was referring to Miami University, the liberal arts college just forty miles from Dayton where Avery's two children were students.

"Yeah, but I don't want them to know about this, or to feel the shame this'll cause them. As for Gloria, I really don't know where she stands. Our marriage has been shaky ever since DiSalvo."

"Avery," Burt said, "you know asking for bond in a case like this is useless. It'll be a capital case where the proof is evident and the presumption of your guilt great. You know the law. The DA will probably bring the video in and show it to the jury. Bail will be denied."

"So, I'll lose my job and just sit here forever?" Avery asked, somehow just now realizing the extent of his problem.

"You're going to be sitting here for a long time," Jack said. "You better get in touch with Gloria and find out where she stands on this. You better find out how much money you have, and decide if you and Gloria are a team, or if you're on your own. You need to decide if you're going to be represented by the public defender, or you're going to hire a private attorney."

Avery wanted Jack on the case, which meant getting him as his PD, but he'd heard the rumors that Jack was quitting and going into private practice. Burt was a good lawyer—fire-and-brimstone type. Burt was erratic, though, and his personal life, with his revolving door of girlfriends, long the subject of gossip and speculation in Montgomery County, made Avery edgy. What's more, there had long been rumblings that Burt blew white powder up his nose. He could see they would make a nice team—Jack's cool, thoughtful, creative, thorough, and dogged approach in conjunction with Burt's emotional, sledgehammer attack, so Avery knew he had to have Jack. Jack was the brains, the rudder and the anchor. Avery was not sure how much money he could put together for a private defense. "Look, you guys, you're really saying something about yourselves by showing up here right away to help me. I know I'm in real trouble. I must be fucked up, but I don't know how or why."

"We'll help you figure it out," Burt said, not sure he was telling the truth. This case was as big a mystery to Burt as Avery Jackson was to himself. "We'll be in court tomorrow morning with you when you make your first appearance. We'll ask for bond and for a preliminary hearing. I'll get Dr. Phil Gilmour to come over to see you so we can see where you were, mentally, at the time of the shooting."

"I won't get bond, will I?" Avery asked.

"No, you won't get bond," Burt said. "This is a non-bondable offense. You know that as well as we do."

"As to your comment," added Jack, "that you're in a mess and need our help, I can't think of another person who needs help more than you right now. You need to get all the support you can from family and friends."

Avery grimaced. "I'm not sure how much of that is out there for me now. I just hope Gloria sticks by me through this. The last thing I need is for her to bail out on me. The next to the last thing I need is for you to withdraw, Jack," he added.

"Let me give it some thought," Jack said, his stomach tightening. He felt himself getting sucked into something he had promised himself and Marci he would not do, but how could anyone guard himself against something as unforeseen as this?

Monday—4:00 P.M.
The Hardacre home

Defense attorneys frequently ignore the devastation victims of crime and their families feel. It's not malicious on their part—only self-preservative. Jack was wrong when he told Avery Jackson that no one presently needed more help than he did. The Hardacre family did. They were in total shock. This morning Gene had been fully alive. He and Betty had been alive together; they had made love. Now, he was gone; and the strength of the love between them could only be experienced through a memory. It was preserved perhaps with sensations in her body and remnants in her soul, but their physical connection was gone— as ephemeral as life itself. It didn't seem possible—not even remotely possible. She, on an intellectual level, knew it was true. Emotionally, she had no clue how to understand the gravity of her loss. No one in her shoes could. That would be left for the interminable grieving process that lay ahead. All she could feel right now was numbness. She now had two kids without a father, both of whom needed to go to college. There was some savings, a house and a survivor's pension for officers killed in the line of duty.

She could feel nothing for Avery Jackson—not even hatred, though she vaguely knew that would inevitably come. Right now, she was just too numb. She wouldn't watch the news that night. She'd heard what had happened from the deputy sheriffs who'd come to her house that afternoon with news of the horror that had taken place. Maybe someday she'd watch the video of Gene's murder, but not now. Maybe she'd wait until the trial. Certainly, she wouldn't allow Ashley and Derrick to watch. The devastation to two children who had just lost their father was unfathomable.

Ashley was a high school senior and Derrick a freshman. Now they had no father. Ashley had spent a lot of time sitting on her father's lap as a child. He had gone to all of her band concerts and school plays. She was applying to college next fall. She had counted on her father's strength and encouragement when she left home. She adored her father. As for Derrick, all of the soccer, basketball and Cincinnati Reds' games he'd shared with his dad would now only be a memory; there would be no more in the future. He was only a freshman. He needed his dad to lead him into manhood.

There was no way either Ashley or Derrick could understand, but then there was no way anyone—adult, adolescent or child—could understand Gene Hardacre's murder. Right now, they were all sure they never wanted to see the tape of their father's killing. Derrick hated Avery Jackson and wanted vengeance. Ashley, like her mother, was too numb to feel anything but confusion. Betty, Ashley and Derrick together were an open wound; a wound that would never completely heal.

CHAPTER 2

Alec Hunter was a very handsome man. He looked like the quintessential banker or investment broker of TV illusion. He was always impeccably dressed in dark suits and white shirts starched to perfection. His ties were expensive and conservatively tasteful. He was politically aware, having just been re-elected district attorney for the fourth time. He kept his ear to the ground about the mood of the community and went whichever way the wind blew. He talked tough law and order; that was how to get re-elected. It was just good politics. He had inculcated the loyalty of the police and the sheriff's department and worked closely with them. He cut cops a break when they used too much force in making an arrest or when they killed someone. The police were there to protect, and he understood better than anyone how important it was for the citizens to believe them to be omnipotent and beyond reproach.

Alec's children were grown. Throughout their college years, they'd both been members of the best sororities and fraternities. His son, Benjamin, was working as a lawyer in an insurance defense firm in Columbus and was able to get his father season tickets to the Ohio State Buckeyes' games. His daughter, Stephanie, was married to a lawyer doing securities' work in Dayton. She and her husband were expecting their first child. Alec's love for his children fluctuated, depending on how they made him appear to others.

Benjamin was the first born, a good child who played athletics and got straight A's. This endeared Ben to his father. Stephanie, on the other hand, was a rabble-rouser in high school. She'd gotten busted for using drugs. The case had been taken care of quietly and discreetly with a few calls by Alec. She'd gotten the message from Alec that she'd be cut off if she didn't shape up.

Alec and his wife, Alice, lived in Oakwood. His salary of one hundred ten thousand dollars a year barely supported their standard of living. They belonged to Oakwood Country Club. She drove a Lexus, he a Cadillac. Although Alec could have made a lot more money in one of Dayton's prestigious civil law firms doing insurance defense or tax work, he had stayed with the district attorney's office for sixteen years. He claimed he loved his job, but inside, he resented being where he was. He felt he was entitled to more respect in the party and had aspirations to hold a high political office. He believed he had the talent to become a senator or even President of the United States, and the time was now to make his move. It would be a matter of breaks and connections that would get him there. At this stage in his career, he had to make the most of his opportunities.

Alec was a mediocre lawyer himself, but what he lacked in sound, legal thought, he made up for in eloquence and appearance. He looked like what influential Daytonians wanted their district attorney to look like. He could take a really ugly or violent case and sanitize it with his appearance and common sense alone, which is what juries wanted—the feeling that the rot in their society was being exorcised by the public officials they had elected to keep them safe. Impressive looks and glib speech were the key. Armed with those, it was as easy as shooting fish in a barrel to prosecute people. He knew juries wanted to convict. Proof beyond a reasonable doubt be damned in most cases.

As a practical matter, it was up to a poor person, especially a person that was a member of a minority group, to prove *himself* or *herself* innocent. All the people who were being released from death row and prison after serving fifteen to twenty years for murders and rapes because DNA evidence showed they were wrongly convicted proved what Alec knew—juries wanted to get rid of the bad in themselves and put it on the briars, niggers and the unpopular. They wanted to convict people, especially when the crime was violent or sexual.

Society needs to protect itself. It was Alec's ability to read needs and instincts in people and capitalize on them that had made him successful.

Alec also understood that no juror wanted to find anyone Not Guilty by Reason of Insanity—NGRI. When John Hinckley was found NGRI after shooting President Reagan in 1982, the insanity defense died across the country, and possibly the world. U.S. citizens wanted him dead, or at least severely punished, not coddled and cured. When Hinckley got off, so to speak, the people were furious, which slowly created a mass psyche that refused to let it happen again.

All a prosecutor needed to assert now in order to blow that defense out of the water was to say—and somehow prove—that the defendant was faking a mental illness. It was what jurors wanted to hear. Most any juror would buy it. Few lawyers even attempted insanity defenses in Montgomery County or anywhere in the United States anymore, for that matter. Alec knew it.

But there'd been bumps. No one in Ohio had been successful in an insanity defense in front of a jury since 1984 when Pete Cassidy Rose had been found NGRI after he'd shot three people in a bar. He'd claimed psychomotor epilepsy, and the jury bought it. Dave Morgan had been the district attorney then. Morgan had assumed Rose's conviction was a foregone conclusion, and when he didn't deliver, it had cost him his job.

Alec used that verdict as grist for his campaign mill.

He'd been relentless in his attack on Morgan as an incompetent, slovenly DA who'd let a triple murderer walk down to the state mental hospital from which he would certainly be released in a couple of years. His campaign slogan was "David Morgan—The DA Who Makes Life Cheap in Montgomery County" and "Three's a Charm" or "Life's Cheap in Montgomery County." Alec won that first election by a landslide, and then had gone on to win the next three elections by a wide margin.

There were always a lot of shootings and stabbings, as well as an ample supply of drug dealers and burglars. Alec prosecuted them to the fullest extent of the law, and he made sure the press knew about it. He was skilled at using the media, who needed him for stories and he needed them to advance his career. Most cases weren't really high profile though, certainly not like the People v. Avery Jackson. No case on record involved the assassination of a newly-elected white, Republican sheriff by a black, Democratic, liberal ex-judge who'd been reviled by the press and public for releasing Benny DiSalvo, a two-time rapist, on probation. *And*, in no case Alec had ever handle, were there a hundred and fifty eye witnesses composed of the most prominent businessmen and government leaders in town.

It was up to Alec to seize the moment. The upside of this case was tremendous. There would be national exposure, not to mention the local media saturation. He had the opportunity to become a national figure, maybe run for Congress or the Senate if he should be successful in his prosecution of ex-judge and Professor Avery Jackson. He was also aware of the downside. A loss of this case, a finding of guilty to anything less than first-degree, capital murder could signal the end of his career. He knew if that happened, an opportunistic, upstart lawyer would be waiting in the wings to dethrone him.

It was with these thoughts in mind that Alec sat with his senior staff at the DA's office just a few hundred yards from where Avery Jackson had killed Sheriff Hardacre. They had watched the local five o'clock news and then the NBC evening news with Tom Brokaw. Both the local and national people had elected to show the video to the point where Avery Jackson approached the podium and reached into his pocket. Then there was a gap until Sheriff Hardacre hit the floor and was lying there in a pool of blood with Judge Kessler holding the smoking gun.

It was reminiscent of the scene in Los Angeles when Bobby Kennedy had been shot by Sirhan Sirhan: a victim on the floor, his head being cradled, shocked people doggedly holding on to the shooter, mass confusion, dazed eyes everywhere. There was that glassy, distant look of human animals frozen with trauma and fright as the horror unfolded.

Sheriff Hardacre was clearly dead, his eyes fixed and open, and without a soul behind them. The actual firing of the gun and the explosion of Sheriff Hardacre's head was cut from the media presentation, but of course, saved—it would be critical evidence at the trial. Whether *Court TV* had the guts to show the full tape on cable remained to be seen, but certainly they would show the trial. Maybe it would not be as spectacular as the O.J. Simpson case, but what was? No question it would be a close second.

Hunter's senior staff consisted first of James Brodan, a career prosecutor, cool under pressure, without much emotion; he appeared to have ice in his veins. He was a brilliant lawyer. He, and others, fancied him as a Spock, believing that legal decisions were based on pure logic, devoid of emotion, bias or world view. His personal life was a reflection of his sterility. He had been married twice and was now single. It remained a secret that with each wife, he had been in unsuccessful couple's therapy. Each wife complained he was devoid of feeling and emotional response while they became depressed, empty and lost within the relationship. Each woman had become increasingly frustrated and enraged. The distance he maintained was maddening for them. Each complained that his interest in sex, not to mention in pleasing them sexually, was minimal. For Jim, the clitoris might as well have been a type of insect. When confronted, Jim Brodan could not understand the problem. After all, *he* was satisfied, and he couldn't understand why they weren't. Both marriages ended in divorce without children. Jim was better off single. His only successful relationship could be with the law.

The third member of the senior staff was Hank Dorsey, a man with emotional savvy, who was a gifted orator. Hank Dorsey and Jim Brodan frequently tried cases together. As a team, they were very good. Hank supplied the emotional intelligence and trial skills; Jim argued the law. Hunter boasted that they had never lost a murder case when they had worked together—something like twenty in a row.

The final member of Alec Hunter's inner circle was Stephanie Marshall. She had tried cases years ago but no longer did. She helped Alec with political strategy and was his media relations guru. She was forty-five, divorced and very attractive. She dressed well, kept a nice figure and let her blonde hair hang long and casual, like a '70s beach girl. She had a daughter, Angela, who was a senior in high school. They lived fashionably; Stephanie was a woman of independent means. She rarely dated. The question around the courthouse was what she did for intimacy in her life. She was beautiful, tasteful and professional. She was the whole package. Single, middle-aged men were afraid to ask her out because she intimidated them. She was a prosecutor—powerful and intelligent, yet stunning and classy. Men saw her as high risk if they should venture the courage to approach her—too much penis herself and the ability to cut theirs off. Such is the plight of the beautiful, successful woman.

Alec's secretary had ordered Chinese food to go for the senior staff. They had watched the news with their dinner. Alec started the conversation. "We have a major case on our hands. By tomorrow, the national media will be here wanting to interview us, and the local people will want a comment from me for the late news. We need to discuss what we're going to say. We also need to figure out the appropriate outcome of this case and anticipate defense strategy. Stephanie, make sure our investigators get us an uncensored tape so we can see the actual shooting."

"Sure, no problem," Stephanie answered. "With regard to the media, I think our position should be obvious—utmost sympathy for Sheriff Hardacre and his family—we're reviewing the evidence and talking to witnesses. We don't intend to try this case in the media; we believe the evidence will speak for itself and justice will be done, etcetera, etcetera and *blah, blah, blah, blah, blah*. When the media asks if we believe the defense will raise an insanity defense, we can just simply say, 'Sure, that's one defense that may be available to them.'" Stephanie had already given this considerable thought. She typically handled mundane, media matters and spoke for the DA's office for Alec, unless he wanted some airtime. "Do you want me to represent the office, or do you want to, Alec?"

"I want to represent the office in all releases to the press, TV or radio for this case, unless you hear from me to the contrary," Alec replied. "Everyone understand that?"

No response signaled their agreement; this was hardly a big surprise.

"Stephanie, will you make sure that none of our deputies opens his mouth to the media or a friend over a beer?" Alec asked. "There are to be no leaks about what we're doing."

Stephanie nodded. On a case of this magnitude, such a procedure was implicit.

Hank was still in shock by the horror of the day and what he had just witnessed on television, unable to eat much of his dinner. "I can't believe I saw what I just saw. I know Avery Jackson. Hell, we all know Avery Jackson, and he's a good guy—wasn't a great lawyer or judge, but still, a basically good guy. I've met his wife and kids. I know Gene Hardacre, and I've met his wife and kids. It's a cliché, but this just goes to show that there are things about people we just don't know. What you see isn't always what you get." He shook his head and gazed off into the distance.

Jim Brodan sat quietly, coolly assessing their legal position. "There are a number of issues we have to consider in this case. The first one is whether our office can prosecute this case. Did anyone from our office attend the Rotary Club meeting today?" No one answered. Brodan was contemplating the legal/ethical principle that forbids lawyers in a case to also be witnesses in the case. "If we've got any lawyers who're witnesses, we might be conflicted off the prosecution."

Hunter was quick to respond. "I can tell you," he said, "there'd better not be any deputies from our office who were at Rotary today. As you know, the in-service we did today was mandatory. It took some doing to get that psychologist here." Alec was referring to Dr. Wolcott, a clinical psychologist who had done research on jury selection techniques and profiles for various types of cases including homicides, sexual assaults, domestic violence and insanity cases. She'd spoken over lunch to the entire district attorney's staff for approximately an hour and a half. Her presentation was cut short when a secretary burst into the conference room to tell everyone that Sheriff Hardacre had been shot to death at the Renaissance Hotel. "Stephanie, would you check to make sure everyone was at the in-service?" Alec asked. She nodded.

"I assume then that's not a problem," Brodan said. "The next question, Alec, is who do you want to try this case? We don't want the person who tries this case to have had a personal relationship with Avery Jackson or Sheriff Hardacre that would compromise our prosecution."

"I want my number one team to try this case," Alec said. "That means Hank and you will be on the front line. I want to be working closely with you two on the investigation. I'm also reserving the option of coming in and trying the case with the two of you."

"Sure," Hank and Jim said.

"I have had almost no relationship with Avery Jackson," Alec went on. "He's a Democrat. Obviously, when Jackson was on the bench, our deputies appeared in front of him regularly, but I didn't. As for Sheriff Hardacre, I attended his inauguration party, we're both Republicans, but I have no friendship or relationship with him other than law enforcement business. We had almost no contact with each other in the ten days or so he was in office. I don't believe I'm legally conflicted. How about you two?"

"Same as you. There was nothing personal between us; it was all mainly professional," Hank said.

Brodan nodded in agreement.

"Let's talk about bond."

"That's a no-brainer," Brodan said. "Guy can't get bond on murder one."

"If ever there were a capital case," Alec said, "where the proof was evident and the presumption great, this is it. Adamantly oppose any bond, and if the defense attorneys push hard, request a bond hearing where we can put on the video of the actual killing. Jackson will be making his first appearance tomorrow morning in front of Judge Bonin. Even a liberal like her will refuse to give this son-of-a-bitch bond." Hunter was referring to Judge Madeline Bonin, a newly-appointed county court judge, who would be considering bond and conducting the preliminary hearing. "Speaking of defense attorneys, I wonder who'll get this case."

"You won't believe who's on the case," Brodan said. "The public defenders. Goddamn Burt Porter got thrown in jail today for being an asshole with the sheriffs' deputies. Porter was trying to break up Jackson's interrogation, and the deputy over there slapped handcuffs on him—apparently they weren't going to let him run their jail, the fools. Jack Maine and a new, black woman deputy from the PD's office went over to federal court and Grice released Porter on a writ of habeas corpus."

"Can you imagine," mused Alec, "being so invested in a killer like Jackson that you'd go to jail for him? It makes no sense to me. The man is a murderer, and Porter is willing to go to jail for him?"

"More astounding," Brodan said, "is Jackson's fall. Can you imagine a lawyer, judge and professor falling this fast? Now, he can't even afford his own private attorney."

"I wonder if that's a permanent thing," Alec said, "or just temporary until he can get the money together?"

"I'll tell you this," Hank said, "there are a helluva lot of lawyers in Montgomery County I'd rather deal with than those two. They'll have nothing to lose on this case because it's so indefensible. Guys like that can be very tough. Porter's a burnt out PD. Maine's relentless, but he's leaving the PD's office. Most guys would have just bonded Porter out when the sheriffs arrested him. Maine goes to federal court and writs him out." Hank appreciated good lawyers. It made no difference what their persuasion was. Advocacy was advocacy. The more competent their representation, the more he admired them. "I don't care how solid our case is, if Maine and Porter are taking it, we'll be in for the fight of our lives."

"Not to worry." Alec smiled. "It's really comical when you think about it. The public defender running around trying to save Jackson's ass—trying to prevent him from giving a statement to the cops when there is an actual videotape of the killing. The amusing thing about it is that they can make all the flimsy constitutional rights' arguments they want—there's no way anyone is going to suppress a videotape of the actual murder. Here we have a liberal Democrat who released a rapist to probation, was run out of office and then he kills the sheriff of Montgomery County in cold blood. This is a great opportunity to make a real statement to the community about crime. It doesn't make any difference what the killer's social position or education is. He should be treated the same as all the other street scum we prosecute. I say to hell with the defense attorneys, be they Porter and Maine, or some other damned team. I know we have to give this careful consideration, but I think this should be a death penalty case. What do you think?"

"If you ever had aggravating factors or special circumstances for the death penalty, this is the case. We have a defendant lying in wait, as well as obvious premeditation and deliberation, and we have the death of a law enforcement officer," Brodan said.

"From a public relations' standpoint," Stephanie added, "I believe it could be harmful for us politically *not* to seek the death penalty given the aggravation and the death of an elected, law enforcement official. Both wealthy and poor whites will have a fit."

"I agree," Dorsey said. "Regardless of my mystification over Avery Jackson's doing this, the fact remains that this case represents a frontal assault on law enforcement. The community, indeed the country, needs to be aware that attempts to destroy our guys on the front line will be met with a helluva lot of legal shit."

"I think we must present the death sentence to this jury and let them decide. Anyone disagree?" Hunter asked. No one did. "I think," Alec said, "we need to be ready for some sort of mental defect defense. We need to have Dr. Procheska ready." Hunter was referring to Irwin Procheska, a psychiatrist who had testified successfully in many cases for the prosecution. "I also liked the psychologist we heard today, Dr. Wolcott. I wonder if she'd go to bat for us if we needed her." Alec glanced at Stephanie.

Stephanie picked up on the lead. She was aware that it would be important as a matter of strategy for the prosecution to contact these people immediately, discuss the cases with them and send them police reports and statements by the defendant. "I'll get right on that, Alec," she said. "If we get to them first, they'll be our witnesses and eliminate them as experts Porter or Maine might want to use. At least we can use Wolcott to help us on jury selection strategies. I thought she was quite impressive."

"I'd rather have her working for us as opposed to her working for Porter and Maine," Alec said. "But then, they couldn't afford her, and we can. And we know we can always count on Procheska in a case like this." He winked at the other three. All four got up from their seats. "I think that fairly well says it all. Does anyone disagree?" No one did.

Alec Hunter walked into the lobby where lights were on and cameras were set to run. He was in his zone—the very successful district attorney molding, then using the press to his advantage.

Monday—6:45 P.M.
The King's Table Restaurant

"Damn, it's cold," Burt said to Jack as they left the office. It was only a short walk to the King's Table, and each could feel the biting sensation in their throats and chest as they hit the night air. The warmth of the lounge and restaurant welcomed them as they entered through the heavy, wooden doors, hung up their coats and walked to the bar. The carpet was full and rich under their feet. Oldies were playing on the surround-sound system.

The Table, as it was called, was dark and tastefully done with rich-burgundy leather booths and a marble and glass bar. The Table prided itself on the appearance of its hostesses and waiters. It catered to powerful men and women who wanted to let their hair down with a few drinks and maybe dinner. It was a comfortable place for adversaries who had beaten each other's brains in all day long, or were thinking about how they were going to do so tomorrow. It was the hangout of businessmen and businesswomen, lawyers and judges. Tonight, it was full of people still trying to digest the day's events. They had congregated to hear who knew what about Sheriff Hardacre's death and Avery Jackson's arrest. There were several Rotarians there who had witnessed the shooting. They were holding court, going over the trauma of the day's events quietly, again and again, to an enthralled audience. They had already given their story to the detectives, but they needed to tell what they witnessed to anyone who would listen.

Burt and Jack settled onto their barstools.

"What'll it be, gentlemen?" Rick Buscemi, the bartender, asked.

"Miller Lite on draft," Burt said.

"Make that two," Jack said, "and some bar snacks, Rick."

"Sure thing, guys," Rick said as he poured the beers and grabbed the pretzels. Their mouths watered as they watched the tall and thin, frosted glasses fill with liquid gold. "The word here is that you guys are representing Judge Jackson. Any truth to the rumor?"

"Could be. We'll be there with him tomorrow morning for his first appearance," Burt said as he took his first swallow.

"Who told you that?" Jack asked.

"Oh, it's all over the place that Burt got thrown in jail for being a bad boy and that you had to go to federal court to get him out." A big smile passed quickly across Burt's face. It was certainly a badge of honor, a rite of defense attorney passage, to be thrown in jail for vigorously representing a client.

"You can't believe everything you hear," Burt said. "The guards over at the jail just got a little carried away. It was really nothing."

"Burt, there ain't nothin' you do that's nothin'. It's all big," Rick said. "Can I get you guys another one?"

"Once more," Burt and Jack said, having practically inhaled their first drinks.

"Is Chris coming for dinner tonight?" Jack asked, referring to Burt's newest girlfriend, Chris Conley.

"Yeah. I called her a little while ago. How about Marci? Call her."

Jack pulled out his cell phone, talked to his wife and made the arrangements. "She'll be here in half an hour. Let's talk before the women get here, okay?" Burt nodded. "I'm leaving the office February first, and you aren't going to talk me into staying for this case, or any other," Jack said. "Avery's case is a loser. You and I both know it."

"He's our friend, though," Burt said. "We can't let him twist in the wind. He deserves the best defense."

"He's our friend," replied Jack, "and I feel for him. There is something screwy going on in the case that doesn't meet the eye, but we have to be realistic. He's in deep trouble. The only possible defense is a mental one, and we will never sell that to a Montgomery County jury—ever. The reason Alec Hunter is the DA is because of Pete Cassidy Rose and his psychomotor epilepsy defense. Do you think Hunter will allow us to blindside him the way old Dave Morgan was blindsided by John Hodge?"

Jack was referring to the defense attorney who had gotten Rose off with an NGRI verdict years ago. Hodge was now a highly-respected district court judge. "Hunter's made his career off that case. The difference here is that Rose had a severe head injury when he was a kid, and Avery didn't. Hell, he hasn't even seen a psychiatrist in his life, except for some psychiatrist in the Army forty years ago. We'll probably never even get that record. If we're going to sell an insanity defense, we need something physical. If we claim Jackson killed Hardacre because of schizophrenia, depression or post-traumatic stress, it'll never fly. Those diagnoses are too vague—like vapors in a jar. You just can't get a judge or jury to say NGRI when your client's killed or raped someone, unless the defendant has an IQ of forty and looks like Rasputin, and even that's not good enough. Prosecutors have insanity prosecutions down to a science. They just find a doctor who'll tell the jurors that the defendant is faking his mental illness, which is what jurors need to hear because then they don't have to make any hard decisions. The doctor says the magic words, 'faker,' and voila—a conviction. It'll be even easier for them to say that about Avery because he's bright. For god's sake, Avery is a lawyer and college professor."

"Keep trying to talk yourself out of doing this case, but you're hooked. Rick," Burt said, "how about another beer for my friend here?"

"If I don't make the move now out of the PD's office," Jack said, "I'll never do it. I'll be a burned-out public defender when I'm fifty-years old like you. I might even start blowing powder up my nose like you."

"What do you know about drugs?" Burt asked. "I bet you've never used a drug in your life except for a little grass in college. You're a Boy Scout, Maine. Besides, a little coke used recreationally is harmless."

"Recreationally, my ass. Your eyes are getting so baggy you look like an owl. You're an addict just like the drunks down on Ludlow Street. If I consider doing this case with you, you'll have to stop it and get into drug treatment or something. I'm not making any sort of commitment to you on a case like this if you're hungover all the time."

Burt hadn't been confronted so directly in years, and it pissed him the hell off. "I ought to kick your ass and then fire you for insubordination, Maine."

"Always the tough guy," Jack said. "Go ahead, buddy, and then I won't have to make a decision on whether I'll take this godforsaken case with you—and by the way, cut the tough-guy stuff; it's phony, and god knows I've known you too long to fall for it." Burt took a long swallow of beer. He motioned to Rick, who promptly came over. "Another round." Rick drew the drafts and placed them on the counter. "I'm not an addict," Burt protested, albeit lamely.

"Yeah, you are," Jack said calmly. "The only way I'll even consider doing this case with you is if you take your life seriously. You act as if you're trying to kill yourself." Jack took a sip of his beer and sat quietly. He looked at Burt. "You have to want to get straight for you—not just to keep me on this case. If you're doing it for me, forget it."

"Fine," Burt said, fuming.

"I'll need to talk with Marci about it, anyway. I'll give you an answer before the preliminary hearing. You need to understand one thing. I'm not going to end up doing most of the work while you sit around with a hangover."

"Fine, now let's enjoy the rest of evening."

Chris Conley and Marci Maine walked into the King's Table. Burt and Jack got up to greet the women. The two men picked their beers up off the bar. Burt put down five dollars for a tip, furious with Avery Jackson and Jack Maine for putting him in a position he couldn't ignore.

The four of them crowded into a booth.

Monday—10:00 P.M.
Montgomery County Jail

Avery paced in his suicide cell thinking obsessively of just that. He'd heard once of a prisoner just convicted of murder cutting his wrists with the broken lens of his glasses. He would have done that except the deputies had taken away his reading glasses. He would have used his shirt or pants to hang himself if he could have found something to tie them to. When on the bench, he had seen many defendants accused of murder. They had been tried, and many of them convicted, and sentenced in his court—some to life in prison. How could this be happening to him?

He was faced with his first night alone in jail. All he could hear was the occasional clanging of metal doors, activity in the jail having slowed down as evening approached. He lay down on the hard slab of what was supposed to be a bed. The light in his room could not be turned off. He had to sleep; his advisement and bond hearing were first thing in the morning.

Then he thought about the fact that he hadn't heard from his wife. He'd been allowed a phone call to her, but when he called, he got her voice mail. He told her he had a bond hearing in the morning and wanted her to be there. He asked her to come to the jail after the hearing so they could talk.

Some people who are depressed cannot sleep, but others, like Avery, sleep too much. He was gone from the world almost immediately, so exhausted from the day, and at least when he was asleep, he couldn't feel his headache—but then came the dreams and the voices: "The moon is full. The moon is full." *Bang*! And the blood began to run onto the cement floor and into the metal spout. He awoke gasping, sweat on his forehead. *It would be better if I were dead*, he thought, *these dreams are my worst form of torture—certainly worse than a death sentence.* He wondered how many more nights he'd be alive in jail isolated from humanness, tortured by his thoughts. Sometime in that first night, his soul allowed him just a morsel of dreamless sleep.

CHAPTER 3

Tuesday, January 16—8:30 A.M.
Montgomery County Court

County court is different from district court. It is a lower court where defendants charged with misdemeanors, as opposed to felonies, are tried. County court judges handle felony cases at their inception, which means initial advisement of rights, bond hearings and preliminary hearings. Then the cases are bound over to the district court judges if there is a finding of probable cause at the preliminary hearing. Almost all felonies are bound over for trial; all evidence is construed in favor of the state and even some hearsay is allowed. County court judgeships are frequently steppingstones to district court positions. Madeline Bonin was interested in her county-court appointment as just such a steppingstone. She was a forty-year-old woman from a prominent Democratic Montgomery County family that had contributed large sums of money to the party and had supported its candidates. Ohio's Democratic governor had appointed Judge Bonin to the bench. Madeline herself had gone to Harvard Law School and, upon passing the bar exam, had eschewed a lucrative private practice for a position with Legal Aid helping the poor. She had been offered a position by Burt Porter and had turned it down. She was more interested in practicing civil law, helping women attain equal rights and protection from abusive men. She was married to a lawyer practicing environmental law; they had one son. For Madeline Bonin, her family and the law were her life. She was not about to sabotage either of them—certainly not by making any stupid or

51

unpopular decisions that would jeopardize her popularity with the press or electorate.

When she arrived early that Tuesday morning, she knew she'd be hearing the Jackson case because she was the duty judge that week, which meant that all new cases would come before her for advisement and bond. The case of Judge Avery Jackson represented her first visible challenge. Any decision she made on the issue of bond or probable cause at the preliminary hearing that made her look soft on crime, or gave the appearance of showing favoritism for one of her colleagues, might spell the end of her career. She had witnessed what happened to Jackson on the DiSalvo case. When he appeared soft on the rape issue, the press and the electorate crucified him. And now here he was—an example to all judges of what not to do—about to appear before her. *How can a man so naïve also be so cunning and vicious?* she thought as she drove to work. It didn't make sense, but better him than her. She didn't care what Jackson was going through at the time that led him to commit such an horrific act. He was now grist for the wheels of justice, and she was about to turn them.

Bonin guessed there would be a great deal of media at the hearing; she just underestimated how many. Camera crews were waiting in the parking lot outside the courthouse as she pulled in. She was able to evade direct contact with them because she, like all the other judges, parked beneath the building behind a security gate. For now, she would be safe from them. It was when the hearing was over and she left the courthouse that she might have problems. They had no access to her in her chambers or when she was on the bench. She would not allow cameras in her courtroom, although they would be allowed to film through the glass portals in the thick, wooden doors to her courtroom.

Her clerk and bailiff warned her that the courtroom was full, and there was a crush of media outside in the halls. She had instructed her staff that no cameras were to be turned on during the proceeding and to inform the sheriff's office that she would advise Judge Jackson last and to bring him in after she finished the morning docket of insignificant bonds and advisements. She also asked her bailiff to communicate to the deputy sheriff the need for increased security.

The run-of-the mill drunks, prostitutes, petty thieves and male abusers were handled by the newest deputies from both the district attorney's office and the public defender's office respectively. Yolanda Crone was the public defender that morning. Her adversary was another black woman, Ivy Sanders, who had only been with the DA's office a month. When the Jackson case was called, Yolanda and Ivy gave way to the first teams and moved to the chairs behind the counsel tables.

Avery Jackson appeared. He looked haggard, as if he had not slept. His hair was matted and he was unshaven, showing that his beard was quite gray. The suit and tie he wore when arrested had been replaced by a baggy orange jumpsuit with MONTGOMERY COUNTY JAIL stenciled in black on the back; he had to waddle to the counsel table because his hands and feet were shackled.

Burt Porter and Jack Maine walked with their briefcases and calendars to join him. Alec Hunter, Jim Brodan and Hank Dorsey assumed their positions at the People's table, the one closest to the jury box, which was now empty.

When the defendant had shuffled to his chair between Burt and Jack, Judge Bonin spoke to a hushed courtroom. "This is case number 05CR66 the People of the State of Ohio v. Avery Jackson. Counsel, would you please enter your appearances." The cameras outside the courtroom began filming and the media artists began quickly sketching the defendant sitting at counsel table.

"Alec Hunter for the People, Your Honor," Hunter said, "and if the court please, also appearing with me are Deputy District Attorneys Henry Dorsey and James Brodan."

"Thank you, Mr. Hunter. And for the defense?"

Burt rose to his feet. "If the Court please, Burt Porter on behalf of the defendant, Avery Jackson. Also appearing with me is my co-counsel, Jack Maine. We're representing Judge Jackson because he does not yet have the funds for private counsel. Given the seriousness of the alleged crime, it is imperative Judge Jackson have counsel at all stages of the proceeding. If Judge Jackson makes arrangements to secure private counsel, we will apprise the Court immediately. As a preliminary matter, we're asking the Court to request that the sheriff's deputies handling Judge Jackson have his handcuffs and leg irons removed for future hearings and that he be allowed to appear in court in his suit." Burt was very careful to emphasize the word *Judge* whenever he referred to his client.

As Alec Hunter rose to his feet, Judge Bonin asked, "Mr. Hunter, what's your position on the requests of defense counsel?"

"Your Honor, certainly, we have no objection to Mr. Porter and Mr. Maine representing this defendant so long as he is indigent. As for cuffs and leg irons, we have no objection to his cuffs being removed, but we believe it appropriate that he wear leg irons in view of the seriousness of the crime and the possibility of him being a flight risk. Furthermore, Your Honor, we have no objection to this defendant wearing a suit in future hearings as opposed to his prison jumpsuit."

Hunter immediately countered Porter's reference to Avery Jackson as a judge with his own characterization of him as a mere defendant, no different from the other twenty-two defendants who'd just appeared in Judge Bonin's court that morning, all of whom were charged with crimes and wore orange jumpsuits, had bad breath, greasy hair, were unshaven and reeked of cigarettes.

"The Court will order defendant's handcuffs removed at this time. I will further order leg irons removed. I see the sheriff's office has enough men here to control this rather small defendant should that become necessary. He will also be allowed to wear his suit to further proceedings. As for the issue of public defender representation, I will assume the public defender's office knows how to use its limited resources, and the Court will not interfere with its discretion at this time. Mr. Hunter, what charges do you intend to file in this matter?"

"First-degree murder, Your Honor, with special circumstances of killing a peace officer, to wit, Sheriff Eugene Hardacre, while the defendant was lying in wait and with premeditation and malice aforethought. The State of Ohio is seeking the death penalty."

Such words always froze a courtroom. There was something about one human being killing another human being, followed by a third human in the form of the DA, with more power than the first two, proclaiming he would be attempting to kill the first human being for killing the second human being. That's just a lot of killing, and such a pronouncement always appeals to the most primitive prurient, aggressive and survival instincts of *Homo sapiens*.

"Mr. Porter and Mr. Maine, has your client been advised of his rights in this matter?" Bonin asked.

"Your Honor, as the Court knows, Judge Jackson has advised hundreds of defendants of their rights in another courtroom in this very building; and yes, we have advised him of his rights and therefore waive any further advisement."

"Very well, Counsel. What is the People's position on bond?"

Alec Hunter rose, squared his shoulders and in a senatorial manner, stated, "Your Honor, the People oppose bond in this matter. This is a capital case where the appropriate punishment might well be death. Furthermore, this is a case where we would argue the proof is evident and the presumption great. There are roughly a hundred and fifty witnesses to this crime. It's been recorded on videotape. When there is such overwhelming evidence of guilt in a capital case, defendant's Eighth and Fourteenth Amendment Rights to reasonable bail give way to the right of the People to protection and justice. We oppose any motion for bail. If the court is entertaining any notion of granting bail, then we would request a hearing on the matter at which time we can show the videotape of the actual killing of Sheriff Hardacre by this defendant."

"Mr. Porter, are you seeking bond for this defendant, and do you want an evidentiary hearing on the issue?"

Requesting an evidentiary hearing on the issue was suicide. Neither Burt nor Jack wanted the tape of the actual killing aired over and over again prior to trial. "No, Your Honor, we only wish to be heard on the issue," Burt replied.

"Very well, Counsel, proceed."

Jack made his pitch on the issue of bond as he'd done so many times in his career, knowing fully that his arguments would bear no fruit. "Your Honor, as the Court knows, Judge Avery Jackson has been a lifelong member of this community. He is an attorney, former judge, now a college professor at Sinclair University instructing police recruits, and working for law enforcement. He has a wife and two children who're in the courtroom today. He owns real estate in Dayton. This is a man who poses no flight risk. If he is able to keep working in his present job as a college professor, he would be able to afford private counsel and not rely on the funds of the taxpayers."

Avery's heart sank. He hadn't seen his wife and children in the back of the courtroom. He was mortified that they should see him in chains and shackles. He hoped the media wouldn't be able to identify them and ask them questions.

"Do the People have a response?" Bonin asked Hunter.

"Yes, Your Honor. It defies logic that a man facing a possible death sentence should not be considered a flight risk. We ask that bond be denied."

Bonin didn't hesitate. "The Court, having heard the arguments of counsel, finds that the charges concerning defendant Jackson are the most serious imaginable, that although the presumption of innocence still pertains to this defendant, the proof is evident and presumption of guilt great, and therefore the motion for bond is hereby denied. If counsel would like to raise this issue again at the time of the preliminary hearing, the Court could reconsider it then, depending on the evidence. Counsel, the Court is setting the preliminary hearing for next Tuesday, a week from today, in this courtroom. Is that date suitable for all counsel?"

"Fine with the People," Hunter stated.

"Acceptable to the defense," Maine said.

"Court is in recess, and the defendant is remanded to the custody of the sheriff of Montgomery County to be held without bond."

"All rise," the bailiff called out.

Judge Madeline Bonin took her leave by the door behind her bench and retired to her chambers.

Tuesday—11:00 A.M.
Montgomery County Jail

Friends and relatives aren't allowed contact visits with prisoners in the Montgomery County Jail. They can look at one another through thick glass while speaking by telephone. Only professionals—doctors or attorneys—are allowed contact visits with their clients because of a presumption that doctors or lawyers would not pass the prisoner any kind of contraband.

Perhaps, it was best this way—it gave Avery some protection from his wife.

She sat in the visitation booth. Avery entered on the other side of the glass. Gloria was a fifty-year-old, light-skinned, black woman who was menopausal. Where once she had been rather big-boned but still shapely, her middle had filled in and her once-pretty face was now full and double-chinned. She dressed expensively, but the costliest of dresses could no longer hide her paunchy fat and revive her beauty. She had to dye her gray hair. She made sure her acrylic nails were done weekly. Once a devoted teacher, she was now just putting in her time. She had grown irritable with the students. For years, she had secretly harbored the belief they were there to gratify and adore her. When she found out that neither the students nor Avery could make her feel better about herself, she grew annoyed with everyone around her and suffered from bouts of depression. She would have liked to have changed careers except, "Where does a fifty-year-old teacher go for new employment and make the same amount of money?" she would ask her friends, hairdresser and manicurist.

Avery had once appeared to her to be a good capital investment—now his stock was worth nothing. She should have sold her shares in him earlier when he still had value. She could have gotten something in the way of alimony or child support for Aaron and Rebecca. Now, there would be nothing; the kids were adults, and he was incarcerated. Her dilemma was whether to hang in there and hope his value went up. That wasn't a likely proposition given the charges. Alec Hunter's words kept ringing in her ears, ". . . proof evident and presumption great." The way she saw it, it was time to cut her losses and blowout all her stock in him. Besides, if she dumped him now, she would not have to go through the humiliation of sticking by him as he was sentenced to prison, or even death.

Gloria and Avery looked at one another. It was not a look of love shared by two people who'd been separated by fate or tragedy. Gloria's disdainful contempt was apparent. He looked at her sheepishly, hoping that somehow she would still love him.

Each picked up a telephone. She began stridently, screeching, "Avery, what did you do?"

"Gloria, if I knew, I'd tell you. All I remember is teaching class yesterday morning, and the next thing I know I'm being led by a bunch of cops to the jail here. How are you and the kids doing with this, and how are they? I really didn't want to hurt you or them."

"God, Avery, I don't believe it. Your life is a mess. The political hassle with the DiSalvo case was all I could take. You haven't been there for me for years."

"The question, Gloria, is the same one I have been asking you for the last two years since DiSalvo, 'do you still love me?'"

Repulsed at even the thought of touching her husband, she puckered her mouth and nose like she'd just had castor oil forced down her throat. "I don't know if I love you, Avery. I haven't known for a long time."

Avery stiffened, realizing clearly there would be no tenderness from Gloria, probably ever again. He looked at her for an interminable time, breathed deeply and said, "I'm going to need a lot of support through this mess, both emotionally and financially."

"Avery, the fact is, I can't provide any emotional support for you. Maybe the kids can; they certainly love you. I certainly can't provide support for you financially. My money was given to me by my parents. It's all I have and under the circumstances, I'm not about to share it with you. I have two kids to put through college on a teacher's salary. The chances are you'll never make another dime in your life."

"That's pretty cold. There's no chance for us. You don't believe in me."

"How could I?" she laughed.

"How much do I have in my retirement and savings accounts?"

"Three grand in savings and about twenty thousand in retirement—and half of that is mine because, as you know, this is a joint-property state. We've got about twenty thousand in equity in the house after we pay a realtor if we decide to sell it. Your car is worth maybe ten thousand, and so is mine."

"Got all the figures at your fingertips, huh? You've already talked to a lawyer, haven't you?"

Gloria just stared at him, her silence saying it all.

"I can see where your head is, Gloria. You've already made plans to get out."

She said nothing.

"Just give me the retirement and savings. You keep the house and give the car to the kids. Fair enough?"

"You know, I've been thinking about the two of us for a long time. This shouldn't come as a surprise to you; we've talked about it. Things between us before DiSalvo weren't much good, and since DiSalvo, they've been a disaster. But I'll help get whatever cash to you I can out of your retirement account."

"That's big of you."

"If you don't want the help, I'll walk out of here right now," she shot back.

"Let's not talk about money right now. How are Aaron and Rebecca? I saw them in the courtroom and it tore my guts out."

"They're outside in the lobby and would like to see you, but I have to tell you, they're both very upset with you. Don't try to change the subject. We need to work out this money thing. The way I figure it is, you have twenty-three thousand dollars, plus a car, and they're all marital assets. I'll be living in the house, and it's worth less than you've saved. I want you to give me thirteen thousand for living expenses and the kids' tuition. That leaves you with ten grand for an attorney. I'll pick up the rest of the expenses and tuition."

"Ten thousand dollars on this case won't even pay for the experts," Avery answered angrily. "It occurs to me that you make fifty thousand a year and have a bunch of money you inherited from your parents. How about your retirement? What about that? I'm entitled to half the interest and dividends off your accounts."

"Avery, you know I only have a few thousand dollars in retirement because I elected to take my salary in cash rather than retirement."

Avery could feel the anger. He could not contain it. "Yeah, right, and you spend most all of it on clothes, jewelry and perfume for a body you have let turn to dimpled, puckered fat. It has always been about you, Gloria." Avery had wanted to say this for years. He went on. "When I really need you and can no longer benefit you, you dump me. I can't believe that you'd come here the day after I'm arrested for a crime I don't remember committing and attempt to take whatever money I have while you divorce me. Bitch."

"Fuck you, Avery." Those would be the last words she ever said to him.

Suddenly, the anger just disappeared. It was useless. "Okay, Gloria, fine, you take the house, I'll give you eight thousand for the kids' tuition and give them my car. I want the rest. I'll have my lawyers get the money, not you. I promise you'll have a check within two weeks. Now get out of my sight and send in the kids." She hung up her phone and got up without looking at Avery. She knew under the circumstances, she was getting a more than fair settlement. She turned for the door.

Tuesday—7:00 P.M.
Burt Porter's Condo

Burt Porter owned a condominium in downtown Dayton. It suited his lifestyle. He could finish work, have drinks and dinner, and go home with a date or alone. He really didn't need a car. His condo complex was right on the river in an affluent area, just blocks from the courthouse and the office. It was next to the YMCA where he occasionally worked out. That had become less frequent, however, the more he drank and the more dependent he became on cocaine. The results were evident. Where he had once been buff, broad-shouldered and tough-looking, he was now soft. He had a slight paunch. His hair had thinned in the front, although it still maintained its brown color.

His frequent hangovers were becoming harder to get over, and though he thought cocaine was an ideal recreational drug, he was beginning to feel the toll the booze and drugs were taking on him physically and emotionally. He didn't want to quit, of course, even though at some level he was aware of his dependency, and didn't like it. But, he did what all addicts do. He sought more coke to recreate, or even exacerbate, his original high.

His problem now, however, was the promise he had made to Jack Maine to keep him in the office.

Chris, his new, steady girlfriend, shared his fondness for cocaine. She was much younger than Burt, in her late twenties. She had light-brown hair that she enhanced to a beautiful blonde. Her body was flawless. She wore tasteful, modest suits when on the job in Judge Judith Jeffers' court as a court reporter. The vests and jackets covered full and well-formed breasts. Her legs were model-perfect and she always kept them tanned-looking with a sunless lotion. Burt saw her often in Jeffers' court and the attraction between them was immediate. Burt, like most males, was taken by her looks and the oozing sexuality she could not cover with clothes, no matter how hard she tried. As she transcribed the proceedings, he'd steal glances at her legs when he sought relief from the intensity that was trial law.

Chris was attracted to Burt by his ruggedly-handsome good looks. He came across as if he had no peer among males in terms of slyness, cunning and sheer strength. It further turned her on that she turned him on. She and Burt turned into sex buddies. He introduced her to cocaine, and she loved that as much as sex. Her fantasy that Burt would grow to love and marry her always percolated, though all her friends told her it was pretty unlikely.

On this Tuesday night, they were together at his place after having dinner out. Still very cold and icy outside, it felt good to be in the warm inside. He kept his condo neat and nicely furnished. A woman came in once a week and cleaned it. His furnishings were decidedly male, a lot of rich leather. He had plenty of big pillows on the couches and on the floor. The carpet was white, full and soft. Burt liked candles and his gas fireplace. Chris lounged comfortably on the couch while Burt lit the candles and turned on the fireplace. All the lights in the house were off, except the candles and flames from the fireplace. He put on a Boney James soft-jazz CD.

Burt went into the bedroom and came out with a small vial. He unscrewed the cap, poured some coke onto the round, glass-topped coffee table in the middle of the room. He separated the coke into four lines with a one-sided razor blade. Without hesitation, he snorted a line through a cocktail straw. The mountain of worry and anxiety over Avery Jackson quickly became a grassy hill that he could easily walk through. His thoughts were pristine and logical.

Chris got up from the couch, knelt down on her knees and snorted a line off the table, immediately relieving the monotony and tedium of listening to six hours of that day's unrelenting testimony.

"Thanks for the dinner, Burt, and thanks for the coke. I sure needed this."

"Don't mention it. There is one thing I have to mention, though. I didn't talk about it at dinner because I wanted us to be alone when I brought it up."

"What? I hope everything is okay between us."

"We're not a problem," Burt said. Chris relaxed and breathed. "The problem is that I promised Jack Maine that I'd stop using coke and get into treatment."

"You're kidding. What did you do that for?"

"Not because I wanted to. He just caught me at a weak moment after he got me out of jail yesterday. He really put the screws to me at the King's Table saying he wouldn't consider doing Jackson's defense with me unless I was clean. I wish I'd never told him I did coke. When I told him, I was just sort of trying to feel out if he was a player, too. I should have known better; he's such a Boy Scout."

"Do you need him on Jackson?"

"Yeah, I need him. He's the best criminal trial lawyer in town and maybe in the state. I know I don't have the stamina anymore to do a case like this one alone. A case like this will drive me into the ground."

"You could tell him you've stopped and are in treatment. It doesn't mean that you couldn't dabble a little on the side. Know what I mean?"

"I thought about that. I won't do it. I'm not going to become one of those damned junkies who lie to his best friends. I'm either going to quit or tell him I can't quit and find someone else to do the case with me. I've always said to myself I could quit if I wanted to. Now, I have to quit within the next week. And, I honestly don't know if I can."

"I wasn't expecting this tonight. I was expecting to do some lines and have some great sex."

"We can still do the lines and have the great sex, but the drug part might end within the week, unless you can think of an alternative. You need to know what I'm thinking."

"Where will that leave us? I'm not sure I can quit. I love the stuff and I love being with you when we're doing it," said Chris.

"What I have in mind is enjoying the next few days, see how I'm feeling, and then make a decision. We don't have to be all heavy tonight about this. It's just on my mind. Let's enjoy the rest of the evening."

"You get no argument from me." She moved close to Burt and kissed him gently on the lips. Her kisses became harder and fuller on him. She moved to his ears and neck with gentle nibbles, flicking her tongue across his earlobe.

He could feel himself harden quickly. He never had a problem if he did a line first, but without it, he did.

He loved the way she kissed and moved. There was something about her that was different—more sensually animal. He had to have her. And did. A blow of coke here, a blow there, tongues and tumbling, wrestling, slippery, sliding, biting, and then forgetting everything but the sublime moment of climax.

They held each other for minutes before they said anything. Each was spent. Each knew that perhaps they could not enjoy this kind of incredible sex anymore without coke. They looked at each other, knowing that each had to quit, but not wanting to. How could anyone ever let go of this experience they had just shared with one another?

Chris finally broke the silence. "Let's do this as much as we can this week before it's over."

Burt nodded. "I don't think we can walk away from this kind of high. I'll get enough coke to get us through the week and then we'll decide what to do. I'll have my dope man, Van, come by tomorrow."

They listened to jazz, made love once more, talked and fell asleep around two in the morning. They didn't want to think about how they would feel when they awoke. Right now it all felt too good.

Tuesday—11:00 P.M.
Public Defender's Office

A brown sedan with two white men in the front seat pulled into the lot behind the public defender's office.

A two-story, light-red, brick structure, it was not the usual high-rise office building with a security guard and security elevator. Instead, it was a burglar's dream. A skeleton key could open both the main lock and the deadbolt on the back door. A single light poorly illuminated the lot and the back door. The frozen Miami River was on the other side of the lot and down an embankment; light reflected off its frozen surface. Naked oak and maple trees blocked a clear view of the back door. There was only the noise of traffic off Interstate 75 in the distance and an occasional car running down Third Avenue in front of the building.

The driver was thin and wiry with dark hair; the passenger was more heavyset with brown hair. The car moved into a space directly behind the back door.

The driver looked around the lot. "Let's go," he said. They got out simultaneously. The driver carried a black bag, opened it, brought out a set of equipment and keys, moved efficiently and purposefully as he disabled the alarm and opened both locks to the door. "After you," the driver said to the passenger. The driver entered the building quickly with his partner right behind him carrying another bag that was zipped shut. They entered a corridor just off a room where there were desks set up in cubicles.

"Got any idea where Porter's office is?" the passenger asked.

"They told me it was the one farthest from the back door in the front of the building."

As they walked toward the front of the building, it became very dark. The passenger turned on his flashlight and went into one of the bigger offices. He shined it on the wall and could see the college diplomas of Arleen Rice and a license from the Supreme Court of Ohio entitling her to practice law. "Not this one," he said.

The two men went into a few more offices, coming out quickly.

"Let's try this one, it looks like the biggest one," the driver whispered, wary of someone else being in the building doing research or working on a trial late at night.

Immediately upon entering the large office, they saw Porter's undergraduate degree, licenses to practice law in federal court and state courts of Ohio, as well as numerous certificates of appreciation lining the walls. "This is it. Do your thing," the driver said.

The passenger quickly unscrewed the lid to Burt's phone and placed a small, electrical recording microphone in both the mouthpiece and the ear piece. He then moved efficiently to the light on Porter's desk and placed a small transmitting device under the shade.

"I think we ought to get Porter's secretary, too," the driver said.

"Good thinking."

The driver turned quickly and walked out of the room to a secretary's desk right outside the door. The passenger shined the flashlight on the in-basket on the desk. In it were a bunch of legal documents and motions signed by Burt Porter. On the desk was the name, Judy Mabin.

"This is it. Mabin is Porter's secretary," the driver said.

Within a minute, they'd installed a transmitting devise in her phone. "Let's go," the passenger said.

In seconds, both men were out of the building and back in the car. They pulled away slowly and inconspicuously, disappearing into the night.

CHAPTER 4

Wednesday, January 17—10:00 A.M.
Burt Porter's Office

Secretly, Burt referred to Ovanul Hazeltree as his "nigger." To his face, Burt called him "my man," "cool dude" and "player." Ovanul preferred to be called Van.

Burt had first met Van ten years ago when Van was only eighteen-years old. Burt represented him in a possession of cocaine for sale case, and, of course, learned Van's history then. Van had all the jargon of a young man who was moving up within the drug-peddling world. He was a junior-high dropout raised by a welfare mother, Althea, in north Dayton. Althea had her own dreadful history of victimization, including being molested by a stepfather and beaten with an extension cord and burned with hot, french-fry grease. Van had never met his father. In fact, Althea wasn't sure who his father was. Van was the first born. In that position, he assumed more responsibility. He was the man of the house. Over the years, there had been numerous men seeing his mother—his five siblings had four different fathers. Most of the men coming into the house were dealers or pimps who used his mother for sex and drugs. As Van grew to adolescence, he became a manipulator and drug user like his mother and the men who visited her.

Althea supplemented her welfare existence with a trick or two on the side and also sold drugs on her own. Once a rather attractive woman, Althea aged rapidly by using her own product regularly. She dealt mostly in the hard stuff—

heroin, speed, a little LSD, and a new drug that was coming out called X. Much of her prostitution and drug profits went to the men who supplied her and pimped for her, but she generally had enough money for her family to get by on. There were always guns and large sums of cash around the house and lots of "motherfucker this, and motherfucker that." When Van acted up, he'd get a whuppin'. When he got a whuppin' from some of his mom's boyfriends who started to throw their weight around, he got homicidal. "I'll kill you, you motherfucker," he'd say, swinging at them until he was exhausted. They'd laugh at him, but Van meant it. By the time he was ten, he'd decided he would always be in control, and that no man or woman, white or black, would ever get the best of him. He would control the women, sex, money and relationships in his life.

Van was precocious; he picked up on everything. He skipped right into adulthood: dealing marijuana when he was ten, had a rap sheet by the time he was thirteen for car theft, burglary, possession of dangerous drugs and fighting at school. He did quite a bit of time in the detention center and finally got committed to the Ohio Department of Youth Corrections for beating up and threatening another kid with a knife in the schoolyard who couldn't pay him for drugs he'd bought. The kid he beat up turned up in a dumpster with his throat slit a few months later. Van could never be linked to the killing.

Van hated being locked up and vowed he'd never go to jail again; he'd die first. Burt only represented Van once because that was the only time Van didn't have the money to afford a lawyer. The case was dismissed; Burt never figured out how, though he had his suspicions. Even when Burt showed up for trial in his three-piece suit on this case, he believed he had no chance of winning. Just before they began to pick a jury, the detective announced there'd been a mistake in the handling of the evidence, and he couldn't be sure the drugs taken from Van were the ones he sought to introduce in the trial; the DA had no choice but to dismiss the matter. *Odd that should happen,* Burt had thought. Later, any time Van got into trouble, he had high-priced legal talent—always the Rosato brothers, Jim and Jeff.

Occasionally, Van would stop by the public defender's office to see if Burt was in. They enjoyed talking to one another—two egomaniacs, one educated and the other not, pumping themselves up. They weren't all that different from one another in terms of native intelligence or the ability to manipulate the system and other people; it was just that one did it according to a mass of rules he'd learned in law school and the other according to a set of rules he'd learned on the streets. One acted according to conscience and ethics; the other according to immediate necessity. As Burt's addiction grew, the differences between the two became blurry.

Nowadays, when they got together, their conversations would go something like: "Hey, bro, whuz happenin'? How much you makin' in this motherfuckin' job here as boss man? Still about ninety-K a year?"

Burt would get a big smile on his face and say nothing.

"Listen, bro, I make that in a *bad* month, sometimes in a *bad* week. Now, my people on the streets and me, we need to make an adjustment for inflation. We takin' in about a hundred large a month, an' lookin' for some talent and would like to know if you could either take a job in sales for us or as legal counsel? The sales job pays a hundred-K a month; the law job about a mil a year. I like you better'n the Rosatos any day, but they're out there to be hired. You, on the other fuckin' hand, are here makin' piddly shit. So, bro, why don't you get your head out yo ass and make some real fuckin' money working for me?"

"Hey, bro, Van, you know, it's just not all about money," Burt would say. "It's about job satisfaction. It's about getting people equal justice in a world where fairness is in short supply. You have apparently forgotten where you came from. So cut the shit when you come into my office and tell me how you got that case fixed?"

"You know what the detective said, 'The evidence was bad, the—what the fuck do you call it—chain of custody was broken,' yeah, motherfucker, the chain of custody was broken." Then Van would get a big smile on his face and wink at Burt.

"You and I both know that's bullshit," Burt would shoot back. "And tell me, man, how much for some of those hoes you got runnin' round on the streets?"

"Burt, my man, as you know, the price is usually negotiable, but for you we could probably arrange a decent price for some of my best pussy."

"You know, Van, a Popsicle will freeze in hell before I'd buy any of your pussy. I get plenty of that for free and don't get AIDS as part of the deal. So tell me, which profit margin is bigger, that for drugs or pussy?"

"You know I never discuss my markup with nobody, but judging by my new wheels—that new Lexus sitting outside in your parking lot, you see that one—you should be able to guess my profit margin on all of my—business...yeah, business—ventures, is cool. Why don't you try a little of my cocaine, or crack, or I could even mix you a speedball or two? I won't even charge you, bro, 'cause I still owe you for past legal services."

"No thanks, Van, I'm fine."

After years of this sort of banter, one day, at a time of weakness, after he had already started to develop a cocaine habit, Burt took a small foil of cocaine from Van. After all, it was free, he rationalized. Van looked at Burt. It was a moment of truth; he knew he had Burt, like a lion falling into a pit. The predator had found his prey. From that point on, Burt got his coke from Van. Van always gave him a discount on the coke that had been cut with Italian baby milk powder. It was the best stuff Burt ever had—not pure, but very good. Their business relationship developed in that way. Burt knew it was dangerous, but he couldn't help himself. He loved the cocaine, and the price.

So, it was on this Wednesday morning around ten o'clock that Burt got into work. He had an eleven o'clock meeting with Jack and the investigators on the Jackson case. Judy brought him a cup of coffee and the morning paper so he could read the latest news on Avery's case. He began sipping his coffee. He knew he couldn't wake up feeling like this much longer: bleary-eyed and somewhat desperate, already craving the taste and the high coke gave him. God, he could already feel the need for it and it was only 10:10 a.m. By tonight, he knew he would feel clean and powerful if he had another fix. But that was okay; he could stop using by the coming weekend. Yeah, by this coming weekend.

He called Van's pager and entered his number. He continued reading and sipping coffee for another ten minutes. Judy beeped him. "There is a call from your buddy, Van, on your personal line. Want me to take a message?"

"No, I'll take it. Hold all of my other calls, will you, Judy?"

"Sure, let me know if you need anything," said Judy, knowing Burt had had a hard night. Over the years, she had gotten to know him extremely well.

"Hello, Van, what's up?"

"You beeped me just now, man. What the fuck you mean, 'What's up?' You tell me what's up and then I'll tell you what's up. I have some information on this end you might be interested in."

"I need enough coke to get me through this weekend. Can you bring some by tonight?"

"Sure, bro, you got the cash, right?"

"You know you don't even have to ask that."

"Just checkin'. I'm a businessman, you know. Is your line safe?"

"Of course, my line is safe. It's always safe."

"Okay, man, listen to me, this is going to blow your socks off, rock your world. But I'm knowin' from first-hand information that your man, Judge Avery Jackson, was set up."

"Oh yeah, and just who set him up?" Burt asked, trying to maintain his cool through his hangover.

"I'll tell you tonight, bro. Your man did nothing more than pull the trigger for some other people who needed Gene Hardacre snuffed."

"I need more than that. Do you expect me, or a jury, to believe that a guy like Avery is a hired hit man? Bullshit. Why did they need Gene Hardacre snuffed?"

"The oldest reason in the world, bro—he knew too much. You have to trust me on this one, bro."

"How do you know?"

"Let's just say that I do."

"Van, my man," Burt said, trying to hide the urgency of his interest, "I need more information than that. I need something that will stand up in front of a jury. Why would you give me this kind of information anyway?"

"Let's just say I have an interest in giving you this information. okay? When I get to your crib tonight, I'll give you more of the inside skinny. What time be good for you?"

"How about seven-thirty?"

"Seven-thirty it is, bro. See you then."

Burt hung up the phone, sighed, stared off into space and grabbed a cigarette. While taking that first, precious drag that seemingly brings all nicotine addicts closer to God and truth, he decided not to get too excited about their conversation. He'd heard a lot of bull from a lot of street hoodlums in the past. Nevertheless, there had always been something about Van that generally stood up. He'd make sure he taped their conversation tonight, minus the drug transaction, of course. He had other things to think about now, like the meeting coming up in a few minutes with Jack and their PD investigator, Joe Betts. For the first time, though, Burt saw a glimmer of hope on Jackson. It was probably just bullshit, though.

An hour later his hangover was still bothering him, but he figured he could bluff his way through this meeting; he'd be in control; he was the boss. He'd give Jack Maine lip service. He could keep his present lifestyle going and keep Jack on board with Jackson, his first priority at the moment.

He knew a number of psychiatrists who owed him favors. He'd get one of them to cover him with Jack—write a letter or give him a phone call saying he was in treatment. He'd call in a favor. He had spread a lot of public defender money around to those guys over the years. If they wanted public defender business in the future, they would play ball with him. *Why not?* Burt thought. *The goddamned DAs got the shrinks to say whatever they wanted because they control the money; he could too.*

"Where's Joe?" Burt asked Jack as he entered the office.

"He'll be along in a few minutes," Jack replied. "Before he gets here, let's talk about our private agreement. How are you doing with drug treatment?"

Bastard is such a Boy Scout, Burt thought. "I'm going to do it. I talked with Chris about it last night. She and I are going to do it together."

"Have you talked with a therapist yet?"

"No. I'll make some calls as soon as this meeting is over."

"I've heard 'I'm gonna' bullshit from junkies for years," Jack said. "That and two dollars will get you a coffee at Starbucks."

"Now I'm a junkie?"

"Yes, you're a junkie."

"You know damned well you want to do this case, whether I get clean or not."

"What concerns me about my doing this case with you is that lately your balls have disappeared up your nose. When you're not hungover, I'll spar with you; right now, you're too pathetic. You know Marci and I have been talking about my going into private practice for a long time. It'll be all I can do to put her off until Jackson is over. So you start treatment by the preliminary hearing on Monday or Avery Jackson will be your problem."

"This is the last time you'll have to ask me. But you need to get this straight. I'm running the case. I'll have the shrink call you, or do you want a letter?"

Jack just looked at Burt. "*I'm* running the case until you can get your head out of your ass. Do I make myself clear?"

Porter said nothing. He could probably handle having Jack run the case, but he didn't want any of the other lawyers to hear the mutiny.

"I think we should have that young, black woman, Yolanda, in on the case, too. She's green behind the ears in terms of trial experience, but she's got guts. I thought she showed spunk when we went over to Grice's court and got you out of jail with a writ."

"Noway. There are a helluva lot of women lawyers in this office who've paid more dues. They'll be pissed at me. It'll cause political problems." In his heart, Burt had an inherent mistrust of women. He believed there were no female attorneys as tough as male attorneys. It was a genetic thing. Men are the gladiators, women the gatherers.

"It's important," Jack said, "that we have a black woman attorney believing in Avery and sitting at counsel table with him. She's the only one in the office, and she's capable. We're bound to have two or three black women on this jury and maybe some black men. The black women will look at her as a role model, and the men will like her looks. She's got a lot of guts, her heart seems to be in the right place and she has some life experience. She's not a kid. I think it's a good idea."

"It's against my instincts. I don't think women are up to a case like this; they don't have the stomach for it. But I suppose she could help us with research and monitor the investigation," Burt mused. Jack nodded.

"Come to think of it, I'm glad I thought of her," Burt said. "She can also be a wet nurse for Avery when we don't want to go to the jail and hold his hand. I'll deal with the politics in the office. Don't worry about it." Jack had to work at it, but he refrained from shaking his head at the silliness of it.

Burt picked up his phone. "Judy, tell Yolanda—what's her last name? Yeah, Crone—tell Yolanda Crone to come to my office immediately. And is Joe Betts back yet? He's supposed to be here, too."

Joe was an ex-con, convicted of manslaughter when he was twenty; did ten years in the Ohio State Penitentiary for it. Six foot six, his skin very dark, almost black, he made a statement all by himself, even if he had not been jailhouse-muscled from pumping iron. Now middle-aged, Burt had hired him as an investigator nine years ago, one year after his release from prison. It had been a good pick. Joe turned out to be bulldog: relentless, a diligent researcher and investigator who never let go until all loose ends were tied up.

He'd done most of his time in the cell next to Dr. Sam Sheppard. Joe always had interesting Sam Sheppard stories that the young attorneys loved. Basically, Dr. Sam was a nice guy who kept to himself and always maintained his innocence. After Sam's death, DNA proved him to be telling the truth. Joe also had other grizzly stories to tell—like how the lights of the prison used to dim when they were throwing the switch on the electric chair.

Joe had just returned from giving some testimony in court. He and Yolanda met at Burt's door and entered together. The four of them sat at a conference table not three feet away from the light on Burt's desk. "This is our team for the Jackson case," he announced. Joe had already been told he was part of the action. For Yolanda, this came out of the blue. She looked at Jack and with a smile, said, "Thanks, Jack. I'll make sure you aren't sorry you picked me." Then she looked at Burt.

"Welcome to the team, Yolanda," Burt said. "We have a lot of work to do. We might as well get started right away."

Yolanda couldn't wipe the smile off her face.

Burt shifted his eyes from her to the Jack. "Okay, first, Jack, have we gotten the forensic psychologist over to interview Avery yet?"

"I've made arrangements for Dr. Phil Gilmour to do that first thing tomorrow morning," replied Jack.

"Why don't you and Yolanda meet him over there in the morning? You might want to sit in to see how well Avery does with him. Do whatever Gilmour wants." Burt was starting to wake up. He was hitting his stride. "Secondly, Joe, we need Avery Jackson's entire history. Talk to his wife, his kids. Find out everything he did on Monday, if he owned a gun and whether it was registered. Find out where his car was parked. Is it still in the parking lot at Sinclair

University or did he drive it to the Renaissance? Get his service records.

"Also, I want you to do an investigation on a Mr. Ovanul Hazeltree. He's a former client who's scored big in the drug and prostitution business in town here. You can get his date of birth and social security number from the old file. Hazeltree has a penchant for picking up serious cases, and then getting them mysteriously dismissed—the Rosatos represent him now whenever he gets in a jam. Van's protected—he's either a snitch or he's paying someone off. Get the records from all his cases, who the DA was, the arresting officer, the investigating detective, the judge and the particulars of the dismissal. Hazeltree claims to have information on Jackson's case."

Joe nodded, taking notes.

"What kind of info does Hazeltree have?" Jack asked.

"I'll tell you tomorrow; I'm meeting with him tonight to find out."

"Get him on tape if you can," Jack said. "Don't you think it would be a good idea to have Joe there to take notes? You can't be a witness, you know, and if you become one, you'll have to conflict off the case."

"Yeah, I know," Burt said, "but Van will never tell me anything with Joe there. I'll see what he has to say and maybe soften him up to have Joe do a videotaped interview, or at least get something in writing later." Burt was aware his drug habit was interfering with his professional life, but he could rationalize his drug usage because, if not for it, this information wouldn't be coming to him on this important case. "I'll try to tape him, but I don't know if he'll do it. Yolanda," Burt turned to her, "I want you to start doing some research on sanity cases. Start snooping around to find experts who have written about people committing crimes and having no memory of them. I guess you'd look under legal amnesia. Can those people assist and cooperate in their own defense? Do they know right from wrong? Which lawyers and psychiatrists have done these kinds of cases around the United States with some degree of success? You know that sort of thing. Look on the internet, research the case law and look at psychological abstracts."

"Will do."

"Let's all meet again after the preliminary hearing to talk about what we've found out—say Monday afternoon," Burt suggested. "Will that work for all of you?"

"You're assuming the preliminary hearing will be over before lunch?" Yolanda asked.

"It will be," Burt assured her. "The preliminary hearing is just a formality. It'll be over before we can say Ovanul Hazeltree. It'll be interesting to see who they'll call to establish probable cause. Will it be the Presiding Judge of the District Court, Carl Kessler, or the Presiding Judge of the Court of Appeals, Bob

Wulf? Maybe we should object to their testimony on the grounds their fucked up characters make them incredible as a matter of law. I think we'll need a lot of humor to get through this. If anything comes up, we can have informal meetings; otherwise, we'll get together Monday after the preliminary hearing."

Joe and Yolanda got up from the conference table to get to work. Yolanda still had a smile on her face.

"After the shit you've been giving me, I think you owe me lunch, Maine," Burt said.

"I'll take you to lunch tomorrow, junkie. I'm taking Marci to lunch today. Just have a note for me from your doctor by Monday, or you and Yolanda will be doing Jackson alone."

Wednesday—12:15 P.M.
The King's Table Restaurant

Marci Maine was a thirty-four-year-old, blonde spitfire at five foot three, about a hundred ten pounds, all of it well-proportioned. She'd once been a pro/expert skier and instructor working winters at Keystone Resort in Colorado before meeting Jack; she still stayed in good shape. She was every bit Jack's equal—her intelligence was exceeded only by her insight into people. She had good judgment and a keen sense of morality and justice. She could have been a good lawyer, but hadn't ever wanted to get all bogged down with the details of tax, contracts and the like. She'd decided to make her money in a women's world, as opposed to competing in a man's world by becoming a sales director for Sherry May Cosmetics. She made over a hundred thousand dollars a year working with, and selling to, women and gay men.

She enjoyed the notion that the women in her company were the highest-paid, female executives in the world, but she was tired now of what she was doing. She wanted to work with Jack, and she wanted a child. Jack agreed, but had put her off for a while saying he needed a little more experience in the PD's office—the womb, he called it—before venturing into the world. The appointed date for Jack's delivery from the womb was February first, and Marci aimed to help with the delivery and catch him when he popped out. She'd found a crib for them in the form of an office. She was supposed to put a deposit on it this afternoon after she had lunch with him.

"Hi," Jack said, as he kissed his wife and sat down in a booth at the King's Table.

"We haven't done this for awhile," Marci said.

"I know. I didn't know if I would get here on time because of a meeting on Jackson."

"How did that go?"

71

"Okay. But you know I don't know what I want with this Jackson case, whether I should stay and finish it, or whether I should bail out now. I feel like I'm betraying you if I stay, and I feel like I'm betraying Avery and Burt if I go. We have our plans. There is a part of me, though, that really wants to do this case— there's something about it that doesn't make sense. No sane person would do what he did."

Before Marci could respond, the waitress, Bobbi, came to the table with menus and water. "*Ah*, two of my favorite people. Can I get you anything to drink?"

"Good to see you again, Bobbi," Jack said. "Water will do, and we're ready to order."

"Okay, what will it be?"

"Two soup and sandwich specials—make that turkey on wheat, light on the mayonnaise with coffee, black," Jack said. "Is that all right with you?" Marci nodded. The Table's soups were superb and perfect when it was still so cold outside.

Marci waited until Bobbi was done scratching down the order before she said, "If you really think this case is that important, I'm willing to wait 'til it's over. I trust your judgment."

He took her hand as he moved closer to her in the booth. "Thanks. It might be a moot issue if Burt doesn't do something about his habit."

"He's hungover again today?"

"He looks pretty bad."

"What are you going to do?"

"I'll leave and we'll go ahead with our plans if Burt can't prove to me by next Monday he's in treatment. If he hasn't started, then we'll put the deposit down on the office. If he has, I'll do the trial. I love you for making this easy for me."

Marci squeezed Jack's hand. "I love you, too. I just don't want to wait much longer. We deserve a life where we're going in the same direction. There has got to be more to life than selling cosmetics and representing poor people."

"Sometimes," Jack said, "I think I'm as addicted to the punishment of being a public defender as Burt is to cocaine. People get hooked on pain, you know?"

"Maybe you ought to get into treatment."

"I'm all right. I'm just finding it hard to extricate myself from the tar pit."

"This is how I see it, Jack. We've paid our dues and invested plenty in our futures. It's time to collect some dividends. And, I want a child soon. Got it?" Marci ran her hand halfway up Jack's thigh.

"I want the same things, and I certainly am interested in the process of making babies, if you get the picture." They gave each other a kiss.

"I'm interested in that process, too," Marci said, smiling.

The waitress came to the table with the turkey sandwiches and steaming, vegetable soup. "That was quick," Jack said.

"We aim to please," said Bobbi. "It looks like you two are still Dayton's most romantic couple." Jack and Marci grinned at her. "I hope so," Marci said.

Wednesday—7:30 P.M.
Burt Porter's Condominium

It was very dark. The temperature hovered slightly above zero. It was too cold for a serious snow—just a few spitting flakes. Burt had eaten at home. It was a bachelor's meal—a salisbury steak TV dinner with two beers. The house was brightly lit and surely not as romantic as it had been the night before, though there would be time for that. Chris was coming over around eight-thirty. First, he had this piece of business to take care of with Van. He didn't want tonight to be his last score of cocaine. He didn't like how he felt when he was sober. Everything became confusing when he wasn't high—a feeling of deadness. He wasn't sure how he looked to other people anymore. He thought he'd looked like he was in control at the Jackson-case staff meeting today, but now he wasn't sure. Then again, he didn't seem to care as much about anything anymore. Maybe it was just part of being middle aged.

Van rang the doorbell. His Lexus was parked across the street. He was wearing a tan, leather coat over slacks and a sweater and thick, leather gloves. His shoes were Bruno Magli, the same shoes worn by O.J. Simpson when he allegedly cut up his wife and Ron Goldman. "Hey, bro, I'm in a hurry tonight. I got places to go and people to see."

Burt could feel that his voice was different. It was pressured. "Kind of uptight tonight, Van?"

"Yeah, bro."

"We're gonna have time to talk about that big hint you dropped this morning, aren't we? Or were you just blowin' shit?"

"No, we'll talk, but let's do our business first."

"Fine."

"I got some extra good shit for you that I want you to try. Blow a couple of lines, see how ya like it. Ya do, I'll give ya a special deal on it."

"What's with the Santa Claus routine? You haven't given me any free coke since that first time."

"Exactly why I'm giving you free shit tonight and a good deal on some more, if you like it. You be'in a regular customer and all, bro. I done collected enough of your green stamps; you can start claiming some gifts at Van's redemption center." Both of them chuckled.

They sat down on the leather couch in front of the glass coffee table. Van brought out his satchel. He reached in and pulled out a vial of white powder, put it on the glass of the table and sorted it into two lines with a blade. He handed a straw to Burt.

"Wanna take off your coat and stay awhile?"

Van unzipped his coat and took off his leather gloves. "Now, try this shit," he said.

Burt bent over and inhaled two lines. He then sat back to enjoy the feeling. Burt could tell this stuff was different from any junk he had ever snorted. He could feel the rush of wellness, intense power and pleasure, but it was much, much stronger. "Just a minute," he said, getting up. "This shit's giving me a helluva buzz and the beer's going right through me. I gotta pee." He headed toward his bathroom. He went in and stood in front of the mirror, looked at himself and could see sweat forming on his brow. *I gotta turn on the tape recorder before I discuss the case with Van"* he reminded himself, trying to keep it together, the blow now ballooning in his brain. On the way back to the living room, Burt pressed the RECORD button on his sound system. He was losing his bearings. He felt his breath shortening, his chest tightening. He sat down. "Now, let's . . . let's talk about . . . Avery . . . Jackson." The words tumbled out of his mouth, yet it seemed like it was not his mouth they were coming out of. His body was outside of his mind, or was it visa versa?

"Okay, bro, in a minute we can talk about that, but first tell me how you like the stuff." Van sat staring at Burt.

Burt's breath accelerated, nausea overwhelmed him, sweat poured from his forehead. Suddenly, he slumped forward, then fell to his side on the couch. His eyes rolled back in his head. Foam began coming out of the corners of his mouth as he began to seize. He shook uncontrollably, then he rolled to the floor between the couch and the coffee table.

Van continued staring at him, then said, "Sorry, bro, but the big boys are putting the heat on me. I had no choice. It's a survival thing for me, and I aim to survive." He reached into his pocket and brought out a thick shawl, placed it over Burt's mouth and nose. Burt gulped for air as he writhed on the floor, his legs and arms twitching. Within a minute his breathing stopped. Burt's chest heaved one last time. He was dead.

Van calmly put on his gloves and coat, spread out one more line of coke on the glass and put out a new straw next to it. He picked up the old straw as well as the vial and blade. He went to the door, opened it quietly and walked out into the cold, night air. He saw no one as he walked to his Lexus and got in. As he turned on his headlights and drove away, a tan sedan parked nearly a half block away with two white occupants inside, also turned on its lights. The sedan left a few seconds later heading in the same direction. Van drove very slowly, making sure he didn't draw attention to himself. He turned on his CD player, turned the volume to high and listened to a rap CD he had just recently bought. He was hungry; maybe he should get a bite to eat.

He visualized what he had just done. As far as he could tell, he was clean. Everything was cool. There was nothing left behind. It would look like a classic drug overdose, just a yuppie, honky lawyer who'd bitten off a little more than he could chew—he'd gotten his hands on a pure speedball, and now he was dead. Van smiled as he thought about how he gave Burt pure, uncut cocaine and heroin in the same cocktail. What a way to go out. He wondered if Burt stroked out, died of a heart attack, or a seizure. Maybe it was all three. No matter. Now, he was going to see one of his ladies, get something to eat— maybe smoke some weed and get some pussy.

He drove toward North Dayton to his female friend's crib. It was a Wednesday night, quiet, cold and dark in a semi-residential/business neighborhood. He pulled up to a stoplight. There was no one else in the intersection. He thought about running the light. There was no one around except the funky, old, tan car behind him. *This is a bullshit light anyway*, he thought. He looked again in his rearview mirror; he could see two people through the windshield sitting in the car behind him.

Suddenly, the car moved up to the driver's side of Van's Lexus. The passenger in the sedan rolled his window down and yelled, "Hey, hip-hop, cool nigger— Van."

Van looked to his left, startled. He hated being called a nigger by a white guy. For a second, he thought he recognized the passenger in the light and made momentary eye-contact. Something wasn't right. He reached for the gun underneath his seat, but before he could grab it, a fusillade of bullets from an automatic weapon blasted through the Lexus' window and into Van's face. He slumped forward onto the horn and the car accelerated with his knee-jerk reflex speeding through the intersection, then sideswiping two cars on the other side of the street and crashing into an oak tree. Van was dead.

The tan sedan made a right turn at the intersection and drove methodically away.

Wednesday—9:00 P.M.
Hazeltree's Murder Scene/Burt Porter's Condo

The scream of police sirens shrilled throughout the downtown area as patrol cars screeched out of the sheriff department's garage. Their blare was urgent, and the sound of tires hitting the cement made it clear the drivers meant business. There is something primitive about blood that causes human beings, like sharks, to congregate. In this case, the police were responding to a fatal, drive-by shooting. Probably the work of juveniles, the officers figured it was just more gang stuff.

When the five patrol cars got to the scene, they could see the Lexus with its front end wrapped around a tree. Every officer knew Van Hazeltree. When the homicide detectives arrived, they taped off the scene, took photographs and went door to door to see if neighbors had seen anything. Although they went about their business quietly and professionally, each thought this was all for the good—the law of nature had prevailed. The dope-pushing pimp had gotten his due. There would not be a lot of work put into solving this shooting. In fact, in a fair world, they thought the person who'd pulled the trigger should be given immunity, as well as a public commendation.

Orlando Solano was on call and caught the case. He seized the evidence carefully and professionally—a gun still clutched in Van's right hand, a vial of white powder and a cocktail straw with powder residue on it. He later checked it all into the Evidence Room, along with Van's clothing, which included a thick, wool shawl.

About a mile away at Burt's condo complex, Chris Conley had made an urgent 911 call at 8:03 p.m., requesting an ambulance, which squealed away from nearby Central Hospital only minutes later, followed by a squad car.

Just before the paramedics got there, she decided she needed to hide the white powder on the table to protect Burt. If he were still alive, she didn't want him to be charged with a drug-related offense. She loved him. She took the razor blade, pushed all the powder into a pile on a piece of paper, and then poured it into an empty vial in her purse, where she had from time to time kept small amounts of marijuana and coke. With her thin leather gloves still on, she placed the razor blade and the unused straw in her purse.

When the EMTs arrived, it was clear to them that Burt Porter was dead. Blood had already settled to the bottom of his body. His face was grotesquely twisted, and he had foamy blood running from his mouth and nose.

Detective Guteman arrived at the scene shortly after the paramedics along with the uniformed officer, McGee.

"We don't usually see you boys for hours or until the next day," McGee commented.

"I aim to please," Guteman said. "What do we have here?"

"Dead body. Girlfriend here claims she found him like this." McGee pointed to Chris.

Guteman examined the body perfunctorily and then said to Chris, "I'm Detective Guteman."

"I'm Chris Conley. I'm Burt's girlfriend." Her eyes were glazed. She was obviously in shock.

"So I've heard. What happened here?"

"I got here about eight-thirty and saw him like this. I thought he had just passed out."

"How did you get in?"

"I have a key."

"Looks like he was doing dope. Were you doing it with him?"

"No."

"I just have to ask certain questions. We have a dead man here."

"Are you sure?" Chris asked.

Guteman nodded. Chris began to cry.

Guteman wasn't interested. "Did you two do a lot of dope together?"

"No, I think I need a lawyer, Detective." She couldn't believe this questioning had turned to her.

"You can call a lawyer at any time. You probably know plenty of them. I recognize you from the courts, don't I?"

"I'm a court reporter."

"Did you and Mr. Porter intend to do coke together tonight?"

"I need a lawyer, Detective."

"If you will allow me to search your purse for weapons and evidence, you can go. We'll ask you to come to the station for more questioning once we get the toxicology report."

"I don't want you to search my purse. Look. I'm a court reporter in Judge Jeffers' division. I'm a good citizen. I love Burt. I called in the report."

"That won't get you anything. Your boyfriend is dead. It could be that you two were doing dope together and he overdosed. It could be you intentionally slipped him a hot shot and he died. That would make it a murder."

"This is crap, Detective," Chris yelled, beginning to get really frightened.

Guteman went on without breaking stride. "It could be you brought some hot stuff in and gave it to him. Then he vapor-locked. That would make it criminally negligent homicide. I need to check your purse."

Chris' purse was on the couch next to the coffee table some twenty feet away from where they were talking. She started to move in that direction when she remembered she'd put the coke in it. She stopped dead, panic engulfing her, her heart suddenly started racing.

Guteman stepped past her and grabbed the purse.

"You bastard, you do *not* have permission to look through my purse. You know damned well I didn't threaten you in any way. I'm not within fifteen feet of that purse."

"I'm running the show here, not you." He emptied the purse's contents onto the couch. Out fell the razor blade as well as the vial of white powder.

"If you want to call for a lawyer now, you may. Have him or her meet you at the county jail, though, because you're under arrest."

"This is crazy!"

"Scream and cry all you want. It won't do you any good. You and your boyfriend are dopers. See what it got him? See what it's gonna get you?"

She could feel Guteman's steel heart; he reeked coldness. "I found his body just like this," she said as she gathered herself. "I found the dope on the table and put it in my purse to protect Burt. I haven't done any dope with him tonight at all. He told me he would be buying dope tonight from his supplier, Van somebody."

"What's Van's last name?'

"I have no idea."

"How much dope do you do?"

"That's none of your business."

"I get the feeling that you and your public defender, lawyer buddy here did quite a bit. He's a dead man."

Chris was beginning to absorb the reality; her tears streamed unchecked down her cheeks.

Unfazed, Guteman said, "Sorry, Miss, but we'll have to take you in." He motioned to the uniformed officer. "McGee, put the cuffs on her and book her for possession of a controlled substance and suspicion of criminally negligent homicide. Make sure the tech at booking draws blood so we can get a tox screen on her."

In the hallway between Burt's bedroom and the living room, the recorder stopped. No one had noticed.

Wednesday—9:15 P.M.
Public Defender's Office

While all the police sirens were blaring and the tires screeching downtown, a white van with a logo of Myron's Deli and Catering pulled into the parking lot behind the public defender's office. Painted above Myron's logo were pictures of a steaming, pepperoni pizza and a submarine sandwich. In the van, Harry Bova and Mike Swenson, both fairly large, white men, accompanied Tony Losavio, a small, gray-haired man dressed in overalls. All three men were experts in breaking and entering and electronic surveillance. The three quickly exited the van, Joe carrying a small, black bag. He deftly penetrated the locks on the back door. They entered the building and immediately headed to the front offices of Burt Porter and Jack Maine.

Losavio quickly took Porter's phone apart. "Somebody's already been here," he said quietly.

"What?" Bova asked.

"This phone is already tapped. What do you want me to do?"

"Is there a way we can find out where the tap is transmitting to?"

"Sure, I got just the thing. But we'll have to leave this tap in place."

"That's okay," Bova said, "just leave it there and put a separate one in for us so we can monitor what Porter is doing."

"Not a problem."

Bova put in his own transmitter and also a device that would trace the destination of the transmissions from the bug already in place.

"Let's sweep the entire room for other bugs and also bug his secretary," Bova suggested.

Joe swept all of the pictures, diplomas and vases with a scanning device. There was no reaction until he got to the light on Burt's desk, which set off a beeper. They quickly located the bug. Another tracer was put on it to trace the destination of transmissions, should it be different from the one in the phone. The rest of the room was clean. They quickly found the bug in Judy's phone, too, put a tracer put on it, and installed another bug in her phone.

The three men then went to Jack Maine's office. They swept it for bugs and found none.

"Whoever got here first was sloppy," Swenson said. "Probably didn't know about Maine. Let's put a couple of bugs in this office, too." The bugs were quickly put in place, one behind Jack's law license, the other in his phone. The three men exited the building quickly, piled into the catering van and left.

Wednesday—11:00 P,M.
Montgomery County Jail

Chris Conley was booked and fingerprinted. Her bond, according to the bonding schedule, was ten thousand dollars for Possession of Cocaine and twenty-five thousand for Criminally Negligent Homicide. She had a couple of choices to make regarding these bonds. She could attempt to post the bond immediately by coming up with 10 percent of the thirty-five thousand dollars and getting a bondsman to secure the balance, or she could post the entire thirty-five thousand dollars with cash or property.

She could also stay in jail overnight without it costing her a dime, appear in court tomorrow and attempt to get out on a personal recognizance bond. But of course the problem with that was she'd have to go through the humiliation of appearing in Judge Madeline Bonin's court tomorrow morning in prison garb with no sleep, no make-up, no toothbrush and matted-down hair. She might not get out of a holding cell all night long, spend the evening with prostitutes and drunks, and be propositioned by any lesbian women who might find her legs as attractive as men found them.

She knew Judge Jeffers would find out about the charges against her. Word would travel around the courthouse at the speed of light tomorrow. She would tell her before she could hear it from anyone else. All things considered, she could maintain some control over the situation if she made bond tonight. She just hoped she could keep her job.

She contacted a bondsman, Dandy Don Lonard, who often appeared in Judge Jeffers' court. He had known Chris for years and had always wanted to sleep with her. He allowed her to charge the thirty-five hundred dollars surety premium on her MasterCard on the promise she would secure the other thirty-one thousand five hundred dollars with her condo or her mother's house. She was out of jail by one o'clock that morning. It took that long to process all of the paperwork and draw her blood. Dandy Don took her back to Burt's condo to get her car. He reminded her that she needed to appear in court for her initial advisement on the twenty-fifth, or she'd lose the other thirty-one thousand five hundred dollars in bond money that she had to come up with by the end of this day.

She drove home in a frightened, frozen daze. Her life, as she knew it, was over. Her boyfriend was dead. She was going to be charged with some sort of homicide crime she did not commit.

Chris entered her apartment shaking. Her body was overcome with exhaustion. She barely felt like she was alive. She just needed to get some sleep, but she didn't know if she could relax. She would call a lawyer tomorrow and start preparing for Burt's funeral. She took a Xanax and went fitfully to sleep.

CHAPTER 5

Thursday, January 18—7:00 A.M.

It was a new day in Dayton. It had been very damp, cold and gray for several days with slight sprinklings of snow, but this morning brought with it a clear, blue sky with warmer breezes blowing. For the first time in weeks, the temperature was above freezing. As Jack drove in to work, he turned on an oldies station; the Beach Boys were playing. "Round, round, get around, I get around," he sang to himself. He loved their stuff. It picked him up.

Today was Gene Hardacre's funeral. The media would be all over it. Since Monday, there had been a continual bombardment of stories chronicling his life. Gene Hardacre was taking on the aura of a martyr both in Dayton and nationally. In just a few, short days, his image had been transformed from newly-elected, but not really well-known, law enforcement officer, to a martyr who had come to save the city only to be gunned down in the metaphorical street. There were stories in the *Dayton Daily News* about his childhood, his days as a police officer and his rise to power. The national media ran daily stories about his life and repeated the video of his shooting nearly as many times as the 9/11 terrorist attacks on the World Trade Center. He had become a *cause celebre* for honest law enforcement and decency. His wife and children had been rabidly (though with all expressions of appropriate dismay) exposed to the public in their time of grief. Certainly there would be photo opportunities that showed their tears as they sat in front of his casket.

"Good, good, good, good vibrations," Jack went on singing as he thought how fitting that song was on this sunny day. He felt real empathy for Hardacre's wife and children. He was sure this was a devastating thing for them. He hadn't known Gene well but had liked him. He thought he was an honest man and would have been a breath of fresh air in the law enforcement community.

Jack could only imagine what it would have been like for him to lose his own father while he'd been in high school like the Hardacre kids had just lost theirs. He didn't know how he would have borne the pain of it. His father was still alive and had always been one of his biggest supporters. *There's nothing like a good dad,* he had thought many times over the years. If healthy, they give their children, both boys and girls, the strength and confidence to move forward, venture into the world and persevere in tough times. His father had encouraged him to venture out, had always supported him in Little League, high school athletics and had always taken pride in his son's academic achievements.

His mother had been right there with his father. She was an intelligent, nurturing woman who was well educated and accomplished in her own right. *It was probably because I had a good mother*, he thought, *that I married a good woman like Marci.* That thought gave him a twinge of anxiety as he considered his predicament. How long would this Jackson case take? How much longer would it hang him up in the public defender's office? Was it stupid for him to make such a promise to Burt out of loyalty to him? Was it really loyalty to him or his own fear of going out on his own? Was Avery Jackson worth the energy he would have to spend to defend him? Were the principles of the case that important? And for that matter, what were the principles of the case? Was waiting to leave the office really fair to him? Fair to Marci? And when he hung out his own shingle, would he be successful? He felt sure he would have clients, but would they be people who could pay his bills and keep him and Marci, and perhaps a child, afloat?

His Beach Boy reverie was broken when the station switched to the news. He was only half listening as he thought about his responsibilities that day. Avery Jackson would be meeting with the psychologist this morning. It was an important meeting. *Certainly Avery's state of mind at the time of the shooting was the key to the case,* he thought as the world news discussed another terrorist bombing in Israel, the market was down again—god, I'm not sure this is the time to go into private practice.

"In local news, there was another drive-by shooting in North Dayton last night. The victim has been identified as Ovanul Hazeltree. The killing is believed to be gang-related."

At first, Jack didn't recognize the name. Then he thought, *Wasn't that the guy Burt talked about in the meeting yesterday? Burt was supposed to meet with him last night. Claimed he had information on the Jackson case. Ovanul? Sure, that was the guy, not a name you forget.*

The news went on about the raising of Rapid Transit rates. Jack was hardly listening. He couldn't wait to talk to Burt to see if he had hooked up with Hazeltree before he had been killed. *Maybe this wasn't the same Ovanul. Oh, it had to be with a name like that.*

There was a commercial, then suddenly the newscaster was back. "*Uh,* we have a breaking news story: Prominent, veteran criminal defense attorney and head of the Public Defender's Office, Burt Lee Porter, was found dead at his home last night, possibly from a drug overdose. His girlfriend, Chris Conley, a court reporter for the state court system, has been arrested in connection with his death. She's being held—*uh,* no, she's been released on a thirty-five thousand dollar bail—on suspicion of criminally negligent homicide and possession of dangerous drugs."

Jack almost drove off the road. Then everything went into slow motion as he pulled into the parking lot of a strip mall. He got out his cell phone and called the office. Paula, the receptionist, answered, "Public Defender's Office, how may I direct your call?"

"Paula, is it true what they're saying on the radio about Burt?"

Paula had just found out herself from Detective Guteman, who was sitting in the waiting room waiting for Jack to arrive. She broke into tears. "Yes—it—it is true. Detective Dave Guteman is here wanting to search Burt's office. I told him he'd have to wait until you got here."

"They don't waste any time. Does he have a warrant?"

"No, I haven't seen one," Paula said through her tears.

"Tell Guteman I'll be right there."

Jack's head was spinning. He was stunned but also mobilizing. His deal with Burt was off. Dead men are unable to perform their end of a contract. He should have insisted upon immediate treatment for Burt, not in a week. Had he done so, Burt might still be alive. And Chris, Chris wouldn't have done anything to hurt Burt intentionally. But negligently? God, I hope not.

Then, like any good lawyer, he started thinking about the law. *Did Guteman have a right to search Burt's office without a warrant? Sure he did. Burt was dead. He had no privacy or Fourth Amendment rights anymore. Sure, he'd let Guteman search Burt's office. He'd just watch and make sure he saw everything that was taken.*

Jack pulled into the parking lot. As he walked through the door, he could not feel his feet touching the ground, his mind was absent from his actions.

As soon as he walked through the door into the waiting area, Paula rose to her feet. She hugged Jack with tears running down her face. Jack hugged her and patted her back. Detective Guteman rose to his feet. "Jack, this is Detective Guteman," Paula said.

"Introductions are not necessary, Paula, I've known the detective for a good many years," Jack said as he thought of the irony of the situation. He was now working alongside Guteman trying to find out what happened to Burt when for years Guteman had been his and Burt's bitter enemy. *Burt would hate the fact Guteman was investigating his death,* Jack thought to himself.

"Jack, do you mind if I search Mr. Porter's office? I'm looking for evidence in connection with his death."

"Sure, go right ahead, Detective. We'll cooperate in any way we can."

"Fine, I'll get started."

"Paula, would you take Detective Guteman back to Burt's office?"

"Yes. Oh, and here's a message that came in for you. She says it's urgent." Paula pushed a pink message into Jack's hand and led Detective Guteman to Burt's office. He looked at the message. It was from Chris Conley and marked URGENT. He went to his office, closed the door and dialed the number.

Chris answered, panicky. "Jack, Burt's dead! It was the most awful, grotesque thing I've ever seen! I'm still shaking over it. When I found him—"

"Slow down, slow down, Chris."

He heard her take a breath. "When I found him, he had foam coming out of his mouth. I didn't know if he was dead yet. I called the police," she said, staccato fashion. "I shouldn't have done that because they arrested me. I had *nothing* to do with his death, Jack. God, I loved him." She began to cry hysterically.

Jack waited a minute to let her compose herself. "You need a lawyer. Do you want me to refer you to someone?"

"No, I want you to represent me."

"I can't; you're not indigent; you can afford private counsel. You don't want to be represented by the public defender, nor can you be. You own a condo and make good money as a court reporter."

"Burt told me you were thinking about leaving the office and that he was trying to get you to stay to do Jackson. Is that true?"

"Yes, that's true. But I don't know what I'm going to do now. I just found out a few minutes ago that one of my best friends is dead. Maybe I need to stay here to help with the transition in the office. I don't know what I'm going to do. Why don't you get the Rosatos to represent you until I can figure out what I'm going to do?"

"Oh god, no. Burt said that if they were ever forced to try a case, they couldn't do it. They'd just take your money and work out a plea bargain."

"Burt's right. But there are other guys out there. Mike Munro. Why don't you try him?"

"Mike would be all right except that I dated and slept with him before I started dating Burt."

Jack realized that a number of the criminal lawyers in town would be unable to represent Chris for that very reason. "All right, Chris, where are you?"

"I'm at home. I called in sick this morning."

"You better talk to your judge to make sure your job is secure."

"Yeah, I will. I hope I still have a job or I might actually *have* to have a court-appointed lawyer. How much would you charge me if you represented me?"

"I don't know. I'm new at this. I'm used to doing it for free."

"I'd give you a ten thousand dollar retainer."

"Let me think about it. I have to think about whether it's ethical for me to represent you. You're charged with the negligent homicide of my employer and friend. If I represented you as a public defender, it would have the appearance of conflict and impropriety written all over it. Maybe I can't represent you even if I do leave. I'd have to be sure that in no way you participated in Burt's death before I would even consider it, and even then I might not."

"I *didn't*. I promise you, Jack, I had nothing to do with Burt's death. Please call me later this afternoon and let me know what you want to do? I'm not going to take no for an answer."

"You might have to. I'll call you when I know something. I gotta talk to Detective Guteman. He's already here to search Burt's office."

There was silence. Then Chris said, "He's already there? God, that man is such an asshole. The way he went after me last night was unreal. He ignored me when I asked for a lawyer. He didn't care what I said about Burt's drug supplier."

Jack heard only the last bit. "Did Burt tell you that a guy by the name of Van was coming over last night to talk to him about Avery's case?"

"Partly. He told me Van was coming over to sell him some coke," Chris admitted.

"Do you know that Van was killed last night about the same time Burt died? At least, I think it's the same Van, a dope dealer, street hustler."

"I heard on the news this morning there was a drive-by shooting last night."

"The guy who got his face blown off in that shooting was named Ovanul. Burt just said they called him Van. It has to be the same guy. How many Ovanuls are there in Dayton? Did you happen to know if his tape system was running?" Jack asked.

"No. Why?"

"Do you still have a key to Burt's condo?"

"Yes," she answered, not quite knowing where this was going. "Why?"

"Because I told Burt to tape record his meeting with Van."

"Burt would never record himself making a drug transaction. He's way too smart for that."

"Perhaps, but we need to find out if it exists. Wouldn't you rather have the tape than Guteman?"

"*Uh-huh.* I'll go right over and get it."

"No, I'll send Joe Betts over. You have to be protected, and if a tape exists, it's imperative that Joe retrieve it so there aren't problems with the chain of custody and so you don't have to take the stand to authenticate the tape should it become evidence. Joe will be right there. Okay?"

Within twenty minutes, big Joe Betts had picked Chris up, and in another ten, they were at Burt's condo. Chris' queasiness got worse when they pulled up in front of the complex. She was glad she had Joe with her; now that she'd had time to think about it, she didn't think she could've handled going in alone. Neither she nor Joe paid any attention to the white van with Myron's Deli and Catering painted on the side that they parked behind. When they got to the door of the condo, there was yellow tape on it stating CRIME SCENE— DO NOT DISTURB. It had been cut. They looked at one another.

"Got the key?" Joe asked.

Chris reached into her purse and pulled out her keychain. She quickly found Burt's key among the six others that were held together by wire attached to a miniature mace sprayer. She had carried it since being stalked by a weirdo who used to hang out at the courthouse.

"Are you sure it's all right we do this? Am I going to get into more trouble?" she whispered to Joe.

"Don't worry about it. The cops' name isn't on the deed."

"Neither is mine."

"Just a technicality. They don't have a right to be here anymore than you."

She inserted the key in the lock and turned it. It made no sound—the door wasn't locked. "God, it's open. The cops must have left it open," she whispered. She stopped suddenly and said rather loudly, "I don't believe I'm back here. I can't look."

"Go ahead," Joe encouraged her.

They entered furtively, walked through the living room where she'd found Burt's body, past the glass coffee table and into the hall next to Burt's bedroom where the tape deck was located. Chris reached for the eject button and could see that the tape cartridge was open. She looked at Joe. "Let me check the bedroom. This isn't right."

She pushed open the door and began to go in. She was suddenly, violently shoved from behind onto the bed. Two other men, one blond and young, and a small man dressed in a Myron's Catering Uniform, bolted past her into the hall. Joe reacted quickly and tackled the blond man, who struggled. Joe slugged him in the face.

The blond man yelled, "Bova, get this guy off me!"

Harry Bova reached into his waistband and produced a gun with his right hand. He held a tape cassette in the other hand. He moved quickly toward Joe, pistol-whipping him with the butt of the gun, blood flying everywhere. Joe fell to the side, holding his head.

"Get up, let's get out of here," Bova yelled, throwing the stunned Joe off him. Chris sprang to her feet and sprayed mace directly into Bova's face before he could turn his gun on her. Blinded, he screamed, "You fuckin' bitch! I'll kill you." He swung wildly at Chris with his gun grazing the side of her head and knocking her back. He reeled and fired the gun blindly into the ceiling. Joe and Chris froze.

"Here, give me the cassette. Let's get out of here," the blond said as he grabbed the tape cassette out of Bova's one hand, took him by the arm and led him through the door. They exited the condo, ran to the catering van and drove quickly away.

Chris and Joe lay on the floor. Although both were conscious, each was groggy. Neither was in shape for a melee like this, but who is? It all happened so quickly and violently. Chris had a red mark fast becoming a large, blue welt running from the side of her jaw to her temple. The hand that Joe held the top of his head with was full of blood.

When he removed it, Chris said, "Jesus, Joe, you're cut bad. We need to get you to the hospital right now to get you stitched up."

"No, we can't do that. There's too big a chance the police will get involved—we're taking evidence from the scene of a crime. Hell, those guys might have *been* police, though they sure as hell didn't act like it. They knew they didn't have a right to be here. The cops would have tried to arrest us or some shit like that. These guys were something else—some undercover kind of guys. The little one didn't say shit. He just had the same logo on his shirt as that white van we pulled up behind when we parked on the street—Myron's something. We gotta get out of here. Do you still have the keys?"

"Damned right, I still have the keys," Chris said, clutching the small mace canister on her keychain.

"We gotta remember their names."

"The guy I maced was named Bova. At least, that's what the blond guy called him, I'm sure of that."

"The guy I punched in the face was a blond, honky boy. Like to see the damage to his face tomorrow. I got a real good shot to his eye. The question I got now is how the hell they knew to come here to look for a tape? When did you and Jack have this conversation about Burt recording the conversation with this doper?"

"About forty-five minutes ago."

"Jesus, how the hell could that be?" Joe picked himself up off the floor and helped Chris up. The sound of sirens in the distance was plain and growing closer. "We gotta get outta here. If you get busted here, you'll get your bond revoked. Let's just walk outta here like nothin' happened."

Chris locked the door as they left. They walked to Joe's car. He drove them away just minutes before the squad car arrived. Chris had a friend who was a nurse who worked afternoons at the hospital. Chris called her on her cell phone; she was home. They headed to her place to get Joe stitched up.

Thursday—10:00 A.M.
Montgomery County Jail

Avery was no longer in an isolation cell; he'd been moved to a pod with other prisoners who were doing time for drunk driving. There had been quite a bit of debate within the sheriff's office as to what to do with Avery. Should they keep him in isolation, or move him to a cellblock with other pre-trial detainees who had been charged with violent crimes, or put him in a place where he would be relatively safe?

There was a fourth choice: kill the son-of-a-bitch. To the sheriff's deputies, he was a cop killer, plain and simple.

A faction of the deputies wanted to keep him in isolation. It would be like putting a criminal in the hole, they reasoned. The sensory deprivation would drive him nuts—make him paranoid. The murdering scumbag deserved it. But if they drove him nuts that might be helpful for an insanity defense.

Another faction wanted to put him in with other guys charged with a variety of heinous crimes. These guys were likely to sexually assault, kill or just beat the hell out of him just because he was an ex-judge—some of them might even have appeared in front of him when he was on the bench and were carrying beefs; certainly people in their extended families had. The briars, they reasoned, would love it. They could fuck the nigger up the ass, or at least get a blow job from him—let him know his place immediately. That would be a just comeuppance for a "boy" who'd risen too far, too fast. Then again, that might upset the black inmates and start a race war within the jail.

Alec Hunter had stopped all the chatter by calling the jail requesting that Jackson not be put in peril in any way because if he were killed, or hurt in any way, it would reflect negatively on Dayton both locally and nationally and bring into question the efficacy and decency of the criminal justice system in

Dayton. Nor did he want any sensory deprivation or other rough treatment of Jackson that could affect his competency to stand trial. Thus, Avery was housed with the serious traffic offenders.

Jack met Avery in the same Contact Visitation Room they'd been in on Monday. Avery was dressed in an orange jumpsuit and wore flip-flop sandals— laced shoes were out because many a prisoner had hanged himself or been hanged by shoe laces fashioned into a noose by someone else. He didn't look as bad as he had for his bond hearing. He obviously had slept. The jail physician had prescribed Buspar, a medication that helped with depression, anxiety and sleeplessness. It took the edge off and allowed him to survive an impossible situation with some equanimity. He had shaved and brushed his teeth for the first time and no longer felt as if he were walking through death's door—only standing in front of it.

Jack was sitting on a plastic chair at a round table when Avery entered; he rose to shake Avery's hand. They made warm eye contact with one another. Jack knew Avery had probably not gotten word of Burt's death, and he'd have to tell him. There needed to be a determination of who would be handling the case. The preliminary hearing was Monday. Jack himself felt that he'd lost his bearings since he'd heard about Burt. The shock of his loss, the mysteriousness of his death, the call from Chris that morning had left him reeling. He needed a grounding meeting with his client as much for Avery as for himself.

Jack righted himself. "How are you, Avery?"

"Not so good. I'm charged with first-degree murder, my wife left me, I'm being held without bond, and finally, I got a letter this morning from Sinclair University that I have been suspended without pay pending the outcome of this case. But other than that, Mrs. Kennedy, how was Dallas? At least I'm sleeping. I got some good drugs from the doctor here and that's helped."

"Good, you're going to need the rest to get ready for your meeting with Phil Gilmour. He's coming over here to meet you in an hour to start evaluating you psychologically. I need to talk to you about something else now, though." Jack took a deep breath. "I have one more piece of bad news for you."

"Nothing's happened to one of my kids, has it?"

"No. Nothing like that. It's Burt."

They looked at one another for a couple of seconds, Jack struggling to say the words. It couldn't be final, could it?

"Let me guess. He was arrested snorting cocaine and sodomizing simultaneously." When Jack didn't smile, Avery knew it was serious.

"Burt died last night."

The room was quiet for what seemed like forever.

"How?"

"It looks like he had a heart attack, or a stroke, or seizure, or something like that, maybe from OD'ing. His girlfriend, Chris Conley, Judge Jeffers' court reporter, has been arrested in connection with it, and the cops are trying to pin a negligent homicide on her. The kicker is that we met yesterday and he said he had a meeting with a street guy by the name of Van who was going to give him information about your case. To make matters more interesting, a guy by the name of Ovanul was killed in what looks like a drive-by shooting about the same time Burt died last night—somewhere between seven and eight o'clock. We think it's the same guy."

"This is bad news," Avery said. The quiet during the pause seemed amplified. Avery finally went on. "I've known Burt for nearly twenty years. I knew, like you probably did, that he was fooling around with cocaine. I was worried about his representing me because of it. In terms of keeping the ship on course throughout this entire mess, well, I need a steady hand."

"Which brings us to what do you want to do about representation? If you don't want to deal with it today, I understand. But we have Dr. Gilmour coming over here in a few minutes to meet you and he doesn't work for nothing. Did you talk to your wife about your financial condition?"

"Yeah, Gloria was in here after the bond hearing. She essentially told me she wanted out of the marriage. She had all the money divided up already. She got the house and there's somewhere between fifteen- and twenty-K to spend on a defense. I need to sign a Power of Attorney for you to get the money out of my retirement."

Neither Jack nor Avery had an understanding of the economics of law, neither having ever been in private practice, but Jack had heard of attorneys getting twenty-five thousand dollars just to enter a plea of guilty. Retainers of a hundred thousand dollars on big cases were not uncommon. The amount of money Avery was talking about was peanuts.

"Here's the problem. That amount of savings eliminates you from legal indigence, as you know. You can't be represented by the public defender. You also don't have enough money to find a good, private lawyer to represent you. Expert witness fees and investigation on your case will cost you all the money you have. You're in what I'd call the black hole of legal representation. Your money will be gone before you even begin paying your attorneys a dime."

"I'm asking you to take the case on privately. I can get money from friends and colleagues in the black community who know me and believe in me. I talked to my kids. I think both of them will help in whatever way they can."

"Avery, get real. Your kids are in college. They don't have much time to help. They're inexperienced in fund-raising, they're not paralegals and they don't have any experience in investigation, do they?"

"No, but they're smart and can learn, can't they?" Avery argued, knowing that their contributions would be minimal, but he wanted them involved anyway.

"Avery, this is a helluva time for on-the-job training, with their father's life on the line."

"What the hell do you want me to do? Do you want me to give up my life right now? Maybe I should. I blew the man's brains out. I can't be represented by a decent attorney and put on a first-class defense. I can't do what O.J. Simpson did. If O.J. had my money, he'd be doing life without parole right now, or even looking at a lethal injection. He got the best defense money could buy, and he walked right out of a cold case just like mine."

"True. You know as well as I do that it's all kinda tough-shit justice in a free-market economy. Some people shop for lawyers at K-Mart, others shop at Neiman-Marcus. What I'm hearing from you is that you want me to provide a Neiman-Marcus product at K-Mart prices. That about the size of it?"

"That's not want I want, but that could be the result," admitted Avery. "If I'm convicted of this, you'll probably never see another dime. But if you get me off, I'll owe you and I'll pay you whatever way I can."

"I know your intentions are good, but they won't pay the bills for me."

Avery looked Jack in the eyes. With all the force and sincerity he could muster, he said, "Look, it's my life, Jack, and I need you to help me save it. I won't beg you. I won't ask you again. But I'm willing to put my life in your hands right now."

There was a long silence. Jack was thinking he couldn't turn down such a plea. But this case was suicide economically and professionally. He and Marci could lose everything. She'd have to go back to selling cosmetics. "Well, I'm still at the PD's office. I'm not in private practice, yet. I agreed with Burt to stay in the office until your case was finished, but I'm not obligated to stay since I have no cases left except yours. I could leave the office tomorrow, and I might. I need to talk with my wife about whether we're going to make the transition to private practice now."

"Fair enough. I assume you will be representing me through the preliminary hearing on Monday regardless of your decision though, right?"

"I'll be with you through the preliminary hearing, regardless. If I stay on the case after that, it'll be as a private attorney. The law firm of Jack Maine, not the public defender's office, will represent you."

"When will you let me know?"

"I'll let you know by tomorrow at noon, okay?" Avery nodded. Jack went on. "I asked Dr. Gilmour to be here at eleven, and it's eleven now. Yolanda Crone, an attorney with our office, will also be here. She's been working on the case with me; she's been researching the state sanity laws."

"Wait a minute. Are you sure you want to do this? You haven't decided whether to take the case yet, and you got a psychiatrist coming in?"

"Look, Judge, the way I see it, you'll need a mental evaluation regardless of who's representing you. Right now the PD's office is paying for it, so don't worry about it. Besides, Gilmour is a good man. He'll lead us in the right direction. If he can't figure out what's going on with you, he'll give us a good referral."

The sound of a metal door opening and sliding shut on its tracks interrupted their conversation. Yolanda Crone and Phil Gilmour, M.D., walked into the room He was the caricature of a psychiatrist: gray hair with a goatee, tall and thin with black, reading glasses that contrasted nicely with his gray hair. His brown, corduroy sport jacket with tan, leather pads on the elbows was somewhat worn. His Dockers covered a slight paunch.

He was a man who had spent a lot of time reading books and thinking he could quantify human behavior. For him, psychiatry was a science, not an art. He was conservative in his approach to problems, not wanting to take a chance. He had treated people with talk therapy in the past, but was now just doing medication consults. He had never attempted to do hypnosis or any sort of intervention that might result in a rage-filled reenactment of a traumatic event in someone's life. Too messy. He felt he could determine sanity without becoming involved in such unpleasantness, and he was careful in determining if someone were faking. About half of his practice these days dealt with forensics, where psychiatry and the law meet and answer difficult legal questions. Dr. Gilmour believed he could objectively answer whether a person was mentally ill and knew right from wrong. He had a reputation as an honest man. He was not a whore. He called a spade a spade.

Gilmour worked for both the defense and the prosecution. He had infuriated many district attorneys when he told them a person was schizophrenic and the voices telling him to kill were real. "The person controlling the purse strings does not control my opinion," Gilmour was proud to say to any attorney who attempted to influence him. If he thought a defense attorney's client was sane, he told the attorney he could not help him.

Avery and Jack stood up as Crone and Gilmour entered the room. Jack began with the introductions.

"Avery Jackson, this is Dr. Phil Gilmour. He'll be doing the preliminary, psychological evaluation on you."

They looked one another in the eye. Avery knew how important he was to his case.

"And this is Yolanda Crone. She's second-chairing your case. She's doing research and will be taking a bigger role in the case now that Burt—" Jack stopped as he felt the tears welling up in his eyes.

Dr. Gilmour rescued him. "I was so sorry to hear about Burt's death. I worked a lot of cases with him. He was always fun to be around—a really good lawyer."

Yolanda and Avery shook hands. It was the first time she had ever shaken the hand of a killer. A shiver went up her spine as she made that realization. She expected an icicle or cold steel to touch her hand. Instead, she simply felt warmth. They smiled at one another.

"Professor Jackson," Gilmour said, "if you'd like to wait for another day to begin this evaluation, we can do so. The loss of your attorney must be quite a shock to you, and it might be better to postpone this evaluation."

"No, I want to go ahead. I feel bad about the loss of Burt, but I always figured Jack was the lead attorney on my case. The preliminary hearing is Monday, and I want a speedy trial."

"Very well, we'll proceed. It'll just be the two of us today."

Yolanda and Jack got up to leave. "We'll leave the two of you alone. I'm having lunch with my wife to talk about the business matters we discussed, Avery. Yolanda has a lot of work to do on the case. The autopsy and initial offense reports are finished. Yolanda will be working closely with you and Dr. Gilmour on a daily basis."

As Jack and Yolanda left, the heavy, metal doors slammed shut behind them.

CHAPTER 6

Gilmour began the evaluation. "Professor Jackson, I need to advise you that everything you say to me is confidential. I will share it only with your attorneys. If, however, based upon my opinion, a mental-defect defense is proper in your case, everything you tell me will no longer be confidential. It will be subject to complete disclosure to the district attorney and can be talked about in front of the jury. Of course, you're a lawyer, a judge and a professor and are familiar with these concepts."

"Yes, I'm familiar with them, but it doesn't hurt to explain them to me. It's different sitting in this chair as opposed to the bench or running a classroom. And you can call me Avery."

"I'd rather not. In a forensic evaluation like this, I prefer to maintain a sense of formality. I'd prefer you call me Dr. Gilmour, and I'll call you Professor or Judge, or whatever appellation you're comfortable with. I know that sounds stiff, but it'll serve you well in the long run. Objectivity is the key to a sound, forensic evaluation."

"That kinda takes out the human factor, doesn't it?"

"What human factor are we talking about?"

"The fact that I am sitting here in this jail charged with first-degree murder, looking at the death penalty, with no recollection of what I did to get here. My wife has just deserted me. How the hell are you going to objectify all that?

94

Right now, I'm just trying to figure out how all this has happened to me. I feel like shit."

"You thinking about suicide?"

"Yeah. A lot."

"That's understandable under the circumstances. If you need medication or psychotherapy, I can arrange that for you through the jail. My evaluation will be more accurate and complete, however, if medication is kept to a minimum. My role is not to treat you, but to try to render an opinion as to your mental status at the time of the shooting."

"That's all right, Doc. I'm going to call you *Doc* so you're not stiff as a board. Anyhow, the prison doctor here has given me Buspar to help me sleep, which's helped quite a bit."

Gilmour had never been referred to as "stiff as a board" before, nor had he been talked to this directly by a subject charged with first-degree murder. They usually cajoled, ingratiated and tried to manipulate him. "Have you ever had a psychiatric evaluation before?"

"I remember seeing a psychiatrist when I was in the military."

Gilmour began taking notes on a yellow, legal pad. "Do you recall the reason?"

"No. That time in my life is very vague. I know boot camp was relatively easy for me. I was in good shape when I went in. I ran track throughout high school and college and stayed in good shape during law school, so the physical part of it wasn't bad. I remember seeing the psychiatrist before going to and after I left 'Nam and had returned to Fort Bragg before exiting. Fort Bragg is where I did my basic."

"Why do you think that period of your life is vague?"

"I don't know."

"Were you suffering from emotional problems when you saw the psychiatrist the first time?"

"Not really. My commanding officer just wanted me to see a psychiatrist. I was picked along with a number of other guys in my unit to see one."

"What was his name?"

"Who? The commanding officer or the psychiatrist?"

"Either."

"My commanding officer's name was Doerning. A real tough guy. I don't remember the name of the shrink. All I remember is he wore black glasses. Everyone back then wore black, horn-rimmed glasses. I saw the same dude when I was exiting. He wore a white coat and the same black, horn-rimmed glasses."

"Did you have any psychological symptoms, depression or anxiety, when you left the service?"

"When I left, I felt really messed up. I don't remember a lot of the service. I know I was in a special unit. We apparently did a bunch of top secret missions in Saigon and behind enemy lines."

"What do you mean 'apparently'?"

"That's all kind of a blur, kind of a blank. I know I had some actual combat. I was decorated for it. I have a couple of silver stars and several other commendations. I believe I killed some folks over there. I have some memories of blood and gore. I took a bullet in the leg, for that I got a Purple Heart. The leg doesn't bother me too much anymore, but I have dreams that do."

"Can you remember anything specific about killing?"

"I remember killing Cong in the jungle. I got in a firefight and a lot of our guys were killed. I lived, but I don't remember a lot after that."

"Do you find that odd, that you can't remember anything more specifically?"

"I remember the firefight and some of my buddies getting killed, and some guys losing body parts. The rest is hard to piece together. I just think there were other killings after that. You'd think I'd remember something so graphic, but I don't think it's particularly odd. I have a number of friends here in town that fought with me over there, and they don't remember much of it either, and the stuff they do remember, they try to forget."

"Why's that?"

"Because some of the shit that went down over there would take your breath away." Avery said, starting to hyperventilate.

"Do you often start breathing like that when you talk about these things?"

"I haven't particularly noticed it before, but come to think of it, whenever I think of my experience over there, I can't remember much, but I do start breathing hard sometimes."

"You said that before you exited, you were really 'messed up.' What did you mean by that?"

"I just meant that I felt dazed and confused. I felt real nervous and jumpy. Noises really bothered me. They still do. I hate it when these metal doors slam open and shut; I jump almost every time. I'm much calmer now than I used to be. It bothers me that I don't remember parts of what I did over there. After I got out, I was really depressed. It's amazing I was able to come back here and start a law practice. I'm grateful to Burt for allowing me to work with the public defenders—" Suddenly, tears welled up and fell from Avery's eyes. He began to cry; a dam was bursting inside him. "Jesus, I don't know what's happening to me. I feel like crying all the time. I haven't cried in years."

"The strongest men cry the hardest," Gilmour said as he looked directly into Avery's eyes that were still filled with tears.

Avery brushed aside the tears and straightened up. "Let's go on."

"Tell me about the dreams."

"I hate them."

"What do you mean you hate them?"

"They give me no peace."

"How often do you have them?"

"It seems like every night, but it's probably more like three or four nights a week."

"Tell me what they're about."

"At first, there's this misshapen man and a deformed leper-woman yelling at each other. They look like gargoyles. They don't have faces, but the man has this huge dick with warts and bumpy blobs all over it. He just keeps screaming at the women that he's going to give the dick to her, and she pretends she doesn't want it, but she finally takes it and sucks on it and protests until *she* comes. I usually wake up when she comes. I always feel like heaving she's so disgusting."

"How long have you had that dream?"

"Oh, since I was in high school or college."

"Do you know who the strange-looking people are?"

"No, they're not like any people I know."

"Is that the only dream plaguing you?"

"God, Doc, I wish. That one just makes me sick to my stomach. The others scare the shit out of me. First, there's a dude in a white coat with black, horn-rimmed glasses and a hypodermic needle. When I see the hypodermic needle, I sometimes wake up screaming. Then there's a gunshot, followed by red and green blood running down downspouts into a barrel. The backs of people's heads are blown off, but I can see their eyes. The gunshot never wakes me; it isn't that loud. I wish it did. It's the eyes of those bodies peering into me that wake me up. They're frightening, and when I see them looking at me, I always like jump awake, sweating and screaming." Avery paused and took a breath. "My wife, or soon to be ex-wife, Gloria, got so tired of my waking up screaming in the middle of the night that she started sleeping in a separate bedroom, which I suppose was the beginning of the end of our marriage." Avery began to cry. It was the first time he had felt grief over her loss.

Dr. Gilmour stopped taking notes. "If you need a moment, please take one, Judge Jackson."

Being called Judge Jackson shocked Avery back to stoicism. "No, I'm okay. It's the first time I've cried about the loss of my family."

"Do you find that sort of odd?" Gilmour was back to taking notes.

"Not really. I've been in shock since I was arrested. When my wife came here to tell me she wanted a divorce, I was still in shock. This is all just now kind of sinking in."

"Have you ever cried about 'Nam and what went on over there?"

"No, not really. I don't think I know enough about what I did over there to cry about it."

"What did the psychiatrist at Fort Bragg talk to you about when you exited?"

"I can't really remember. I know it wasn't about my experiences or feelings about what happened over there. It was more about whether I remembered anything at all."

"What did you tell the psychiatrist?"

"I told him the truth—that I remembered very little about what had happened over there after the firefight in the jungle. I remember telling him I hated going down into those tunnels and that I suspected I was chosen because I was black. Now I think it was because I was small, in good shape and, me being black, provided a better cover for me in the jungle and in a tunnel with the Vietcong. I told him the rest was very vague. He asked me if I remembered killing anyone. I told the truth—that I didn't remember killing anyone except in the firefight. He let me go a few minutes later. He told me I might experience some depression, nightmares and flashbacks but that most of the guys coming out of there had that problem and not to be too concerned with it."

Gilmour stopped taking notes and looked up at Avery. "That's all he said?"

"Yeah."

"Did he refer you to any place for treatment—like maybe the V.A.? Did you think it was strange that he didn't ask you how you were feeling about your experiences over there, and then discouraged you from getting professional psychological help?"

"At that time, I knew nothing about mental health. I was a lawyer in the service. I did my job. That's all the service gives a shit about."

"What's the relationship between the man with the horn-rimmed glasses in your dreams and the psychiatrist you saw before and after you went to Vietnam?"

"*Huh.* I never thought about it. Probably none. Everyone over there had them—the glasses, I mean."

"Tell me about your current life."

"It's been pretty lousy since I lost the bench over the DiSalvo rape case. It killed my career, and it was the beginning of the end of my marriage."

"Why?"

"Because when my wife found out she could no longer use me for social-climbing, or get any money from me, her feelings for me changed." Avery stopped, furrowed his brow while thinking a few seconds. "I don't know if her feelings for me changed. It's just that she could no longer tolerate me. In retrospect, I would have handled the DiSalvo case differently, and I wouldn't be in this jam. I believe people can change if given help. Some people can change, some can't. DiSalvo is out of prison now and doing fine, according to all reports. Maybe he'll screw up again. Maybe he is another Ted Bundy, but I don't see how anything more terrible than this could happen."

"To what are you referring, Judge?"

"My killing the sheriff."

"Did you kill the sheriff?"

"Apparently so."

"What does 'apparently' mean?"

"It means just that. By all appearances, I killed the sheriff."

"Tell me about it."

"I don't know a thing about it. I remember teaching my Evidence class and feeling really depressed about my lot in life, my marriage failing, my being underemployed teaching a bunch of police recruits and undergraduates Criminal Justice and Evidence. I remember I wanted to have a cup of coffee. I can smell that coffee right now. I always wanted to have coffee after teaching the early morning Evidence class. The next thing I remember was being questioned by the detectives."

"You can smell the coffee now?"

"Yeah, it's freshly brewed and black. It's like the stuff we had in 'Nam in the morning after being up all night. That's the only thing I remember about 'Nam clearly: smells, images, that kind of shit. When I spend too much time and energy thinking about it, I start getting a tremendous headache, and that's what I have right now."

"How often do you have headaches?"

"Whenever I start thinking about killing the sheriff or other things in my past like the war."

"Have you had memory lapses before?"

"As I said, I don't remember a lot about the war. I had trouble remembering deadlines on important criminal cases when I was a public defender. I was really pretty disorganized at times. It used to piss Gloria off. She always thought I just didn't want to give her or the kids the attention they needed. She didn't have much patience with me. But I wouldn't say that my memory lapses were more than usual or more than most people have. I think I kept it together reasonably well. My being run off the bench wasn't because of a memory lapse. It was the result of poor judgment—not necessarily poor judgment about a defendant, DiSalvo—but about how the press would react to what it perceived to be a threat to the community."

"You seem more upset about DiSalvo than killing the sheriff."

"That's because I remember exactly what happened with DiSalvo. I don't know a thing about what happened with Hardacre. I'm upset about Hardacre but can't feel or see myself doing anything to him. The only feeling I have about killing him is from an intellectual understanding that I took his life and destroyed his family."

"How do you want this case to come out?"

"Most of the time, I don't care. I just want to die, and sometimes hope I'll be executed. Then I think about my kids and what that would do to them, and I keep on going. What I need to know is why, how and for what reason I did this."

"Do you have any feelings about an insanity defense in this case?"

"Most of the time, I don't care yet. I know it's unlikely to be successful. I don't particularly want to go to the state hospital because they don't help you down there. They shoot your ass up with some heavy-duty tranquilizers like Prolixin or Thorazine and let you rot. And it's no real bargain. Being found Not Guilty by Reason of Insanity—called NGRI in my world—can be a life sentence, and on a case like this, it likely would be. The way I figure it, I'm doing life or death no matter how I slice it." Avery shrugged his shoulders.

Gilmour said nothing; he had to maintain the appearance of objectivity. It wasn't his job to give him therapy or empathize with him. It was his job to determine if this man was sane, could he understand right from wrong when he committed this heinous act, period. Gilmour ploughed ahead. "Do you have any history of substance abuse?"

"I wouldn't call it abuse. When DiSalvo went to hell and the media was going after me, I started using some grass and cocaine. I smoked quite a bit of marijuana for a while. It kind of settled me down, made me feel mellow."

"How about on Monday, did you smoke any dope that day?"

"None. In fact, I haven't smoked dope since I was made a professor at Sinclair, which was over a year ago."

"Tell me about your family when you were a kid."

"Christ, Doc, I was wondering how long it would take you to get to that. Isn't it always about the parents with you psychiatrists?"

Gilmour sat impassively, and then asked, "Is there something about your family you don't want to share?"

"There are a lot of things about my family I don't want to share—most of it, actually."

"For instance."

"Like, how we survived. My dad was a skycap out at the airport for years and then hooked on with the post office. My mom cleaned houses and babysat kids in the neighborhood. Both were high school graduates. Both were intelligent and underemployed. We had three kids; I was the oldest. Sometimes it was a war around our house between my parents. My dad drank and had affairs. When he was drunk, there was hell to pay. Momma was really the matriarch of the family. She controlled most everything. When dad would get to feeling sorry for himself because he was trapped in a shitty job, he'd start in on my momma, just to let her know who the boss was. Then he'd start drinking to build up his courage and get physical with her. She'd fight back and cry. She'd threaten to cut him off sexually."

"How do you know that?"

"Because they'd have very loud fights where we could hear them hitting each other, and then she'd start screaming at him that he 'wouldn't be getting any more of her pussy.' They'd fight over sex, money and dad's girlfriends. She was always nagging him. Dad was likely to give my sisters, or me, a whuppin' when he was like this. Mom, too. Then he'd leave us and be gone for weeks at a time. He'd be with Faye, his alcoholic girlfriend, who probably gave him a helluva blow job, but she took him away from me."

Tears started to well up in Avery's eyes. "God, here I go again. Anyway, dad would finally return, and momma would always take him back. We could hear them in the bedroom making up, moaning and groaning. It made me sick, but I was glad to have him back home."

"You're bitter, Judge."

"I *am* bitter. My dad is dead now. I never really got to know him much. He was either working or drinking. One time he took me to a Reds' game, and occasionally, he'd throw a ball with me. When he died, I clung to his dead body at the funeral. Here I was an adult, a lawyer, a judge, a decorated war hero and I felt like a little boy. I was the last person to leave the mortuary before they closed his casket. I was the last person to be with him when he died in the middle of the night and the last person to be with him before he was lowered into the ground—forever."

"What was your mom like when he was gone?"

"Oh, she'd have extra chores for me—I became her little man. She'd call me the 'man of the house.' I liked the special attention from her, but I felt like she was using me as a substitute husband. She had me out working two paper routes to help with the money. I decided I'd just get the hell out of there. I was always a good student, applied myself in school, ran track, kept to myself. I got a scholarship to Wright State. It was part academic, part athletic. I got a half-ride for track and the other half was for academics."

"Did you date?"

"Never had a date in high school. Girls and relationships scared me; I was too nervous around girls to ask them out. The thought of having sex with them made me so nervous that I kind of pushed the notion of it out of my mind."

"When was your first sexual experience?"

"You won't believe this, but I was in 'Nam, and I was twenty-six. I was on leave, a little rest and relaxation, or R&R as we called it. I was in Taiwan, and for fifty bucks, I could have a woman for the entire day. Her name was Rosa. It wasn't her real name. They'd give these Asian women western names."

"What was that like for you?"

"Well, the only reason I did it was because all the other guys would come back after R&R having screwed their brains out. I was still a virgin. Here I was, this Special Forces guy, trained killer, big macho man, and I'd never had sex. I never let on. It took me two R&R's before I got up the courage to try it."

"So, what was your experience with a woman like?"

"I was so scared and nervous the first time that I couldn't get a hard on. When I finally did, I came while she was helping me in her. I was humiliated, but Rosa was patient and we spent the rest of the day playing with each other until I could finally accomplish what I'd set out to do. I spent the next two days with Rosa. She gave me baths, fondled my balls, gave me blow jobs, pushed small balls up my ass and pulled them out on a string when I came. I loved it. She showed me the areas on a woman that made them feel good. It was an eye-opening experience for me, an epiphany of sorts."

"Do you have any idea why you were so anxious around women at first?"

"No, all I knew was I was scared."

"How do you feel around women now?"

"I'm still scared of 'um, I think."

"When you talk about the beatings that went on in your family, you do it without feeling."

"Yeah, so?"

"Tell me this. Can you still see yourself being 'whupped' by your father, and if so, can you still feel it on your body?"

Avery closed his eyes and tried to visualize. "*Huh*. No, I can't see it happening, and I can't feel it. I just know it happened."

"Can you still hear and see your parents fighting?"

"No, I just remember that happened, too. When I try to visualize it, I just go blank. That's when the headaches come."

"Can you still hear them having sex?"

"No, not that either."

Gilmour stood up from the table. He reached for his briefcase to put his notes in it. As he did, he asked, "Judge, have you ever been hypnotized or been in a drug-induced trance with sodium amytal or scopolamine?"

"I know I haven't been hypnotized. I think sodium amytal is a 'truth serum' and I've never had that. I don't even know what scopolamine is. Could it be a potato dish?"

For the first time the entire day, Gilmour smiled. "No, scopolamine is a drug that cuts to your subconscious mind and allows you to be opened up, if you will."

"I sure don't want to be opened up any more right now. I've cried more in the last couple of hours than I have my entire lifetime. I'm afraid of what's in there."

"*Um-hum.* One last thing for today. Did you know Gene Hardacre or have any reason to kill him?"

"I barely knew the man. I had met him before. He was a Republican, I'm a Democrat."

"That's it?" Gilmour asked.

"That's it. This is a mystery to me, too."

"I'll discuss your options with your lawyer. Thanks for your cooperation. I may be back. I will write up a report on my impressions and meet with your lawyer."

Avery stood and shook Gilmour's hand. He rang for the guard in the control room to open the metal door. It slid open with the screech of metal-against-metal. Gilmour walked through it. When it clanged shut, Avery started. He sat there and his whole body began to shake. "Damn, I'm falling apart. I don't understand any of this," he muttered to himself as he continued to shake. The guard came to escort him back to his cell.

CHAPTER 7

Thursday, January 18—1:30 P.M.

Gilmour thought about his interview with Jackson all the way back to his office. *He's a killer. He's a killer. This claimed amnesia has got to be a fraud. But what if it isn't?* Gilmour kept thinking. It was unlike any case he'd had before. He had interviewed defendants who'd claimed amnesia for a crime, but he hadn't believed most of them. If he gave any credibility to an amnesia case for the defense in a case of this magnitude, he'd be laughed out of the community. Certainly, all other forensic psychiatrists and psychologists would think he was crazier that Jackson. But how could he explain what happened? What was the meaning of the dreams? What effect did the beatings and Jackson's dysfunctional childhood have on him? They might have traumatized him, but certainly they couldn't have created a condition of insanity. Jackson wasn't schizophrenic. He didn't think he was God or Jesus Christ who needed to kill to save the world, nor did he claim command-hallucinations told him to kill the sheriff, nor did he claim thought-insertion where someone else is inserting thoughts asking that he kill.

People are tired of insanity, Gilmour thought. *When the hell are people going to take responsibility for their actions? Jackson surely wasn't.* Gilmore wondered if he was going to enable a murderer to avoid taking responsibility for his crime. The problem was that Jackson apparently didn't know what acts he should be taking responsibility for.

Gilmour stopped for a bowl of organic vegetable soup at a deli close to his office. He ate it quickly. When he got to his office, he sat at his desk and wrote a lengthy report to Jack Maine. When finished, he proofread it, signed it and faxed it to the public defender's office. It rang in at Judy Mabin's desk; the fax machine automatically began spitting out the report there.

Mike Swenson, Tony Losavio and Harry Bova sat in a surveillance truck with Myron's Deli and Catering logo on the sides. It wasn't filled with roast beef and enchiladas—rather with hundreds of thousands of dollars of electronic equipment. Swenson took a copy of the fax out of their machine and handed it to Harry Bova. The left side of Swenson's face had ballooned out and his left eye was black and swollen shut. Joe Betts had left his mark.

"Do we have a reading on the other bug yet, Tony?"

"We got it. A phone number and address."

"Good," Bova said.

"We need to talk to Dr. McGinty at Langley to see what he wants to do with this information."

Thursday—12:20 P.M.
The King's Table

Marci Maine had asked to be seated in their favorite booth in the corner. Bobbi walked over and asked for her order. "Need something to drink today, Marci?"

"Jack will be here soon. I'll have a Coke; he'll want a Dr. Pepper."

"Is it true what I just heard about Burt being dead?"

"I'm afraid so. I don't know all the details yet. Jack called me this morning to tell me. It's a shock for all of us. When he gets here, I'll know more."

"Keep us posted. This place won't be the same without Burt hanging around and holding court here. Women loved him. I loved him." Bobbi got tears in her eyes.

It was no secret that Burt and Bobbi had had a brief romantic liaison. For Burt, it was mainly sexual, for Bobbi, more.

"I can't believe I'm crying in front of the customers, but everyone around here is pretty broken up. Let me get your drinks." Bobbie turned away from Marci while wiping her eyes with a Kleenex Marci had pulled from her purse.

"You're deep in thought," Jack said seriously when he sat down next to Marci and kissed her cheek.

"I am. Can you explain to me what's going on around here? The sheriff is gunned down by a man we all know, in broad daylight, not three days ago. His funeral is going on right now. Now, Burt is dead. His funeral is Saturday. What I'm thinking about, dear, is, what is the meaning of all of this?"

"That's not all," Jack said, taking hold of Marci's hand. "The cops are trying to pin a criminally negligent homicide on Chris."

"Chris? Chris who? Chris *Conley*?" Marci asked incredulously.

"Yeah, Burt's Chris."

"I hadn't heard that. She wouldn't do anything to hurt Burt."

"That's not what the cops are thinking."

Marci was horrified. She and Chris had become friends. "What *is* going on?" she asked.

"I can't tell you because it's privileged."

"What do you mean it's privileged? You don't represent Chris."

Jack smiled. "I can share this with you if you're part of my law firm, otherwise, I can't. It would fall within the ambit of attorney-client privilege."

"Does this mean that we're going ahead with our plans?" Marci asked.

"I think we need to make a decision right now on what we're going to do, what I'm going to do. Burt's dead. It feels like the time is right for me to leave. I'm thinking tomorrow will be my last day in the office."

"If that's what you want to do, I'll call the guy about the office space. It's sitting empty, and he said we could move in tomorrow if we needed to," Marci said.

"Before you call him, there are a few things you need to know." Marci's eyes grew larger as she looked at Jack. "No," Jack said, "it's all good news—well, almost all good. The county commissioner asked me this morning if I'd be interested in running the public defender's office. It pays a hundred thousand a year. I told him I'd get back to him this afternoon. Secondly—I'm assuming you're going to be my office manager and investigator now. Chris Conley called me this morning and asked me to represent her on this case involving Burt. She says she can pay me a ten-K retainer. Third, Avery Jackson wants me to represent him privately. He has fifteen or twenty thousand to do his case."

"Let's deal with things in order," Marci said. "Are you interested in the PD job? A hundred thousand isn't pocket change."

"I don't think so. I want to try cases like these."

"Okay, tell him you're making good on a long overdue commitment to your bride." She reached for Jack's hand and squeezed it. "On the second problem, Chris' case, can you ethically represent her when she's charged with negligently killing your boss and friend? Isn't that a conflict of interest?"

"If I leave the PD's office before she's charged, I don't see a problem. She assures me she had nothing to do with his death. If the forensics come back and corroborate her story, I'm going ahead. Nobody could want to get to the truth about Burt's death more than I do. I have a feeling about this whole mess."

"Like what?"

Jack told her the details of Burt's death and the Van Hazeltree connection, of Hazeltree's murder, and finally, about Joe and Chris' fracas over the audio tape.

"Well, some people obviously want to know what happened in the condo that night with Burt," Marci said. "They wanted that information before you got it. Sounds to me like you're hooked, Counselor."

"I think it's about time for the two of us to go for it. *Can* you get the office set up and running by Monday? I thought I'd do the preliminary hearing as a public defender on Monday morning, and be in private practice Monday afternoon."

"So, what I'm hearing is that I have like two days to get a law office up and running? Here we've been talking about doing this for over a year and when it all comes down, I have two days to make it happen?" Marci said, feigning anger.

"That's about the size of it."

"As for the money, Chris is good for her fee. She may need to pay some of it over time. Jackson's case is a different story. How much will it cost to do a case like that?"

"A lot. Phil Gilmour is over at the jail right now interviewing Avery. The expert witness fees alone could be twenty grand."

"It hardly seems worth it if we're going to spend all the money on experts," reasoned Marci.

"We're also going to have to spend money on investigations. After what happened this morning with Joe Betts and those three at Burt's apartment getting into a fistfight, I don't want you risking your life. This is a dangerous case, and people we love are turning up dead. We can get Joe to work for us part-time on an as-needed basis until we get going."

"The agreement we had was that I'd run the office and do some of the legwork on investigations."

"That's still the plan, but when it gets hairy, I want a big, tough guy out there. All our plans for the office, for a family together, will go out the window if you're dead," Jack said.

"Okay, but on a matter or case where there is no chance that I'm going to be hurt, I'd like to be part of things. Okay?"

"Sure." Jack squeezed Marci's hand. "There is one more issue."

"What's that, Counselor? Haven't you already asked enough of me this morning?"

"This is a big one involving a lot more expense and another lawyer who happens to be female. I'd like to ask Yolanda Crone to come aboard as an associate. It doesn't have to happen right now. She'd need a couple more months in the public defender's office as seasoning, and we can't afford to bring her in immediately anyway. I'm not going to try this case alone, nor do I want to try Chris' case alone if it should get that far. I need a junior associate to help with legal research, to wet nurse Avery throughout this and to help try the case. She's already working on Avery's case; Burt made her part of the team. I just left the jail and Yolanda was with Avery and Dr. Gilmour. Avery and Yolanda seemed good together, and I think her presence would play well with the jury."

"Yeah, I like Yolanda, and it'd be good to have another woman around the office," Marci said. "I'll agree on the condition that I get to pick the first male associate. I'll try to get one with a cute butt. How much do you think it will take to get her?"

"She's getting thirty a year at the PD's office. I think she'd work with us for about the same. I think she'd generate a big clientele of her own when she gets started. She'd probably easily pay for herself."

"So, let's see, we've already spent about fifty thousand before we've paid a dime of rent, phone, furniture, or secretarial expenses. By the way, what are we going to do about secretarial help?"

"I figure we can all answer the phones until we get a steady source of income that'll allow us to hire someone. We'll let the calls we miss go to voice mail."

"Who is *all* of us? Since I will be there most of the time, I'll be it."

"We'll be using voice mail and typing our own motions and briefs. We may lose money on Jackson, but the exposure will be good, and hopefully we'll pick up a lot of other business as a result of it. Of course, if we lose it, people will think I'm an idiot."

Marci smiled. "I'll write a check for the rent on the office space and put all the furniture and word processing equipment on a credit card. By the time the bill comes due, you'll have earned some of the money we take in on retainer. This deserves a toast," she said. "To the business of Jack Maine and Associates—Attorneys and Counselors at Law."

Jack put his Dr. Pepper to Marci's glass of Coke. They were in business.

Thursday—2:00 P.M.
Public Defender's Office

When Jack got back to the public defender's office after lunch, he was excited about the prospect of starting his own practice—after all, he was now an entrepreneur—but no more steady paychecks from just one employer was a little scary. Hopefully, he'd have many paychecks from many employers. His focus changed when he walked into the office; the shock and grief over Burt's death from everyone there was palpable. Deputies sat in each other's offices and commiserated. They told Burt Porter stories, an icon in the making, a cult hero among defense attorneys.

Jack walked down to his office and threw himself into his swivel chair. It was still beautiful and sunny as he looked out the window at the Miami River. The ice on its banks had begun to melt. *What a day of ups and downs*, he thought. He and Marci were about to start an adventure. That was exhilarating. But Burt was dead. Jack needed to make sense of the last four days. He had an obligation to his friend to do so.

He began cleaning up the pile of mail on his desk; he'd start moving out today. On top was Gilmour's faxed preliminary psychiatric report. He tried reading it: lots of jargon, Oedipal complex, dissociative disorder, trauma. He looked at the diagnosis: post-traumatic stress disorder, dissociative disorder—rule out malingering. What the hell was that? He picked up the phone and called Gilmour's pager and touch-toned in his number. He went on looking at the report. Within minutes, Paulette put a call from Phil Gilmour through to Jack.

"Phil, I got your report and read it. What's the bottom line?"

"Your client claims he doesn't remember important parts of his life. If he doesn't honestly know what happened at the time he killed the sheriff, then he would not know right from wrong and would be unable to appreciate the wrongfulness of his act. He would be legally insane."

"Do you think he's telling the truth?"

"I don't know. The case is really beyond me. I can't give you an opinion at this time. On one hand, he gave me no reason to believe he wasn't telling the truth, but then again on the other, he's an intelligent man, a lawyer and he knows the process and might know how to fake amnesia to build a defense."

"Did he have a reason to kill Hardacre?" Jack asked.

"None that I could see."

"Is he faking amnesia?"

"I can't tell."

"Let's assume," Jack said, "that he's telling the truth. Do we have an insanity defense?"

"The courts are starting to recognize amnesia as the basis of an insanity defense if it's related to trauma and a dissociative condition."

"What's a dissociative condition?"

"Essentially, being spaced out. To be legally insane, a person has to be so badly spaced out that part of him is one place and another part of him is another place."

"How could that happen?"

"It happens all the time: traffic accidents, rapes, incest, beatings and sodomizing of children, spousal abuse. Overwhelming, terrifying events that scare a person so badly he or she leaves the body and goes to the corner of the room and hides, while another part takes over and functions. The effect is a numbing of the body so the person can't feel the terror. The soul of the person is split into pieces. The victim might not remember the scary event and certainly can't feel it."

"Is that why people don't remember until later that they were sexually abused or beaten as kids?"

"That's it," Gilmour said. "They begin reclaiming the part of themselves that split off and went to the corner of the room. The thoughts, feelings and memories may begin to emerge later."

"What did you observe, Phil?" He was tired of the psychological doubletalk. "Is the killing related to trauma or a dissociative condition, and do I have a way to get Jackson out of this?"

"Mr. Jackson is dissociative. He talks about his childhood and the abuse that occurred without the feelings he should have about what happened. A normal person would experience considerable fright and there would be tears over what happened to him, but not Jackson. He has just begun the process of feeling. Pain, hurt and anger are not connected to the people and incidents that caused them. That's dissociation, but it doesn't make him insane. There's no way that alone will provide an explanation for what happened. We all dissociate. We all space out every day in order to survive. It doesn't necessarily make us legally insane or give us an excuse to kill someone."

"So why the hell did he commit this crime?"

"I don't know yet. The thing that concerns me the most is the loss of time and memory he has regarding his war experience. My hypothesis is that there is something very traumatic that happened during his time in the military. Whatever it was caused part of him to split off and leave him. Even so, I don't know how that trauma could be related to this killing."

"Did you uncover any motive?"

"No, I didn't find one. He apparently has no feeling whatsoever for the sheriff. That's the most important thing about this case. He expresses no reason he would want to kill the man. There's something we're missing—his recurring nightmares also tell us that. Unfortunately, neither he nor I know what that is."

"Doc, I gotta find out because the criminal justice system is going to kill Avery Jackson."

"The only thing I can suggest is that we bring in someone who's done forensic evaluations on people with amnesia—people with multiple personality disorders and the like— who have committed crimes. There is a psychologist in Denver by the name of Marcus Offen who does that sort of work. I heard him speak and present tapes on his work at a conference in San Francisco a couple of years ago. The work he presented was very controversial. It showed a multiple personality-disordered guy by the name of Darren who had cut off his pregnant wife's head. Darren had been severely abused as a child. He unconsciously created a personality by the name of Buddy who would protect him from further abuse. Darren switched from this passive, nice guy to this vicious personality, Buddy, who would kill anyone who threatened Darren. The psychologist hypnotized Darren, and while in a trance, the killer, Buddy, came out and explained why he did it."

"No jury will ever accept that scenario."

"It really did make sense, but for some people, it was pretty hard to believe. The psychiatrists and psychologists at the conference didn't believe it. They were very critical of Offen's work."

"Did you believe it?"

"Let's just say I was intrigued," Gilmour hedged.

"What's this guy's name again?"

"Marcus Offen. He's a psychologist, a Ph.D."

"How did Darren's case come out?"

"Darren was convicted. As I recall, the jury was out for two days. They found him guilty even though they believed he had another personality, but they still concluded he was legally sane."

"I need something that works. Has this guy, Offen, ever had any success with judges or juries?"

"Claims he did. They were both first-degree murder cases. One ought to be particularly interesting to you. It involved a Vietnamese man who experienced a flashback to the torture he endured in a Vietcong prison and killed his wife while she was working in the kitchen with a knife. He believed she was a Vietcong soldier who had tortured him with a knife during the war. The similar thing about that case was that after the murder, this man behaved just like Jackson did. He didn't try to run; he sat down in a daze on the porch; the police came and arrested him. He simply didn't remember what he'd done. In fact, this guy and Darren were both similar to Jackson in that after they killed, they were confused about what had happened."

"Can't you do this kind of work?" Jack asked. "I hate to go out of Dayton to a place like Denver to bring a guy like this in. He'll be expensive, and a jury is not likely to believe him because his work sounds too bizarre."

"The first thing you have to know, Jack, is that a jury is not likely to believe any kind of defense involving insanity. You remember what happened years ago on the Pete Cassidy Rose case when he was found not guilty by reason of insanity. Alec Hunter will leave no stone unturned."

"Would you consider working with Dr. Offen?"

"Sure, it would be an honor. I'd like to have more experience with amnesia cases. I'm sorry I can't be of more help to you right now."

"Thanks, Phil. I'll think about this. It all sounds pretty bizarre, but there's nothing about this case that's ordinary." Gilmour made arrangements to get Jack in touch with Dr. Offen.

After Jack hung up, he leaned back in his chair and put his feet up on the desk. *What a day*, he thought. *What a week*. Part of him wanted to run. Part of him was irresistibly attracted to the excitement. Adrenaline is an addictive drug, and his veins were full of it. However, when he thought of Burt, he quickly slowed down. He must keep his composure. He needed to take things one step at a time. He called Chris Conley and told her he would take her case right after Jackson's preliminary hearing on Monday. She was delighted, despite everything that had happened, including her altercation that morning, which she told him about. "Jesus," muttered Jack, "the tape, we've *got* to have that tape. It's like a football—it attracts a crowd of people- desperate people- and obviously, we're not the only ones who are desperate." After the call, he prepared a written letter of resignation and faxed it to the county commissioner.

A few minutes later, he pulled an empty cardboard box from a storage closet and returned to his office. He would take tomorrow off, help Marci with the new office and prepare for Burt's funeral on Saturday. The office would be empty tomorrow anyway. He started packing his things. The files stayed, as well as most of the office property. He took personal pens and items from his desk. On the credenza behind him was a picture of Marci and their dog, Sam, as well as a picture of him and Burt at a Cincinnati Reds' game. Every year they went down to Cincinnati on opening day. Tears filled Jack's eyes. He put the pictures in the box and wiped away his tears with a Kleenex.

Hanging on the wall across from his desk was his law degree from Ohio State and his law license from the Supreme Court of Ohio. He packed the law degree by placing it face down in the box. Then he took the license and placed it face down in the box. As he did so, he looked at its back.

Jesus! he said to himself. Adrenaline rushed through his veins again. He stood up and walked through his door only to find Joe Betts with seven nasty stitches adorning a huge knot on the right side of his head. Joe was recounting the morning's melee to Yolanda.

"I need you two," whispered Jack as he put his finger to his mouth.

They followed Jack into his office. He drew their attention to the license silently. Joe looked at it. His face flushed red. Calmly and quietly he walked over to Jack's phone, unscrewed the receiver and found another listening device. He screwed it back on. He walked into Burt's office, unscrewed the receiver on his phone and found two more listening devices, as well as the tracer. He screwed that lid back on, too. He then went to Burt's secretary's desk. Judy had already left for the day, and sure enough, she had two bugs in her phone, as well as one in the fax machine. He found nothing in Yolanda's office. Systematically, he checked every other phone but found nothing more.

Joe motioned to the two of them to follow him outside. Although warmer outside than it had been, without coats they felt the chill as the sun was going down. "No wonder those sons-of-bitches beat us to Burt's condo this morning."

"Did you find a file on Hazeltree?" Jack asked, connecting the dots.

"Yeah, Burt represented him ten years ago on a Possession with Intent to Sell case. Burt got it thrown out. Cops came into court and admitted they lost the evidence. Did you ever hear such bullshit?"

"Cops never do that unless the defendant is a snitch or is working for them somehow," Jack said. "Did Ovanul go by the name of Van?"

"Burt calls him Van throughout the file."

Jack stood in silence, his mind spinning. "Let's go over to the King's Table. At least, we won't be bugged over there. We're going to freeze out here."

The three of them made the short walk around the corner to the Table and sat down at a booth. Jack ordered a Coors Light, Joe a Bud and Yolanda a red wine. Jack began thinking out loud. "Someone knows about the conversation I just had with Gilmour, and I got Avery's psychiatric report through Judy's fax machine. God knows how many people know about that. It could be in the *Globe* tomorrow. Joe, can you and Yolanda get someone down here who knows electronic surveillance so we can figure out where these bugs are transmitting to?"

Joe nodded.

"Do you want to call the sheriff?" Yolanda asked. "It's a criminal offense to be tapping phones without a warrant."

"Maybe the cops got a warrant on Burt's phone because he was a suspect in some drug stuff," Joe said.

"No, let's not call the cops," Jack said. "Bottom line is I'm not sure I can trust the cops with this stuff right now. Let's see if we can get some information privately about who put these bugs in and where they're transmitting to."

"I got just the guy for the job. I'll see if I can get him in here right away," Joe assured them.

"Can you also snoop around and find out if any judges over at the courthouse have signed off on any warrants for wiretaps? It could be a federal warrant—DEA stuff, so go over to the federal court, too, and find out if anything has come out of there. We need the case files on all of Hazeltree's cases from the DA's office. We need to know all the details—the arresting officer, the DA, the assigned detective, the judge on each case. Can you get all that?" Jack asked Joe.

"Yeah. I just started getting it together. Hazeltree had seven felony charges, including a first-degree murder. Every last one of them was dismissed."

"Did the Rosato brothers represent him?" Jack asked.

"On every single case."

"Now, Yolanda, you see why I don't want you to call the cops just yet on this case?" Jack asked.

"I see, but I don't believe it. The last four days nobody would believe."

They nodded.

"That brings me to another issue," Jack said. "Burt asked me to stay with the office until Jackson's case was completed. Obviously, things have changed. Jackson asked to represent him privately and so has Chris Conley. I'll be leaving the PD's office on Monday after Jackson's preliminary hearing, but I want to keep our team intact on the Jackson case."

"How can we do that?" Joe asked.

"I want you to work for me in my private practice. I'm asking you to moonlight with me for a while until I can get established, then make the jump. Yolanda, I want you to come with me as soon as you can give the public defender's office notice."

Joe didn't hesitate. "Sure. I'll be there. I could use some extra bucks. Besides, I want another shot at the sumbitch who hit me on the head this morning." Joe put his hand to the stitches on his head. "I'm looking forward to meeting up with the honky muthafucka again. I'll come to work for you if you'll promise me I'll get another shot at him."

"We don't know if we'll ever see those guys again, but I'll tell you this, you need to find that tape. How about you, Yolanda?"

"I just started to get to know you four days ago. I know I'm a little older and more experienced than most women in the office, but I've only been here for a few months. I've tried just two little misdemeanors. I'm honored you'd want me, but I don't think I have what it takes to try cases like these."

"Don't sell yourself short. I heard about both of your trials. You got an acquittal on a domestic violence case and a hung jury on a DUI. Lawyers who saw you said you were *very* good. I believe them. I think you do have what it takes to try cases like these; you just need a little more experience. You can get some of that while you finish out your cases with the office. You'll get plenty of trial experience working with me. What do you say?"

"Same money?"

"Same money," Jack assured her while realizing that he didn't even know if there'd be any money coming in.

"It's a deal. But I need to give the office at least thirty days' notice."

"That's fine. Take the time you need, but I may need your help in your off hours before then. Can you do that?"

"Sure, as best I can."

"Then let's drink to our new association." Jack waved Bobbi over. "Let's have another round." Jack held up his frosted beer mug to Joe's frosted mug. Yolanda gently clanged her wine glass to their mugs. "To Burt. He would take pride in our association. It is in his tradition that we move ahead."

"Burt," Joe said, "must be rollin' over down at the morgue right now, knowing his girlfrien' is gonna be charged with killin' him. He'd want us to kick their asses."

"We'll find a way," Jack said. "But Joe, you need to find that tape."

"Done deal, boss."

Yolanda looked at both of them. For the life of her, she couldn't figure out how they'd ever find the tape, much less win the trial.

CHAPTER 8

Monday, January 22—8:30 A.M.
Preliminary Hearing, Montgomery County Court

The preliminary hearing is a critical stage in a criminal proceeding. Defendants can take the stand if they wish, but as in a trial, they can't be compelled to do so. They hardly ever testify at the preliminary hearing because their lawyers use the proceeding to gain information about the state's case. A defense lawyer rarely puts on evidence of his own because he does not want to tip his hand. The burden of proof for the state is very low, the lowest the law ever requires. Upon a showing of probable cause, the defendant is bound over for trial. Probable cause means that, construing the evidence most favorably to the prosecution, the defendant probably committed the crime. A defendant should never waive his right to a preliminary hearing unless he benefits from doing so. It is before the preliminary hearing that plea bargains are explored, and if a reasonable offer is put on the table, the defendant will then typically waive the preliminary hearing and plead guilty to a reduced charge after the case is bound over to district court.

This was not the case in the State of Ohio v. Avery Jackson. There were no such offers. On the cover of the Jackson file was the acronym GORT—the defendant would either plead guilty to the charge of first-degree murder or go to trial—Guilty or Trial. Either way, Jackson was looking at the death penalty.

It had been a week since Sheriff Hardacre's murder. The media attention had not waned, but instead, had been exacerbated by the poignancy of his

116

funeral. The public had a hunger for information about it. They had seen the video of the killing many times on the local and national news. *Dateline NBC* had done a story on it and the lives of Sheriff Hardacre and Avery Jackson, respectively. *Dateline* had paid particular attention to the rapist, DiSalvo, and Jackson's demise subsequent to his giving DiSalvo probation. The angle of the story was that perhaps Jackson had been paid off for such a sentence. After all, Jackson was a murderer. Why then would he not be corrupt? Pressure was put on Alec Hunter through editorials in the *Dayton Daily News* and *Journal Herald* to investigate the possibility of bribes. Hunter had come out publicly saying that he'd launch a full investigation.

Jack arrived at the courthouse at eight-thirty in the morning for the nine o'clock preliminary hearing. Yolanda had already arrived and had earlier spent time with Avery. She'd made sure he'd been given a suit as well as a clean and starched white shirt and a dark-brown tie; she didn't want him appearing in the orange jumpsuit that's worn by most indigent defendants. The press and the public were already sure he was a vicious killer; there was no sense in his looking like one, too.

Avery had taken an immediate liking to Yolanda. He knew having a woman on his team was a good idea, and he needed some female, emotional support after his wife's dumping him. Gloria hadn't visited or communicated with him in any way since she last saw him and laid out the terms for their divorce. The ongoing conflict within him that battled between the things he enjoyed and those he hated about her was maddening at times as he grieved the loss of her. He missed her smell, her voice and sitting across from her at meals. It was the sensory things about her that he was finding the most difficult to let go of— the visual, tactile and olfactory. The pain he felt in his gut over the loss of those things was soothed only by the memory of her selfishness and the thought of how she callously used him.

The deputies brought Avery to Judge Bonin's courtroom at eight forty-five and placed him in the jury box. Three deputies were assigned to see that he did not escape.

Every seat in the room was taken. Videocams abounded outside the room, their operators jockeying to get a position at the courtroom door's glass portals.

Jack and Yolanda were with Avery in the jury box when Jim Brodan came over and asked to have a word with them in the attorney's conference room just off the courtroom. Hank Dorsey was already seated in the room when they got there. "Please have a seat," he said.

"Where's Alec?" Jack asked.

"He's back at the office organizing a press conference announcing an investigation into the DiSalvo case and possible bribes your client may have taken," Hank said. "I know that makes your day right now. I'm sure you have enough on your plate handling Burt's death and his coming funeral. I want to extend my condolences to you."

"Thanks for your concern. Last week was a nightmare, but I believe we're ready to go on," Jack said.

"The word is you're leaving the public defender's office and going into private practice," Hank said. "Any truth to the rumor?"

"That's true. This will be my last appearance for the PD's office."

"Who's going to be taking Jackson's representation to the district court?"

"Hank, you're assuming Jackson will be bound over for trial. We intend to get the matter dismissed today at the preliminary hearing," Jack said.

Hank Dorsey smiled. Jim Brodan looked worried for a second, as if there was something he didn't know.

"That brings me to the point of this meeting, other than to express my sadness for your loss. Would your client waive his right to the preliminary hearing?"

"Now, Hank, why would he do such a thing? What could possibly be in it for him?"

"Because he doesn't want to have more media exposure when the mood in the community toward him is bitter. You and I both know that this hearing is a formality, and it will serve you no good to have it," Dorsey said.

"If you gentlemen would take the death penalty off the table, we might waive the preliminary hearing."

"Are you saying that your client would plead straight up to first-degree murder if we drop the death penalty request?" Brodan asked.

"I haven't discussed that with him. *Are* you offering that?" Jack asked.

"No," Hank retorted, "we're not. We've begun the investigation on possible DiSalvo payoffs to Jackson. We need to find out where that comes out before we consider making any offers."

"If you're not making any offers, there's no sense in his waiving the preliminary hearing. We figure things can't get much worse for Judge Jackson now. Oh, and by the way, I'll be continuing as Judge Jackson's legal counsel at the trial, as well as representing Chris Conley, at least at her preliminary hearing."

Brodan sat straight up in his chair. "Is that ethical?"

"Yeah. Obviously, we don't believe Detective Guteman's theory about the case, and you certainly should not bind me in terms of my ethical obligations. We don't think the case should have ever been brought."

"Fine. Look forward to trying both of those cases against you." Hank smiled. "I hope you're getting big retainers because these are the kinds of cases that can break a private, criminal lawyer's back," Hank said solicitously.

"Thanks for your concern, Hank," Jack said, equally as disingenuously.

"Sure, just keep those things in mind," Dorsey said.

"Why don't you go out and ask your client if he wishes to waive his preliminary hearing?" Brodan asked while looking at his watch. "The judge will be on the bench soon."

"I'll ask, but count on calling your first witness," Jack said as he and Yolanda left to return to their client.

"You know how confident a district attorney is when he asks you to waive a preliminary hearing while offering you nothing," Jack said. "I'm not even going to tell Avery. It's an insult to him."

As they entered the courtroom, all was quiet. Avery was already seated at the defense-counsel table, his cuffs removed. Marci had arrived and saved a place for Avery's two children, Aaron and Rebecca, immediately behind them.

Avery looked at his two children, tears welling up. Gloria wasn't there; she'd obviously meant what she said about wanting out.

Dorsey and Brodan came into the courtroom. Accompanying them was Carl Kessler, Presiding Judge of the Montgomery County Court. Always impressive in appearance and ability to articulate, Kessler would be the perfect witness to get Avery bound over for trial. He would leave no doubt as to guilt. The media were going to love him.

"All rise," the bailiff called out.

Judge Bonin entered the courtroom from a door behind the bench. She sat in her high-backed, black judge's chair without making eye contact with any of the lawyers.

"This court is now in session," Bonin's bailiff announced. "The Honorable Madeline Bonin presiding. Please be seated."

"Calling the case of the People of the State of Ohio v. Avery Jackson," Bonin said. "This matter comes on for preliminary hearing. Good morning, Counsel. Please enter your appearances."

"Good morning, Your Honor. Henry Dorsey and James Brodan for the People," Dorsey said.

"Jack Maine and Yolanda Crone for the defense," Jack said.

"Are Counsel ready to proceed?" asked Bonin.

"The State is ready," Dorsey said.

"The defense is ready," Jack said.

"State will call Judge Carl Kessler," Dorsey said.

Judge Bonin swore Kessler to honesty.

"Will you state your name please?" Dorsey asked.

"Judge Carl Kessler."

"Where are you employed?"

"I am the Presiding Judge of the Montgomery County Courts."

"How long have you held that position?"

"Sixteen years."

"Did you have occasion to meet one Avery Jackson in that position?"

"Yes."

"How?"

"He was, until a couple of years ago, one of my colleagues on the bench of the district court. I have also been a member of the same political party he is and have been involved in fundraisers and meetings with him regarding political matters. We are both Democrats."

"Could you please point Avery Jackson out to us?"

Kessler pointed at Jackson. "He's the black man in the brown sport coat sitting at counsel table next to Mr. Maine."

"Let the record show that Judge Kessler has identified the defendant, Avery Jackson."

"The record will so reflect," Judge Bonin acknowledged.

"Did you have occasion to be attending a Rotary Club meeting last Monday, January fifteenth, at the Renaissance Hotel?"

"Yes."

"Was that hotel located in the City of Dayton, Montgomery County, Ohio?"

"Yes."

"Would you tell the court what happened at the meeting?"

"Yes. We had finished our lunch. Aubrey Shell, our present Rotary Club president, made some announcement about fundraisers and that sort of thing. He then introduced the speaker for the day."

"Who was the speaker for the day?"

"The sheriff, Gene Hardacre."

"Did you know Sheriff Hardacre prior to that day?"

"Yes."

"How did you know him?"

"He had appeared in my court on various cases, and I'd seen him on television while he was running for office."

"Could you tell us what happened then?"

"Sheriff Hardacre got up, took the podium and began his speech. He was maybe five minutes into it when Avery Jackson approached the speaker's podium."

"Let me interrupt you here, Judge. Where were you seated at the time?"

"I was seated, along with Judge Wulf and Judge Duncan, at a table immediately in front of the dais."

"Okay, and what happened then?"

"Mr. Jackson walked right up to the sheriff while he was speaking. He pulled out a gun, and fired one shot into Sheriff Hardacre's head, killed him right there."

"What happened then?"

"A number of us grabbed Mr. Jackson, I picked up the gun. An ambulance was there a few minutes later and Sheriff Hardacre's body was taken away. Half of his head was missing and he wasn't breathing. Then the deputy sheriffs arrived and took Mr. Jackson into custody."

"Can you identify the man who fired the shot at Sheriff Hardacre?"

"It's the man I have already identified. He's seated right there." Kessler pointed at Jackson again.

"Let the record reflect that Judge Kessler has identified Avery Jackson as the man who shot Sheriff Hardacre."

"The record will so reflect," Bonin said automatically.

"No further questions of this witness, Your Honor," Hank said.

"Very well," Bonin said. "Cross-examination, Mr. Maine?"

"Thank you, Your Honor. Judge Kessler, how long did you observe Judge Jackson before he fired the shot?"

"Just a matter of seconds."

"Did you recognize him immediately?"

"Yes."

"You have known Judge Jackson for many years, have you not?"

"Yes."

"You've observed him many times over the years, haven't you?"

"Yes."

"He was both a lawyer in your court and a judge working with you in the district court, isn't that correct?"

"Yes."

"You would describe him as a fairly thoughtful and considerate person, would you not?"

"Yes, prior to last Monday, but I really don't believe I could describe him that way anymore. Thoughtful and considerate were not traits that Mr. Jackson was displaying last Monday."

"You never observed him to be acting strangely until January fifteenth, did you?"

"Not really."

"Wouldn't you describe him as a fairly bright and animated person?"

"Yes."

"And he was an excellent jurist in terms of running his courtroom and the application of the rules of evidence, was he not, Judge Kessler?"

"Yes, he was an extremely bright guy who was very knowledgeable on the rules of evidence."

"His demeanor was very different on January fifteenth at the Renaissance Hotel, wouldn't you say?"

"If you mean he was different when he blew another man's brains out in front of all of us, I'd say you were correct."

There were a few anxious snickers in the back of the courtroom. The reporters wrote furiously to get that last piece of testimony down on paper. Judge Bonin glared at the gallery, but said nothing.

"You are saying then, that what he did was totally out of character for him."

"Certainly, it was out of character. We don't normally have murderers on the bench."

There were again a few anxious snickers in the courtroom. Judge Bonin looked up and said sternly, "If anyone thinks this is any matter to be laughing about, you're to leave the courtroom immediately. I am instructing the officers to remove anyone who is disrespectful in this court. Proceed, Mr. Maine."

There were numerous red faces and sets of eyes looking down in embarrassment. The courtroom was quiet. It was as if everyone had stopped breathing.

"Judge Kessler, describe Judge Jackson's facial expression immediately before and after the shooting," Jack asked.

"It didn't change. He was deadpan both before and after."

"Didn't you find that strange?"

"I find it strange even now."

"You're saying then that he had no particular look of animosity, hatred or acrimony on his face prior to pulling out the gun, after pulling out the gun, at the time of the shot, or after the shot?"

"That's correct."

"Judge Jackson said nothing prior to pulling the trigger?"

"Nothing that I heard."

"And he said nothing at the time he pulled the trigger, did he?"

"Not that I heard."

"And he said nothing after he was subdued by you and the other men, did he?"

"He said nothing."

"He did not attempt to run, did he?"

"No, he didn't."

"He did not struggle in any way, did he?"

"No."

"What were his eyes like before and after the shooting?"

"They were fixed, somewhat dazed, but I expect everyone there had dazed eyes, including me. We were all in shock."

"Would you say he was in a daze both before and after?"

"I would say he was in a daze after the shooting. I didn't have a clear view of him before he shot."

"Would it be safe to say, Judge, that everything Judge Jackson did was somewhat automatic?"

"I wouldn't go that far."

"It would be safe to say, would it not, Judge, that it was as if Judge Jackson were sleepwalking both before and after the shooting?"

"Certainly, it was as if he were sleepwalking afterward. I just couldn't tell exactly what he was like beforehand. It all happened so suddenly."

"What if anything did you see Sheriff Hardacre do and hear him say to Judge Jackson before he was shot?"

"I believe Sheriff Hardacre put his hand in front of his face for protection and he said something like 'Avery?'"

"Did Judge Jackson try to avert his aim in any way in response to Sheriff Hardacre addressing him by name or putting his hand up for protection?"

"No, it was as if Sheriff Hardacre was not even talking to Jackson. It was as if Jackson had a target, and nothing was going to interfere with that target."

"Were you aware, Judge Kessler, that Sheriff Hardacre was shot through the webbing of his hand before the bullet went through his skull?"

"No, I wasn't aware of that, but it wouldn't surprise me because Sheriff Hardacre put his hand up in front of his face for protection."

"No further questions."

Dorsey called three more witnesses. The first was the medical examiner, Dr. Sheila Katz. She testified that Sheriff Hardacre died from a gunshot wound to the head. She also mentioned that Sheriff Hardacre had a superficial bullet wound to the webbing of his right hand. She said his death was immediate because of massive trauma. The next witness was a ballistics' expert who testified that the bullet used to kill Sheriff Hardacre was a hollow-point and that it was so fragmented it could not be traced to the .38-caliber gun taken at the scene. He testified that the gun was registered to Avery Jackson. The next witness was a fingerprint expert who testified that the gun had recently been cleaned and showed no prints except those of Avery Jackson, the defendant, but there was an unidentified single print on the barrel. He identified numerous points of comparison between the defendant's prints after his arrest and the prints lifted from the gun.

When asked whether he had any questions of the experts, Jack simply said, "No questions."

With no surprises from the defense, or deals having been made, Bonin closed the hearing. "The defendant, Avery Jackson, will be bound over to district court for arraignment in two weeks," she ordered. "As you know, Mr. Jackson, your case will be assigned to a judge in the district court. You are to be remanded to the custody of the sheriff to be held without bond. Court is in recess."

"All rise."

Judge Bonin left the bench as quickly as she had taken it. The media dashed out of the room, some dialing their cell phones as they left. The videocams rolled. As the courtroom door opened they had an opportunity to get a shot of Avery as he stood up and was again being handcuffed by the deputies.

Avery turned to see Rebecca and Derrick. A railing separated them. Rebecca reached over the railing to hug her dad. As soon as she touched him, one of the three deputies intervened. "Excuse me, Miss, but there can be no contact with the inmates."

Rebecca withdrew. She had tears in her eyes. "I love you, Dad," she said.

"I love you, too, Becky," Avery said, forcing back the tears. She allowed no one except her father to call her Becky.

"We'll come to see you, Dad," Aaron promised him.

"I look forward to it."

The deputies led Avery to the holding cell and then back to the jail.

When Aaron and Rebecca went to the jail after the hearing to see their father, they were turned away because it was not time for visitation hours. They drove their father's car back to college. Any fantasy they had about their father's innocence, or possible acquittal at trial, had been destroyed.

CHAPTER 9

Tuesday, January 23—1:00 P.M.
Hilton Hotel, Room 911

There was just enough light so he could watch his body moving methodically between her legs in a full-length mirror on the closet door next to the bed. He liked to watch as they had sex. He liked the way he looked, still handsome and trim though well into his fifties.

The remainder of the room-service lunch sat on the table across the nicely decorated room. They had met like this for two years—same time, same hotel, same room. She had a standing reservation under the name of Dr. Claryce Fordyke. It was better that she made the reservation—he was much more of a public figure than she was. The desk clerk and other Daytonians who happened to be in the lobby would certainly recognize him, but probably not her. She went to the hotel desk every Tuesday and picked up the room key and paid cash; he'd reimburse her for it later. She would order room service. He would come to the room, knock on the door and she would let him in. Lunch would be served. They always talked first about the politics of the office, Ohio State football and basketball, sometimes about his marriage and occasionally, about her and her daughter. They always had sex in front of the mirror. The routine rarely varied.

For Alec Hunter, the sexual liaison with Stephanie Marshall was important. Intimacy between him and his wife, Alice, had ceased years ago. She was interested in her tea parties, drinks and bridge at the Oakwood Country Club.

Alec and Alice were the mirror image of one another. Each was primarily interested in how he or she was perceived in the community. Each needed to be adored and revered by the public. Each was socially ambitious. Her sexual interest in him had ceased soon after the birth of their second child many years ago. She had never really fully understood the need for orgasm, or the wetness and sloppiness that went along with it. Orgasm for her meant the loss of control. Their bed always needed to be changed after sex in order that a wet spot didn't become an embarrassing dry one. That being too onerous, she insisted upon his wearing a rubber despite the fact she could no longer become pregnant. For Alec, though, realness in Alice was not as important as her adoring him. When her adoration waned, so did his passion for their relationship.

Stephanie, on the other hand, felt she loved Alec. He was powerful and she needed the feeling of power and protection from a man. Her father was CEO of his own firm. Rarely home and preoccupied with building his empire, her father had not been there for her when she was young. She vowed as a child she would not be treated as she and her mother had been, though damned if, as an adult, she didn't fall into that same trap. She married a third-year law student who was handsome, ambitious and intelligent. She was so in love. When they graduated together, he went into a corporate firm, she became pregnant. His career was more important than her or the baby. Divorce came quickly and painfully and she raised her daughter alone. Stephanie rarely dated before going to work for Alec. An affair with him was ideal. He was powerful and unavailable. She wouldn't risk being hurt again the way she had been in her marriage.

Stephanie had been discreet about the relationship, as had Alec. She had told no one. She had one attorney friend in the office, Amy Casper, with whom she had coffee and lunch. Amy probably suspected the liaison, but it never came up in conversation. Amy was divorced and looking. She wondered why Stephanie wasn't interested in looking. Stephanie played the role of the woman who is never asked out, or when she was, the guy would be a dork, nerd, too narcissistic or have some other characteristic that made romance impossible. Stephanie spent her time working on her career, taking care of her daughter and having one tryst per week with Alec. Occasionally, she and Alec would be able to get away together. Alec would tell Alice he was going to a DA's conference only to go to a rendezvous where they could spend time together.

On this day, their lovemaking continued rhythmically, sometimes slowly, sometimes rapidly. He came. As they lay in each other's arms after he finished, Alec started talking with her about the Jackson case. She had an extraordinary ability to listen dutifully.

"Hank and Jim came back this morning after Jackson's preliminary hearing and told me that it was very clear where Maine was going with his cross," Alec said.

"Where?"

"Almost all of Maine's questions went to Jackson's demeanor at the time of the shooting. We're going to get a defense based on lack of intent or knowledge by Jackson that he was about to kill Hardacre. Probably an insanity defense. No surprise. We expected that."

"There's no other place they can go. What's going on with the investigation of Jackson as to whether he took money from DiSalvo?"

"We got nothing. We got a warrant and went through all his bank and retirement accounts. There were no large deposits, just the steady sort of stuff from each paycheck."

"How do you want me to handle that with the media?"

"Just tell them the investigation is 'ongoing.' We don't want to say anything that would cast Jackson in a favorable light. Let's let him twist in the wind."

"How long do we wait until we inform the media there's nothing there?" Stephanie asked as she stroked Alec's chest, resting her head on his shoulder.

"Long enough that we can make it look like we're investigating competently and thoroughly. When three or four weeks have passed, we can inform them that there isn't enough evidence to allow us to prove the case beyond a reasonable doubt. That'll leave the impression that there *might* be something there."

"Sounds a bit Machiavellian to me—somewhat on the edge of unethical. I guess, though, we don't owe him anything," Stephanie said.

"Are you kidding me, Stephanie? You're starting to sound like a defense attorney," Alec said playfully as he stroked the side of her right breast.

"My job is to keep you out of trouble, dear, and I must say that I believe I've done a great job."

"You really have, and I love you for it." Alec was using that loaded word in its most generic sense—like he loved chocolate—not necessarily that he loved Stephanie.

"Speaking of love, Alec, my dear, at some point we're going to have to do something about us. I'm not getting any younger. Neither are you. You keep saying your marriage is dead. I think we need to be together," Stephanie suggested coyly, as she continued to stroke the hair on Alec's chest.

"Let's play it by ear to see where Jackson takes us. If it takes us to Washington D.C. and the Senate, then I'll ask my wife for a divorce after I win the election. If that doesn't happen, then we'll be together sooner. I'm in a place financially where I don't really have to work. We can just live our lives and enjoy them."

Stephanie felt the slightest twinge of exuberance—he'd never mentioned his money to her before. "If we're to be together, though," she said tentatively, knowing that she might be taking a big chance on his becoming angry, "it'll be expensive for you to leave Alice. Is that the reason you haven't already left her?"

She could be dominating in the courtroom, but with Alec, it was another matter. "I'm sorry, Alec, I didn't mean to be so forward, but there are times I wonder if we're going to be together, and I worry that we won't be because you'd lose so much in a divorce."

"Money's not a factor in my leaving my wife. The only reason I haven't already left is because of my political career. I have plenty of money that Alice isn't privy to."

Stephanie just looked at him, the wheels in her mind spinning rapidly. "How did you manage to do that without her knowing about it?" she asked, trying to temper her intrusiveness with strokes down his chest to his stomach.

"I've been consulting with a number of corporations now for years and they've paid me a hell of a lot for it. Ooooh . . . that feels good."

"What kind of consulting are you doing? It's nothing that would create a conflict of interest for you in your position as district attorney, is it?"

"Not in the least. Everything is completely legitimate and aboveboard. I'm providing security information to some foreign and domestic corporations that export and import goods and advising them on how they should be handling their money."

"I didn't know you knew anything about business law. I'm impressed. How did you handle the tax problem? Alice would certainly see that money on the income tax return, wouldn't she?"

"It's never been a problem. The accountant prepares the tax form and Alice has just signed it for years without looking at the bottom line. I need to get back to the office. The autopsy report on Burt Porter and all the forensics are done. We need to have a meeting on Chris Conley's case later on this afternoon. Could you get Hank, Jim and yourself together?"

"Sure, dear," Stephanie said as she moved her hand down to Alec's pubic hair.

As she stroked it, he could feel the blood rush into his penis. "This is one reason you are irresistible. You make me feel like a man when you touch me."

"You don't have to go just yet, do you?"

"Soon. What did you have in mind?"

Monday—3:00 P.M.
District Attorney's Office

Alec Hunter had gotten back to the office nearly a half hour before Stephanie, perfectly attired and coiffed. The receptionist had a stack of messages for him, most from reporters and other media outlets. In his in-basket was the Burt Porter autopsy report from the medical examiner, as well as the forensic reports and the drug screen on Chris Conley.

When Stephanie walked into the office, she was also perfectly put together. She had numerous calls from the media on the status of the "suspected DiSalvo bribe" of Judge Jackson. She returned the calls immediately, spinning the matter in the way that Alec had told her to do when he was in bed with her only an hour or so earlier. She called Jim Brodan and Hank Dorsey. Each agreed to meet on the Chris Conley case in thirty minutes. For Stephanie, the biggest challenge in these meetings was to be efficient and intelligent without addressing Alec as "dear" or "honey."

Monday—4:00 P.M.
Conference Room, DA's Office

Coffee and soft drinks were on the table to provide late afternoon caffeine for the elite four of the office. Alec was seated at the head of the conference table when the other three filed in. Detective Guteman was also there as the arresting detective on the Conley case. Hunter distributed photocopies of the relevant documents and began.

"We have a very interesting situation here. We have Judge Jeffers' court reporter involved in a very ugly scene with our departed colleague and adversary, Burt Porter. It's also an important case in terms of image for the office. I'm getting calls from media and citizens both, wanting to know if there's a connection between the Conley and Jackson cases. As far as I can tell, there isn't. It only appears there is because Porter was Jackson's attorney, and each homicide occurred within the same week. The conspiracy nuts are having a field day with this, of course. It's important we handle this thing carefully, not only legally, but from a political perspective. It could turn into a real can of worms for the office. Okay, now I'm going to turn the meeting over to Detective Guteman. Tell us what went down in Porter's house."

All eyes shifted to Guteman. "On the night of January eighteenth, I took the dispatch to Porter's condo because Detective Solano was handling an unrelated drive-by, gang shooting not far from where Porter lived. Porter's girlfriend, Chris Conley, had phoned 911 to report that he was seriously ill and needed an ambulance. When I arrived, the paramedics were already there. Porter was dead on the floor. He had foam coming from his mouth. He had also urinated all over himself. I questioned Conley about what had happened. She claimed she had just arrived and she'd found him sick on the floor. I asked her if they had a date. She said they had. I asked her if they did a lot of drugs together, and she started getting skittish. I could smell she was lying. I asked her if she minded if I looked in her purse that was right next to her for my own safety. She said that she had nothing to hide. She'd obviously forgotten about the dope. I found a vial of what I thought was cocaine and a straw for snorting it in her purse.

"It looks like she went there that night with the dope to party with Burt. They bit off a little more than they could chew. He died. She freaked out and called the police. My theory is that she at least acted recklessly, criminally and negligently when she put out the dope that caused Porter's death. If you really want to try to hit the long ball in this case, you could attempt to make it first-degree murder after you hear a few more details."

"What did the toxicology report show was the cause of death?" Brodan asked.

"Drug overdose. Cocaine and heroin, called a 'speedball' on the streets. He had a high level of it in his blood."

Hank Dorsey intervened. "I know Chris Conley just from hanging around Jeffers' court. It's hard for me to believe that she could do something like this to Burt. What you've told us so far won't get us a showing of probable cause at a preliminary hearing, let alone a conviction before a jury."

"I know her, too," Stephanie said. "She seems like a decent person. So far, you've given us very little."

"Here's the kicker," Guteman said, leaning forward conspiratorially, "the dope in Chris Conley's purse was exactly the same as the dope on Porter's coffee table. It was pure, uncut heroine and cocaine. It would have killed a horse according to our toxicologist, Dr. Bixby. It was exactly the same purity and consistency, and in the same proportion as that found on the coffee table and in Burt's blood."

"Tell us more," Alec said.

"The vial had two sets of fingerprints on it," Guteman said.

"Let me guess," Brodan said, "Porter and Conley's."

"You got it. And speaking of fingerprints, we found Conley and Porter's prints all over the coffee table; it looks as though they used the table to party on. We also found evidence of Porter's semen and Conley's vaginal fluid on the floor and on the couch next to the coffee table. It looks like the two of them were a couple of party animals."

"There is a real problem with your theory of the case, Detective," Stephanie said.

"What?" Guteman asked.

"Here's Bixby's tox screen on Chris. It shows her blood was completely clear. If that speedball was strong enough to kill an elephant, and the two of them were partying, she should be dead along with Porter, or at least have a significant level in her blood." She had never liked Guteman. She thought he was an arrogant, little-guy bully.

"I thought of that, Counselor," he replied. "My theory is that she brought the dope in, handed it to him, and he tried it before she could. Maybe she went to the can or something, or was putting on her makeup when he snorted the stuff. When she got back, he'd already gone into convulsions. It scared the hell out of her and she called 911. By the time anyone got there, Porter was dead."

"You said a cocktail straw was taken from her purse?" Dorsey asked.

"That's right."

"Were there any prints or dope residue on it?"

"No. Just hers."

"That makes no sense at all," Dorsey replied. "Porter should have handled it. We know he snorted it, don't we?"

"Yeah, the autopsy showed it in his nasal passage," Guteman said.

"Well then, he should have handled the cocktail straw," Hank said.

"Could be that Conley threw away the one Porter used and the one in her purse was one she used some other time," Guteman said.

"Did you find any others in Conley's purse or in Porter's pockets?"

"No, but you can't tell what might have happened to it. I think we need to proceed regardless of the straw confusion. There's too much other evidence. She admitted to me they were going to party that night. The substance that killed Porter is the same as that in her purse, and the same that's under his nose. Besides, I have a feeling about this case. When I talked to her, I could just tell she was dirty."

"Hunches don't stand up in court, Detective, and that cocktail straw could be enough for reasonable doubt," Hank said.

"I agree," Stephanie said.

"I agree with Detective Guteman," Brodan said. "What he's shown us here will amount to probable cause and we can get this matter to a jury. If they find reasonable doubt, then she walks, but we've done our job. There's too much of this sort of crap going on in Dayton, and we need to put our foot down."

Stephanie didn't like Brodan either, but she could tolerate him. She felt like he lacked something personally, like essential humanness or a conscience. "I agree with you, Jim, there's too much dangerous drug activity going on in Dayton, but it just seems to me that we could deal with it just by convicting Chris of the possession of a dangerous drug charge. As I see it, there's no need to try to hang a homicide on her. She may lose her job, and it will ruin her life. She's too good a person."

"Jackson was a good person, too," Brodan retorted. "Look what he did. You're letting your feelings and friendship interfere with the intelligent prosecution of this case. Maybe we should be investigating her for first-degree murder. No one gives pure cocaine and heroin to another person unless she wants to kill him. It could be that she wanted him dead to collect an insurance policy, or because he was screwing some other woman."

"Why would she call 911?" Stephanie asked.

"To cover her ass, just like so many criminals do," Guteman said.

Hunter could feel the heat going up quickly in the room despite the freezing temperature outside. "All right, let's all settle down. The charges should be possession and criminally negligent homicide. If we find she was the beneficiary of his life insurance policy or that she was angry with him for some reason, we can change the charge to first-degree murder. Obviously, there are some proof problems on the homicide charge. I assume there are none on the possession charge, Detective?" Alec asked.

"None whatsoever."

"If she can beat the homicide at the preliminary hearing, or bring us other exculpatory evidence that clears her, more power to her. But I think we need to start with the criminally negligent homicide and use that hammer as a bargaining tool," Alec said.

"Are you sure you have a good search of her purse?" Stephanie asked.

"I can promise you there's nothing wrong with the search. Strictly kosher, and I'm Jewish," Guteman said. Guteman had always passed himself off as a Jew. An orphan adopted by barren Jewish parents, little David had been indulged. They had covered for him when he got in trouble for several petty thefts and putting cats in burlap sacks and setting them on fire.

There is something repulsive about a humorless man making a feeble attempt at humor, Stephanie thought.

"Has anyone entered an appearance on the Conley's case yet?" Hunter asked.

"Maine's doing it," Brodan said. "He said so at the preliminary hearing."

"How can he do that?" Alec asked. "She's not indigent, and neither is Jackson."

"Apparently you haven't heard. Maine went into private practice yesterday after the Jackson preliminary hearing. He's opening up an office down in that new building by the river," Stephanie said.

"Where have I been?" Alec asked.

"Who's handling the Conley case on behalf of our office?" Hank Dorsey asked.

"Good question," Alec said. "I want Jim here to handle it. He's the best search and seizure guy in the office. The press, and maybe Maine, will try to connect Porter's death to the Jackson case. I don't want Hardacre's life to be tarnished by such nonsense. I think it's important we keep Conley as a homicide defendant as long as possible. It will keep the public, and the conspiracy theorists, from drawing a bunch of false inferences. Jackson needs to pay the full price for killing the sheriff. It's that simple."

CHAPTER 10

Wednesday, January 24—12 noon
Jack Maine and Associates

The Great Miami River rippled below with its brown, muddy water gliding beneath frozen sheets of ice. The heavy snow from last night had left the naked branches of winter clothed in white. The view from the office would be beautiful in the summer when the trees were full. Marci had picked a good location. For a starter office, it was ideal—brand new, nice carpeting, and clean walls. It didn't have the amenities that large, well-established law firms have like rich-cherry wood, marble floors, fireplaces, law library and a bar. She had bought used, oak, office furniture from a law firm that was closing. The desks, filing cabinets, couches, conference tables and chairs were purchased at a good price. The only new items in the office were the computers. The phones were being hooked up today. Marci and Jack could be sure they would not be bugged, at least for one day. Outside the door was a burgundy sign JACK MAINE AND ASSOCIATES neatly displayed in an oak frame. Jack and Marci were in business.

Jack had ordered out for pizza and drinks. Joe and Yolanda were coming over for lunch and a conference on the Jackson case. It would be their first time together in the new office.

"When's the food coming?" Marci asked. "I'm starved, Counselor."

Jack was sitting for the first time at his own desk in his own law firm. His feet were up on the desktop as he reclined in his high-backed, black judge's chair, admiring what Marci had put together. "It'll be here any moment," he replied.

"I'm famished. I figure it's about time you took care of me. You're using me, but if I get tired of it, I'll let you know, Counselor," Marci said as she moved over to sit on his lap. She kissed him firmly.

The door to the waiting room opened and in came the deliveryman with two large pizzas. Immediately behind him were Joe and Yolanda. "I'm always right behind the food," Joe said.

Jack paid for the two pizzas and gave the deliveryman a tip. "So, what do you think of the place? I think Marci did a great job of putting it together."

"This looks like it will work fine for us," Yolanda said, as she looked around at the office with her name already on the door. "I love the view. I'll have an office with an actual window."

They all sat together at the conference table for the first time, sharing the exuberance that goes with new digs.

"We've got a lot to talk about," Jack said. "I hope the place isn't bugged yet. We'll risk it today since we just got the key for the place this morning. Joe, what did you find out about the bugs at the public defender's office?"

"My man traced them to two places. One set is transmitting to the Federal Center government offices in town here. The other is transmitting to a—are you ready for this?—to a group home for adolescent boys in North Dayton called Experiences in Growth."

"Not your usual growth experiences," Marci quipped.

"Which agencies have offices at the Federal Center?" Jack asked him.

"I went out there to check. The Air Force has space, along with the Bureau of Land Management, the Department of Agriculture, Housing and Urban Development, the Drug Enforcement Administration, the FBI and the CI-goddamn-A."

"*Whoa,*" Jack exclaimed. "Did you find out if any judges signed warrants for electronic surveillance?"

"As far as I can tell, none were signed. I went to each clerk and asked if there'd been any requests in the last couple of weeks for wiretaps. Each said there hadn't been, even at federal court. They could be bullshitting me, but I don't think so."

"You don't suppose the DEA or FBI was tapping Burt for drugs or anything, do you?" Jack asked.

"Could be," Joe said, "but I don't think so. He was strictly a recreational user, but you never know. You know how those DEA dudes think. If they can bust him, a prominent attorney and all, it could lead to higher-ups."

"Whoever broke into Burt's house and stole the tape away from you and Chris had to be listening to my phone calls that morning. Those calls made someone very uptight, that's for sure. Drug enforcement guys would have likely had a warrant and yellow DEA letters on the back of their windbreakers. They would have identified themselves before they cold-cocked you, and wouldn't have run out of the place like a bunch of guilty spooks. But they're probably not from the CIA either. The CIA is not allowed to do domestic incursions—just foreign stuff."

"That never bothered Richard Nixon. Something made someone so uptight that people had to die for it. We have three dead bodies in the last week," Marci said.

Jack, Joe and Yolanda just looked at her. It was the first time anyone had mentioned the possibility that all of these deaths could somehow be connected.

"Joe, I want you to go out to the Federal Center and park your car close to the CIA parking area; hang around, see who's coming and going; you might recognize one of the guys who pistol-whipped you. If you don't recognize anyone there, you might try the FBI or DEA."

"Yup. And I'm going to have my gun with me just in case."

Jack looked to the ceiling, rolled his eyes and shook his head. "I don't want you going back to the joint. We need you. I have this vision of you getting into some sort of shootout. No, I have a better idea," he said as he stared off into space, the wheels turning.

"What?" Joe asked.

"Are the bugs in my office—the ones that send information to the government offices—still in place?" "Yeah, they're still there, except for the one behind your diploma. The phone transmitters, though, are still there."

"Let's get these bastards to come to us. Be in my office at two today and I'll call you. Just play along with me. What do you know about the Experiences in Growth home, Joe?"

"It's a non-profit corporation owned by a for-profit organization called Recovery Corporation. You may have heard of Recovery Corporation. It's based out of Chicago and owns a number of boot camps around the country for kids who're tryin' to dodge hard time. It also owns a number of kiddie prisons around the country. Its biggest cash cows are kids' prisons in Lima, Ohio, and Brush, Colorado. The one in Colorado was just shut down because smaller kids were getting corn-holed by the bigger kids. There were a bunch of suicides. When the smaller kids got tired of sucking the bigger kids' dicks, they hung themselves. Just like that. They have a bunch of dead-brains with GEDs working as counselors in these places—pay them peanuts and bill their time at a hundred fifty an hour. States all over the country were sending their scumbag kids to these places to get them out of their hair—couldn't get rid of them soon enough. Put them in Podunk towns—pay any goddamn amount to get rid of them. Recovery is charging two hundred dollars a day for each child. Each of its facilities in Ohio and Colorado had around one hundred eight beds. That's thirty-six thousand dollars a *day, per* facility! All the money they get comes from state treasuries either through youth correction departments or social services. States need these blood-sucking operations like Recovery to get rid of their toxic waste."

"Why are we opening a law business?" Marci asked. "We need to get into the kids' treatment business. I could live on thirty-six grand a day."

"Who's on the board of this place?"

"You need to know this first. Recovery Corporation is owned by Frontline Enterprises. Frontline owns the Starburst and Big Money Down, two casinos in Vegas, as well as movie studios in LA. My sources tell me that Frontline also owns an import business in Miami and Arizona, as well as Hiawatha Enterprises, which owns strip clubs and porn shops."

"Mob," Jack said.

"Definitely," Joe said.

"Tell me about the Board of Frontline and Experiences in Growth."

"There are two names common to the boards. One is a dude from Chicago by the name of Marshall Conn. He looks like the force. I don't know much about this dude, but he's a big money guy. He's got a mansion on the North Shore of Lake Michigan. Then there's Frank Newton, an ex-vice cop from Maryland. He helped Recovery take over a large treatment center in Baltimore. A bunch of problems came up there and the place was finally closed by the state. He also got Recovery a state contract down in Florida to run a kids' jail, housing Florida's worst. That also closed because the kids were corn-holin' and killin' each other. Newton is Recovery's Head of Operations."

"Interesting," Jack said, "this organization appears to be failing everywhere it goes, yet it keeps getting big money contracts from various state governments. There must be a lot of government people on the take."

"And I saved the best for last. There are two other members of the Board of Experiences in Growth and it's like a goddamn list of Who's Who in Dayton law enforcement."

"I can't wait. Tell me," Jack said.

"Let's see," Joe said, looking at his computer printout like a poker player looking at his cards waiting for the right time to unload a royal flush, "there's our favorite hard-ass Detective Guteman, *and* our former Sheriff Hugh Lane."

"*Now* I remember this place," Marci said. "There was a big article in the paper about it soon after it was opened a few years ago. Social workers and the juvenile justice system were so happy to have it as a resource where they could place their kids. The article talked about how skilled the treatment staff would be. Come to think of it, Hugh Lane used his involvement with Experiences in Growth as a campaign tool. He went around to the Optimist and Rotary Club meetings talking about how tough he was on crime and how invested he was in the youth of the community and all that. What would a big money corporation like Recovery want with a small non-profit like Experiences in Growth in a city like Dayton, Ohio? Doesn't make sense."

"Oh, it makes sense," Jack said. "Big money mobsters don't open a group home for philanthropic purposes. They use places like that for money laundering and as public relations gestures to make them and their organization look legit. They run dirty money through two, three or four corporations and a non-profit or two and make it come out clean. I'll bet you Recovery writes off a fortune in bogus treatments for kids, training tapes and whatever. They're probably running so much drug and prostitution money through a place like that, it'd make your head spin."

"Definitely smells like organized crime shit to me," Joe said. "I'll promise you this, there'll be others that'll turn up dead."

"That's reassuring," Marci said.

"What did you find out about Avery's car and gun, Joe?" Jack asked.

"Avery's car was parked in the Sinclair University lot outside the Criminal Justice Department. At this point, no one knows how the dude got from the college to the hotel. He could have walked the four blocks, taken a bus or been dropped off. It looks like he didn't take his own car, though. The cops towed his car, took it completely apart and found nothing. As for the gun, that's bad news. I talked to Jackson's wife. She says they have had the gun in their nightstand for a while. She hasn't seen it. She thought Avery might have loaned it to someone, but she isn't sure. I went over and talked to Avery about it and he says that he had the gun for years. The dude, though, is just plain seriously weird," Joe said.

"Of course, he's weird," Jack said, "he blew away the sheriff in front of a hundred and fifty people. How weird is that? Why else do you think he's weird?"

"Because when I asked him when the last time was he saw the gun, he couldn't remember a damn thing. He said there was just a blank. Now, that's weird. I loan my gun to anybody and I'm gonna remember it."

"That's just another on a laundry list of things that Avery can't remember. Maybe we can get some answers from the psychologist we're hiring. One more thing, Joe, did you find the discovery on all of those cases involving Van Hazeltree?"

"Yeah, I got it."

Wednesday—2:00 P.M.
Public Defender's Office

Joe sat quietly in Jack Maine's old office. Jack's personal effects had been gone for two days. A new attorney had not yet moved in. No one had removed the transmitters from the phone. He had known since he had been hammered at Burt's condo a few days ago that this case was dangerous. Now, the mob. "There is just too much weird shit happening here," he muttered to himself as he waited for Jack to call. He felt for the gun in his shoulder holster to make sure it was firmly within the leather.

But the tape, I've got to get the tape. The thought of the tape had grown into an obsession. His head still throbbed from the pistol-whipping; and the notion, or perhaps the delusion, that the tape could save Avery Jackson's, and now Chris Conley's life, had become so big that it had taken on a life of its own.

He didn't wait long for the call. Paulette buzzed and Joe picked it up. "That you, Mr. Maine?"

"Yeah, Joe, it's me. Did you find the other tape from Burt's condo in the bottom drawer of my desk? Chris Conley was supposed to drop it off there this morning."

"Yeah, I found it and listened to it. The shit's dynamite. Just like Chris said it would be. At least now, we have an idea who set Avery up."

"Shocking, isn't it, Joe? I heard about it from Chris, but I haven't listened to the tape myself," Jack said.

"The stupid shits who hit me in the head missed it. They didn't see it on the floor next to Burt's bed. Chris said she found it right there."

"Can you get it over to my new office after work?"

"Yeah, but I can't stay. I gotta get home to look after the old lady tonight. Where you at?"

"Fifty Osceola, number two hundred. There won't be anyone here tonight between five and seven 'cause Marci and I are going out to eat. Why don't you drop if off at five, and I'll come back to get it after dinner?"

"I can do that. I don't have a key to the office, though."

"I'll leave one on the top of the molding around the door. Just open it up, put the tape on my desk and I'll come get it after seven. Just make sure you lock the door after you leave. We need to guard this tape with our lives. Oh, and keep the key for your own."

"Will do. Is there anything else?"

"No, Joe, I'll watch the tape tonight and let you reproduce it tomorrow. This is the sort of thing we may want to leak to the press tomorrow."

"Gotcha. Talk to you tomorrow." Joe smiled as he hung up the phone.

Wednesday—4:45 P.M.
The King's Table Restaurant

Myron's Catering and Deli van was traveling on Interstate 75 from the Federal Center north toward the downtown area. It was cold and almost dark. The snow had stopped, but traffic was still moving slowly. Lock and bug expert Tony Losavio was driving. Mike Swenson was riding shotgun. Harry Bova was in the backseat on the cell phone with Langley, Virginia.

"Dr. McGinty," Bova said, "we're on the way to the office of the asset's attorney. We've picked up a communication indicating there is another tape from Porter's condo that we missed."

"Who's the new attorney?"

"A guy by the name of Jack Maine. He was Porter's junior attorney on the case and now he's taken over."

"Could be a set up," McGinty said. "It doesn't seem likely that Porter would have made another tape. He was too busy dying."

"We've had the same thought. The problem is that Maine is so interested in the contents of the tape that he is talking about going to the press tomorrow. If that happens, our asset's Company operations could be exposed. I think we have to take the chance. This has to be a greenhorn lawyer; it sounds like he's opened a mom-and-pop practice with his wife."

"Sounds like our asset is in good hands." McGinty laughed sarcastically. He derived a strange sense of power using the word *asset* to describe a human being. "Maine should be able to be bought. He's vulnerable—just a neophyte lawyer from a flyover state who wants to be a big-time criminal defense lawyer. Probably seen too many Perry Mason's. Those kinds of lawyers are a dime a dozen. But let's not underestimate him—not yet anyway. Have you made any progress in figuring out who penetrated our Jackson?"

"We got our noses to the ground and are sniffling around. We have nothing concrete," Bova replied.

"Bova, we need that information. Do I make myself clear?"

"Crystal," Bova said while flashing his middle finger to Swenson and Losavio. McGinty had always been long on orders and short with Bova. Bova had resented it for years and had grown to hate McGinty about half the time. Apparently, because McGinty had a Ph.D., it meant he could treat Harry Bova like a peon.

"Did you get any information on the guys who had the other bugs in Porter's phone?" Dr. McGinty asked.

"Yeah, the bugs are in a place called—are you ready for this—Experiences in Growth. It's a kids' home. It's owned and run by Recovery Corporation, a company specializing in privatized prisons for kids, and correctional boot camps around the country. Recovery is owned by Frontline Enterprises. The main stockholder and CEO of Frontline is a connected guy out of Chicago. He was once indicted for tricking Elvis Presley into a shady land deal in Wyoming. He was charged with fraud. He beat the rap but has operated on the edge ever since. He owns stock in dozens of companies that are into everything from real estate to B movies, porno, to making instructional videos on treating screwed-up kids. He's hired people to grease a lot of state legislators to get his kids' prisons opened in their states. He pays them off with favors and large sums of cash under the table. The FBI has done very little with him because he makes it look like he's paying his income tax and because we've told the Bureau to stay away from him because he's ours."

"What's his name?" McGinty asked.

"Marshall Conn," Bova answered.

"*Whoa.* We've done some business with Conn before, and are still doing it. He's funded a number of our top secret, out-of-budget and off-the-record operations with drug money, arms money, etcetera, laundered through the Company. Don't go into that attorney's office tonight! It's too pat. It's gotta be a set up. Besides, if there is any possibility Conn is involved in this, I don't want to step on his toes. I don't want us in any way interfering with Conn's business affairs."

"Are you sure, Doctor?" Bova asked, showing the mandatory deference to the Ph.D. "We may be passing up on the answer as to who got to Jackson."

"Absolutely. Not tonight. I'll let you know if and when I want you to go back in with the surveillance. But I need you to figure out how our asset was subverted and whether the Company is protected. If the Company isn't safe, then we need to discuss alternatives—all of them."

"Understood. We'll call you tomorrow."

"I'm relying on you, Bova."

Bova rolled his eyes and hung up. They were already outside Maine's office on Osceola. It was five-fifteen. As they were pulling into the parking lot, they could see Joe Betts walking from the back door of the office complex to his car, his size and gait making him easily identifiable.

"Look, there's the black guy," Swenson said. "It looks like the coast is clear."

"Operation's off. McGinty's call."

"Fine by me," Swenson said, touching the knot on his head. "I want nothin' to do with that gorilla anyway."

"McGinty thinks it's a set up. Losavio might go in again later."

"I hope you guys don't have the same sort of racial prejudice toward Italians," Losavio said.

"Don't worry about it, we hate wops, too," Swenson assured him.

All three men cracked up.

"Now, let's get some steaks," Bova said. "They just don't have meat like this in D.C., but that's the only good thing I can say about this god-forsaken place."

CHAPTER 11

Each member of the team held a Starbucks' cup in their hand. Its warmth was soothing, which was good, considering the rawness and despondency that permeated the room.

"You know," Jack said, "no one died last night, for a change. We didn't get what we hoped for. We didn't catch a mobster, or a crook, or a spook from the FBI or CIA. But let's look at it this way—if we had, we could be dead right now. Let's face it. We aren't equipped to deal with that kind of situation. We just need to redouble our efforts to find the people who have the tape."

"Really, Counselor? What have you in mind?" Marci asked as she sipped her latte.

"Mothafuckas should have been here," Joe said. "Maybe we should have waited around a few more hours. For all we know, they just got here late. They were probably pissed off the tape wasn't here when they arrived."

"Forget it, Joe," Jack said. "Our friends are at one of three places: the CIA, the FBI, or the boy's home. And, I can promise you none of these people is stupid. They wouldn't go walking into such an obvious trap. But we need that tape back, and we gotta figure out how to get it."

"I know the routine," Joe answered, "and it is a pain in the ass. I'll check all the Bovas in Ohio through Motor Vehicle and see if I can get my friends over at Social Security to step up. I'd hang out at the Federal Center, but you can't get close to the FBI or CIA offices since 9/11. For all we know, boss, Bova wasn't even the dude's name. Hell, that could have been his nickname or something."

"I'm counting on you, Joe. I know you'll find a way."

"Done deal, boss," Joe said, knowing there must be dozens of Bovas in Ohio and hundreds throughout the United States, and that the deal was anything but done.

"What have we found on Guteman?" Jack asked.

"Detective Dave Guteman is a piece of work," Yolanda said. "Marci and I have gone through all the cases that involved Ovanul Hazeltree over the years. Guteman was involved in every one of them. If there was another detective on the case at its inception, he always got replaced, and Guteman finished it off. Always some glitch—lost evidence, bad chain of custody. Two first-degree murder cases were dismissed because a witness came up missing or developed amnesia."

"Son-of-a-bitch is dirty," Joe said. "He's a killer. Gotta be. I can feel it. Who was the DA on all of Van's cases?"

"That's an interesting thing, too," Marci said. "Jim Brodan was the DA on three of the seven."

"Gotta be dirty along with the Rosatos," Joe said.

"Wouldn't that be something?" Jack mused. "Jim Brodan. The problem we have here is this is all conjecture. We don't know how this all fits in with Avery or Chris' case. We have nothing going for us on either case. Joe, what have you found out about Jackson's connection with Lane?"

"Their only connection is that they fought together in 1970 and '71 in Vietnam and did basic training together. They were both in Special Forces—tough guys, Rangers. They're still friends—helped each other get elected. Lane was a womanizer, drank a lot of hard liquor and was wheelin' and dealin' while Avery was quiet. Not a lot in common."

"Somehow, we have got to start getting some hard evidence on the Jackson case," Jack said. "The psychologist from Denver is flying here in two weeks to start working with Avery, but I just don't like insanity defenses; juries don't buy them. What have you found out about their viability, Yolanda?"

"The facts are grim. Since the Hinckley case, the insanity defense has been raised .09 percent of the time. That's nine defendants out of a thousand. It's only successful in 20 percent of the cases in which it is raised. So, the bottom line is that out of a thousand defendants, only about two of them are found Not Guilty by Reason of Insanity. The even more sobering fact is that most of them are found to be insane by stipulation between the DA and the defense because the guy is so crazy no one could disagree. That means that juries never find anyone Not Guilty by Reason of Insanity. Less than one out of a thousand are found not guilty by a jury. The problem is the public's perception of the insanity defense. The public believes it's raised 37 percent of the time as opposed to less than 1 percent, the real number. They overestimate by forty-one times how much it is raised. The really staggering statistic is that they believe it is successful eighty-one times more often than it is. The media is probably largely responsible for this misperception because of one particularly salient case—Hinckley. That's about the size of it," Yolanda finished.

"Not good," Jack said. "It will be impossible to get a receptive jury." He reached into his briefcase and brought out a box of embossed business cards. He opened it and pulled out a card. "So, it's up to us to change those stats. Ladies and gentlemen, I'd like you to meet Nancy Havekost, our new social worker. She's about to make a home visit." He handed a card to Marci.

"Good, I'm ready to get out of this office and get out there and do something."

"Joe and I believe you'll like this assignment. It's safe and you're the perfect person to pull it off."

"I'm not sure anything about this case is safe."

"I wouldn't let you go if I thought you were in danger," Jack reassured her.

"One last thing, Joe. Get your wiretap guy over here today to see if they got to us last night."

"Done deal, boss."

CHAPTER 12

I think we should up the ante on the Conley case," Jim Brodan announced. "We need to indict her for first-degree murder and let the chips fall where they may." He had assembled the senior staff of lawyers—Alec Hunter, Stephanie Marshall and Hank Dorsey. Conley was now his responsibility. It, too, was a career-maker. Brodan had invited Detective Dave Guteman to the meeting. Each had a coffee mug in hand.

"Why would we do that?" Stephanie asked. "We staffed it a couple of days ago and decided criminally negligent homicide was a stretch."

"We have a vial of pure heroin and cocaine—strong enough to bring down a horse—found in Conley's purse. The same substance that killed Porter. Both of their prints are all over the vial. And now we have a motive for first-degree murder. I'll turn the meeting over to Detective Guteman. Detective."

Guteman took a sip of coffee. He began slowly and without emotion. "Both of Porter's parents are dead. Porter died without a will. Great lawyer, huh?" Guteman said. "Anyway, he had a brother who's a lobbyist in Washington, D.C. He stands to inherit everything of Porter's, which is apparently not much. Porter lived big and wild. He spent a lot on trips, golf, eating out and drugs. He had a condo with a little equity. His only real asset is a life insurance policy through the public defender's office. He had recently increased the payoff amount to two hundred grand and had changed the beneficiary from his brother to none other than our Ms. Chris Conley."

"Do you have any evidence that she knew she was the beneficiary of the policy?" Stephanie asked.

"Yes, apparently the company, Ohio Equity, sends out a letter to beneficiaries when there's a change made by the policyholder. Ohio Equity sent Conley a notice a few months ago," Guteman said as he reached into his briefcase. He pulled out a photocopy of a letter. "They've sent me this Notice of Beneficiary addressed to Chris Conley at her present address, registered, return receipt signed by Conley."

The room was quiet. Brodan took over. "Now, we have motive, premeditation, opportunity, and we have the weapon—pure, uncut drugs."

"And, we have malice," Guteman added. "I've talked to another court reporter friend of Conley's, Patty d'Angelo, from Judge Bonin's division, who hung out with Conley a lot. She was reluctant to discuss their friendship and conversations. She did tell me, though, that Porter recently told Conley he never wanted to get married. He wasn't the marrying type. She apparently went nuts and threatened to leave him. I guess they had quite a fight over it. Porter told her that even though he didn't want to get married, he wanted to be with her and that he was going to put his life insurance in her name. It looks to me like it was sort of a peace-offering thing. According to d'Angelo, Conley was still very upset and wanted more. Conley told d'Angelo she'd had it with men who used her and dumped her, and swore she would not let that happen to her with Porter."

"I think she got tired of waiting," Brodan said. "She took the bull by the horns and decided to cash in while she had the chance."

"This is very interesting," Alec analyzed. "It seems to me we can get this case to a jury on murder one. I know Stephanie had some misgivings about going ahead against Conley with a negligent homicide, not to mention a first-degree murder charge. What do you think now, Stephanie?"

"I don't think Conley's a murderer. Just because she and Burt Porter dabbled in drugs doesn't make her a murderer, but this makes me a little more suspicious of her. It's thin, but probably enough to get to a jury though," Stephanie said, hating the notion that she could give any validity to Guteman's work. "If we charge her with first-degree murder," she said, "there will be people in the courthouse who will be upset with us. She's quite popular."

"Good point," Alec said as he sat stroking his chin and thinking. "I think that to cover ourselves and make it look like it's not our decision, we should take her case to the grand jury and see if it wants to indict her on either first-degree murder or negligent homicide. If they come back with first-degree murder, we'll go with it and let the chips fall where they may, as Jim said."

"Yeah, I think that's the thing to do," Hank Dorsey said. "I'd feel much better about it. I agree with Stephanie that it's a weak case. What worries me is the search of her purse. If there was a violation of her rights, and the dope is suppressed, we have no case against her and potential liability. What about it, Detective?"

"We've been through this before. The search of her purse was legit. She consented to it, and I had to do it for my own protection, and so that she didn't destroy the dope before I could get a warrant," Guteman said.

"That brings me to another point, Detective," Hank said. "I watched the video of your interrogation of Avery Jackson. The guy asked for an attorney three times and you just kept right on going. You know better than that."

"The way I saw it was we had so much evidence against him, it didn't matter," Guteman said. "Jackson's got no way of worming out of this, and you and I both know it." He hated being talked down to by lawyers who sat on their asses, used their mouths and never had to put their bodies on the line.

"Listen, Detective, there's no sense in creating issues by doing lousy police work. It just screws things up for us, gives the defense something to yell about, and appeal, after we get a conviction. Cut it out," Dorsey ordered him.

Hunter intervened. "We appreciate Detective Guteman's aggressiveness. He has made more cases for us than any detective. The good detective has to be mindful of the fact, however, that he doesn't have to prove these cases. We do. End of discussion. Are there any other issues we need to discuss today?"

Nobody said a thing. "Thanks for your counsel. I always appreciate it," Alec said.

The lawyers left the room. Guteman took a final sip of coffee, gathered his papers and walked out. He was angry. He was tired of dealing with attorneys who were more concerned with dotting I's and crossing T's than putting lowlifes in prison. He was in a hurry. He had a moving job to do. The Chicago guys wanted the surveillance equipment moved to a safer location.

Friday—12:15 P.M.
Experiences in Growth Home

Marci Maine pulled up in front of Experiences in Growth. It was a huge, old-Victorian house in a wooded area. There were many other similar houses on the street in various stages of disrepair. At one time, this had been the most upscale neighborhood in Dayton, but it had long since declined. It took a great deal of money to make the houses livable. Heating these huge, old houses was impractical; they had little insulation and antiquated windows. The cold air came through the walls faster than the radiators could heat it up. Plumbing, heating, doors and windows all needed to be replaced. The surprising thing that Marci noted was that while many homes were in shambles around it,

Experiences in Growth had been restored. Painted bright white with black shutters, it had wrought-iron fencing and professional landscaping. A neatly painted sign, EXPERIENCES IN GROWTH, was on the fence in front of the house. Snow had been shoveled off the walkway leading up to the steps of the veranda and the front door.

As Marci climbed the stairs, she could feel her heart thumping in her chest and her breathing getting shallow. *Am I the hunted animal*, she thought, *or am I the hunter?* When she realized she was the hunter, she calmed herself. She looked very put together as her hair flowed over her black, woolen coat down to her black mink collar. The dark-blue, business suit and silk blouse fit her perfectly.

The cards Jack had printed with the name, Nancy Havekost, Dayton Department of Human Services, Investigations and Compliance, were embossed with gold print and looked very official. She walked in the front door without hesitation. She believed she could pull this off if she acted as if she was in total control. *Isn't that how a person in Nancy's position would act?* she mused. She and Jack had rehearsed her role. She was ready.

A billow of warm air hit her in the face as she opened the heavy wood and glass door. She walked into a marble foyer. Refinished, oak trim framed a spiral staircase. A glass chandelier hung in the middle of the foyer above the staircase. A bell was attached to the door and it jingled as she entered.

A petite, black woman dressed in a blue pantsuit emerged to the left of Marci only seconds after she entered. She looked official. "May I help you?"

"Yes. My name is Nancy Havekost, and I am an inspector for the Montgomery County Department of Social Services. I have been ordered to inspect your facility as a preliminary step for your license renewal. I am also interested in placing a young man here. It's really quite beautiful." Marci reached into her purse and brought out a business card and handed it to the woman. "And you are?"

"I'm Loretta Day; I'm the assistant to the director." Loretta knew that the Department of Social Services paid their bills. "And thank you," she said, "we get a lot of compliments on the place. Our director, Pat Hankins, is at lunch right now. Did you have an appointment with her?"

"No. It's our policy to drop in unexpectedly at times in order that we can see the facility as it really is. I trust that you will allow me free access to it according to the department's licensing regulations."

"Of course. But just let me call Pat to tell her you're here."

Marci had come during the noon hour anticipating that the director would be at lunch. That part had worked out. "Feel free to do so, but I am on a tight schedule. I must be back at the department by one-thirty for a meeting, and I really must get this done today. My supervisor is trying to find placements for all the kids who blew-up in their homes after the holidays. We have a whole host of kids who need to be placed immediately. What's the availability of beds here?"

"Normally," Loretta said, "we have a waiting list, but not right now. We just sent a couple of kids home. You could probably get a child placed here within a few days, if he's suitable. Just let me call Pat on her cell phone."

Loretta punched in seven digits on the touch-tone keypad. She was looking at Marci with a smile as she held the phone to her ear. She began speaking into it. Marci had the impulse to run out the door. "Pat, this is Loretta. There is a woman by the name of Nancy Havekost here from Social Services. She wants to do a licensing inspection and place a child. Call me if you have any concerns or objections, otherwise I'm going to get one of the kids to show Ms. Havekost around."

Marci could feel herself breathe again. It was only a message.

"She's got her cell phone turned off. I'm just going to call Darnell. He's the only boy here right now. He can show you around. Most of the kids are in school or on field trips. You have to take Darnell with a grain of salt. He's come a long way since he came to us, but has a longer way to go, if you understand what I mean."

"Of course, I understand. We see a lot of kids like that," Marci said.

Loretta picked up the phone, pushed a button and said, "Darnell, please come to the lobby immediately." To Marci she said, "Please have a seat. Darnell will be right with you, I'm sure."

Marci sat in one of the two padded, powder-blue armchairs in the foyer. She picked up a *Newsweek* magazine and paged through it for a few minutes.

"What . . . it . . . is," a young, male voice said to her.

Marci looked up from her magazine and there was a tall, wiry, black kid maybe thirteen years old, standing in front of Loretta. Looking like he was straight from the 'hood, he wore long jeans that hung so low that the cheeks of his buttocks were plainly visible beneath his plaid boxer shorts. His jeans covered high-top, Nike tennis shoes that looked as big as snowshoes. His red muscle shirt revealed long, wiry arms. His hands hung nearly to his knees. He had hair growing on his upper lip, certainly not a mustache, but enough to let you know he was becoming a man.

"Darnell," Loretta said, "this is Ms. Havekost. She's from Social Services and you're to show her around the facility and answer any questions she has about what it's like to live here."

Darnell looked at Marci. A smile crossed his face as he surveyed her face and body. "Be glad to," he said. If it were an older man leering like that, he'd have been called lecherous.

"Please bring Ms. Havekost back here after you've given her the tour, Darnell, so she can ask whatever questions she might have."

Darnell and Marci shook hands. "Pleased to meet you, Darnell,"

"I'll show you the kitchen first," Darnell said. "Just follow me." He took Marci through a door that swung open into a hallway. There were meeting rooms with fancy tables and chairs. One of them was the boardroom with pictures of the directors on its wall.

"Let's stop here," Marci said. She didn't recognize most of the directors, but there was no mistaking Sheriff Hugh Lane and Detective Dave Guteman, and if that wasn't enough, their names were engraved on gold plates beneath their pictures. Next was a group therapy room with one-way mirrors, floppy pillows and comfortable couches. Then, the kitchen. It was well-equipped with large pots and pans hanging from hooks over the burners. Darnell led Marci in and grabbed a sandwich and a soda out of the refrigerator. "We're not allowed in here. I figure it's all right because I'm with you. I haven't had my lunch today. Want something, ma'am?"

"No, thanks, Darnell, I already had my lunch. I appreciate you showing me around. Tell me what it's like to live here."

"I'd rather be with my homeboys. I'm finishing a two-year hit in the reformatory."

"What for?"

"I did a bunch of auto thefts and got into some trips with the cops. Nothing big."

"How old are you?"

"Sixteen."

"How old were you when you did them?"

"Oh, I started when I was ten. I can break into a car, hotwire it and have it running within two minutes. I hold the record on my block."

"You must be quite proud," Marci said. "Where are your parents?"

"Oh, they live in Toledo. They sent me down here 'cause this is s'posed to be such a good treatment place. They really just wanted to get me out of town. I was a one-man crime wave for a while. I don't really know my daddy. I just know who he is. My momma couldn't handle me after I got to be nine or so. I was out stealin' everything."

"Do you like it here?"

"Like I said, I'd rather be home, but it's okay. Some uh the dudes in this crib are cool. Others are assholes."

"Show me the rest of the facility."

Darnell took her through another door. "You married, Ms. Havekost?"

"Call me Nancy, Darnell. And yes, I'm married."

"Too bad, babe, I just wanted to let you know I'm available."

"If I were younger, Darnell, I might take you up on your offer."

"These here are the rooms of all the guys. They got bunk beds in 'um. No more'n two dudes to a room. The real assholes sometimes get their own rooms 'cause none of the brothers want to spend time with 'um. White boys are a minority here and we let them know it. It's the only time in their lives they don't have more status than the brothers."

"That must be quite a shock to them."

Marci looked with interest in all the empty rooms. The beds were neatly made. There were boom boxes in nearly every room on the main floor and the upstairs. Darnell was proud to show Marci his room. There were ten bedrooms in the house, but nothing in them resembled the sort of equipment necessary to receive and record wiretapped information. There was a large recreation room on the main floor with a pool table, video machines and ping pong.

"What's in the basement?" Marci asked.

"Off limits," Darnell said. "We not allowed to go down there under any circumstances. They say it's because it's a fire risk if we hang out down there. Hell, this whole house is a fire risk. We all know that's bullshit 'cause there are some dudes who been hanging out down there lately."

"Tell me about the dudes."

"Two, in the last coupla weeks. They drive up in a plain car—what looks like an unmarked police car—a funky-ass, old-man, tan sedan. They come through the side door. They got keys, but the dudes aren't counselors here. They just come in the door and go right to the basement door and go down. We don't see them like for hours. They come up then and leave. Stone-faced dudes, don't say a word to no one. You can tell they don't like kids; they don't give us the time of day. Cocky, white-faced dudes."

"I know the kind. Could you show me this door?"

"Sure, it's right here where they come through," he said, pointing to a door on the side of the house next to a driveway. "This where they park that ugly-ass car. Here's the door to the basement."

Marcy looked at it. It had a solitary lock on it. "Darnell, it's very important I get down there to inspect the basement to report to my boss. It's important for other reasons, too, which I may be able to explain to you some day."

"You ain't really no social worker, are you, Nancy? Social workers always act like they got a stick up they asses when you talk to 'um. They use bullshit phony words like 'appropriate' alla time. 'This wouldn't be appropriate, that wouldn't be appropriate.' It usually be my behavior gettin' dissed. I guess it just means proper, but I don't know what the hell proper is. To white folks, it be one thing. To poor, black folks, it be another."

"You're a smart guy, Darnell. I promise I'll tell you one day what I'm really up to."

Darnell reached in his pocket and brought out a pick perhaps four-inches long. He inserted it into the lock and moved the pick around inside the lock like a brain surgeon at work. "I was doing locks tougher'n this when I be ten," he bragged. The door sprung open within seconds. "You go down there, Nancy. I'll stay up here. I don't wanna get in no trouble; I'll get knocked down to Level One if I get caught down there. I'll be a lookout for you. If you hear me knock on the door, get your ass up here as fast as you can."

Marci took a deep breath. She knew she was taking a big risk if she went down those stairs. Who might be down there? She peered down into the dungeon of darkness. She could hear nothing. The dank smell of the basement of a one-hundred-year-old house hit her right in the face as she flicked the light switch on the wall to her left. Slowly, she descended the stairs. When she reached the bottom, the room was fairly dark, lit only by the dim light of the stairwell illuminating it. It gave her the creeps. It was like something out of a Thomas Harris novel.

There was an old tool cabinet and bench. Old hoses, rakes and a decrepit lawn mower were placed haphazardly along the wall. There was nothing that remotely resembled receiving and recording equipment. Marci felt like cutting and running. She caught herself. There in the corner of the room was another door. It was painted gray and was peeling and cracking. The musty smell was almost making her gag as she walked toward it. She pushed it open. The room in front of her was almost completely dark except for the light from one small window. There was just enough light for her to see a light switch and flick it.

Her heart began to race when she saw state-of-the-art receiving and recording equipment in front of her. It was just like Joe's wiretap expert had described to her. On the table next to the machine were audiocassettes. There were reel-to-reel tapes on a machine. Obviously only voice-activated, they were presently motionless, yet a red light on the machinery told her it was operative. It was placed neatly on a desk. There were two chairs in the room. She reached into her purse and brought out a camera and began taking pictures as fast as she could. Then she hurriedly stuffed the tapes into her purse.

Upstairs Darnell was standing by the side door when Detective Guteman drove into the driveway. Darnell had seen Guteman there before. He knew his name from his picture in the boardroom. He knew he was a cop. He knew that Nancy—or whatever her name was—was going to be in a lot of trouble if Guteman were to go downstairs; Guteman was a predator. The little bit he had been around him, he hated him.

Guteman pulled out a keychain, unlocked the door, and entered the house. Darnell was there to greet him. "Officer," Darnell said, "the assistant director needs to speak with you right now about something. She told me to tell you."

"How do you know who I am, kid? I don't know you at all." Guteman walked right past Darnell. "I'll talk to her later. I have to move some stereo equipment out of the basement. I'll pay you five bucks to help me move the stuff." Guteman put his key in the lock and turned it. He could tell that the door had been opened.

"You been down here doing anything, kid? You have, I'll bust you so far back to the joint you won't be getting out until you're eighteen, you little fucker."

"Never been down there, Detective. Somebody must have left the light on when they were down here last. And the reason I know you is 'cause I seen your picture in the room with the big, long table."

"Okay, but if you're lying, I'll kick your ass. Here's five dollars. Help me with the stuff down there."

They went down the stairs quickly. Darnell repeated himself as loudly as he could. "No sir, Detective, I've never been down here before!"

When they got to the bottom of the steps, the room was dark and the door to the room where the equipment was kept was closed. Guteman opened it quickly with Darnell immediately behind him, and turned on the light. Darnell almost froze with terror. The room was empty, except for some old rolls of carpeting on the floor in the corner.

Marci lay covered between two of those rolls, and among the mice, their acrid turds and dried urine. Her breathing was shallow, as if a mountain lion was sniffing nearby, ready to tear her throat out and leave her entrails strewn about the room. She knew Guteman. She had seen him at Avery's preliminary hearing. *He's a killer,* kept going round in circles in her mind. If she was found down there, she would be next. She would disappear, never to see Jack again; he would never know what had happened to her.

Guteman turned off the power on the unit. He began unplugging cords. "Here, kid, take this piece up to my car. It's right outside the door and come back." Guteman continued to work on disengaging the equipment. When Darnell returned, he looked around the room mystified at how she could have disappeared.

Darnell quickly went over to Guteman, who had a second load of equipment for him. "Where are the cassettes, goddamnit? Those idiots probably took them. Kid, look around and see if there are any cassettes on the floor behind this desk."

Darnell got to his hands and knees and snooped around. "None here, Detective."

"Okay, pick this up and I'll take the rest. Let's get out of here. Christ, it stinks down here." Darnell took the last load. Guteman followed him out of the room, turned off the light and went up the stairs with Darnell.

Marci heard the door close and lock. She crawled out from beneath the carpet, grabbed her purse and its valuable contents of photos and cassettes, and climbed to the top of the stairs. She tried to open the door; it wouldn't budge. She was locked in. She needed desperately to get out, but couldn't. She could try to break down the door, but Guteman might hear her. Nor did she want Loretta to discover her in the basement. She stood at the top of the stairs trying to decide what to do.

Suddenly, she heard Guteman. "Don't spend all of that money in one place, kid, and remember what I said. What did you say Loretta wanted?"

"I don't think it's important," Darnell replied.

"I'll check anyway."

Marci could hear the door swing open and then shut, then Darnell opened the basement door. "Thank god, he didn't see me. You gotta be very careful. If he finds out you knew what was down there, he'll hurt you."

"Let's go back to my room and wait 'til he's gone." They quickly went up the back steps to his room. They could look out the window at Guteman's car. About five minutes later, Guteman got into his car and drove away. As they were going down the stairs, Darnell asked, "What's your real name and how do I get a hold of you?"

"My name is Marci." She pulled out a real card and gave it to Darnell. "If you see anything else around here that seems suspicious, give me a call. You might save someone's life."

Darnell just looked at her. He had already played a lot of cops and robbers in his lifetime. For the first time, though, he sensed the cop was the criminal and not him.

"Let's go to the lobby so I can thank Loretta for the tour and tell her what a great job you did," Marci said.

"Maybe you just better go."

"No. Let's just play this out," she said. They made their way to the front lobby. "Thank you, Loretta," Marci said when they'd found the assistant. "Darnell did a terrific job showing me the place. It exceeded my expectations. I had heard it was excellent, and it truly is."

"I'm glad you liked it. I trust we'll get a good report and that we'll be seeing you in the near future with more placements."

"You can count on it. I'll be in touch with you soon." Marci buttoned up her coat and went out into the cold, January day.

As the door closed, Loretta looked at Darnell and said, "Why did you tell a board member like Dave Guteman that I wanted to talk to him when I didn't? I didn't even know he was coming, and I surely didn't tell you I wanted to see him. I was embarrassed. I looked like an idiot in front of a board member. Darnell, what are you up to?"

"I didn't tell him you wanted to talk to him. He misunderstood. I tol' him maybe he oughtta check with you, see if they be any messages for him 'cause I knew he be on the board."

"And when did you become so thoughtful? I'll let it pass for now."

Darnell shrugged his shoulders and went back up the stairs to his room, clutching Marci's card in his right hand.

Friday—4:00 P.M.
Jack Maine and Associates

"I wouldn't have let you go if I'd thought you were going to be in danger. Right!!" Marci said in a sarcastic, joking tone to her husband, trying to soothe her fright. "Famous last words to me—almost. I don't know if I should be mad or relieved."

"You're probably both," Jack said. He could only shake his head and smile— he was just relieved she was alive.

Marci was still shaking when Joe returned to the office from the field. She was just about finished telling Jack about her experience when Joe walked in.

"Joe," Jack said before Joe could say a word, "I want you to listen to these tapes Marci swiped. I'll bet you'll find Burt's conversation with Van Hazeltree on one of them. Seems like Dave Guteman and his boys have set up shop in the basement of the group home. Now, we *know* he's dirty. There could be a smoking gun in those tapes, Joe—could be the tape stolen from Burt's place— the one you took the shot in the head over."

Joe grumbled. "Muthafuckas." Then, he smiled for the first time all day. "That Marci girl—she got talent," he said proudly. "I always knew it. Hope these tapes 're good, 'cause I ain't found a damned thing all day. All the Bovas I came up with are women, old men, kids, and none of them live in Dayton. There are some forty year olds in Cleveland and Columbus, but nothing here. FBI and DEA won't give the names of any of their people. I didn't even try the CIA; I know the spooks are off limits."

"Well, you have all weekend to listen to them," Jack said.

"Joe, I pulled voice messages," Marci said. "You have a call from a Mr. Hardin Long. Says it's urgent. Left a beeper number."

Marci handed him the phone message. Joe went to the refrigerator, pulled out a Dr. Pepper and went back to his office with the box of tapes. He wanted to start listening to them immediately. He called the pager number and punched in his number. He popped his soda, put his feet on the desk and began queuing the first tape when the phone rang. Marci answered it in the waiting room.

"Mr. Hardin Long, Joe," she announced as she routed the call through.

"Joe Betts. How can I help you?" Joe said as he cradled the receiver between his head and shoulder, sipped his soda and pressed PLAY.

"I have something you might be interested in, Mr. Betts," said a man with a muffled, gravelly-hoarse voice, who sounded as if he were deliberately disguising it with some sort of towel or cloth.

"Lots of stuff I'm interested in." Joe took another sip of soda and continued listening to his tape.

"Well, this you would be *very* interested in."

"First, tell me who I'm talking to."

"Hardin Long."

"Do I know you?"

"I met you once, Mr. Betts."

"Where? I don't remember you." Joe could hear the voice of Burt Porter on his tape—his voice was unmistakable—it was as if he were still alive.

"Last time I saw you, you had a big headache. How many stitches did it take to close that hole anyway?"

"Stitches?" Joe said, his heartbeat going from first to fourth gear in one second. He pressed STOP on the tape player, then pressed the speaker phone button, shot to his feet and motioned Marci and Jack into the office.

"Let's cut the bullshit," the muffled voice said. "You want a certain audio tape, and I have it."

"How can I be sure that the tape I want is the one you have?"

"It's the one, all right. As far as I can tell, it is very valuable. Has a murder on it."

"Whose murder?" Joe asked as Jack and Marci gathered around Joe's desk.

"You can't figure it out? If you don't know, you're kind of a dumb ass, aren't you?"

"Been called worse."

"And what the detective did with that girl, Chris, or whatever her name was? Ohh, ohh. Disgusting!"

"Mr. Long, is it?"

"Yeah, Mr. Long."

"Well, Mr. Long, how can I arrange to pick up the tape? I'd like to listen to it."

"That can be arranged. But, you see, I'm a businessman."

Jack rolled his eyes.

"Here it comes," Marci whispered.

"What's your business?"

"I sell information to the highest bidder."

"And what would be the price of that information?"

"Fifty big ones—to be delivered in hundreds at a place designated by me."

Jack's muscles tightened and he gasped. Both the Conley and Jackson cases together hadn't grossed half that.

"Lot of money, Mr. Long," Joe said. "Perhaps if we could have a number other than a beeper number—perhaps an address—we could get back to you after we try to raise that kind of money."

"The beeper number is the only one you're gonna get. It's untraceable. You see, Mr. Betts, and you can tell this to Mr. Maine, this is a one-time offer. It's fifty grand, or no deal. If you don't believe me, listen to this." There was a click on the line, then a voice that clearly sounded like Burt's, talking with someone. The voice played for only seconds, then there was another click and silence. "It's legitimate," Long said.

"I can't tell it's legitimate from that. There are a lot of tapes with Burt Porter's voice on them. Hell, I was listening to one when you called."

"Well, then, you could tell it was his voice."

"Perhaps if you could tell us more, we could believe you and make a deal."

"What do you want to know?"

"Who were the three assholes who took the tape? Why did they want the tape? How did you get hold of it?"

"I can't tell you any of that."

"Well, Mr. Long, I need more information."

"If you have any intelligence over there, you'll take this deal."

"You're talking bullshit, Mr. Long."

"I just gave you the only information you'll get."

"Well, I'll tell you this," Joe said, "fifty grand is more than we could afford."

"Fifty grand is what it'll take. This tape is *that* valuable. Take it or leave it."

Jack walked over to the speaker. "Mr. Long, this is Jack Maine."

"Mr. Maine, glad to meet you. Perhaps you are a more reasonable man than Mr. Betts."

"Eminently, Mr. Long. We'd like to do business with you, but we can't afford fifty. That's way out of our league. What would you take?"

"Fifty—take it or leave it."

"Who's your supervisor at the Central Intelligence Agency, or is it the FBI? Perhaps if I could talk with him, we could negotiate a deal."

"Good try, Mr. Maine, but I work independently."

"Well, who at the CIA or FBI would be in charge of this sort of thing?"

"Who said anything about the CIA or FBI?"

"We already know the government is behind this. Now, who do I talk to?"

"Told ya, I'm an independent."

"I see," Jack responded. "Should I ask for Dr. Dick Draggin over there, or should I continue to talk with you, Mr. Hardin Long?" Jack asked. "Perhaps you could tell us your real name."

"I'm impressed, Mr. Maine. You catch on quick. Tell you what, I'll be calling Mr. Betts tomorrow. If he has the money, we'll do business."

Mr. Hardin Long hung up.

Joe immediately pressed star sixty-nine hoping he could retrieve Long's phone number. The number was blocked. "Blocked. Goddamnit, we let the sumbitch get away," Joe shouted. "We need that tape; that was Burt's voice, I could tell."

"Sounded like him," Jack agreed.

"That was good, boss. I fell for that hard and long shit until you asked to talk to Dick Draggin."

"You don't really expect a guy like that to go on the record with a legitimate name, do you, Joe? It could get him killed, or at least fired."

"Well, he had me faked out," Marci said. "We can't raise the money, and no way can we go to the cops after what I saw with Guteman today."

"We won't go to the police," Jack said, "but we do have something. He essentially told us the deal at Burt's was done by a government operation. At least, he didn't deny it. Joe, follow up on that pager number. I bet it's government owned."

"Done deal, boss. What do you want to do now?"

"He'll call back. See if he'll take three thousand. Figure it out—he's selling to a limited market. We're the only ones interested in his product. Unless he's stupid, he'll take what we offer him."

"Might be a double agent," Joe said.

"Might be," Jack affirmed.

Marci sighed, then said, "Today has been a little more than I can handle. I think I need a glass of wine."

"Done deal," Joe said.

"Joe, I haven't seen any done deals in this mess yet," Jack said as they headed out the door to dinner.

CHAPTER 13

Monday, January 29—Early Morning
Alec Hunter's Cadillac

The holidays, although only a month past, seemed as distant as they always do as January turns into February. Warmth and sunshine are only a memory, which must suffice until spring. At least that's the way it is in Ohio in winter; and, a day like this Monday only reinforced the feeling of doom and imprisonment by the weather.

For Alec Hunter, however, it was a bright day. Avery Jackson's arraignment was later in the morning. In the afternoon, he would be presenting Chris Conley's case to the Montgomery County Grand Jury. He had subpoenaed Detective Dave Guteman to testify. Grand jury proceedings are generally just a rubber stamp for the district attorney. The DA presents the evidence, makes his argument to the jury, tells them what he wants and they usually go along with it. Hunter had decided he'd present the case himself. It was always a good political move because there were fifteen people on the grand jury and it gave him an opportunity for exposure.

He was looking forward to his time with Stephanie tomorrow. His fantasies always took him back to her naked body—the beauty of her pendulous breasts and reddish nipples. She kept herself so marvelously in shape. He could see her flat belly and wonderfully shaped hips framing her delicate, blonde pubic hair. He wanted, no—he deserved—that sort of beauty. When he fantasized the wetness between her legs, he could feel the blood rush to his penis. *Pretty good for a fifty-five-year-old man*, he thought. Alice, although still pretty, had become saggy. Pleated thighs and a saggy ass had always turned him off. He needed Stephanie. When elected to the Senate in two years, he might divorce Alice and marry her. Maybe they would discuss it more tomorrow in bed.

He switched from talk radio to easy-listening music. He contemplated his position. He was pretty much set financially. His career was on track. He had money and influence behind him—although, he'd noticed that the more perfect his life seemed, the more power and wealth he attained, the more anxious and paranoid he was becoming. He realized for a fleeting moment he really had not one friend in the world. There was no one with whom he could really talk and share his anxieties. He had thought about seeing a shrink, but he didn't trust them. They were soft and had more problems than he did. No, his power would be his elixir and bastion of safety. It would be his anti-depressant, his Prozac. Both of his parents had needed Alec to be strong and perfect for them. When he was little, weakness or insolence would get him a slap in the face from his mother, his ultimate humiliation. As he thought about it, he could feel his cheeks become hot. He burned with rage for a moment, then buried it again.

He wondered what Avery Jackson would do at his arraignment. He knew the media coverage would be saturating again. It was important that his office appear in complete control of the situation. He fully expected an insanity plea. His experts had assured him there were no real risks of a NGRI verdict if such a plea were entered. They knew the stats, too—no one had convinced a jury of insanity since Hinckley. Still, it was important that he knew what Maine was doing. He just wanted to be one step ahead. After all, Alec was on the right side, and Maine was on the wrong side. Alec couldn't understand how one could possibly represent low-lifes. He understood the necessity of their having an attorney and constitutionally-protected rights. But these people were different from him. He knew that, and what's more important, the public knew it.

The commute was over. As he pulled into his parking place outside of the district courthouse, he could see all the media outlets had trucks there. Alec Hunter was in his element. There would be even better days in the months ahead. The Jackson and Conley cases were part of his destiny. There would be no slaps in his face today.

Monday—10:00 A.M.
Montgomery County District Court—Judge John Hodge's Division

The People of the State of Ohio versus Avery Jackson was assigned to Division Four, Judge John Hodge. Hodge had been on the bench for twenty years.

Originally a district attorney of high repute, he'd tired of the job and switched to defense work. He'd been one of the first lawyers in the public defender's office. He stayed there for a few years before going into private practice and then being elected to the bench. He made his bones representing Pete Cassidy Rose in the most famous insanity case in Ohio history. His victory, and Dave Morgan's defeat, won Alec Hunter the election.

Bald, with gray hair and a mustache, Judge Hodge loved athletics and had played them all. Now paunchy and middle-age, he could only sit and watch. Hodge was married and had one daughter who identified with him so strongly she even attended his alma mater, Ohio State Law School. When drinking a beer with his friends, he would confide in them how bored he was with being a judge. He could remember only one case in the last five years that had interested him. It was a products' liability case involving Wonder Chemical. Lawyers from Chicago and New York tried the case. It involved a Dayton woman who had become ill from her silicon breast implants. One had broken and the silicon had permeated her body causing her to need a mastectomy. She nearly died. The lawyers picked a jury, and after she testified quite convincingly, Wonder settled the case for two million dollars. Hodge was disappointed; he'd wanted to see a jury sock it to Wonder.

He once enjoyed criminal cases; now, they bored him. He had heard a number of homicide cases and had sentenced people to life in prison. He had never had a death penalty case. Although he was personally against the death penalty, he had sought counsel within himself and decided he could impose it if necessary. After all, it was the will of the people.

Hodge didn't particularly like Hunter. Although admittedly Hunter ran a good office with competent deputies, Judge Hodge felt he was unusually harsh on powerless people. Hodge was excited about the Jackson case. He saw it as a chance to get some real action into his courtroom and see that Avery Jackson and his victim, Gene Hardacre, were both treated fairly. In that regard, the parties to the lawsuit—the State of Ohio and Avery Jackson—could not have drawn a better judge. John Hodge had an acute sense of justice—misdeeds needed to be confronted, exposed in an open forum, and dealt with.

Arraignments are simple things. The defendant simply enters a plea— usually not guilty, even if he is guilty as sin. When Judge Hodge's bailiff called the case, Avery walked from the jury box, where he was detained by the deputy, to counsel table. He was dressed in his dark suit. Yolanda had taken it for dry cleaning. Had someone told her in law school she would be handling a client's laundry, she probably would have thought them daft. She felt for Avery though. She believed him when he said he had no memory of shooting Gene Hardacre. She liked his kindness and the gentleness of his eyes and respected the sharpness of his mind. She had brought him his suit early that morning. In spite of what nearly everyone else in the courtroom thought of them, she felt proud when she and Jack and Avery stood before Judge Hodge.

"This matter comes on for arraignment. Will Counsel please enter your appearances," Hodge said. He had never seen his courtroom so full, nor had he seen as many videocams and artists recording an event.

"Alec Hunter for the People," Alec said.

"Jack Maine and Yolanda Crone for the Defendant, Avery Jackson, who now appears before this court, Your Honor."

"Does your client waive formal reading of the charges against him, Mr. Maine?"

"He does, Your Honor."

"How does he plead to Count One, the charge of Murder in the First Degree with special circumstances, to wit, he killed a law enforcement officer, that he lay in wait, and that his crime was especially heinous?"

"Mr. Jackson enters pleas of Not Guilty and Not Guilty by Reason of Insanity," Jack said.

Hunter and Brodan glanced knowingly at one another.

"Those pleas will be accepted and the matter will be set for trial. Counsel, as you well know, Mr. Jackson has a right to a speedy trial by jury within ninety days. Does he wish to waive that time requirement in order to allow psychologists ample time to evaluate him?"

"No, Your Honor, we insist the trial take place within ninety days. We'll have our experts together by that time."

"In that regard, Your Honor," Jim Brodan said, "we suggest that the defendant does not have a right to a speedy trial if he's asserting insanity as a defense. We will need to have him examined also, and do not know if we can have our evaluation done within ninety days."

"Your Honor, we believe he does have the right to a speedy trial regardless of the nature of his defense. If he were asserting self-defense, he would have the right to a speedy trial. We do not believe that his assertion of one right—the right to defend himself by virtue of his mental status—should mandate that he give up another important constitutional and statutory right—the right to a speedy trial."

"I agree with Mr. Maine. The matter will be set for trial within ninety days. Could we have a trial date, please?"

The court clerk scanned quickly through her docket and announced April twelfth. "Is that date suitable with Counsel?" Hodge asked. Both sides agreed to the date. "All right, Counsel, the matter will be set for trial April twelfth. Both sides are to provide discovery to one another, including the reports of all psychologists and psychiatrists thirty days before trial. All other motions must be filed within thirty days."

"Your Honor," Jack said, "there may be a real problem in picking a jury because of the overwhelming pretrial publicity this case has generated. Among the motions I will be filing will be a motion for a change of venue."

"I was expecting that, Mr. Maine," Hodge said. "We will attempt to pick a jury here in Montgomery County. If it becomes clear during the voir dire process that we're unable to get an unbiased jury, we will move the matter to another county, though there's the potential problem that this case has aroused so much media attention and debate that I suspect nearly every citizen in this state knows about it. Times have changed, Counsel, it's not like it was fifty years ago when print media were the main source of information, and a significant portion of the population was illiterate. Now with the Internet and high-speed access to information through cable news and videotape, everyone will know about the case. The question will be whether we will be able to get a jury that can apply the law fairly. What I'm hearing today, Counsel, is that the real issue is not going to be whether Mr. Jackson committed this homicide, but what was his mental condition at the time of its commission. Would that be correct, Mr. Maine?"

"It's likely that's the direction we're going, Your Honor."

"We'll cross that bridge when we come to it," Hodge said. "Are there any other issues before the court?"

"No, Your Honor," said both counsel.

"I need to raise two issues. The first is whether it is appropriate for me to sit on this case, in view of the fact that a number of years ago, this defendant was a member of the bench here in Montgomery County at a time I was also a member of the bench. The second issue is whether this case can be tried in Montgomery County at all because of the fact that Avery Jackson was once a judge here. This is a highly unusual situation—probably unprecedented in the United States—to have a former judge charged with a capital offense in the very courthouse where he once presided. I would think that if there would be a necessity for a change of venue, it would be because of this issue."

Hunter quickly sprang to his feet. "Your Honor, the People have given this serious thought. Certainly, we do not want the appearance of impropriety. There is too much at stake for the People in a crime so serious. However, we have no objection to your hearing this matter."

Hunter was currying favor with the court. If he didn't, he feared Hodge would make him pay down the road, either on the Jackson case or other cases in Hodge's court. He would have preferred a judge who would be a bigger puppet. Hodge, however, was brutally tough on defendants who had committed heinous crimes. Hunter would roll the dice with Hodge. It could be worse. Hunter went on. "That's a decision you have to make in view of your prior relationship with Avery Jackson. With regard to the second issue, the People believe it is imperative this matter remains in Montgomery County. The facts are that Avery Jackson left the bench in this county two years ago when he was voted out of office. He no longer has any contacts or interest with this Court, and prior to his arrest, was employed as a professor at Sinclair University. It would set a dangerous precedent, indeed, to require former employees of this court to be tried elsewhere. The issue is whether you feel it is appropriate for you to hear the matter."

"Mr. Maine, what say you?"

"If I may have a moment, Your Honor," Jack said, feeling the need to talk to Avery and Yolanda. With his hand over his face, he whispered to them, "The worst thing that could happen in this case is for it to be sent to some redneck county in coal country southern Ohio where they have no appreciation for mental health issues. I say let's keep the case here."

"That's fine with me," Avery whispered.

Yolanda nodded her agreement. "We could do worse elsewhere in this state on insanity issues," she said. "We might do better in Shaker Heights or Upper Arlington, but who's to say we could get the case sent to those places? I say keep it here. We have as good a shot here as anywhere."

"Okay, we're in agreement. Let's keep it here," Jack whispered back, but not feeling good about his decision. *No matter where the case was tried, it was a loser.* "Your Honor, I have conferred with Mr. Jackson and co-counsel about these issues. We are not asking for a change of venue merely because Mr. Jackson was a member of this court. If we're unable to get a fair jury, we will assert our motion for a change of venue. With regard to you hearing the matter, Your Honor, we believe you will be unbiased, and therefore we are *not* asking you to recuse yourself."

"Thank you, Counsel. I have given this matter considerable thought and can say that my past association with Mr. Jackson was only professional. I have never had a business relationship, a social relationship or any sort of friendship with Mr. Jackson. We were merely colleagues in the law and on the bench. No more, no less. I will not recuse myself unless I am asked to do so by the parties involved."

"We have no such request," Hunter said.

Maine followed with, "Nor do we, Your Honor."

"Very well, gentlemen. If you wish a further hearing on motions, we will see you back here then. Otherwise, be ready for trial on April twelfth."

"All rise," the bailiff called out.

Hodge left the bench relieved that he would not have to recuse himself. He looked forward to being challenged for the first time in years. He had persuaded both counsels to agree that the matter could be heard in Montgomery County. There would be no appeal on those grounds.

As the deputies began to cuff Avery, he grabbed Yolanda's warm hand and squeezed it. She squeezed back. It had been her frequent visits to the jail when Jack was busy with other aspects of the case that had sustained him. The dreams had continued with greater frequency and intensity since Dr. Gilmour had evaluated him. Avery could not imagine why the government, be it the FBI, DEA or CIA, with all its money and power would be interested in him. After all, he remembered no involvement with them. When he thought about it, though, he experienced blinding headaches.

There were now three dead men connected with the case. It would be easy to have Avery set up in jail if someone wanted to get rid of him. Everyone close to the case speculated about whether or not Jack, Marci, Yolanda and Joe were safe. Already one lawyer had been killed who apparently knew too much. Why not kill another lawyer, or anyone for that matter, who might know something about this case? One thing was for certain. There were some powerful motivations for such violence. There had to be a lot of money and secrets involved to kill people of such important stature—even Hazeltree was important in his world— so gratuitously. The problem was they didn't know what the secrets were and who held them. They didn't know who profited by the murders of Gene Hardacre, Burt Porter and Ovanul Hazeltree. They just knew that Avery Jackson did not.

"I'll be over to see you later today or tomorrow, Avery," Yolanda said. "Hang in there." Avery acknowledged her with a nod of the head.

CHAPTER 14

Tuesday, January 30—9:00 A.M.
Montgomery County Jail

Jim Rosato sat in the attorney-client visitation room of the Montgomery County Jail. When the guards brought Avery in, he thought he'd be meeting with Jack and Yolanda again preparing for the psychological evaluation. Instead, there was Jim Rosato. Rosato smiled as he saw Avery, stood and extended his hand to him. Avery didn't shake it.

"What brings you to see me?" Avery asked. He was well aware of the Rosatos, and Jim Rosato in particular. He had appeared in Avery's court many times, usually on drug cases. The poor, black and white communities of Dayton, which frequently used and sold street drugs and had little appreciation for the skill and art of being a trial attorney, believed the Rosatos, as a matter of course, bought off judges and district attorneys. Avery had resented them because they took large amounts of money out of the poor, black community on the basis of the fraud they regularly perpetrated on it. He believed the Rosatos to be mediocre trial lawyers dressed in expensive suits. There is at least one of them in every city. Dayton had two brothers.

"Could we sit down and talk?" Rosato asked.

"Certainly, go ahead," Avery said.

"I'll get right to the point. Two benefactors have approached us to ask that we represent you. They are willing to pay your attorney fees as well as allow you to keep the money that is left over from your defense to help with your children's education, or for whatever purpose you choose to use it."

The room was quiet. Avery just looked at Rosato. "Who are these benefactors?" he asked.

"They insist on anonymity or the money will not be made available to you."

"And how much money are they offering?"

"Four hundred thousand dollars."

"Only four hundred?" asked Avery sarcastically. "Are they white folks or black folks?"

"They are white," Rosato said, "but I'm not sure that has any relevancy."

"I think it does."

"Why?"

"Why would some white folks want to pay for my representation when I killed a white sheriff? Certainly, there must be something in it for them? What's the catch?"

Rosato evaded the question. "There's no restriction on your defense; you can present an insanity defense, or whatever other defense you like."

"That seems hard to believe. How much money would you charge me for your representation?"

"I've talked the matter over with my brother and we decided we could do the case for two hundred thousand, through trial. If you're convicted, we'd charge another hundred thousand for the appeal."

"What would happen to the remaining hundred thousand?"

"It'd be left to you to use however you wish. Certainly, your children would be able to use it for their education."

"This all seems a little too good to be true. You know what my mama used to say to me about deals that look too good to be true, Mr. Rosato?"

"Like I said, there are no restrictions on your defense."

"I believe I have the right to know who the benefactors are if I'm your client. How could I ever trust you as my lawyer if someone else is paying you and I don't know or trust that person? They certainly must have an interest in my defense, and I believe I have the right to know what that interest is."

"I'd tell you their names, but I'm afraid the funds would not be made available to you."

"Does the name Bova have any meaning to you, Mr. Rosato?" Avery asked, taking a wild shot at the name of the man who had mugged Joe in the fight over the precious, missing tape.

Rosato's eyes shot up. "Look, Avery—"

"Don't call me Avery. It's Judge Jackson to you. Just because I'm here in a vulnerable position does not mean you can come in here and buy me. My lawyers have already told me that several spooks, one of them by the name of Bova, stole a tape out of my dead lawyer's apartment the day after his mysterious death. Are these the same guys who are offering you the money?"

"I can't tell you that or their offer will be withdrawn. All I can tell you is that the only condition they've put on the funds is that you use their experts to show your insanity at the time of the shooting. They've offered to pay for the experts, as well as the four hundred thousand. They've agreed to provide the finest psychiatric experts in the world."

"Doesn't that strike you as a bit odd, Counselor?" Avery asked.

Jim Rosato sat expressionless. "It is highly unusual, but I believe it to be an offer you should seriously consider."

"Why? Their experts have an interest that is probably at odds with my interest on the case."

"Let me speak frankly to you, Judge Jackson. I have seen the videos of you killing Gene Hardacre. Every citizen of Montgomery County, Ohio, has seen the killing. I also understand the relative impossibility of you being successful with an insanity defense. You will not beat this charge even with the best expert witnesses. I figure the best you can do here is work a deal with Hunter. He'll back down when he finds out you have the finest government psychiatrists coming in to testify. He'll be afraid of losing a case that no one should lose. It will be bad for his image. He will eventually cut a deal with you. If you plead guilty to first-degree murder, he'll drop the request for the death penalty. He can sell that to the people with you being a former judge and all. You'll be eligible for parole in twenty years. You may even be able to get clemency after you do ten to fifteen years if you do well in prison. You'll have a chance to walk again on this earth as a free man. You can take the two hundred-K and have enough for your retirement or to get your kids through college and graduate school."

Avery sat listening.

Rosato went on. "We have had no conversation with Alec Hunter and can't promise this, but we think when we give Hunter a list of the best experts money can buy, he'll back down. You can enter a plea in a couple of months here. If we don't have to prepare for trial, we'll give you three hundred-K, and we'll keep a hundred. Plain and simple."

"A hundred thousand for entering a plea of guilty and not having to prepare anything. That's pretty easy dough for you," Avery said.

Rosato shrugged his shoulders. "It's pretty inexpensive if it saves your life."

"That will preclude me from putting on a defense in a case where I really don't know that I killed anyone," Avery said.

"Save it, Judge. You and I both know this system is not about guilt or innocence. It's about appearances. It's about who *appears* to be guilty or innocent. In this case, there's no question about appearances. What you see is what you get, and you'll look like a cold-blooded killer to everyone on the jury. Don't be stupid. Take the money."

"You know, I always wondered how you guys did business. I always suspected it was like this. You know fucking, damn well your proposal is unethical. You have a conflict of interest between your moneyed benefactors and my need to defend myself at trial."

Rosato shook his head. "Take it or leave it. This is the real world."

"I'll think about it overnight and get back to you in a day or so," Avery said. "Thanks for your time." He stood up. Rosato offered his hand. Avery didn't move. "Forgive me, but I had a shower this morning and I don't want to feel dirtier than I already feel after hearing this."

"Your attitude will change, Judge, when the three hundred thousand dollars is deposited in a bank account for your children."

"Perhaps, but I'll never know how this happened to me, nor will my children."

"Does it really matter when you have this kind of money on the table? Call me tomorrow." Jim Rosato went to the door. The steel door slid open and then slammed shut.

Avery was startled. He wished every sound didn't startle him.

Tuesday—12 noon
The Hilton Hotel

The attractive blonde woman signed the name Claryce Fordyke to the register, plunked down the cash and picked up her key. She felt a little apprehensive as she pressed the nine button. For the first time, she realized their room number was 911. Perhaps that was an omen; she'd been struggling lately with her feelings about this whole affair. Where once she felt a rush of excitement when she went up the elevator, now she felt different. She loved Alec, to be sure. She still saw him as having a special glow about him. She thought they were beautiful together—having the potential of being a powerful couple that could do positive things for the people of Ohio. But, would she ever have a relationship with him that was meaningful and enduring? Her daughter Angela would be going to college in a year. It was time for her to start planning a life outside of her career.

Stephanie ordered room service as soon as she settled into the room. Alec wanted a Reuben sandwich and a bowl of their special, house soup, tomato basil. She ordered only tomato-basil soup and some rolls for herself. Then, she went to the bathroom to freshen her makeup and her breath. Alec would be there soon. She hoped the food would come before he arrived so they could have a romantic, meaningful lunch. Lately, Alec had been engaging in more sex play before they ate. She just wasn't in the mood to immediately put his penis in her mouth anymore.

As she opened the cap to the mouth freshener, she heard a knock on the door. She finished spraying it into her mouth, looked in the mirror and did a last second comb-through of her blonde hair. Although beautiful, she never really felt that way. She was relieved it was room service at the door with a tray of food. As she was tipping the young man, she saw Alec coming around the corner from the elevator and down the hall toward them. *What a great looking man*, she thought to herself.

The porter finished putting the food on a table in the room, stuffed his tip into his pocket and departed. They were alone once again. At the office, they were engulfed by the intensity that goes with crime and the trauma that accompanies it. There they were unable to express any feeling for one another. In this room for two hours of every week, they could talk to and touch one another. Alec reached for Stephanie and kissed her. She kissed him back. He kissed her more deeply, trying to part her lips and reach her tongue. She did not respond. She pulled gently away. "Let's eat and talk first today, Alec."

"In case you didn't notice, I was trying to eat," he said.

She smiled at him. It was rare for Alec to show that much humor. "Don't worry, we'll take care of that. I'd just like to know how you are and what your morning was like," Stephanie said.

"The grand jury issued a True Bill this morning charging Chris Conley with first-degree murder. Judge Sobocinski raised her bond to two hundred grand. He wouldn't hold her without bond. He issued a warrant for her arrest. Rather than go over to Judge Jeffers' court and just throw the cuffs on her in front of everyone and inconvenience the court, we called up Maine and made arrangements for her to turn herself in at the end of the day."

Sadly, Stephanie said, "I know the insurance evidence and her frustration with Porter over his not wanting to get married look bad, but I also know Chris Conley is not a killer. She might snort a little cocaine, but she is not a killer."

"I knew you wouldn't like it, but we just have to go with the evidence on a case and try not to get emotionally involved. You don't need me to remind you that's our job as prosecutors. We'll have to let a jury decide if she's responsible for his death. I'm sure Maine will file every motion imaginable and she'll get a good defense. If she beats the case, more power to her. Did you order me a Rueben sandwich?" Alec asked as he took the silver cover off his plate of food. "Look's good. I know I can always depend on you."

Alec took a bite of his sandwich, and Stephanie took her first spoonful of the tomato bisque soup. It was, as usual, hot and tasty. "I don't normally feel this way about defendants," she said somewhat apologetically, "but that's because I don't know them as real, flesh-and-blood people. We tend to just categorize them all as dirt bags and forget that some of them are good people who, for one reason or another, have gotten involved in some dangerous stuff. I look at her and say to myself, 'But for the grace of God, there go I.'"

"Come on, Stephanie, you don't get involved with street drugs," Alec said.

"You know, if you were a cokehead—and I'm sure there are district attorneys out there who smoke grass and snort cocaine—and you wanted to do some dope with me when we get together on Tuesdays, I might just do it. Let's say you divorce your wife and change the beneficiary of your life insurance to me, and just coincidentally, you have a heart attack after we do some coke together, and you die. Does this mean I should be charged with first-degree murder?"

"I would never do any dope, and I would never have anything to do with you if you wanted to do it with me," Alec said.

"Alec, are you trying to tell me you have never smoked grass—not even in college or law school? When you were in school, you were a total dork if you hadn't tried it."

"I smoked a little, but I never inhaled and I never got high."

"You and Clinton, *huh*?"

"Don't associate me with a Democrat like him, Stephanie. We might be having an affair, and I might cheat on my wife, but I don't get gratuitous blowjobs from our interns."

"That's true, just from me on Tuesdays," Stephanie said. It was certainly the most honest thing she had ever said during her entire relationship with Alec. He just looked at her, surprised. "What did you do, just get drunk on the weekends?"

"We got drunk a lot at fraternity parties, but that was a legal high."

"You know, when we go on trips together out of town, you drink quite a bit. What if we got loaded together and you died after having changed the beneficiary of your life insurance to me? Could I expect to be charged with first-degree murder?"

"What the hell are you trying to do today, start a fight?" Alec asked. "This is unlike you. I thought we could have a nice lunch without you antagonizing me. What's with you?"

"I'm sorry. I guess I'm feeling a little insecure about us and where we're going as a couple," Stephanie said, honestly.

"I've been thinking about that quite a bit myself. I like you; you make me feel good. Alice and I are already separated and, in a sense, are already divorced.

In the last two weeks, things have really changed. We'll convict Jackson, perhaps even Conley. I've gotten the support of the party and some well-placed people for a Senate run. It's a big jump from DA to the Senate, but I think it can be done what with the national publicity we'll get on the Jackson case. The bottom line is that after I run for the Senate, win or lose, I'll divorce Alice and then we can be together. I've put aside enough money so I never need to worry about that again. All of the things I've done are beginning to pay off."

Stephanie glowed. She took another sip of her soup. Alec worked on his soup and sandwich. *This is what I wanted from him,* she thought. There were no divorce papers filed yet, but they would be coming later. He looked and acted like such a straight arrow. She felt she was getting to know him better. He had allowed her into his life—not a lot—but enough to let her to feel closer to him. *This could work out well,* she thought. *Angela will be going away to college about the time of Alec's Senate bid.*

They went on eating and making small talk.

When they finished, Stephanie got up and went over to Alec. She unbuttoned his top button, slipped off his silk tie and unbuttoned the rest of his shirt. He could feel the blood rushing to his penis. She took him by the hand to the bed where she undressed him and kissed him all over. She knew what he wanted as she took him into her mouth. Their lovemaking went on longer that usual. He took time undressing and fondling her. This time, it felt like he could accept her, and she him. She hoped the feeling would never go away.

After finishing, they lay naked under the covers for a while. "Is Brodan still going to handle the Conley prosecution?" Stephanie asked.

"Brodan's perfect for it. He's a prosecutor's prosecutor. She'll be arraigned tomorrow in district court. We'll see which judge we draw. We could have done better on Jackson. Morris or Sobocinski would have been better. They're pure district attorneys, not half-breeds like Hodge." Alec was referring to Hodge's brief stint as a defense attorney. "Morris and Sobocinski have ways of giving cues to the jury that say 'this guy is a guilty son-of-a-bitch and do not listen to any of the defense bullshit.' You know we're going to be getting plenty of motions from Maine trying to get Jackson out of this one. Hodge will probably be all right for us, though. He's just a little too understanding of defendants for my blood."

Alec got up and began getting dressed. "We'll get good experts to tear them apart. Juries won't want to believe Maine anyway."

"You act as if something could go wrong."

"You just never know what these shrinks are likely to come up with on Jackson. Next thing you know, they'll be claiming Jackson was under the control of a foreign government or voodoo or something."

Stephanie laughed. "They also might claim the moon is made of green cheese. No one could possibly believe that. Okay, why would a foreign government want Gene Hardacre killed?" Alec shrugged his shoulders. "I just don't understand why you're so uptight about this case," Stephanie added.

"There's a lot riding on it," Alec said.

Alec tied his tie, put on his suit coat and his overcoat. Stephanie was still naked in bed. "I always love these Tuesdays with you, Alec," Stephanie said. She had given him the perfect opportunity to tell her he loved her. He had never said those priceless words to her before. She waited.

"I look forward to them, too," he said. "See you back at the office." He leaned over the bed and kissed her. The kiss felt good, but she felt let down. He was just talking about divorcing his wife and being with her. Did that mean he loved her and wanted to marry her? She knew she loved him. Minutes before, she felt he had given himself to her. Now, she wasn't sure she was anymore than just his employee and sex-buddy. There was a coldness about him. He missed the cue. Were all men that frustrating, or just the men she picked? Stephanie got out of the bed, went to the bathroom to urinate, freshen her make-up again and dress. She needed to get back to the office.

CHAPTER 15

There were six judges in the Montgomery County District Court. The chances were something like one in thirty-six that Judge Hodge would get both the Jackson and Conley cases. But it happened—when they spun the wheel for Ohio v. Conley, Judge Hodge's Division Four came up again. When Jack Maine found it had been assigned to Division Four, he made his way to that court quickly; Chris would be appearing shortly for advisement of her rights, arraignment and bond. They had had extensive conversations where he had intimated she was not in extreme peril. Now, she was in jail. Chris was bound to be upset.

When he got there, Chris was sitting in the jury box with a female deputy sheriff standing about ten feet away. She was dressed in an orange, prison jumpsuit with the words MONTGOMERY COUNTY emblazoned in black on her back. Her blonde hair was disheveled. She had no makeup on. She looked as though she hadn't slept. On the other side of her sat four male prisoners guarded by two male deputy sheriffs. Two were black, two were white. They were all heavily tattooed. They reeked of cigarettes, sweat and stinky underarms.

Jack approached her in the jury box. The deputy, who had known Jack for years, allowed him access to her.

"Can you get me out of this hell hole? I'm going to lose my job if I can't get out of here. When they brought the hookers in last night, they looked at me and said they couldn't wait—couldn't wait to have their tongue in my pussy. They meant it. Get me out of here."

"I'll try to get your bond lowered," Jack said. "However, I'm sorry to tell you this, Chris, but I talked to the judge just a few minutes ago, and she says she's been ordered by Presiding Judge Carl Kessler to suspend you without pay until the disposition of your case is determined."

That shook her up even more. She hadn't understood why she had to turn herself in last night with a new bond of two hundred thousand dollars. "I'm not going to be able to pay your fee past the retainer if I'm not working and I'm locked up in here," she said angrily. "Why did they arrest me yesterday anyway? I had already made bond."

"The Montgomery County Grand Jury handed down a charge of first-degree murder on you; it was filed with the court yesterday. It alleges that you killed Burt with malice and premeditation."

"That's outrageous and they know it!" she screamed. "I'm being set up!"

People sitting in the gallery stared at Chris and Jack.

"Counselor, I'll have to take her back to the jail if she doesn't quiet down. The judge will be out in minutes," the deputy warned him.

Jack grabbed Chris' hand. She was shaking, but his touch seemed to soothe her. "Chris, you must keep it together. I'll try to get the bond lowered. Can you come up with twenty thousand to make the bond? You get credit for the money you've already posted."

"I don't know. I'll have to talk to my mother and father. It'll take almost all the money they have. My life is over. I'll never work in the courts again. Even if I get out of this, everyone will always know that I was charged with first-degree murder. I'll always be guilty."

"We must take things one step at a time. You have a chance of winning this on pretrial motions for the bad search." Jack knew that in reality, the chances of that were slim unless they were able to secure Hardin Long's tape. Guteman had always lied his way out of bad searches, and the invisible Mr. Long had disappeared despite Joe's efforts to reach him. He had not called back, as he had promised.

"If that is true, why did Burt tell me that cops nearly always get away with bad searches by lying?"

"Burt was telling you the truth. But you don't look like a drug dealer or a hooker. You have more credibility than the average defendant. For god sakes, Chris, you work in the courts. Hodge knows that, and he also knows Guteman. He was a defense attorney at one time, and Guteman's reputation precedes him."

Unimpressed, unfazed and unsoothed, Chris went on hysterically. "I've just been charged with first-degree murder? Are they going to ask for the death penalty like they did for Avery?"

"I haven't heard any mention of that," Jack assured her.

"At least he got to kill someone. I didn't do a thing," Chris said wildly, her voice again escalating.

"We'll ask for a speedy trial and get a motions hearing in a week or two."

"My life is over and I know it."

"Something very good will come out of this. Trust me."

"I trust you. It just feels like shit. First, I lose my boyfriend, and now I'm blamed for it."

"I know, but we'll get through this," Jack said. He thought how much different her case was than others. Most of the time, his clients were guilty and all he could do was try to create reasonable doubt. This time his client was innocent. He'd find it hard to live with himself if anything bad happened to Chris.

Judge Hodge's bailiff and court reporter entered the courtroom. The judge would soon follow. "All rise. This Honorable Court is now in session. Judge John Hodge presiding. You may be seated."

"Good morning, ladies and gentlemen. I'm going to call a case that comes into this court by way of indictment. Call People versus Conley. Will counsel please enter their appearances?"

"James Brodan for the People, Your Honor."

"Jack Maine for the Defendant, Chris Conley."

"This matter comes here for advisement and arraignment. The defendant has been charged with Possession of Dangerous Drugs and Murder in the First Degree. Do you wish the charges read to you, Miss Conley?"

"No, Your Honor," Jack said. "We'll waive the reading of the indictment and enter pleas of Not Guilty to both charges. We ask the matter be set for trial within ninety days, and also ask for an expedited hearing on a motion to suppress evidence. We have reason to believe that such a motion will be dispositive of both charges," Jack said.

Brodan looked at Maine incredulously. He had never heard such a bold statement by a defense attorney on a murder case. Serious charges usually leave defense attorneys helpless. "We have no objection to that, Your Honor," Brodan said confidently.

"We would like to address the issue of bond immediately, Your Honor," Jack said.

"As you're aware," Hodge said, "bond in this matter has been raised from thirty-five thousand to two hundred thousand. This is a first-degree murder indictment that the people of Montgomery County have leveled against Ms.

Conley. Is there any reason why I should change it at this time?"

"There is, Your Honor. As the court is well aware, Ms. Conley has been a reporter in Judge Jeffers' division for years. She has many contacts in the Dayton area, including her parents. She originally made bond on charges of Criminally Negligent Homicide and Possession. She has not chosen to run or evade the court in any way. In fact, yesterday afternoon, at the request of the sheriff, she turned herself in. I have been retained to represent her. I have known her for a number of years. Her word and promise to appear are good."

Brodan stood. "Your Honor, I'm glad Mr. Maine can assure the Court that her word is good. He would probably be willing to post her bond then, too. We think that two hundred thousand on a first-degree murder charge is reasonable."

"So does the Court, Mr. Maine. I appreciate that Ms. Conley has been a reliable citizen until this point. This, however, is an indictment. The charges are extremely serious. Motion for Reduction of Bond is denied. What I can do is give you an expedited hearing on your motion to suppress evidence, Mr. Maine. The matter will be set for February fifth. The defendant will be remanded to the custody of the sheriff."

"Can't you do something?" she whispered to Jack.

He couldn't; he was powerless. The wheels of justice had just turned a quarter turn and Judge John Hodge had just squashed her like a bug under them. "I'll call your mother and see what she can do," Jack said. "Otherwise, you'll have to cool your heels until next week. We'll be over to see you."

The deputy moved over to put the cuffs on Chris and take her back to the jail. She glanced at Jack with one more forlorn look as she passed through the door.

CHAPTER 16

Thursday, February 1—4:00 P.M.
Montgomery County Jail

The dreams were vivid: the black, horn-rimmed glasses and the hypodermic needle, then the shots, and the blood running down the gutter into the barrel, the dead eyes staring into his soul.

Avery lurched awake just as the guard approached his cell. It was February, snow on the ground, cold and gray outside and yet, he had sweat on his forehead. The door screeched open as the guard said, "Jackson, your attorney is here."

Avery righted himself. He wiped the perspiration from his forehead with his shirtsleeve. He rose. It seemed to him he had just walked the one hundred feet from his cellblock to the Contact Visitation Room. He must be mistaken. He hadn't seen anyone the entire day. Why the hell was his attorney there?

Both Jack and Yolanda were waiting for him when he arrived at the visitation room. "What's going on?" Jack asked.

"Nothing much. I was just sleeping. The dreams are driving me crazy." Avery yawned.

Jack and Yolanda looked at Avery, suggesting silently that he begin the conversation. He didn't.

"Avery," Yolanda said, "you left a message at the office this morning saying it was urgent that you speak with us this afternoon."

Avery sat still for a moment, attempting to orient himself. "I did? Oh, yeah—I did."

Yolanda and Jack looked at one another.

"Jim Rosato was here on Tuesday," Avery said. "He claims he has an anonymous benefactor who's offering me three hundred thousand dollars if I will allow the Rosatos to represent me."

"Such largesse." Yolanda said. "What's the catch?"

"I have to plead guilty to first-degree murder."

"That all?" Jack asked. "How much is his take?"

"One hundred thousand."

"What are the Rosatos going to do to earn it?" Jack asked.

"They're going to have a cup of coffee with Alec Hunter and ask him to drop the death penalty request."

"What if Hunter won't drop it?"

"Then, I get a hundred thousand and they get three hundred thousand for trial and appeal."

"Let me guess," Jack said, "the one condition is they get to control the expert testimony. In fact, they'll even pay for the expert testimony."

"How did you know?" Avery asked.

"Because we know the CIA, FBI or DEA bugged my office, and now we have a source who feels to me like renegade CIA. Joe's following up on it as we speak."

"CIA?!" Avery gasped incredulously. "How could it be the CIA? I've never been involved with the CIA in my life, and they don't do domestic cases. It's gotta be the FBI or DEA. It couldn't be them, though. I've never bought more than a gram of coke or an ounce of grass."

"Ever sell," Jack asked.

"Never. Nooo….it couldn't be the CIA. You guys know they can't do domestic stuff."

"That didn't bother the Watergate burglars."

"True. Who's your source?"

"A guy with a phoney alias. That's why I think he is CIA. Spooky cloak-and-dagger stuff—maybe a double agent. Says he's an independent."

"What's his alias?"

"Right now, it would be better if you didn't know. He's attempting to extort us. Strange things happen to people in jail, and right now, the less you know, the better. Did they tell you who this generous benefactor was?" Jack asked.

"Of course not. He said the offer would be withdrawn if the benefactor were revealed. I told Rosato I thought he was acting unethically—that he had a conflict of interest because the interests of the benefactor might be at odds with my interests."

"What did he say to that?" Yolanda asked.

"He blew me off. That was the deal—take it or leave it."

"What are you going to do?" Yolanda asked, upset with the possibility of losing the Jackson case. She was leaving her job at the public defender's office in order to work with Jack on the case. She was also feeling a growing attachment to Avery.

"I told them I'd think about it and let them know today," Avery said. The cobwebs in his mind had cleared.

"Three hundred thousand is a lot of money," Jack said. "If you had the money, you could put your kids through college and have a little nest egg should you get out after doing twenty years. That's assuming Hunter will drop his request for the death penalty."

"I know. What do you think I should do?" Avery asked.

"That's entirely up to you," Jack said. "You do what you think is best for you."

"Tell me this," Avery said, "how much do you think this case will cost?"

"Probably, a hundred thousand dollars. Avery, we've already spent all the money you've given us. Dr. Offen is going to cost us at least twelve thousand. With office expenses, money for Joe and Yolanda, your retainer is burned."

"How the hell are you going to represent me?" Avery asked. "You're going to lose your ass."

Jack shrugged. "Hopefully, you can get some more money out of the black community."

"Most of the black people in the community are trying to disassociate themselves from me. It's not politically correct for them to be contributing to the defense of a nigger who shoots the sheriff on national television."

"If you take the deal, your defense would be paid for, including the expert witnesses, and you'd have money left over. Plus, the CIA, if they are behind this, would bring in the best experts to testify on your behalf."

Yolanda's skin had turned from brown to reddish-brown. "I'm going to tell you exactly what's going to happen if you do this deal," she said, the vein popping out the side of her neck and forehead. "You're going to the state pen, and you'll have a needle in your arm within five years. But it's up to you."

"I've thought about it. I've thought long and hard about it. I'm sure a lot of people in my shoes would take it."

"Avery," Jack said, "there's probably never been anyone in your shoes. This is a one-of-a-kind case. If we lose this trial, and you resent us or are mad at yourself for not taking this deal, then I want out right now. I want this to be very clear. I do not want to represent you if you have any second thoughts. You just need to let me know because I have Dr. Offen coming into town tomorrow to begin his evaluation of you. I'm sure the Rosatos' benefactor doesn't want anything to do with him. I'll need to call Offen and ask him to refund the retainer that has already been sent to him. There will be no hard feelings on our part."

Yolanda said nothing. *That was easy for Jack to say*, she thought. She doubted that he meant it.

"I'm not going to do their deal," Avery said. "I know they'll sell me out. The Rosatos and their psychiatrists will argue to the jury I never formed a criminal intent at the time of the shooting. The jury will be out about two hours and they'll convict me. What I'm concerned with is the money. For you to be able to get paid on this case and avoid financial disaster, you'll have to get me out of prison somehow. Getting me sent to the state hospital for life doesn't get it either. I might as well be dead. I can never pay you like that. I must be working to pay you. Even then, it'll take years. I have no doubt what *I* want to do. I want the two of you to represent me to the best of your ability. Just so I know I have your commitment if this turns into a financial disaster," Avery said.

"You have our commitment," Jack said. Jack and Yolanda looked at one another. Yolanda nodded. The trial was in seventy days. Yolanda would be leaving the public defender's office soon. She had saved enough money to get her through a couple of months. Jack had assured her he had enough to pay her for a couple of months from the retainer money on the Jackson and Conley cases. Certainly, other business would be coming in, they hoped. They weren't about to turn their backs on what they'd started, but they were all operating on faith.

"How are your spirits, Avery?" Jack asked. "Has anyone visited you besides us?"

"My kids have been here a couple of times. Dr. Gilmour was here for the psychological evaluation. Otherwise, I haven't had one person visit. I guess you find out who your friends really are at times like these, and I'm finding out that I have no friends at all."

"Dr. Offen and Dr. Gilmour will be working with you this weekend. I want you to get plenty of rest for that," Jack said.

"Get some rest," Yolanda said.

"All I *can* do around here is rest, and be alone with my thoughts. They drive me crazy."

All three of them stood. Jack and Yolanda shook Avery's hand.

"We'll be with you," Yolanda said.

"We'll give your our best," Jack added.

Thursday—6:00 P.M.
Dayton International Airport

When Dr. Marcus Offen got off the plane, Jack was waiting at baggage claim. He recognized Dr. Offen only because he had seen his picture on the jacket of one of his books, *By Reason Of,* about the criminal mind. Tall, clean-shaven, sinewy, athletic and tanned, he did not look like a psychologist. Nearly fifty, his prematurely-gray hair contrasted nicely with his tan. Whereas, Dr. Gilmour looked the role with his salt-and-pepper goatee, herringbone jacket with leather elbows and black, reading glasses, Dr. Offen looked like a middle-aged model for a ski magazine.

"Dr. Offen," Jack said, "it's my pleasure."

"Jack, I'm Marcus. Good to meet you. If we're going to be working together on this case, it's Marcus. Got it?"

Jack liked him immediately. He didn't talk with the phony propriety of a psychologist. "How was your trip?"

"Sucked. There was snow in Chicago, and O'Hare was its usual pain-in-the-ass self. Otherwise it was fine. I'm glad to be here. I've never been to Dayton before. How's the skiing?"

"Our biggest slope is probably like the bunny run at Keystone or Copper Mountain," Jack said, referring to two popular Colorado resorts. "My wife and I get up there occasionally."

"When this is over," Marcus offered, "you'll have to come out for a vacation. Sounds like you're going to need it."

Marcus grabbed his bag, along with his video-recording equipment and tripod. When they walked into the winter air to the parking lot, they could feel the damp cold of the Ohio winter. "It's this cold in Denver, but not this damp. I'm not sure I'd like it here," Marcus commented. "People in Denver start getting suicidal when they have about three days in a row like this."

"You might be suicidal when you get done with this case. It's got a little bit of everything. Did you get a chance to read Dr. Gilmour's evaluation?" Jack asked as they went through the tollbooth and out the road toward Interstate I75 and downtown.

"I did."

"What did you think?"

"That your client, Avery, is in some deep trouble. I don't need to tell you how difficult it is to prevail with an insanity defense. Juries just hate to hear it, no matter how crazy the guy is. I've done a bunch of them. I've documented them in my book. One, in fact, involved a South Vietnamese soldier who killed his wife and didn't remember it. I must warn you, I've been successful on less than half of them, just so you know what you're getting into—hiring me is a ticket to failure more often than not."

"I know about your cases. Gilmour filled me in on them. And I know about the odds here. We did the research. Something like two defendants out of a thousand are found NGRI, and those two are so crazy that the DA usually agrees to the insanity.."

"I'm surprised the numbers are that high. Those figures are even odder when you realize that about a third of the people in the prison population have serious mental illnesses. In Colorado, we have two whole prisons, plus the state hospital, full of mentally-ill people convicted of crimes."

"There've been some new developments in this case since we sent you the materials and Dr. Gilmour's report," Jack said.

"Oh?"

"We found bugs in my office, and we believe we can trace them to the FBI, DEA or CIA. Then, some guy called us and attempted to extort fifty thousand dollars from us for a tape."

"The CIA?"

"Yeah, I think so. Could be FBI or DEA, but it doesn't feel like them. They bugged my office and the office of the attorney who originally represented Jackson, and now that attorney is dead. They've since gone to the two biggest shysters in Dayton and offered them four hundred thousand dollars to throw the case, or at least allow their experts to present the sanity testimony. The stuff that's happened on this case is just unprecedented. Spooks trying to bribe lawyers. Mobbed-up businessmen in Chicago wiretapping my phones, a dead lawyer, lying cop and that's only half of it. There's just a whole lot of stuff we don't understand. We're looking to you to help us unravel the case."

"What makes you think we're not going to be killed if we know too much?"

"I can't promise you we won't."

"Do I need to be packing a gun while I'm here?" Marcus asked, not sure if he was joking or not.

"It wouldn't be a bad idea."

"The CIA stuff adds a whole new twist. It's actually to your benefit. But first, let me ask you this. You're a defense attorney who has practiced for a number of years, right?" Offen asked.

"Correct," Jack said.

"What's your intuition about the case?"

"I don't think Avery knew what he was doing when he killed the sheriff. We think he's telling the truth."

"That's what Dr. Gilmour says. I get the feeling Gilmour is a pretty conservative guy?"

"Very. If you want an honest opinion, and not the opinion of a whore, you turn to Gilmour."

"Good. This is really interesting about the CIA. It starts making some sense out of this case."

"How so? I don't see much that makes sense."

"Because a great deal of material has been declassified lately under the Freedom of Information Act about CIA and mind control. Frank Sinatra and Laurence Harvey did a movie back in the '60s called the *Manchurian Candidate* that won an Oscar. It was made from a book by Richard Condon about a soldier who fought in Korea, who was brainwashed/programmed to kill the President, but was amnesic for the programming. The controllers used a playing card as the cue to put him into action. Nobody really believed that such a thing could be real. People believed it was just Hollywood stuff. The fact of the matter was, the CIA, Army, Navy, and Air Force had projects going on at the time of the movie and afterward, that were designed to program people who already had multiple personality disorders to become spies, couriers and perhaps killers. The projects were given names like 'MKULTRA,' 'BLUEBIRD' and 'ARTICHOKE.' These projects are on the Internet and in industry books and articles, but hardly anyone knows about them. They aren't mainstream knowledge yet.

"The documents that have been released, with an occasional exception, do not name the subjects of these experiments. The government used prostitutes, prisoners, soldiers and mental patients—people who were vulnerable. They did so by means of CIA-funded projects concocted by distinguished psychiatrists and psychologists within respected universities and foundations. The psychiatrists developed the means to create amnesia, new identities and access codes—stuff that sounds bizarre to the average person, as well as the mental health professional. The scary thing about these experiments is that all the people involved in them had no clue they were being programmed."

"How did they do that?"

"Unethically, of course. They'd use depressed people who were hospitalized and tell them the shock treatments they were giving them were for their care—never mentioning experimentation, of course. They'd tell prisoners and soldiers they were coming in for a routine physical and give them a drink with some Phenobarbital in it. It would knock them out, then they'd subject these people to mind-control techniques."

"For instance?" Jack asked, trying to appear unfazed by what he was hearing.

"Multiple sessions of regressive hypnosis, solitary confinement, truth serums like sodium amytal and scopolamine. Some were given LSD, mescaline and other hallucinogens and then subjected to traumatic events or mind-control techniques. Some had electrodes put in their brains, and others were given massive doses of electroshock to the point where they had no recollection of their childhood or history. The CIA developed techniques to eliminate the original personality and replace it or supplement it with another personality."

"So, they get somebody high, hypnotize or give him or her electroshock. It happens all of the time, doesn't it? That certainly wouldn't make someone legally insane."

"Not like this. This was far more extensive," Marcus said. "The goal was to take a person who was psychologically fragile because of prior abuse or trauma in his or her life and then destroy part of his consciousness, and program another personality into that space in his psyche with directions for him to carry out some task upon cue. Then, they'd create an amnesic barrier for this programming and send the subject into the world. The subjects would have no recollection of the programming or the task, or its execution. The psychiatrists created another personality within the subject. In the case of a programmed killer, it was the personality of a conscious-less psychopath—sort of an automaton—who'd stop at nothing to carry out his mission."

"So, how does this fit into an insanity defense?" Jack asked.

"For sanity purposes, if the main personality has no knowledge or control over the programmed personality, then the person would be legally insane because he would not know right from wrong and would not be able to appreciate the wrongfulness of his acts. Indeed, he would have no knowledge of the acts."

"We have no evidence whatever that happened to Avery, and if you try to explain it to a jury in Montgomery County, Ohio, they'll laugh you right out of here."

"No doubt about it. If that's what happened to Avery, we'll have to show it on video. What's more, you'll have to back it up with independent records from the service or from CIA files. We'll have to show how he was programmed, and then delve through his unconscious into his other personality to reenact the shooting of the sheriff."

"Interesting you should say that, Marcus. It just so happens that all of Avery Jackson's service records have disappeared," Jack said.

"Even more suspicious. You'll have to find independent evidence that corroborates any uncovering work we do here."

"What's the plan for the weekend?" Jack asked.

"I'll go to the jail and spend Friday with him. I want to get to know him. I'll talk with him most of the day. I'll make it a marathon like it usually is when these guys are programmed. The goal is to try to get them to start breaking down. If he's a faker, I'll certainly know it within a few hours, if not the first few minutes. If he's authentic, I'll do hypnosis on Saturday and start moving into his unconscious. If at any time I have even a hint he's faking a trance or trying to con me, I'll stop the interview immediately. If he looks real, on Sunday I'll do hypnosis again to access the part of him that killed the sheriff. I'm flying out of here on Monday night. Tell me, what kind of guy is Avery?"

Jack filled Marcus in on Avery's history.

"And you can find no motive for the killing?" Marcus asked.

"None, really. He'd worked on the campaign of the sheriff's opponent in the election last November, but Avery barely knew Hardacre. Avery has no criminal record and was a pacifist. What he did was out of character."

"I read his psychological evaluation. He's either a very clever faker or he's a dissociative personality. I'll figure it out."

"What makes him look like a dissociative personality?" Jack asked.

"It's clear he had an abusive childhood and was probably post-traumatic when he went into the service. That's just the type of guy they'd want—someone who is very bright and makes a good appearance, but who's vulnerable. People who have been programmed are typically forgetful, have gaps in memory and judgment, but are loyal and capable of carrying out orders. It sounds like he'd fit the bill."

"Save your analysis," Jack said, "my wife will feel cheated if she doesn't get to hear it. She's meeting us at an Italian restaurant. I assume you'll allow us to take you to dinner?"

"Sure. We need to get to know each other. We need to believe in each other in order to make this work. I need to believe in you as a lawyer as much as you need to believe in me as a psychologist."

"This should be quite a journey," Jack said.

"Going into the mind always is. It's imperative you understand mind control and multiple personality as well as I do by the time you try the case. You have to believe in this completely or you'll never make a jury believe in it."

Thursday—10:30 P.M.
Jack and Marci's Condominium

Jack and Marci had dropped Dr. Offen off at his hotel after drinks and dinner. Now they lay in each other's arms, deep in thought. When Marcus Offen had talked to them about CIA mind-control experiments, it reaffirmed for them the danger they were most surely in. There were many powerful, dangerous forces at work here and three dead bodies.

"I don't want you to be among the casualties. I'd feel a lot better if you'd keep Joe, and his gun, with you at all times," Marci said. "You're not going to make much of a father and husband to me if you're dead."

"Are we in a financial position to put Joe on full-time?" Jack asked.

"No, but I think we should do it. It'll take all the money we have. I've been looking at getting a line of credit at the bank using our condo as collateral. I think we're going to need it for operating expenses. Do you fully realize the situation we've gotten ourselves into?" Marci asked.

"No, and neither do you. No one understands yet. It could get much worse."

"We're looking down into the abyss. Chris Conley can't make bail and has lost her job. We're not guaranteed another dime from her. Avery is tapped out. We haven't tried either case, and we're already running out of money. We're going to have to find some new clients or we're out of business."

"I just have a feeling this is going to work out. There are just too many secrets and hidden agendas for everybody to be successful at keeping them all tucked away forever."

"I hope you're right, Counselor. I gotta say the last three weeks have been the most exciting of my life. I thought I would die of fright when Guteman almost caught me down in that basement. That kid, Darnell, saved my life. We owe him, Jack."

"Hopefully, we'll get a chance to repay him." Jack squeezed Marci hard and kissed her. "Let's get some sleep. I have a feeling we're going to need all the rest we can get."

"I love you, Jack," Marci said.

"I love you, too," Jack responded. "One other thing, Marci, please make sure we have a few thousand dollars cash around the office for Joe."

"Why?"

"Just in case Hardin Long calls again."

Marci sighed, then giggled. "What if Dick Draggin calls?"

Jack laughed. "Then give him the money. We need that tape."

"We don't have the money."

"So, we'll have to borrow it."

They kissed and fell asleep in each other's arms.

CHAPTER 17

Friday, February 2
Montgomery County Jail

Avery was anxious with anticipation when the deputy came to his cell to tell him he had a professional visitor. He had already been awake for a couple of hours and eaten breakfast. Like Jack, Avery had an inaccurate fantasy of Dr. Marcus Offen. He thought he would be an erudite sooth, full of arcane truths with a beard, goatee and black reading-glasses.

Dr. Offen was waiting for Avery in the Contact Visitation Room. A videocam was already set up on a tripod. A red light was blinking on it when Avery walked into the room.

Marcus rose when Avery entered and shook Avery's hand firmly. "Dr. Offen, I'm Avery Jackson."

"Pleased to meet you. I'm Marcus. We're already recording, Avery. It's necessary that everything be videotaped so there isn't any confusion about what all we said."

"I understand," Avery said. "As you probably know, I'm a lawyer. I'm pretty much aware of how it all works."

"So I understand. Then you're aware that everything you say to me is confidential unless Mr. Maine elects to use my testimony in his defense of the case against you. In that case, everything you say to me can be used for or against you, but only on the issue of your sanity, not to prove you shot Mr. Hardacre. Is that clear?"

"Certainly."

"I have read Dr. Gilmour's report. But it's necessary I get a history on you," said Marcus. "Let's start at the beginning."

They went through his early childhood and developmental years—the abusive, alcoholic father and controlling mother, his dating and sexual history, his marriage, family and how he was coping with his situation. Additionally, Dr. Offen gave Avery a Rorschach Inkblot Test, and had him draw pictures of a house, tree, person and mother with child. He then gave him a series of achromatic pictures of people doing things called a Thematic Apperception Test. Avery was supposed to tell a story about what the people were thinking, how they got into their current situation and how it all ended.

Dr. Offen learned from the tests that Avery Jackson was an attached man with conscience and capable of empathy. He suffered from a post-traumatic disorder and was fairly anxious. He was depressed over losses in his life. Dr. Offen found it significant that in two of the inkblots he showed Avery, he saw people who had a devil lurking within them. He certainly found it interesting that when Avery looked at the thematic card of a woman sitting on the floor next to a gun, Avery saw her as just having shot someone, dropped the gun to the floor and sat despondently to wait for the police. When the police got there, she didn't know what they wanted with her.

Avery liked Dr. Offen's style—completely unassuming, human and non-judgmental. Dr. Offen gave him the feeling they were partners in a discovery mission. It was late in the day when Dr. Offen began to hone in on three areas: Avery's tormenting dreams, his experience in Vietnam and the shooting of Gene Hardacre. Dr. Offen found it most significant that Avery had large memory gaps about his experience in Vietnam. Avery remembered his basic training and training as a Ranger. He remembered he had a series of inoculations at Fort Bragg and then more shots in 'Nam. He thought they were immunizations for disease.

"Undoubtedly, many of them were," Offen said. "During Dr. Gilmour's evaluation, you talked about a psychiatrist you saw both at Fort Bragg and in Vietnam. Did you have any psychiatric problems before you left for 'Nam?"

"None that I know of," Avery said. "I always did very well in school and performed well on jobs I held. I don't know why I was asked to see him. But then in the Army, a lot of times a person couldn't tell why he was ordered to do something. You didn't ask questions, you just did it. Anyway, there were just a few of us who saw this weird-looking psychiatrist with black, horn-rimmed glasses. I know I got some shots from him. Other than that, I don't remember much about him, or how much time I spent with him. All I know is I saw the man again in 'Nam and back stateside when I exited. I remember him asking me how I felt upon exiting, and I told him I was really fucked up. He asked what I meant. I told him I remembered killing some gooks—excuse me, that's what we called them over there—in a firefight. He didn't seem particularly interested in my killing any North Vietnamese soldiers in a firefight. He wanted to know if I had killed anyone else, or seen any others killed. I told him I didn't remember, but I had a vague feeling I had. I just couldn't remember much of what happened over there, except the firefight and my going down the tunnels. They used me as a tunnel rat at first. Then, as far as I can remember, that stopped."

"Apparently you were decorated numerous times?" Offen asked.

"I have a couple of silver stars in oak-leaf clusters and some other commendations. I have a purple heart, but everyone over there had a purple heart. I know a guy who got a purple heart just because he got a case of clap that was so bad they had to clean his penis out with little razor blades."

Dr. Offen smiled. "Gilmour reports that the psychiatrist you saw made no referrals for follow-up, psychiatric care when you exited."

"He just said my symptoms were the same as most guys coming out of the Special Forces and not to worry about it. He may have mentioned going to the VA Hospital, but I don't remember."

"Did you seek out any psychological services after your exit?"

"No, but I should have. I've been depressed off and on. During and after the DiSalvo mess, I could have really used them. DiSalvo was the case that got me voted out of office."

"Jack filled me in. It must have been a tough time."

"Yeah, my life has sort of gone down the toilet in the last two years. This is just the final kick in the balls."

"Tell me what you remember about shooting the sheriff."

"I don't remember anything. It's a complete blank."

"What *is* the last thing you remember?"

"I remember smelling coffee that morning after I finished my Evidence class. It was really cold outside and the smell made me feel warmer. It reminded me of the coffee we used to have early in the morning in 'Nam. I don't even know how I got to the hotel. All I remember is these guys grabbing me in the ballroom, and the sheriffs throwing me in the patrol car and calling me a nigger."

"Don't you find it strange that you have such enormous gaps in your memory? You remember very little of your war experience, yet you have all sorts of awards and commendations. You kill someone, and the period of time in which you did it, is lost to you."

"The doctor with the glasses told me it wasn't at all unusual for the guys who've been involved in heavy fighting to not remember a lot of it; I believed him. I have this friend here in Dayton who also fought with me over there and he claims there're a lot of things he doesn't remember about it. It apparently doesn't bother him."

"Does it bother you?"

"Not until now."

"Did your wife complain about your being forgetful?"

"Constantly. She thought I was a real pain in the ass. She attributed it to my being an 'absent-minded professor.'"

"Okay, about your dreams. Dr. Gilmour says you have a chronic problem with recurrent and intrusive dreams?"

"Yeah, they drive me nuts. I've had one with the misshapen people having sex since I was a kid. After I got back from Vietnam, the man in the dream became a gargoyle. He had this huge dick with warts and lumps all over it. The gargoyle keeps screaming at this leper woman that he's going to give it to her. She sucks on it and protests as if she hates it, and then she comes while he comes in her mouth. The semen runs from her mouth and she's satisfied. It makes me sick to my stomach." Avery sat there looking exhausted. He had been doing the evaluation the entire day, and now he had to deal with the dreams. He was ready to quit and get some food and rest.

Offen ploughed ahead. "That's a hell of a graphic dream. What about it makes you sick to your stomach?"

"The woman is a fraud. The whole time she is acting as if she doesn't like this ugly man, and she does. She defrauds him. She acts one way when she really wants something else. She has a hidden agenda, and it is up to him to figure it out. Of course, it wouldn't be unusual for a woman to treat a man like that. I feel kind of that way about my wife."

"Oh, I wasn't aware of that. What kind of woman is she?"

"Kind of like the woman in my dream in the sense that what you see is not what you get. She was the sort who'd give me a blowjob before we got married, but after I said 'I do,' her real intention was to cut my dick off, not put it in her mouth. She'd act one way when her intentions were really different."

"Dr. Gilmour says you have other dreams."

"Yeah, but since I met with him and told him about them I've been able to put a couple of the pieces together. There is this grim-looking man in a white coat with black, horn-rimmed glasses and a hypodermic needle. The needle is what scares me the most. Anyhow, it seems to me, the sterile-looking psychiatrist with the Special Forces' unit is that guy. I don't know why that son-of-a-bitch scares me so, but he does in my dreams. He didn't scare me in the service—at least not that I can remember."

Avery stopped talking for a while. He looked pale and ashen.

"Is there something wrong?" Dr. Offen asked.

"The next dream is the one that really bothers me," Avery said as he took a deep breath. "I hear a gunshot and then see red and green blood running down downspouts into a barrel. The backs of peoples' heads are blown completely off, but I can see their eyes. It's their eyes that wake me as they peer into my soul."

"Can you see their faces? Are they white, black, Asian?"

"That's a good question. I think most of the time they're Asian, but sometimes they're white or black. It varies."

"Okay. I'll return first thing in the morning. Dr. Gilmour will be with me. We're going to do hypnosis. Have you ever been hypnotized before?"

"Not that I can remember."

"It's really nothing more than a state of relaxation involving your body and mind. It allows us to probe into your unconscious. It may or may not work. We need to have your permission to do it."

"It makes me nervous. I'm afraid of what you'll find—of what might be in there. I have this notion of who I am, and I don't want it disturbed."

"That's typical, but in your case, I believe it's imperative we go ahead and find out how this happened to you and why you shot this man."

"Obviously, I'm going to go ahead. I'm just telling you that it's scary as hell."

"Understandably," Dr. Offen said as he finished packing up his videocam.

Offen stood up and pressed the button for the guard to let him out of the visitation room. As the door opened and slammed, metal-to-metal against the door jam, he could see Avery jump. "The doors slamming open and shut drive you crazy, don't they?"

"Yeah, the loud noises just cut into me. I hate them."

"See you tomorrow," Dr. Offen said.

CHAPTER 18

Saturday, February 3
Montgomery County Jail

The videocam was running and Dr. Gilmour was there with his medical bag. Dr. Offen first did a series of relaxation exercises by having Avery concentrate on each part of his body. Avery's eyes were closed, and he was as deeply relaxed as he'd ever been since he was put in jail. Dr. Offen began his hypnotic induction of Avery in a melodic, gentle, cadenced tone.

"You are sitting in a green field with no one around. You're in this wonderful, euphoric state of relaxation. The sun is bright, but your eyes are shaded. The grass is emerald green. There is a clear pond not far away. You are able to see into the pond. The breeze is gentle. The field is full of beautiful daisies. There is one daisy that draws your attention. It has unusually big, beautiful petals. You're transfixed by it and its delicacy and beauty. You look at it, stare at it and ponder it. Daisy, daisy, daisy, beautiful daisy, lovely daisy. As you're looking at it, it's as if you can see every cell in it, and you're looking right through it and its fabulous, yet simple beauty. Daisy, daisy, daisy. As you're looking at it, you grow more and more relaxed. Flower, flower, flower, flower, flower, flower, flower, flower. You feel yourself going deeper and deeper into this daisy. Deeper and deeper, deeper and deeper. The power of your penetration of this beautiful flower is overwhelming. You are now lost in the daisy. Daisy, daisy, daisy, flower, flower, flower. It is lost in you, and you're at one with it and with yourself. And, if you have reached the point where your arms and body are so heavy you cannot move, just move your index finger."

Avery moved his index finger slightly. His eyelids fluttered, but stayed closed.

Avery was in a trance. Now, Offen needed to take him deeper, and regress him to his time in Vietnam, and then forward again to the shooting. "Avery, you're going deeper and deeper into this wonderful state of relaxed oneness with this flower as you melt into it. Deeper and deeper, deeper and deeper, deeper and deeper. Deeper and deeper, flower, flower, flower."

So effective was Offen's trance induction technique that Dr. Gilmour felt himself slipping away. He had to pinch himself to keep from drifting off.

"Now, we're going to count the years backward starting with this year. You're still in this wonderful state of oneness." Dr. Offen counted backward year after year until he reached 1970. The process seemed interminable and had the effect of further regressing Avery into his unconscious.

"It's 1970, and you're at basic training. Can you see the name of the base at the gate?"

"Yes, it's very clear. Fort Bragg. I can see the brass letters engraved in stone outside the base. B-R-A-G-G."

"Okay, and now you're with the psychiatrist with the black, horn-rimmed glasses. He has called you into his office. Do you remember his name?"

"Yes. I can see his name on his white coat. It is Breyfogle. B-R-E-Y-F-O-G-L-E."

"What's his first name?"

"A-R-T-H-U-R, Arthur. I can see it so clearly."

"And what happens between the two of you?"

"He is giving me a questionnaire asking about my childhood, my sex life, how I feel about women, my friends, how close I am to my family, whether I ever get depressed—stuff like that. He is sitting there the whole time taking notes. He's just reading off the clipboard. He's a weird, scary-looking man. He gives me the creeps. 'You are ordered to come here tomorrow at 0900 hours, is that clear, Jackson?' he orders."

With the order, Avery's demeanor changed to that of a twenty-five-year-old soldier.

"What is your response to Breyfogle?" Offen asked.

"Yes sir." It was now clear to Offen that the regression was complete. The past was now the present. Avery could hear the 1970 conversations as if they were happening right now.

"You are ordered to go back at 0900 hours, soldier," Dr. Offen said authoritatively. "You are back at 0900 hours. What day of the week is it?"

"It's Tuesday."

"What is Dr. Breyfogle saying to you, Avery?" Dr. Offen asked.

"'Do you want a Coke, Corporal?' 'Yes, I would like a Coke.' I am drinking the Coke. It is really cold. God, this is a good Coke. It's the best Coke I've ever had. It's so hot outside. It's the best Coke I've ever had. I'm feeling very groggy. No, not the needle!" Avery began to hyperventilate and sweat broke out on his head.

"What is happening now, Avery?"

"The sky is dark and the moon is dark," said a robotic voice.

"I believe this is daytime, is it not, Avery? Or are you Avery?" Offen was not sure what was happening. Avery's tone of voice had changed.

"The sky is dark and the moon is dark," the automaton repeated.

"What if the sky were bright and the moon were full, Avery?" Dr. Offen asked. He had a hunch Avery Jackson had switched to a different personality.

The automaton became noticeably anxious. "You can't do that. You are not authorized."

"Yes, I am authorized," Dr. Offen said firmly.

"There are only a few people who are authorized. You are not Garg— you're not authorized."

"And who are those people? Who is Garg?"

"The sky is dark," the automaton exclaimed. The steely cold in his voice was clear. This persona was different—hard, cold, calculating—and it was apparent to both doctors. They looked at one another.

Dr. Offen went on. "Okay, let's move from 1970 forward." Offen took Avery from 1970 up to January of this year. He could see the man's demeanor softening. Avery was coming back. When Offen arrived at January of this year, he drew Avery's attention to January fifteenth. "It is now January fifteenth, in the morning. You are teaching your class. Which class is it?"

"I am teaching Evidence," Avery said.

"What aspect of evidence are you teaching?" Offen asked.

"I'm teaching Hearsay. Marvella Dixon understands. Class is over. I feel bad about teaching and no longer being a judge. The DiSalvo case still hurts. I smell the coffee. I am supposed to meet Garg—" Avery stopped abruptly. A steel door had slammed shut again.

"The sky is dark. The moon is dark," the automaton/robot insisted.

"The sky is *not* dark now, Avery, it is the morning of January fifteenth. It is a very cold day, but it is morning. The sky is not dark. It is light."

"No, it's dark," the automaton said coldly.

"But it's light," Dr. Offen insisted, "and, soldier, you're ordered to tell me what happened on the fifteenth of January this year."

The being shook. He clenched his fists. Offen and Gilmour looked at one another. What should they do now? The doctors could see this was a dangerous man, perhaps ready to pounce on either one of them. There could be no backing off. The truth was more important than anything else, and getting into and becoming a part of Avery's world was the key to getting the truth.

"Soldier, you are *ordered* to tell us what happened on the fifteenth!" Offen yelled in his best drill-sergeant voice.

The automaton righted himself. "No, sir. I can't, sir. I have been ordered not to."

"Okay, soldier, who gave you that order?"

"The sky is dark, the moon is dark."

"No, it's bright outside, soldier. I am your commanding officer, and you're ordered to tell me what happened!"

The automaton again began to shake. He clenched his fists. "No, sir. No, sir. You are not authorized to give me orders about this, sir. The sky is dark and the moon is dark, sir."

Offen was at the door to Avery's past; he just did not have the key. Avery's system had been locked down, and Dr. Offen had to think about withdrawing and regrouping for another attack. "Soldier, if that is the case, I will honor you. I understand I am not authorized. I will be bringing someone in here who is authorized. I can assure you, you will be safe to open your door to him. We are now going to count you forward from January fifteenth until today . . . January fifteen, January sixteen, January seventeen. When we get to February third, you will be in the present, in the beautiful pasture with the clear pond and the flowers, the beautiful daisies. It will be the pasture in which we started our journey. January eighteen, January nineteen."

When Offen got to February third, he said, "Now, Avery, you're back from your journey to that beautiful field. I'm going to count to ten. When I get to ten, you'll be fully conscious and no longer in a trance. You will feel refreshed, as if you had a nap." Offen counted to ten. "You may open your eyes now, Avery."

Avery opened his eyes. It was as if he were awaking from a nap. Tears came to his eyes.

"Do you know why you're crying?" Offen asked.

"I have no idea," Avery said as he wiped the tears away with his shirtsleeve.

"What do you remember of the last few minutes?"

"I remember seeing the name of the psychiatrist with the black, horn-rimmed glasses on his white doctor's jacket."

"Do you remember his name?"

"No."

"Does the name Arthur Breyfogle mean anything to you?"

"Not really. How did I do?" Avery asked like a child.

"You did very well. We just need to do a little more work, and I think we will be finished. You need to get some rest. I would expect you to be tired. Enjoy your lunch."

"I wish I was having lunch with you," Avery said.

Dr. Offen nodded his head in acknowledgement of Avery's wish. "We'll see you later."

Saturday—12 noon
The King's Table Restaurant

Marcus Offen called Jack. He thought it important they meet over lunch to discuss the morning's work and what was needed in the afternoon. Jack wanted the whole team together; they all had a burning curiosity about the hypnosis session. Not only was each of them invested in Avery as a person, but they also each realized his or her jobs, and the viability of Jack Maine and Associates, pretty much depended on the outcome of the Avery Jackson case.

On Saturdays, the King's Table was not very busy. Jeans, sweaters and leather jackets replaced the three-piece suit and white shirt. No one was having a beer or wine this lunch. They were drinking hot drinks—coffee and tea. While Jack's team wanted to hear something from the doctors that would give Avery a shred of hope—something for them to hang their legal hats on—the doctors' interest, on the other hand, was more clinical and scientific. The morning session had left them feeling like two children in a toyshop, allowed to look but not to touch. They had felt so close to opening Avery up, only to have him, or at least part of him, slam a door in their faces.

As they sipped their coffee and tea and ate sandwiches, Dr. Gilmour said, "Marcus, would you tell me what we just witnessed, because I felt it to be quite extraordinary."

"Sounds like your client, Avery, was duped. He's probably had all kinds of mind-control experiments done on him he doesn't even know about. The question is whether they made him a killer. He isn't faking. He's not a psychopath, nor does he have a criminal personality."

"How do you know that?" Jack asked

"My testing yesterday made that clear. And I'm sure that when he switched to that other personality today, it was genuine. I think he's a brilliantly, clinically concocted multiple personality who doesn't consciously know that the other side of himself is a killer. We saw the killer when he was clenching his fists and saying 'the moon is dark.'"

Everyone at the table listened intently. This was unworldly.

"The psychic system that was created in him can only be opened and activated by a certain person, or persons, who possess the key to his psyche. He is locked down. He kept saying that the 'sky is dark, the moon is dark.' Those sound like code words that lock down the system to me."

"He did make a mistake," Phil Gilmour said, "when he mentioned twice that Garg was his commanding officer."

"He did slip there, then righted himself quickly. Do you have any idea who Garg might be?"

"It could be that the commanding officer was just named Garg. GARG could be an acronym for something. It could be Greg. It could be almost anyone," Gilmour speculated, "Come to think of it, do you suppose it could be the gargoyle he mentioned in one of his dreams, the one the misshapen man becomes when he is having sex with the leper woman?"

"Maybe so," Offen agreed.

"So, when you say he is 'locked,' what does that mean as a practical matter?" Jack asked.

"It means," Offen said, "that unless we can find out who has the key, we're not going to get into his past by normal means. We're stymied. Has he had any visitors while he's been in jail who could have locked him down so tightly?"

"He told us just a couple of days ago that he had had no visitors at all, except his kids," Jack said.

"I wouldn't trust that. That information is probably also locked. As Avery would say, 'the sky is dark, the moon is dark,' for the Garg's identity *and* whether he visited Avery."

"Joe, could you go over to the jail and check the list of all visitors Avery's had?" Jack asked.

"Sure," Joe said.

"Also," Jack added, "we need you to go over to the college where he worked and find out if there was anyone in Avery's Evidence class who saw him meet someone after class. Garg may have reared his ugly head the morning of the fifteenth. Perhaps they had coffee together. Avery mentioned the smell of coffee."

"Avery also gave us the name of Marvella Dixon as one of his students who knew the answers to all of his questions about Evidence while he was under hypnosis," Phil Gilmour said. "You may want to start with her."

Joe was taking notes.

"The problem we have," Jack said, "is that you're not going to find the person with the key easily, and even if you do, I can promise you that he or she is not going to walk into the jail with us and unlock the door to Avery Jackson's past and help us get him freed."

"So, where does this leave us?" Yolanda asked.

"Nowhere, legally," Jack opined.

"There is possibly another way," Dr. Offen said. "Dr. Gilmour and I discussed it. I suggest we use scopolamine to open Avery up and get to his other side. The released CIA documents about the mind-control experiments often refer to scopolamine. It's only a hunch, but it's possible scopolamine was used to program Avery. I have asked Phil to have scopolamine available if we should need it. What do you think?"

"What is it?" Jack asked.

This was Phil Gilmour's area. "It's an alkaloid made from a plant called henbane. It acts by interfering with the transmission of nerve impulses in the parasympathetic nervous system."

"Translate for us, would you please, Doctor?" Jack said. "If you start talking like that in front of a jury, Avery is dead."

"Sure." Gilmour said. "It alters the chemistry of the nervous system and slows you down. It was typically used as a sedative. In the 1950s and '60s, it was combined with morphine and used for women in childbirth. Under its influence, they could be awake and help with the birth process, but have no recollection of it later. Births where scopolamine and morphine were used were called 'twilight births.' Women gave birth in the 'twilight of consciousness' when they were sedated by these drugs. It's not used anymore because it is considered dangerous and causes depression. In the wrong dosages, it can cause hallucinations, delusions, or even paralyze someone."

"I'll tell you this right now," Jack said, "if we use scopolamine this afternoon and try to get the tape recording of the session into evidence to prove what happened to Avery in 'Nam or on January fifteenth, we're going to get a mighty big challenge. Alec Hunter is going to claim that Avery, under its influence, is unreliable—that he was having a delusion or hallucination. Hunter's also going to claim the contents of the tape are hearsay. Has this technique ever been used in a forensic setting before, Phil?"

"Sodium amytal, the infamous truth serum, has been used. Scopolamine, however, is a better truth serum. It renders the person who has been injected with it psychologically wide open. It's as if they have had their ego cut away and their unconscious, forgotten history spills out from them. According to the literature, they recall forgotten events that happened ten years ago as if they were happening right now, today," Gilmour said.

"In my opinion," Dr. Offen said, "we need to reveal two things to show why he did this. Obviously, we need to show what happened to him on January fifteenth. But before that, we need to show how he was programmed in the Army."

"We're hoping that Avery actually has memories for what happened to him when he was under the influence of scopolamine, and that those memories can be accessed by scopolamine. It's clear we're not going to get there with hypnosis, and certainly not with just talking to Avery," Phil said.

"That's correct," Dr. Offen agreed. "The CIA probably used scopolamine on Avery to create a killer's psychopathic personality. I think it would be most effective to access that personality the same way it was created. We can't be sure we will be successful, but we think it's our best bet right now. What Phil and I are mainly concerned with is psychological truth, not legal truth."

"I," interjected Yolanda, "have researched the law on the admissibility of evidence obtained this way and it's not good for us. Most courts won't allow it."

"So," Jack asked, "what's the use of doing this if we can't get the results into evidence? You guys can get all the psychological truth you want. If a jury never sees the results of your work, what good is it to Avery Jackson? He's the one who gets the needle."

The waitress came with drink refills. The team realized it had reached unexplored areas of the law and psychology. They were pioneers pushing their covered wagons across the Rocky Mountains, not knowing if they would break down, or be swallowed by predators or the cold. The law is forced to respond to the changes brought about by technology and advances in psychology. Unfortunately, the law would be looking at this problem with legal standards on hearsay evidence and insanity created in the nineteenth century. They were at a crossroads in the case. Either they decided to stop the psychological evaluation now and proceed by traditional methods of gaining evidence, or they needed to push forward to the new frontier. There wasn't much conversation. Everyone at the table knew what the stakes were.

When they were almost done with lunch, Marcus Offen started again. "Counselors, what's it going to be? Should I be out of here on the next plane to Denver or do you want to go ahead?"

"We're going ahead," Jack said emphatically. "I've already made up my mind. We're not going to turn back now. We'll try to get the tapes into evidence as the basis for your opinion. Hunter will scream hearsay and scientific unreliability, and he may win. It's up to the jury to decide the credibility of what you have. They'll think you're certainly crazy. In fact, they'll probably think we're all crazy."

"Why?" Marci asked. "Do you think we sound like a bunch of paranoid, conspiracy theorists? We're only talking about the CIA, mind-control experiments, an ex-judge who's maybe got a multiple personality disorder and who was perhaps programmed as a Manchurian Candidate to kill somebody, including our local sheriff. Just your usual stuff. Who looks crazy here? It's not Avery. It's us."

"I'm glad we have one person grounded in reality," Yolanda said.

"Avery's goose is cooked unless we go ahead with this," Jack said. "Do you think a jury is going to believe these two doctors without something pretty graphic on tape? We don't have anything yet, except Avery saying the 'the sky is dark, the moon is dark.' That sounds so hokey. Hunter is going to scream that Avery is faking a bizarre, psychological condition by uttering screwy words. If we stop now, a jury will believe Avery should get a lethal injection just for insulting their intelligence."

"Okay, and what if Avery dies or goes crazy during this session?" Yolanda asked.

"We'll get him to sign a release. It's like any medical operation. There is a risk," Gilmour said.

"What happened to you, Phil? You used to be the most conservative psychiatrist around. Are your drugs wearing off?" Jack asked. Gilmour's face reddened. Jack dug the knife in a little deeper. "You're putting your career on the line here if something goes wrong. I'm not worried about Marcus. The mental health community already knows him to be an eccentric. But for you, this is rather out of character."

"I know," Gilmour said. "This is exciting though, isn't it? When I saw this morning's hypnosis session, I knew something extraordinary was happening."

"Let's do the scopolamine," Jack said. "We'll explain it to Avery, get him to sign the release, and take our best shot. We have nothing at all to lose, and everything to gain."

"I think so," said Marcus looking at Phil Gilmour. Each had a smile on his face. Now they would get a chance to play with the exciting new toy they had seen that morning but couldn't touch. They had witnessed the personality of the killer. Perhaps, they could now get to know him.

"Has anyone ever done a procedure like this in a criminal case before?" Jack asked.

"No," Marcus said, "but then there's never been a case like this before. People who have made important advances in the understanding of the human condition have all taken personal and professional risks. This is our time."

Saturday—2:00 p.m.
Montgomery County Jail

Jack and Yolanda attended the afternoon session along with the two doctors. All four of them were nervous with anticipation. Dr. Offen set up his videocam quickly and put a new tape in it. They set up five chairs. Offen pressed the RECORD button prior to Avery's coming into the room. He wanted no allegation that Avery was coached. "This is Saturday, February third. We are at the Montgomery County Jail in Ohio. Present are Dr. Phil Gilmour, Yolanda Crone and Jack Maine. We are awaiting Avery Jackson, who is just now arriving."

As Avery entered the room, it was apparent the morning session had left him drained. "Tired, Avery?" Offen asked.

"Not too bad, really. I just had a nap. The dreams came again. The one with the gargoyle and the leper. Then the gunshots."

"Do you remember anything at all about the morning session?" the doctor asked.

"I remember your hypnotizing me with flowers," Avery said. "Past that, not much."

"You're very hypnotizable. What we learned was that you go into a very deep trance that allows you to access other parts of yourself. The problem we had during the session is that, for some reason, your subconscious would only allow us to access certain things. We need to go further this afternoon. We'd like to do so with a drug that Dr. Gilmour will inject. We believe it will provide us with an explanation as to why you killed Sheriff Hardacre."

"What's the drug?" Avery asked.

"Scopolamine," Gilmour answered.

"Never heard of it. Does it have side effects?"

"Administered in the correct dosage, it is very safe. You'll have a dry mouth and might feel some depression after the session."

"I feel depressed anyway," Avery said.

"Yolanda has prepared a release we need you to sign in order for us to do this," Jack said.

Yolanda handed Avery the document. He read over it perfunctorily and signed it. "Let's do it," he said.

Gilmour reached into his bag and brought out a small vial of liquid. He opened the plastic around a syringe. He drew the scopolamine out of the bottle and approached Avery with the syringe and a rubber cord to tie off his arm above the elbow. Avery rolled up his sleeve and looked Dr. Gilmour in the eye as he wrapped the rubber tube around Avery's arm.

"It's easy to get a vein on you," Gilmour said.

As Gilmour drew within inches of Avery's arm with the needle, Avery's eyes moved up as if he were trying to look through the top of his own skull. Before Gilmour could get the needle in, the automaton emerged and grabbed Gilmour's arm with his free hand. He stood and kicked Gilmour's feet out from under him. The syringe flew across the room as Gilmour landed hard on the tile floor. The automaton then pounced on him as quickly as a mountain lion preys upon the neck of a young deer. He seized Gilmour's throat with both hands. The automaton was a killer and moved with such precision and quickness that everyone else in the room was stunned for a second.

Yolanda screamed, "Avery!" at the top of her lungs.

Simultaneously, Marcus and Jack lunged on his back. The killer was not about to let go. He squeezed Gilmour's neck purposefully, methodically, forcefully, despite two men on his back each pulling on an arm. This would be a grip to the death if they couldn't get Avery's arms free. Jack kneed the killer in the ribs as forcefully as he could. Still, the killer wouldn't release Gilmour.

Offen kneed him on the other side; he groaned like a wounded animal and relaxed his death grip on Gilmour, who was starting to turn blue, his eyeballs bulging out of their sockets. He gasped for air as the automaton's grip loosened.

Yolanda hit the panic, alarm button. Jack and Marcus pulled Avery off Gilmour and rolled him onto his back. Each subdued an arm while Yolanda sat on his middle. When the deputies arrived a minute later, the murderous, no-longer-Avery animal was contained, hyperventilating, still dangerous. It was not the Avery they had all known; there was no one behind his eyes. One deputy cuffed his right arm while the other deputy grabbed his left arm and brought it to the other open cuff. The killer was finally subdued.

"What in the hell is going on here?" asked Deputy Dan Callahan. Both Jack and Dr. Gilmour had known Callahan for years. He was a good man.

"Thanks for getting here so fast," Jack said. "Phil Gilmour was going to give Mr. Jackson a sedative and he went nuts. That's all. I think we have everything under control now." Jack was afraid Callahan would stop the evaluation after all this, and neither time nor money would allow that.

Callahan looked at Gilmour who was in the process of picking himself up off the floor. "Doctor," asked Callahan, "do you wish to bring assault charges against Mr. Jackson?"

Gilmour tried to find his voice. It cracked. "N-no No, Dan, I'm fine. It's really my fault. I believe Avery here is just scared of needles. The situation is well under control now. I believe we'll be fine if you'll just allow us to finish the evaluation. Let's keep the restraints on in case he becomes phobic again, though. If you have a belt that you could chain the handcuffs to, we'll be fine."

"Deputy Jarvis," Callahan said to the other deputy, "get a restraint belt. It's my job to make sure Mr. Jackson, as well as all of you, are kept safe here. Avery, do you want to tell me what happened?"

Avery had returned. "We're just doing the mental evaluation," he said.

"Are you all right?" Callahan asked.

"Sure, why do you ask?" Avery asked.

"Did you agree to Dr. Gilmour giving you a sedative?"

"Yeah, I did. I had just signed a release and he was about to give me a shot when you came in. Is there a problem?"

The room was quiet.

"There is a problem. It looks to me like you attacked Dr. Gilmour here. Fortunately for you, he doesn't want to press charges."

"Attack?" Avery stood quietly. He knew not to protest his innocence because he knew he could not trust his memory.

Detective Jarvis came back with the belt. He put it around Avery's middle and then attached the cuffs to it. "I thought I'd also bring some leg irons so Jackson can't pull any funny business with his feet," he said.

"That's probably a good idea," Jack said as Jarvis methodically put on the leg irons.

"I believe we'll be fine," Gilmour said. "If there's a problem, we'll call for you."

"I've known the two of you for years. I trust you. But if there's any more bullshit in here, I'm going to stop things." Callahan looked at Avery who was now without the ability to move his arms or do any more than shuffle his legs. "Now, Jackson, sit your ass down in this chair and I don't want to see or hear another peep out of you or you're going into the hole. About a week in solitary might help you to see the light." Callahan moved over to him and helped him shuffle over to a chair. "Now sit," Callahan said as he helped Avery into the chair. "Just hit the alarm button if Mr. Jackson loses control again."

"Thanks, Dan," Jack said. "We will."

After Callahan and Jarvis left the room, everyone sat down and took a deep breath. They had saved the evaluation.

Offen began with Avery. "Tell us, Avery, what you remember of the last ten minutes?"

"Like I said to Callahan, I remember signing the release and then Dr. Gilmour saying he was going to give me the scopolamine. Then the next thing I know I have handcuffs on and everyone is gathered around me looking at me like I'm Charles Manson. I'm tired of this bullshit," he said, tears of frustration and rage visible in his eyes. He struggled against his chains.

"Do you remember kicking Dr. Gilmour's feet out from under him?"

"No."

"Do you remember trying to strangle him?"

"No."

"Okay, Avery, we're going ahead with this evaluation. I like it when you say bullshit. You say it with such conviction," Offen said, lightening the mood in the room from frozen and heavy to moving and light. "Phil, give him the shot. Jack, go over there and hold him in his chair."

Gilmour repeated the procedure with the needle and rubber tourniquet. He took the syringe and quickly put it into Avery's bulging vein. He struggled again against the chains as his eyes looked to the top of his head, again switching to his killer-mode, but it did him no good this time; the liquid went into his veins and quickly into his central nervous system. Avery's throat went dry and his heart rate slowed. The walls of psychic protection were dissolving, the steel curtain of secrecy melting. His mind was now a chain of open doors for the doctors to walk through; they just had to figure out what was behind each door and extract it.

Offen checked to see if the red blinking light of the videocam was pulsating. It was.

"What is your name?" he asked.

"I'm not sure right now."

"How do you feel?"

"My mouth is dry and I feel groggy."

"What is today's date?"

"February third."

"Where are we?"

"Montgomery County Jail."

"Why are you here?"

"I'm charged with killing the sheriff."

"Did you?"

"I can't give you that information."

"Do you remember what happened here a few minutes ago?"

"Yes."

"What happened?"

Avery rolled his head, and his demeanor changed from pensive to very agitated. "Jesus Christ, that motherfucker is trying to stick a needle in me! He looks just like the motherfucker with the black, horn-rimmed glasses, but he has those stupid, wire-rimmed glasses that honkies wear." The killer had returned. He began straining against the chair and the chains. "I have to kill the motherfucker. I have to kill the motherfucker or I'll die," he shrieked, straining against his restraints.

"Avery, what do you see?" Offen asked.

"My name is not Avery, motherfucker, my name is Periscope."

It was as if the air had been sucked out of the room. The automaton killer was not only out, but identified himself. The big fish had been hooked. It was up to Offen to not allow him to get away.

"Who gave you that name?"

"Gargoyle."

"Who is Gargoyle?"

Periscope shook his head.

"What do you see, Periscope?" Offen asked

"I see that motherfucker trying to give me a shot. I will kill you, motherfucker, if you try to give me a shot—you got that, motherfucker?" he screamed at Gilmour.

Gilmour's face visibly paled, but he tried to control any emotion.

"*Why* do you have to kill this motherfucker?" Marcus asked, pointing at Gilmour.

"Because I have been ordered to kill any motherfucker who tries to give me a shot to try to get into my mind."

"Who gave you that order?"

"Gargoyle."

"Who is Gargoyle?"

"I can't give you that information. The 'sky is dark, the moon is dark.'"

"What does the 'moon is dark' mean?"

"That the information is classified."

"Who says the information is classified?"

"My commanding officer."

"Who is your commanding officer?"

"That information is classified."

"You listen to me, Periscope, I am your commanding officer, and I say that information is no longer classified."

"That information is classified."

"No, Periscope, I'm your commanding officer now. The commanding officers you had in Vietnam are dead. I am in charge. You got it, Periscope?"

"No, I have been ordered by Gargoyle not to allow any access to the nature of my mission and not to reveal the identity of my commanders."

"Periscope, those are no longer your orders."

"How can I be sure of that?"

"You have to trust me."

"I can't trust you, motherfucker. If I don't follow orders, I'm dead like all the others."

"Which others?"

"The dead guys with their brains hanging out and blood running all over the floor."

"Who are they?"

"Gooks."

"Let's go back in years. Can you count back with me to 1970 when you were in Basic at Fort Bragg?"

Dr. Offen counted slowly, methodically, and purposefully back to 1970.

When they got there, Avery opened his eyes. His countenance had changed again; this time it showed neither the deadpan, cold, homicidal cunning of Periscope or his own softness. The person sitting before them was someone in between.

"Who are you? You look different," Offen said.

"A cross between Avery and Periscope. Right now Avery and Periscope kind of run side by side, but they're not one and the same."

"Have you ever experienced this state of consciousness before?"

"Never. It's surreal. It's like I can observe Avery and Periscope without being either of them, yet I can experience their feelings and thoughts. I guess you could say I am the historian for their lives."

"That's fine. That's perfect. We'll call you Avescope," Offen said. "Is that suitable?"

"I suppose. I never gave it any thought before."

"Now, let's go to that Tuesday in 1970 when Dr. Arthur Breyfogle ordered you to report back to his office at Fort Bragg. You can see Dr. Breyfogle right now. What does he look like?"

"He's a sinister-looking man with black, horn-rimmed glasses and a white physician's jacket. He's sterile, cold, inhumane."

"What is he doing?"

"He's giving Avery a Coke. The Coke tastes really good. It's got some dope in it—a tranquilizer or something. Oh, shit, now he comes with the needle, oh shit. He is saying it will make him mellow. He gives Avery the needle. He says it will prevent him from getting diseases over in 'Nam. I'm feeling now like he felt then—mouth gets real dry and breathing slows down. He doesn't feel a lot—kinda like I feel now. Now he is talking to Avery."

"What's he saying?"

"'You will be reporting to a commanding officer in Vietnam. His name will be Lieutenant Doerning. I will be over there, too. Another soldier like you by the name of Gargoyle will be over there. Now remember this, Jackson, you're about to take on a new identity within you that will live separate and apart from you. That identity will be called Periscope. Is that clear, Jackson? No one is to know about Periscope's identity. Is that clear, Jackson? And if you fail to follow any of these orders, Periscope, you will die along with Avery. And if you, Periscope, reveal your identity, or that of Avery, you will die. We will give you to the Vietcong; they will cut off your balls with a rusty razor-blade and shove them in your mouth and down your throat until you choke or bleed to death. Is that clear, Periscope? You will follow all of our orders. Is that clear, Periscope? And if I, or Doerning, or Gargoyle, say "shit" you will say "shit," is that clear? And if he wants you to eat shit, you will eat shit. Is that clear, Periscope? You are being created today, Periscope, to serve your country when Avery does not have the balls to do so. You are to protect Avery and your country whenever you're asked to do so. Avery is a weakling. His father whipped him and he was his mother's little pussy-boy. It's your job to protect this helpless little bastard. Do you understand, Periscope? And when you get over

'Nam, you will do whatever Lieutenant Doerning tells you to do. You will not resist any injections he may give you. In fact, you will insist that Avery have the injections; they are in your best interest. Is that clear?'"

"What do you answer, Avescope?"

"Yes sir, yes sir, yes sir."

The room was quiet. Everyone was transfixed except Offen, who was in his element.

"Go ahead, Avescope," Offen said.

"Breyfogle went on, 'You now realize your ass belongs to your country and that whatever you're told to do by Lieutenant Doerning, me, or Gargoyle, you will do it without question. Is that clear, Periscope? You will not remember anything we have talked about today. Is that clear? And if anyone asks about me or Doerning, you will remember nothing.'"

Jack, Yolanda and Dr. Gilmour glanced at one another, raised eyebrows saying it all.

Dr. Offen pushed on. "What is happening now? Is it still Avescope we have out here?"

"Yes. Avery and Periscope are still running together through me. I can watch and hear what Avery and Periscope are doing and they can watch and hear what I am doing. Avery cannot see or hear Periscope, but Periscope can see and hear Avery. I can see and hear both of them and they're aware of me."

"What is happening now with Breyfogle?" Offen asked.

"I can see him right now," said Avescope. "He's ordering Avery to come back the next day."

"Can you see Avery going back?"

"Yes, I can see Avery going back right now."

"What happens the next day?"

"He is asking Avery if he remembers anything from the day before. The only thing Avery remembers is the Coke. Breyfogle seems to be satisfied with that answer."

There was quiet as Avescope stopped and listened to a voice inside him.

"What's happening?" Dr. Offen asked.

"Periscope is inside right now telling me he was born on that Tuesday— the day Breyfogle said he would cut off his balls and stuff them in his mouth."

"What happens next?" Offen asked.

"Avery goes to 'Nam. He doesn't remember anything about Dr. Breyfogle except he was a doctor with a white coat who offered Avery a Coke and asked him stupid questions. Avery knows nothing of the newborn Periscope in 'Nam or the developing Periscope now, for that matter. Periscope is telling me right now, however, that he knew all the time what Avery was doing."

"How did you get to 'Nam?"

"We flew," Avescope said.

"What happened when you arrived there?"

"I have to move the clock ahead a few days." There was a pause as Avescope looked to the top of his head. "Okay, I can see us arriving and going into a Special Forces' unit. Lieutenant Doerning comes to meet Avery. He is a real hard ass, but not evil like Breyfogle. He is a square-jawed, honky dude, really tightly muscled, sweat running off him like a Newfoundland dog salivates. He is coming right up to Avery. 'Jackson, it's a pleasure to have you in my detail,' Doerning says. He is giving Avery special attention. He barely talks to the other dudes. 'Your ass is mine,' he says. 'You are to accompany me tomorrow morning at 0600 hours. Be waiting for me at the front door to this hut? Is that clear, soldier?'"

Avescope begins to show signs of distress.

"What is happening now?" Offen asked.

"I can see the next morning at 0600 hours. Avery is meeting Doerning outside our hut. We are getting into a Jeep. He is driving the Jeep into the jungle. 'We must go five miles.' Doerning is saying nothing to Avery. He's looking at the jungle. The country is lush green, but damn, it's hot and humid. I can feel the heat of it right now in him. He's turning into a sweat hog like Doerning." Beads of sweat were on Avescope's forehead. "Finally, I can see us arriving at a makeshift hut in the middle of nowhere. 'Come with me, Jackson,' Doerning says. I'm walking with him. We are entering the hut. There is Breyfogle. He is sitting in a chair with his glasses on. He still has on his doctor's white coat in the jungle. Another person I have seen before is also sitting there."

"Who is that person?" Offen asked.

"I know that person. He's Gargoyle."

"Who is that person?" Offen pressed.

Periscope bolted out of Avescope and blocked the answer, "The sky is dark, the moon is dark!"

"Periscope, why did you come out?" Offen asked.

Periscope said nothing.

"Periscope, maybe you can identify Gargoyle later. Right now I want to talk to Avescope. Avescope, come back out here," Dr. Offen said.

There was a noticeable change in affect from flat and purposeful to more human. Avescope was back.

"Avescope, why didn't you just ask Periscope for Gargoyle's identity?" Offen asked.

Avescope shrugged his shoulders.

"Why don't you ask him now?"

Avescope rolled his eyes up to the top of his head. He took a few seconds. Then he said, "I asked him. He said he wasn't ever going to release that material."

"Can you retrieve the material yourself?"

"No. I can't quite get it," said Avescope. "I can see the guy has letters on his green fatigues. The first letter is I or L."

"Okay, maybe you can see it later on. What then happened in the hut, Avescope?"

"Avery can see Breyfogle with his hypodermic." Avescope stiffened. "Breyfogle loves his hypodermic. He shoots Avery in the arm. Avery feels the dryness in his mouth . . . just like now. He feels the mellowness, just like I feel now. It's a good thing we're under the influence of this stuff or we'd really be upset right now."

"Why's that, Avescope?" Offen asked.

"Because Avery and Periscope can feel the fright. They couldn't stand it if they didn't have the scopolamine. Breyfogle and Doerning are standing there talking. Gargoyle—I can't see his name yet—is walking into the hut. He has this skinny, Vietnamese guy tied up. He is pushing him by the hair onto a tilted platform with linoleum tile on it. It has spouts coming out of it. The skinny Asian man is scared, real scared. Doerning is saying calmly, 'This man is our barber. He cuts our hair during the day. At night he kills us. He is Vietcong.' Oh, shit! Oh, fuck! Motherfucker! Gargoyle, this isn't happening. Gargoyle is putting a revolver to his head! *BOOM*! The other side of his head disappears. He falls to the floor like a sack of flour. The blood begins to flow out of his head into a pool onto the floor. It runs into the spouts. Periscope is now there to absorb the fright. Avery feels nothing; Avery sees nothing. Periscope sees it all, feels it all. Periscope starts gasping for air. He can't breathe. The corpse's blank eyes are looking at us. Oh-h-h-h!"

The room was quiet; Avescope was quiet. Gilmour, Jack and Yolanda were quiet and didn't look at one another. Could this be real?

"What is happening now, Avescope?" Dr. Offen asked.

"Breyfogle is talking now."

"What's he saying?"

"He's saying, 'Periscope just witnessed that. Corporal Avery Jackson didn't. Avery is a coward. He has gone away now . . . gone away . . . gone away . . . gone away . . . gone away . . . gone away. Avery Jackson has witnessed nothing; he has felt nothing. Periscope, you're the only tough one, the only one with a purpose, the only one who can stand up. You are the mad part of Avery who is now able to stand up to Avery's father. You are the part that witnessed this gook being shot. I want you to look at his dead eyes. He is a dead gook. Look at his eyes.' Periscope looks into his dead eyes."

211

Avescope pauses. He rolls his eyes up in his head, then moves them from left to right.

"What's happening now, Avescope?"

"Doerning is going off like a drill sergeant."

"What's he saying?"

"'You, Periscope, will be able to kill just like this. You are ordered to kill just like this. You will kill anytime you're ordered to do so by any of us. Whenever any of us orders you to kill, we will say 'the moon is full,' and then we will give you instructions for the killing. Is that clear, Periscope?' I can see Periscope nodding his head obediently. Now Doerning is going on. 'You, Periscope, are a killing machine. You take no shit off anyone. You take no shit off Avery or his father. In fact, you're not even a part of Avery's asshole father, nor are you a part of Avery. You don't come from them. You take no shit off the North Vietnamese, the Vietcong, people within our own troops, or South Vietnamese soldiers. If we order you to kill one of them, you do so. Is that clear, Periscope? You are a killing machine. You can kill anyone we order you to kill. You kill just like we killed this gook cocksucker, is that clear, Periscope? Now, Periscope, there is one more thing to remember, and this is crucial. Your life depends on it. When we tell you that the "sky is dark, the moon is dark," you're to reveal no information about your orders, the asshole you killed, or the identity of the three people in this room. Is that clear?'"

Avescope went silent. No one else spoke. Then he began again. "Breyfogle is talking now."

"What's he saying?" Offen asked.

"'Periscope, this sedative will be wearing off in a few minutes. When it's worn off, you'll feel tired. You'll no longer be needed. Avery will be coming back out. He'll have no memory of you or of this killing today. You will rest until the next time we need you. If you violate any of our orders, however, you'll end up like this piece of trash here on the floor. Is that clear, Periscope?' Again, I can see Periscope nodding like a machine." Avescope then sat quietly in the chair, hands and feet chained and bound.

The room was quiet. It was now late in the afternoon. Marcus Offen could see the sun setting behind scattered clouds through the small, jail windows. They had one more day to work before he would be leaving. He looked at Dr. Gilmour. "How much time do we have left, Phil?"

"Just a few minutes, I suspect."

"When we lose Avescope, then it's over for the day—maybe for awhile. Let's push as far as we can," Offen decided. "Now, Avescope, I need you to look at the name of the soldier—Gargoyle—who shot the Vietnamese man. Look at his fatigues. What is his name?"

"The sky is dark, the moon is dark," Periscope shouted as he came out.

"Avescope, I need you to come out."

Avery's eyes rolled around in his head. "I'm here," Avescope said, "but I'm getting tired. Periscope is screaming at me to shut up. 'Shut the fuck up or I'll kill you, motherfucker. Shut the fuck up, or I'll kill you, motherfucker.' He keeps screaming at me."

Offen took a risk. It was something no other forensic psychologist would ever approve of doing, but then again, no forensic psychologist had ever been in this place before. "You listen to me, Periscope, *you* shut the fuck up. You are ordered to shut the fuck up. If you want to go on living, you need to disclose that information or you'll end up dead like the gook you just saw shot. Avescope, read the name off the name tag and the corporal's green, uniform shirt, *now*."

Avescope rolled his eyes up. "It's B-L-A-I-N-E, K. Blaine, but I can't be sure."

Jack and Yolanda looked at one another incredulously. There must have been several dozen Blaines who fought in Vietnam, but they were not Hugh Lane.

"Okay, Avescope, what do you see now?"

"It's not what I see, it's what I hear. Periscope is berating Avery, telling him he'll kill Avery, 'I'll kill you, cocksucker. I'll kill you, cocksucker. I'll kill you just like they killed all those gooks,' he's saying to Avery."

"Why?" Offen asked.

"Because he is not allowed to give that information to anyone."

"Periscope," Dr. Offen said, "don't worry about it. Avery can't hear you. But tell us about all the dead gooks."

"The sky is dark. The moon is dark," Periscope insisted.

"Avescope," Dr. Offen said, "tell us what Periscope is trying to hide from us."

The room was quiet for several seconds.

Avescope rolled his eyes.

"Is there more programming?" Offen asked.

Avescope again stiffened. "I can see there is," he said.

"Tell us what it is, go ahead," Offen said.

Avescope rolled his eyes. "It is three days later. Lieutenant Doerning brings Avery to the hut. Breyfogle gives him the shot. Gargoyle brings in a tiny, Vietnamese woman and pushes her head down onto the linoleum platform. Doerning tells him she is Viet Cong. Doerning shouts, 'The moon is full!' Gargoyle puts the gun to her head and *BOOM*!

"Her blood rolls down the tile into the bucket. Periscope is watching, saying nothing. He feels nothing. Doerning then starts in. 'That was you,

Periscope, who killed that woman. You are a killer. You are programmed to kill. You always follow orders when the moon is full.' Now Doerning is saying something new. 'You are now ready to kill. In three days, you will kill and Avery will know nothing of it. If you fail, you will be killed just like this gook was killed. Now, when you wake up, Avery will know nothing of you or your orders.'"

Offen looked at Gilmour. "If I can get ten more minutes, I think we can get through everything for the day."

"Go ahead," Gilmour said.

"Okay, Avescope, look within yourself. Move ahead three days to the next session with Breyfogle, Doerning, and Gargoyle. Can you see it?"

Avescope looks to the top of his head and begins. "Yes, it's the same, except Breyfogle doesn't give him the injection."

"All right," Dr. Offen said. "No injection. What's happening then with no shot?"

"Doerning is screaming 'the moon is full.' Gargoyle is killing Vietnamese people. Periscope can see the execution of one . . . now two, Vietnamese men. He's told they're Vietcong. *BOOM*! *BOOM*! Right in the head. Brains and skull fragments are flying all over the hut. Blood is running everywhere." Avescope stops.

"What is happening now, Avescope?" Offen asked.

Avescope takes a breath. "Not *another* one, not a *third*," he says. "Wait a minute!"

"What is happening?" Offen asked.

"Gargoyle is bringing a Vietnamese boy in. 'Periscope,' Gargoyle yells, 'the moon is full. This is a Vietcong boy who has already killed three GIs. Don't be fooled by his appearance. He is evil. You are to take this gun from me and shoot him in the head. *Now*, Periscope.' he orders. I can see Periscope getting up from the chair, walking over to the gun, now taking it from Gargoyle. Oh Jesus Christ, Oh, Jesus Christ, he doesn't do it, he doesn't do it. *BOOM*!" Avescope began to cry. He sobbed openly and deeply. "He did it. He's a killer. I'm a killer. We're killers. I just saw Periscope kill that child."

The room was still. *So, this is how you program someone to kill*, they all thought. *Step by step over a period of weeks. You drug them and create a personality within them to absorb the horror of the trauma that is befalling them.*

"What is happening now?" Offen asked.

"I can see Breyfogle. 'The sky is dark, Periscope,' Breyfogle says. 'You have done your duty. You have protected Avery and your country. When Avery returns, he will remember none of this. Is that clear, Periscope?' I can see Periscope nodding and handing the gun back to Gargoyle."

"How many people did Periscope kill in 'Nam?" Offen asked.

"I'll have to ask him," Avescope said, who then looked to the top of his head. "He's saying 'the sky is dark, the moon is dark' for that information."

"We need it now. Look into him and see what you can find."

Avescope paused and then rolled his eyes up in his head. "Okay, there are all sorts of visions. I can see them like on TV. I can see him shooting a South Vietnamese general . . . and a Saigon politician. They are both corrupt, he is told. He shoots two of our own men who are problems—assassinates them when no one is around. Right now, that is all I see. I'm so tired, I can't go on. I'm losing touch with Periscope. There are more, but I need to stop," Avescope pleaded.

"You did wonderful work today, Avescope," Dr. Offen said. "When the sedative is gone, Avery will come back out and you'll be gone. He'll feel exhausted and need to sleep the rest of the day. Then, Periscope will be especially hostile to Avery. Avery may feel suicidal. We'll try to talk to them again in the morning. We'll call the guards to take you back to your cell."

When the guards came, they took off the cuffs and leg irons. "He'll be exhausted tonight," Gilmour said to Deputy Callahan. "If you could take him back to his cell, we'll see him in the morning. And Dan, keep an eye on him. He could become very depressed tonight."

Jack and Yolanda were still mesmerized. Would a jury buy this, though? Gilmour and Offen packed up the videocam. They dated and secured their precious tape.

Tomorrow they would try again. They would regress Avery to the killing of Sheriff Hardacre at the Renaissance.

"I hope we haven't gone too far today," Offen said. "When you get this much so fast, sometimes the system will shut down. The moon and sky could be dark tomorrow."

They were all quiet as they left.

Jack drove to his office. He called Marci. "Marci, can you come down to the King's Table for drinks and dinner?"

"Sure," she answered. "I'm dying to know how things went."

"You'll have to see these tapes because I can't begin to explain to you what we witnessed. Just come down for dinner. Oh, and please call Joe and ask him to meet us."

"Sure. But just tell me, was it good or bad?"

"Both. The good news is that Garg is Gargoyle. The bad news is that Gargoyle is not Hugh Lane."

"*Wow*! See you in a few minutes."

CHAPTER 19

Sunday, February 4—12:05 P.M.
Montgomery County Jail

The energy from yesterday's discoveries was tempered by today's reality. Jack and Yolanda debated the admissibility of the tapes. They hoped they could get them into evidence if, for no other reason, as the basis for the doctors' opinions. The disclosure of the name Blaine meant little. It was not a silver bullet or a smoking gun. It was hearsay based on statements made by a man under the influence of mind-altering drugs. And, how would Joe track down K. Blaine before the start of the trial anyway? He could be anywhere. But now Hugh Lane was out as a suspect and K. Blaine was in. Their client still had one foot on a banana peel and the other in the death chamber.

Phil Gilmour had picked Marcus Offen up at his hotel to go to the jail. Neither could remember the last time he had worked on Sunday, but both realized the necessity of working today. A forensic evaluation was a matter of pacing and timing. Avery had been opened up significantly with the help of the scopolamine. They hoped today their psychosurgery could be completed, and the inexplicable would be explained.

Deputy Callahan escorted all of them to the Contact Visitation Room. As they wound their way through the cement block corridors, Callahan was in an expansive mood. "You, ladies and gentlemen, are as crazy as I am working today. If you work fast enough, you might get home in time for the Super Bowl. I'll probably just catch the second half."

"To tell you the truth, Dan, I've been so busy with this case I'd forgotten

216

all about it," Jack said. "We'll be working as long as we need to today. We'll be needing Avery in restraints again."

"Tell me this," said Callahan as they entered the visitation room, "and this might be a stupid question, but why does Jackson need restraints when he's with you guys and not when he's with Sheriff Lane?"

Jack looked at Yolanda. His heart began racing. He needed to be cool. "Well, that could be because Dr. Gilmour has to shoot him with a sedative before we start working with him," Jack said. "Could be that he doesn't like shots. Does Sheriff Lane give him a sedative like we do?"

"No, I'm sure he doesn't—at least he didn't have a doctor there with him last night."

"Sheriff Lane was here last night to see Avery?" Jack asked casually.

"Yeah, just for a few minutes. He said they were friends. They looked real cordial together."

"Does the sheriff come to visit Avery a lot?" Jack asked.

"There was just one other time when I was here. Did you hear that Lane has been appointed interim sheriff by the commissioners until the next general election in November?"

"We hadn't heard a thing about it," Jack said. "It makes a lot of sense, though. He certainly has the experience."

"Things ran real easy around here when he was in charge. When Sheriff Hardacre came in, things began tightening up considerably. Some people didn't like it. I didn't mind. I'll go get Jackson for you guys. I'll make sure he's all tethered up," Callahan said as he left.

Jack and Yolanda stared at one another. "I wonder if this room is bugged," Jack said.

"My worry is that Lane came over here last night, terrorized Avery and shut him down," Offen said. "I don't trust this K. Blaine stuff. Avescope may be confabulating letters, getting confused. It can happen to anyone regardless of whether they're in a trance or not. When we start working with Avery here in a few minutes, if he is shut down, it's evidence that Lane, Gargoyle, and the trigger are one in the same."

"More psychological evidence as opposed to legal evidence, Doctor?" Jack asked.

"Exactly," Offen said.

"You guys need to understand that at some point you're going to have to find something that will be legal evidence," Jack said.

Deputy Callahan brought Avery into the room. His handcuffs were already in place and bound to a thick leather belt. After Avery was seated, Callahan put the leg irons on him and fastened them to the chair. "Thanks, Dan," Jack said, "we'll buzz you when we're done."

After Callahan left, Dr. Offen turned on the videocam and began asking the questions. "How do you feel today, Avery?"

"I'm beat. I don't want to do this today. I'm really depressed."

"Do you know why you're depressed?"

"I have no idea. I just know I don't feel like living. I feel dirty all over and I don't know why."

"Do you remember what we talked about yesterday?"

"I know that you were going to give me a shot."

"Do you remember anything significant about Dr. Gilmour giving you the shot?"

"No."

"Do you remember attacking Dr. Gilmour and strangling him?"

"No. Anytime you guys want to stop messing with me, you can. I am not in the mood for this," Avery said. "The way I feel today is that I'm going to prison, and I deserve to go to prison. I feel like I deserve to die."

"It's typical for a person with a history and psychological condition like yours to feel very depressed after such a session," Dr. Offen said.

"How long was I with you guys yesterday?"

"How long would you estimate you were with us?"

"It feels like maybe half an hour."

"Actually, it was more like three hours," Dr. Gilmour said, "and you did attack me, but I'm fine; don't worry about it."

Avery's depression clearly turned up.

"You look crushed," Dr. Offen said. "How do you feel today as opposed to the day after you were arrested for killing Sheriff Hardacre?"

Avery thought about it. "Very similar. It's as if I again killed another person and I don't know about it. Just like with Hardacre."

"Do you remember talking with your friend, Hugh Lane, here yesterday evening?" Jack asked.

"I haven't seen Hugh since he lost the election," Avery said.

"Do you remember seeing him on the morning of January fifteenth, the day you shot Sheriff Hardacre?" Jack asked.

"No."

"Let's go ahead with the sedative," Dr. Offen said. "Are you ready, Phil?"

Gilmour nodded and stood up, the syringe in his hand. He applied the tourniquet to Avery's right arm. When Avery saw the needle, he began to squirm in his chair and was able to upset it. He struggled pathetically on the floor like a wounded animal mired and sinking in mud. Jack, Dr. Offen, and Yolanda once again pounced on him and held his arm while Dr. Gilmour found a vein and injected the scopolamine.

Avery relaxed as the sedative again flooded his central nervous system. The two men were able to stand his chair back up with him in it. Avery's breathing slowed. His mouth dried out. He was ready.

"Avery, do you remember our session yesterday?" Dr. Offen asked.

"No."

"Avescope, you need to come out," Offen ordered the middleman.

Avery's eyes rolled to the top of his head and back down. His demeanor changed.

"Avescope, is that you?" Dr. Offen asked.

"Yes, I remember it," Avescope said sadly. "Periscope is a killer. He killed many people. He assassinated them. I remember that. I saw him kill a Vietnamese boy."

"Did you kill them or did Periscope kill them?" Offen asked.

"It was Periscope. It doesn't make any difference though, does it? He's a part of me."

"Do you have control over him?"

"No. I wish I did."

"Today, we want to know if Periscope is again there and if you can see him, read his brain and his thoughts, see what he's done."

"He's there. I can see him. He's sleeping today."

"Periscope!" Offen yelled, "you're ordered to come out and talk today like you did yesterday!"

"The sky is dark, the moon is dark," said a monotone voice.

"I'm going to draw your attention to January fifteenth, just three weeks ago," Offen said. "What did you do with Hugh Lane that day?"

"The sky is dark, the moon is dark."

"Avescope, we need you to come back out. Periscope is shut down."

The historian returned. "What do you want?"

"I need you to access Periscope and tell me what happened the day Sheriff Hardacre was shot," replied Offen.

His eyes rolled up in his head. He scanned. He searched. "I am getting nothing from him. He just keeps telling me that all that information is classified and that the sky is dark."

"Periscope, get your butt out here or I'll have Gargoyle come into this jail today as he did last night."

Avescope again rolled his eyes. Periscope emerged. He shook violently in his chair, fought against his restraints with his hands and attempted to kick out with his feet. From a visage of hatred came a guttural "Fuck you." He then gathered as much saliva as he could and spat at Offen. The wad whizzed by his left ear, leaving some saliva on the side of his face.

"As far as I'm concerned," Dr. Offen said, as he wiped the spit off his cheek, "we're done for the day."

Sunday—3:00 P.M.
The King's Table Restaurant

Jack and the doctors ordered beer, Yolanda wine. They sat quietly in a booth. The Super Bowl pre-game hype had already begun. The evaluation was over but not complete. They were taking a collective breath as each sipped their drinks and munched salty popcorn. Just meaningless, small talk about football prevailed for a few minutes as each gathered his thoughts.

"I can promise you to a reasonable degree of certainty that Hugh Lane is your killer. Unfortunately, we aren't able to prove it," Offen said.

"Even if you could, Marcus," Jack said, "it wouldn't be admissible evidence. It's up to us on this end to figure out how to prove it. What's your opinion on the issue of sanity? Did Avery know right from wrong at the time he killed Hardacre?"

Both doctors agreed Avery Jackson did not know right from wrong when he committed this murder. "I can promise you, however," said Dr. Gilmour, "that you'll get a formidable challenge from the rest of the professional community. Few doctors have stepped into the evil that we witnessed the last two days. You won't get the psychiatric community to accept this, much less a group of twelve jurors."

Jack shook Dr. Offen's hand. Dr. Gilmour would be taking him to the airport. He was able to get an earlier flight back to Denver. "Take care, Marcus. We'll need you back in two months for trial. It's been enlightening," Jack said, knowing that his association with Offen was a rare treat, but realizing that his real utility in front of a jury might be limited. It was all too bizarre.

Jack left to go home to Marci. It wouldn't be easy, but his brain needed to shift gears. The Chris Conley case was set for a suppression hearing tomorrow. This weekend, Avery's life had been at stake—tomorrow Chris'. And Jack had nothing except Chris' testimony. That and fifty cents would buy her a Hershey bar in the face of Detective Dave Guteman. She, too, was looking at a first-degree murder conviction. Her life and Jack's career could be over prematurely. Where the hell was Hardin Long? He had grown short and flaccid—even worse, nonexistent.

As he drove home, he noticed a tan sedan in his rearview mirror. His heart raced. He tried to slow it. Jack had never felt so close to death. It had been all around him for weeks. Now, it was following him.

When he arrived home, he quickly pulled into the driveway. The tan sedan drove by, slowed and then parked across the street. The darkness prevented Jack from clearly identifying anything about the occupants. Jack parked in the garage and went directly into the house.

He and Marci played in the hot-tub, turned out the lights, lit a candle and made love. It had been a long week, and it was over, pleasurably.

The doorbell woke them with a start. Jack looked at the digital alarm, it was twelve-thirty. Neither he nor Marci could orient themselves for several seconds because they had both been in such a deep sleep.

"Jesus, it has to be the guys in the tan sedan," he said.

"Do you have your gun?" Marci whispered urgently.

He reached into the drawer of the nightstand next to him. It was there. The doorbell rang again—several times. Jack's heart raced as he grabbed the gun. He moved quickly, like a mountain lion in the night, toward the front door.

The bell rang again. Jack looked through the peep hole in the door. He could see a figure standing outside—a big, black figure. He ran to the phone on the kitchen wall. Just as he punched nine, a voice on the other side of the door whispered loudly, plaintively, "Boss, boss, it's me. Open this fuc—open the door!"

"Joe, is that you?" Jack asked as he hung up the phone, and moved with gun in hand back to the door.

"Who the fuck ya think it is, Hardin Long?"

Jack opened the door and Joe rushed in, breathing hard, not from running, but from excitement. "*Whoa*, put the piece away!" Joe implored Jack as he realized he'd scared the wits out of both Jack and Marco, and Jack was ready to pull the trigger.

Jack lowered the gun, laid it the coffee table in the living room and yelled, "Marci, it's big Joe." Marci quickly appeared.

"I know this has got to be good because you would never come over the night before trial and wake—"

"Better than you can imagine," Joe interrupted as he reached into his black leather, jacket pocket and brought out a cassette. "I connected with Hardin Long."

"No shit! Is it *really* good?" Jack asked.

"Too fuckin' good. Makes you want to puke." Joe curled up his nose as if he had just smelled something foul. "It has Burt getting doped to death by Van, and Guteman setting up Chris. Listen to this." Joe took out his cassette recorder and put in the tape. The three of them listened with rapt attention to their friend of many years being murdered. Jack and Marci's fatigue quickly dissipated to outrage as the adrenaline again poured into their veins.

Joe then fast-forwarded the tape to the segment where Guteman came in, interrogated Chris and confiscated her purse.

"Smoking gun—definitely a smoking gun if we can get it in," Jack said.

"What do you mean?" asked Marci.

"Well, if it's a fraud, Chris will know it and would not lie in order for us to get it into evidence, and Guteman will never agree it's authentic; that would kill him," Jack said. "We'll just have to see. Where the hell is Hardin Long?"

"Good question. A better question, boss, would be: 'Who the hell is Hardin Long?'"

"Whaddya mean? Didn't you get to meet him?"

"No way. A total spook?"

"Joe, how much did this tape cost us?" Marci interrupted.

"That's the bad news—five-K."

"All the cash I left you?" she asked.

"All of it."

"How did you get it?" Jack asked. "You said Hardin Long refused to answer any of your pages."

"That's right. And every try I made to trace the pager number always ended up in a black hole—no record of any such pager number. Only the government can pull off that kind of shit—FBI, CIA. You know. Bottom line, I kept callin' the number and he finally got back to me tonight—on my cell phone. All I can figure is the sumbitch needed the money awful bad. Started again at fifty-K. I told him no way—that I had three thousand. He laughed. Said he'd come down to twenty-five thou. I said I had five thousand cash, the hearing was tomorrow, that we didn't need his fuckin' tape; we could win it without him."

"And . . .?" Jack said.

"Mothafucka got pissed. He's gotta be an insider who's a renegade—off on his own thing. He sounded pressured, sort of desperate—came down to ten thou. I said, 'I got five thousand cash and the offer goes to zero tomorrow 'cause your fuckin' tape ain't worth a thing by tomorrow afternoon—take it or leave it. And by the way, your name ain't Hardin Long anyway, is it?' Got pissed. Called me a dumb ass. Said he'd think about it. I said, 'Okay, mothafucka' and hung up. About five minutes later, he called me back on my cell. 'Course, the number was blocked—no record of any such number. Said he'd take the five, to leave it in an envelope in my car in the office parking lot. He'd send a boy around to pick up the cash. When he had the cash, he'd have the boy bring the tape a half hour later. I put the money in the car, watched from the office window. A white boy came around, picked up the cash and came back a half hour later with the tape, just slick as shit."

"Jesus, Joe, he could have stiffed us," Marci said.

"That he could have. I figured we didn't have anything to lose but the five grand."

Marci rolled her eyes.

"Great job, Joe," Jack said. "By the way, did you see a tan sedan outside?"

"There was one there with two dudes in it when I pulled up. They drove away."

CHAPTER 20

Monday, February 5—10:00 A.M.
Judge John Hodge's Court
The State of Ohio v. Chris Conley Suppression Hearing

A suppression hearing is a very important part of a criminal proceeding. Defense attorneys file motions to suppress evidence in order to keep statements or materials taken in violation of their client's constitutional rights from being heard or seen by a jury. Most of the time, the evidence sought to be suppressed is either statements that tend to incriminate or drugs or weapons seized by law enforcement.

In the case of statements, the defense will claim they were either coerced or taken without the client being advised properly of his Miranda rights. In the case of physical evidence, lawyers will claim the evidence was taken in violation of guarantees against illegal searches and seizures. In People v. Conley, Jack was going to try to suppress the cocaine and heroin found in Chris' purse and any admissions of guilt she'd made to Detective Guteman.

If he was successful in showing Judge Hodge that Chris' purse was searched illegally, then the Possession of Dangerous Drugs charge would have to be dismissed, as well as the first-degree murder charge, because the speedball mix was the weapon that killed Burt—without that weapon, there was no instrumentality of death and the State of Ohio has no case. A judge, as opposed to a jury, always decides whether a defendant's constitutional rights have been violated. Some judges don't believe evidence should ever be suppressed. Others, like John Hodge, believe that constitutional rights are an important American foundation and need to be respected. For judges, honoring the constitutional rights of defendants charged with serious crimes like murder is not a politically correct thing to do. It enrages the police and district attorneys who then organize politically against them. They go to the media to let them know the judge is soft on crime. Stories are printed and editorials are written. Voters refuse to re-elect the judge, which is exactly what happened to Judge Avery Jackson on the DiSalvo case.

Jim Brodan represented the People. He was sitting at counsel table along with Detective Guteman when Jack walked into the courtroom. Jim had on his dark, three-piece suit. For him, it was a uniform; he wore it every day with a different tie. The lapels were thick when thin was in, and his paunch extended over his belt. Jim looked confident and rested, which was unusual for him. Usually, he appeared harried and hidden behind a tower of law books.

Brodan was sure the outcome of this hearing was a foregone conclusion.

He respected Jack Maine as an attorney, but the most skilled defense attorney in the world would be unable to win this hearing. Brodan had one witness—Dave Guteman—probably the most experienced cop in Dayton when it came to giving testimony. The hearing should not last over an hour. The evidence was clear. Conley had summoned the authorities. Guteman had a right to be in Porter's condo. He was given permission by Conley to search her purse. Even if she claimed he had no permission, Guteman would claim he had to search the purse for his own protection. Guteman was as smart as any lawyer on search and seizure issues. The way Brodan figured it, the only way Conley could defend herself would be to take the stand. He would then get a shot at cross-examining her before her trial. He would bury her. Just a little appetizer for what was to come in the Jackson case.

Jack looked tired as he seated himself at counsel table; his face was drawn. The weekend had exhausted him. He couldn't handle working full time as a lawyer and then moonlighting as a forensic psychologist. He decided it was as draining to be a psychologist as a defense attorney.

The deputy brought Chris into the courtroom in handcuffs. Whereas she had once sat regularly in courtrooms as a reporter taking down every word on her steno machine, now she sat as a defendant in a capital murder case—to her, the switch was freaky. She wore a suit she'd frequently worn for her job. It was a respite from the orange jumpsuit that had become her garb for the last week. Although not made up, she was naturally beautiful. She had showered and washed her hair before the hearing. It hung casually over her shoulders. She had neither the countenance nor the demeanor of a killer, but then most women don't.

Reporters from the *Journal Herald* and *Daily News* sat in the front row. Brodan had made sure that Stephanie Marshall had contacted them. He wanted the public to know that Chris had been caught red-handed with the drugs. It would make his job that much easier at trial. Marci seated herself in the front row next to the reporters. She planned to not miss any of Chris' court appearances.

Jack gave Chris' hand a squeeze after the deputy removed her cuffs. Tears were in her eyes. Her humiliation was as palpable as the small table.

The bailiff and court reporter entered the room. "All rise," the bailiff called out. "This court is now in session, the Honorable John Hodge presiding. Please be seated."

Hodge was energized. He hadn't heard any good constitutional rights' issues in a first-degree murder case in a long time. Maybe this one would bring him something he could get his teeth into. "The Court calls People versus Conley. Counsel, please enter your appearances."

"James Brodan for the People," Brodan said.

"Jack Maine for the defendant, who appears in custody, Your Honor."

"Very well, Counsel. This is a motion by Mr. Maine to suppress evidence taken from the purse of the defendant as well as statements she may have made at that time. Is that correct, Mr. Maine?" Hodge asked.

"That's correct, Your Honor."

"In view of the fact there is a presumption that Ms. Conley did not waive any constitutional rights, the burden will be on the district attorney to prove that the seizure of the evidence was justified and the taking of statements was done after full advisement and without coercion. Call your first witness, Mr. Brodan," Hodge ordered.

"State calls Detective Dave Guteman."

Guteman rose from counsel table. He was dressed much more expensively than Brodan. His camelhair coat and gray, wool pants with Italian, leather shoes fit him nicely as he swore under oath to tell the truth. "Please state your name," Brodan said.

"Detective Dave Guteman."

"How are you employed?"

"As a deputy sheriff for Montgomery County, Ohio."

"How long have you worked in that capacity?"

"Twenty-one years."

"Have your ever been called as a witness before in a criminal matter?"

"Yes."

"How many times?"

"Hundreds."

"Are you the investigating detective on the Chris Conley case?"

"Yes, I am."

"Drawing your attention to January seventeenth at approximately nine o'clock in the evening, did you have occasion to respond to a call at a condominium at an address in Dayton?"

"Yes, I did."

"And what did you find there?"

"When I arrived, the paramedics were there. A plainclothes officer, McGee, was also there. They were trying to revive the resident of the condo, Mr. Burt Porter."

"Did you have occasion to have contact with a woman by the name of Chris Conley at that address?"

"Yes, I did."

"And do you see that person in court here today?"

"Yes, I do."

"Could you point her out, please?"

"Certainly. She's the blonde-haired woman sitting next to Mr. Maine at the defense table."

"Let the record reflect that Detective Guteman has identified the defendant, Ms. Conley."

"The record will so reflect," Hodge noted.

"What condition was Mr. Porter in when you arrived?" Brodan asked.

"I could see he was dead. The attempts to revive him had failed."

"What condition was Ms. Conley in?"

"Slightly upset."

The courtroom door opened. Alec Hunter and Stephanie Marshall walked in. Interviews would be in order after the hearing. They sat in the front row behind Brodan and adjacent to Marci.

Brodan proceeded, "What if anything did you notice about the face of the decedent?"

"He had been foaming from the mouth. I had the sense he had died from a drug overdose. There was evidence of redness and cracking in his nose, as well as mucous running from it. My experience told me he had been ingesting something through his nose—probably cocaine."

"After looking at the body, what did you do?"

"I engaged Ms. Conley in conversation."

"What did she say?"

"She said she had discovered the body and called 911. I asked her what she knew about his death and she said 'Nothing.' I didn't believe her. I had a gut feeling she and Porter were doing dope together. I confronted her about it."

"What did she say?"

"She admitted they were."

"Lying bastard," Chris wrote on a legal pad.

Jack put his hand on her arm. "Not to worry, Chris," he assured her. "And the next lie is about to come."

Guteman went on, "I then advised her she had the right to an attorney—that she had a right to a court-appointed attorney if she couldn't afford one—and that anything she said to me could be used against her."

"Did she request an attorney?"

"No, she said she didn't need one."

"What happened then?"

"I asked her if I could search her purse for evidence or weapons."

"Did she agree?"

"She pointed it out over on the couch and said to go ahead."

"What did you do next?"

"I searched the purse and found a vial with a white substance in it."

"I show you what has been marked as People's Exhibit One, will you please identify it?"

"This has my initials on it. It's the vial of white, powdery substance I took from her purse."

"I ask that Exhibit One be introduced into evidence," Brodan requested of the judge.

"No objection, Your Honor," Jack said.

"Exhibit One will be admitted," Hodge said.

"What else did you find in the purse?" Brodan asked.

"Besides the eyeliners, lipstick and makeup, credit cards and wallet, I found a red cocktail straw and razor blade."

"What is their significance?"

"Razor blades are used to put cocaine into lines, and straws are used to snort it."

"Did you have occasion to have the powder analyzed by the lab?"

"Yes."

"And what were the results?"

"Objection, Your Honor," Jack said. "The results of the lab test are irrelevant for purposes of this proceeding. That is a matter left for trial. The issue here is whether Detective Guteman had permission to search her purse."

"Sustained. We're not going to do a trial here today, Mr. Brodan."

"What happened next?" Brodan asked his witness.

"I asked her what they were doing."

"And what did she say?"

"She said they were planning on doing coke together."

"Did Ms. Conley ever ask to see an attorney before you questioned her?"

"No, she didn't."

"After you found Exhibit One, what did you do?"

"I placed Ms. Conley under arrest. I told the officer at the scene to take her down to the station, book her and have her blood tested."

"No further questions. Your witness, Counsel," Jim Brodan said.

Jack squeezed Chris' hand as he stood to cross-examine Detective Guteman. Chris felt like she'd been assaulted and raped by Guteman. She was going to prison—probably for life. Guteman was in control.

"Detective, didn't you find it a bit strange that Ms. Conley would call the police if she intended to kill Mr. Porter?" Jack knew it was an irrelevant question, but asked it with the intent of hitting Guteman with the most obvious flaw in his case immediately. Perhaps he'd rattle the guy.

Brodan shot to his feet. "Objection, Your Honor, that is an outrageous and irrelevant question to be asking at a suppression hearing. It also calls for a conclusion of the witness and is argumentative. This is not a trial, as Mr. Maine has already argued."

"Sustained," Judge Hodge said. "Mr. Maine, you know better than that."

"Sorry, Your Honor," Jack said, though not really sorry at all. He thought he would start with a right to the jaw as opposed to jabs if for no other reason than to give his client the feeling she was fighting back. "Now, Detective Guteman, you testified you were called to the scene of a crime at about nine o'clock on the evening of January seventeenth. Is that correct?"

"That's correct."

"How did that happen? Did you just happen to be sitting around headquarters that night when the call came in?"

"No, Counsel, I just happened to be in the area of Mr. Porter's condo when I heard the dispatch. I went over there in an effort to be helpful."

"That's very thoughtful of you, Detective," Jack said. "Detective Guteman, I am told by my investigator you live in South Dayton. Mr. Porter lives in North Dayton. It's odd that you just happened to be in the area, isn't it?"

"Not really. I believe I was running an errand up that way."

"Oh, I see," Jack said. "Did the errand involve supervising the killing of Mr. Ovanul Hazeltree?"

Brodan leapt to his feet. "This is patently outrageous cross-examination, Your Honor. I object."

"I'll connect it up, Your Honor," Jack said calmly.

For perhaps the first time in his twenty-one years of giving testimony, Guteman felt a clutch in his heart. What did Maine know? How did he know it? Guteman had no choice but to play out the story. Maine had to be bluffing.

"You've got a lot of connecting to do, Mr. Maine. I'll allow you about two more questions on this topic," Hodge said.

"Detective Guteman, wasn't there a dope dealer by the name of Ovanul Hazeltree killed that night not far from Mr. Porter's condo?"

"That's correct."

"Weren't you told by Ms. Conley that that dealer was Mr. Porter's supplier that night?"

"Objection, Your Honor. I think this is irrelevant."

"I want to hear it, Mr. Brodan," Hodge said.

"She may have mentioned that."

"Did you know a Mr. Ovanul Hazeltree?"

Guteman began to fidget in his chair. "I believe I was the investigating detective on a case or two of his."

"And didn't he frequently go by the name of Van?"

"I wouldn't know, Counsel."

"Isn't it true, Detective Guteman, that you were involved with Mr. Hazeltree on six cases?"

"I know it wasn't that many."

"Let me refresh your memory." Jack went back to his briefcase and pulled out a stack of files.

"Again, I want to renew my objection," Brodan said. "This line of questioning has nothing to do with the defendant's constitutional rights."

"I can assure the Court that it does," Jack said. "Not only does it go to Ms. Conley's constitutional rights, but it also goes to the credibility of this witness. If the court will allow me a little more leeway, I'll tie everything up."

"Proceed, Counsel, but I hope we'll be getting to the relevant issues soon," Hodge said.

Jack presented six case files. All of them were entitled People of the State of Ohio v. Ovanul Hazeltree. Each file had Guteman's signature on it somewhere.

Case by case, Jack asked Guteman to admit to the Court that was his signature. In each case, he admitted that it was. "Now Detective, each of these cases, including two first-degree murder cases, was dismissed at your request, were they not?"

"I don't know, Counsel. I'd have to look at each case file to refresh my memory."

"Allow me, Detective," Jack said as he handed Guteman each file individually. Guteman looked through them and just sat there. His heart was beating hard again, and he could feel his mouth drying out.

"Now, Detective, each of these cases was dismissed at your urging, isn't that correct?"

"Well, it was a decision made between me, my supervisor and the district attorney's office."

"Now, the truth of the matter is, you had a working relationship with Mr. Hazeltree, did you not?"

"At times we cooperated on certain law enforcement matters."

"Law enforcement matters, Detective?"

"He helped me on certain cases," Guteman said. "He was an informant for me."

"And he was also Mr. Porter's supplier, was he not?"

"I wouldn't know, Counsel."

Brodan again shot to his feet. "Your Honor, this is all very interesting, but it does not pertain to the legality of these confessions or this search and seizure."

"I do find this very interesting, and that it does have a bearing on the credibility of the witness. I'll allow you one more question, Mr. Maine, and it better get to the bottom line."

"In order that we don't have these repeated frantic objections by Mr. Brodan, Your Honor, I'll be accommodating and proceed in another way. I'll be coming back here, though." Jack wasn't sure he would be coming back. He just wanted Guteman to know he had the goods on him.

"Detective Guteman, as soon as you saw Mr. Porter's face and nose, you decided that he had overdosed, isn't that correct?"

"Yes, I thought he probably had."

"At that point, you considered Chris Conley to be a suspect in some sort of criminal activity, didn't you?"

"Yes."

"You advised her of her rights, is that correct?"

"Yes."

"And she said she didn't want an attorney."

"That's correct." Guteman was taking the bait.

"And it was at that point, she admitted that she and Mr. Porter intended to do drugs together that night."

"That's correct."

"Now, you're absolutely positive she did not request an attorney, and that she admitted her involvement in drug usage with him?"

"That's correct."

"And it was then that you asked to search her purse, correct?"

"Yes."

"And you had no warrant?"

"That's correct."

"At that point, you had seen no drugs or drug paraphernalia in the possession of the defendant or Mr. Porter, had you?"

"That's correct."

"How far away was the purse from the two of you?"

"Right next to us."

"Are you sure it was not fifteen to twenty feet away?"

"Positive."

Chris' heart was again sinking. Why was Jack making a case against her and agreeing with Guteman?

"Detective," Jack asked, "you had spoken to Mr. Porter, or heard him speak, many times in the past, had you not?"

"Yes, I would say so."

"Now, Detective, I'm going to ask you whether you have a tape recording of your interaction with Chris Conley on that night?"

"No, Counsel, I don't," Guteman said. "I don't typically walk off the street to the scene of a homicide with a tape recorder. We sometimes tape record at the station."

"That's interesting, Detective. I just happen to have such a recording." Jack turned and went back to his briefcase. "I would like to see if you're able to identify your own voice, Detective Guteman."

Guteman suddenly felt faint as his heart pounded hard in his chest.

Jack brought out a small tape recorder and a cassette. I would like this marked as Defense Exhibit One." The clerk marked the items and gave them back to Jack. He inserted Exhibit One in the tape player.

"Since you have a long-standing relationship with both Mr. Porter and Mr. Hazeltree, I expect you can identify their voices on this tape. If you're unable to do so, there are two other people in this court today who can."

Brodan was on his feet. "Your Honor, I object most strenuously to this. Counsel has not made these tapes available to me. I do not know what is on them."

"Your Honor," Jack said, "I am not obligated to produce my evidence prior to a suppression hearing, only a trial."

"Overruled," Hodge said. "Proceed, Mr. Maine."

Brodan sat down slowly, pouting.

"Now, Detective Guteman, see if you can identify the second voice on this tape as that of your snitch friend, Van Hazeltree?"

"I'll see if I can," Guteman said.

Jack pressed PLAY. A few seconds passed, and then Burt's voice came on. *"Now let's talk about Avery—Avery Jackson, Van."*

"Okay, bro, in a minute we can talk about that, but first tell me how you like the stuff."

Jack pressed the PAUSE button. "That would be Mr. Hazeltree's voice, would it not?" Jack asked.

"Yes, it sounds like him, but I can't be completely sure."

"You already testified you have heard Mr. Hazeltree's voice before, numerous times, didn't you?"

"Yes."

"Didn't the second voice sound like his?"

"Yes, but I can't be sure."

"Okay, Detective, let's continue with the tape to see if you can be a little more certain about whose voice we're hearing."

Jack pressed PLAY again. There was horrific gasping, groaning and struggling. Then came the second voice. *"Sorry, bro, but the big boys are putting the heat on me, and I had no choice. It's a survival thing for me, and I aim to survive."* There was the shuffling of feet, gasping, groaning and heavy breathing. Then the breathing stopped.

Jack went on. "Now, Detective Guteman, that is Mr. Hazeltree's voice, is it not?"

"It sounds like his voice, but I can't be sure."

Brodan jumped to his feet. "Your Honor, this appears to be material evidence in a homicide investigation, and it is an ethical violation, as well as a criminal offense, for Mr. Maine to withhold it from us."

Jack responded calmly. "First, there is no investigation in this matter. You have sought the indictment of my client for first-degree murder without any investigation. Secondly, I am presenting this tape to you today—just three weeks after Mr. Porter's murder. I believe it imperative that we listen to the rest of the tape so we have a complete record. My goal is to make a complete disclosure to you today in a manner that is also most representative of my client. I believe that satisfies any legal and ethical obligation I might have."

"Let's proceed," Hodge ordered.

"Now, Detective Guteman, I'm going to fast forward here in an attempt to help you further authenticate this tape." Jack pressed the fast forward button. The counter on the recorder told him when to stop. He then pressed PLAY. A male voice came on. *"What do we have here?"* Jack pressed STOP. "That is your voice, is it not, Detective Guteman?" he asked.

"It sounds like it."

Jack again pressed PLAY. *"I am Detective Guteman. Who are you?"* Jack pressed STOP. "You have no doubt now, do you, that is you?"

"No," Guteman said, "it sounds like my voice."

Jack pressed PLAY. A female voice came on. *"I'm Chris. I'm Burt's girlfriend—"* Jack pressed STOP again. "Now, isn't that Ms. Conley's voice on the night of Mr. Porter's death? In fact, you're speaking with her?"

"Yes, that sounds like her."

"Okay, Detective, let's just sit back and listen to your conversation with her. I'm certain it will refresh your memory."

The tape rolled.

"Do you want to tell me what happened here?"

"I got here and saw him like this, passed out."

"How did you get in?"

"I have a key."

"Looks like he was doing dope. Were you doing it with him?"

"No."

"Did the two of you do dope together tonight?"

"No."

"We have a dead man here. I need to ask you some questions. Did you two do a lot of dope together at other times?"

"No, I think I need a lawyer, Detective."

"You can call a lawyer at any time. You probably know plenty of them. I recognize you from the courts, don't I?"

"I'm a court reporter."

"Did you and Mr. Porter intend to do coke together tonight?"

"I need a lawyer, Detective."

Jack pressed the STOP button. "Now, Detective, do you still assert that you advised Ms. Conley of her rights and she never asked for a lawyer?"

"Apparently, that slipped my mind, Counsel."

"Detective, do you also continue to assert that Ms. Conley consented to the search of her purse?"

"That's my recollection, Counsel."

Jack pressed PLAY.

"If you will allow me to search your purse for weapons and evidence, you can go. We'll ask you to come to the station for more questioning once we get the toxicology report."

"I don't want you to search my purse. Look. I'm a court reporter in Judge Jeffers' division. I called in the report."

"That won't get you anything right now. Your boyfriend is dead. You are at the scene of the death. It could be that you two were doing dope together and he overdosed. It could be you intentionally slipped him a hot shot and he died. That would make it a murder."

"This is crap, Detective."

"Or it could be you carelessly brought some hot stuff in and gave it to him. Then he vapor-locked. That would make it criminally negligent homicide. I need to check your purse."

"You bastard, you do not have permission to look through my purse. You know

goddamned well I didn't threaten you in any way. I'm not within fifteen feet of that purse."

Jack pressed PAUSE. "Now, Detective," Jack asked, "do you still assert that Ms. Conley consented to the search of her purse?"

Guteman just looked at Maine. He didn't answer. There was silence in the courtroom.

Alec Hunter's mind was spinning. He looked to his left. There, the reporters were taking notes. Alec knew what they were thinking—Guteman was working with a drug-pushing, murdering snitch who had knowledge of the Jackson case. "This is a public relations disaster," he whispered to Stephanie.

"We're waiting for your answer, Detective," Jack said.

Hunter had to do something. He rose and walked through the short, swinging oak doors that separated the gallery from counsel tables. "Your Honor, Alec Hunter, District Attorney for Montgomery County, Ohio."

"Yes, Mr. Hunter," Judge Hodge said, "I believe the problems your office has with this case are apparent. I am going to insist upon an answer to the last question Mr. Maine asked."

"In that regard, Your Honor," Hunter said, "I believe you should advise the witness that he has the right to remain silent at this point. It occurs to me that he might be putting himself in a position where it could be claimed that he has perjured himself here today. I am, however, very distressed with Mr. Maine's unprofessionalism in this matter. For a member of the bar to withhold evidence in a criminal matter is the grossest ethical violation. I will be filing a grievance with the Supreme Court of Ohio regarding Mr. Maine's unethical behavior and am considering charging him with Obstruction of Justice."

"Excuse me, Mr. Hunter, but I was in the midst of cross-examining your detective when you interrupted. You do whatever you wish with me, but the fact remains that your office is putting on a first-degree murder case based on perjured testimony by a witness who may be trying to cover up a murder, as well as an illegal search and seizure and improperly taken statements. The ethical violations are those of your office, Mr. Hunter, and criminal acts are those of your witness."

"Just a moment, Counsel," Judge Hodge said. "I will not have you two bickering with one another. This is an important criminal proceeding involving Ms. Conley, who has obviously been indicted by the grand jury for a crime she didn't commit. Mr. Maine, I agree with Mr. Hunter. I need to advise Detective Guteman of his rights. Then, I'm going to insist upon an answer to the question, Detective Guteman." Hodge shifted his attention to Detective Guteman. "I believe it is incumbent upon me at this time to advise you of your right to remain silent. Anything you say may be used against you. You may assert your

Fifth Amendment privilege against self-incrimination if you so choose. You may have time to confer with Mr. Hunter or Mr. Brodan if you so choose. Do you understand, Detective?"

Guteman looked at Hodge. His gut reaction was to say, "Fuck you, Judge. No one talks to me that way." But even he knew better. "I understand, Your Honor," he said.

"Mr. Maine, would you please ask the question again?"

Jack pressed REWIND. He played the tape over again to the point where the vial was seized from Chris' purse against her will and without permission. "Now, Detective Guteman, having heard this tape again, do you still claim that Chris Conley gave you permission to search her purse?"

Guteman did not answer. He'd been reduced to a petulant, stubborn child who had been caught with his hand in the cookie jar and was going to stonewall it no matter the result. It was the same thing he had done as a kid when caught shoplifting and torching cats.

"Detective Guteman," Judge Hodge admonished him, "at this point you have two choices. You can either take the Fifth Amendment or you can answer the question. If you do not answer the question, I will hold you in contempt of this court and order the sheriff to arrest you. What's your pleasure, Detective?"

Guteman refused to answer. Hunter tried to help him. "You are refusing to answer, are you not, because of your Fifth Amendment privilege?"

"I'll never take the Fifth," scowled Guteman. "I'm not a criminal."

"Then," Hodge said, "you must answer the question."

Guteman sat silent.

"Detective, you leave me no choice but to hold you in contempt. I am ordering the sheriff to detain you immediately. You are to be held in jail without bond. We will have a hearing on this tomorrow morning to see if you will be willing to answer the question then. I believe you have perjured yourself in my court, Detective, and I take that very seriously. I suggest an attorney represent you at tomorrow's hearing. In the meantime, I am suggesting to Mr. Hunter that he explore the possibility of bringing perjury charges against you."

"We will review the matter and decide what charges, if any, to bring, Your Honor," Hunter said.

"Mr. Brodan, do you have any more witnesses on the Chris Conley suppression matter?" Judge Hodge asked.

"No, Your Honor," Brodan said.

"Then I'm going to grant the defendant's motion to suppress the evidence taken from her purse, as well as all statements that the district attorney would seek to use against her at trial. I find that her purse was searched without a warrant and without her consent. Furthermore, I find that Detective Guteman did not have probable cause to search the purse, and there were no exigent circumstances making the search of her purse necessary. There was no evidence that Ms. Conley was a participant in any crime when Detective Guteman executed the search, and therefore, the search of her purse was not warranted. I further find that any statements Detective Guteman claims he may have taken from the defendant were taken without Ms. Conley being adequately advised of her rights."

"Your Honor," Hunter said, "in view of the court's ruling, we're moving to dismiss the charges against Ms. Conley, and ask that she be released immediately. It is our intent that she be reinstated in her job. I will personally be talking with Judge Jeffers this afternoon and explaining to her that Ms. Conley is innocent of the charges."

"So ordered," Judge Hodge said. "The defendant will be released immediately from custody. I will see counsel back here tomorrow morning for further contempt proceedings. Court is in recess."

Reporters Al Conover and Chris DiMarco rushed to Hunter and Stephanie as soon as Judge Hodge's gavel hit the bench. Conover posed the most obvious question: "Did your office realize that Detective Guteman had based this case on perjured testimony?"

"Absolutely not," Alec replied. "This was overly aggressive, if not criminal, police work. Our office does not condone this sort of behavior. We will be pursuing whatever charges are available to us against Detective Guteman."

"What, if any, connection does the Chris Conley case have with the Avery Jackson case?"

"None that we know of," Stephanie said. "But now that we have this information, we'll be sure to follow up on all leads."

"Who are the big boys who wanted Burt Porter killed?" Conover asked.

"We have no idea," Alec said. "That will be thoroughly investigated. However, at this point, we believe Avery Jackson acted alone."

"Who was Ovanul Hazeltree?" DiMarco asked. "How was he connected to the Avery Jackson case?"

"He was a pusher," Stephanie said.

"Was there any relationship between his death and the deaths of Avery Jackson and Burt Porter?"

"Absolutely none that we know of at this time," Alec said.

As Stephanie was answering these questions, she felt like a robot. She knew what the office's official position would be. She was badly shaken, but on the surface, she was cool and collected. It was the way Alec needed her to be. He had mastered the art of it. She had learned well from him.

Chris Conley sat quietly as the reporters questioned Hunter and Marshall. She didn't know if she had the strength in her legs to support herself. She could feel her knees tremble as she stood. She was relieved she could finally breathe. An anvil had been removed from her chest, a football from her stomach and an icicle from her heart. She smiled for the first time in three weeks. She hugged Jack. Marci burst through to counsel table and embraced her. Both women cried.

"This nightmare is over for you, Chris," Jack said. "You need to go back to the jail, get your property and meet us for lunch. We have a lot to discuss." Conover and DiMarco asked for an interview. Jack said they would meet all of them at one-thirty after lunch when both he and Chris would have a statement.

The deputy did not cuff Chris as she escorted her back to the jail to get her things. Detective Guteman, however, scowled as Deputy Brady put cuffs on him. "Sorry, Detective, but you know it's department policy." Guteman said nothing to Brady, an officer he outranked many times.

After Guteman was booked, he made a phone call to Jim Rosato's office. Rosato was tied up for lunch but agreed to visit him after lunch at the jail.

Now the jail had the problem of what to do about security for Detective David Guteman. If they were to put him in a pod with other inmates, he would be dead. The other inmates would love to have the opportunity to slap him around, bend him over a bed, and do whatever with his orifices.

Officer Brady and the shift commander decided they would move inmates out of Pod Three into other pods. This would leave Guteman alone in an eight-man pod. He would have the run of it. They would not keep him in solitary confinement as they did other inmates who were a security risk. He would be protected. It was a temporary inconvenience. He would probably be there only one night anyway.

Monday—12 noon
The King's Table

"Marci, may I borrow your lipstick and eyeliner?" was the first thing Chris asked when she met Marci and Jack at the King's Table after her release. Marci was more than happy to oblige. Chris had been without makeup for a week. People glanced furtively in her direction trying to disguise their morbid interest at why an indicted killer would be eating with them. Now, all who had presumed her guilty and had abandoned her would be expressing their relief at the dismissal of the charges and their belief in her from the start. On the way back from the ladies' lounge, she got many "Congratulations, I believed in you the whole time" pats on the back from those who would have gossiped about her had she been convicted and sentenced to life in prison.

"I need a drink," were her next words. Jack raised his hand to summon Bobbi.

"This one's on the house, Chris. What will it be?" Bobbi asked.

"Bourbon and seven." She turned to Jack. "I can't thank you enough for what you've done for me. I only wanted to fire you about three or four times each day after I was locked up."

"I don't blame you," Jack said. "I'd feel the same way if I were in your shoes. We need to celebrate. You also need to know you're about to come into a great deal of money. You were indicted because Burt had taken out a two hundred thousand dollar life insurance policy on himself, and you are the beneficiary. You should have received notice of it a couple of months ago."

"Oh, *Wow*. I remember getting something from an insurance company that I was the beneficiary of something from Burt. I didn't much care or pay a whole lot of attention to it. I always thought Burt would live forever. I didn't even know the amount."

"The company is Ohio Casualty, and they're now obligated to pay you the money. They wouldn't be if you had killed Burt. Now, their debt to you is clear." Jack handed her a note with the name of the adjuster responsible for the claim. "Call this woman; she'll cut you a check."

"Now, I can pay you the rest of the money I owe you," Chris said, more pleased with that than the actual fact of getting the money.

Marci looked relieved. "We're running on fumes, and that will pay our expenses the rest of the month," she said.

"Burt was always too scared to go out on his own," Chris said. "He talked a big game, but he was really insecure about the start-up costs and whether he'd have any paying clients come through the door. That's why he never left the PD's office."

"That's sort of what it's been like for us," Marci said.

"There is another matter I'd like to discuss with you," Jack said.

"What's that?"

"You have a good false arrest, false imprisonment, malicious prosecution and civil rights suit against Guteman and the sheriff's office. I suggest you file it. We would be available to represent you."

"Just give me the paperwork. If you'll do it on a contingency basis for one third of the settlement, I'll agree."

"It's a deal. Now, let's enjoy lunch," Jack said, relieved that he had won the case, but knowing that any civil, damages settlement on it was a year or two away. Now, if only he could stay in business that long.

Monday—1:30 P.M.
Montgomery County Jail

When Jim Rosato met with Dave Guteman that afternoon, the sky was already darkening. The clouds hung low over the city. *It is sure to snow*, Bill thought as he signed for a professional visit at the front desk. Rosato had been at the county jail so many times over the years that the deputies dispensed with the formality of his showing his driver's license and bar card. They simply gave him a visitor's pass and took him straight to the attorney visitation room.

Guteman was already in his prison orange when Rosato came into the room. Rosato smiled. "Aren't you a sight. I never thought I'd see you in an orange jumpsuit."

"Save it," Guteman said. "I could have used you earlier this morning."

"So I've heard."

"I set the bitch up. Jack Maine fucked me right in front of everyone. Somehow he got a tape recording and I was fucked. I've never seen anything like it. I had to stonewall it."

"What do you mean *stonewall it*?"

"Admit I committed perjury or take the Fifth. I refused to take the Fifth."

"How did you get involved in this mess—is it Chicago business?" Jim Rosato knew only too well the arrangement between Hazeltree, Guteman and the syndicate. He had exploited it many times.

"Chicago put out a contract on Porter because he knew too much. Van had opened his big mouth—got hinky on them—was about to roll over. They wanted him and Porter dead."

"So?"

"I arranged it, wiretaps, hits—the whole nine yards. We used Van to kill Porter and then set up Porter's girlfriend."

"The press is trying to make a connection between the Hardacre killing and Porter's killing. Was there one?"

"Of course there was, but I'm not going to get into it. I'm a dead man if I do. All I want is to get out of here."

"Sorry, Dave, but that isn't going to happen until tomorrow morning. I've already talked to Judge Hodge's clerk about whether he'd be willing to cut you loose this afternoon. He told me the judge was pissed that you came into his court and lied your ass off. He's going to let you sit overnight. Said it would be a good lesson for you. If you're not a good boy in the morning, you'll sit longer. He's prepared to let you sit as long as necessary. He's amused that you finally got caught lying about a search."

"Fuck him. How the hell was I supposed to know they had me on tape?"

"It's gotta be a first."

"What should I do? I don't want to take the Fifth like every other scumbag prisoner I've arrested."

"You're going to go into court tomorrow and take the Fifth. Then you're going to apologize to the court; say you meant no disrespect. Then Hodge is going to cut you loose and tell Jim Brodan he should consider a perjury charge against you. Brodan will give him lip service, play to the crowd of reporters that will be there, and then do nothing with it, claiming that after a thorough investigation, he's convinced you'd just forgotten what happened. He's going to assure the press you've tendered your resignation. It will all be over. I've already talked to Brodan, and it's a done deal."

"I know I'm done," Guteman said.

"Yeah, you're done. Every defense attorney in town will have a transcript of the proceeding, and whenever you're called to testify, they'll pull it out and make you look like a lying son-of-a-bitch in front of a jury."

"I know that," Guteman said. "I just want you to make sure I'm taken care of. I took this fall for the organization and they know it. I don't want you talking with Lane. Forget Lane. I want you to talk directly with Marshall Conn at Frontline Enterprises. Tell him I want a million dollars and I'll disappear. The figure is non-negotiable. If they won't play ball with me, I'll take them down—here, in Chicago and Miami—do the witness protection thing."

"Are you sure you want to go down that road? I'm not sure these are the types of guys you want to give ultimatums to."

"Don't present it as an ultimatum. Just tell them I need a million to be happy. Let them figure the rest out. Conn has always been a reasonable businessman. He's always paid me what he owed me for the work I did for him. Remind him that Lane will be taking over as sheriff again in a few weeks, and he'll be able to get another detective on the front line who'll handle the dealers."

Rosato thought for a second. He had met Marshall Conn before at fundraisers and philanthropic functions for Experiences in Growth. He agreed; Conn had always seemed like a reasonable guy. "I'll give it a try, but I'm really going to soft pedal it. These are not the sorts of guys you play hardball with."

"Just sell it to them in your best bullshit, lawyer style."

Guteman gave Rosato Conn's number at Frontline Enterprises in Chicago. "I'll see you in the morning, Jim," Guteman said as Rosato was preparing to leave. "I can do one night in here standing on my head. They got me a pod all to myself. Just get me out of here in the morning."

"Don't worry," Rosato assured him.

Monday—5:00 P.M.
Rosatos' Law Offices

It was nearly dark when Jim Rosato left the jail. Snow was falling; big flakes drifted down onto the cold pavement, swirling and gathering like strands of sugar spun in a cotton candy machine. He walked to the parking lot, got into his Mercedes and drove just five blocks to his penthouse office atop Dayton's highest office building. On the way, he composed his conversation with a man he knew controlled hundreds of millions of dollars in gambling and drug money, as well as tens of millions from corrections facilities and who knows what other clever, white-collar ventures. He realized he owed his success to Conn. There could be even a bigger payoff for him if he played his cards right. On the other hand, if he angered Conn, he might be ruined, or worse. This call must be handled in such a way that the wishes of his client were communicated without poisoning the well.

When he sat down at his desk, it was five-fifteen. He realized it was an hour earlier in Chicago. He would try to get Conn on the phone. He dialed the number of Frontline Enterprises. When he asked for Mr. Marshall Conn, he was referred to Frank Newton, Conn's right-hand man. Guys like him never put themselves on Front Street, especially with an out-of-town lawyer Conn probably wouldn't even remember.

"Frank Newton here," said a powerful voice on the other end of the phone.

"Frank, this is Attorney Jim Rosato in Dayton. I believe I met you and Mr. Conn at some functions in Dayton involving one of your organizations."

"Which organization is that? We have a number of businesses in Ohio."

"Experiences in Growth."

"I remember," Newton said. "I believe you were the attorney with Dave Guteman and Hugh Lane."

"That's correct. I was hoping to speak to Mr. Conn about a very important matter involving my client, Dave Guteman."

"It's an impossibility for Mr. Conn to speak with you. He's very busy. I handle all his business affairs at their inception. I would ask that you call me back on my cell phone."

Newton gave Rosato the number. Rosato called back immediately.

"So, what can I do for you?" Newton asked.

"Mr. Guteman has become involved in a situation here today that prevents him from cooperating with your organization any further. Mr. Guteman is currently in jail, actually," Rosato said.

"We are aware of the situation," Newton said. "We are sympathetic. What does Mr. Guteman need?"

"Mr. Guteman will appreciate that. His career is essentially ruined. He will need some severance money to help him go on with his life. He will then disappear to a warmer climate."

"What amount of money does he need?" Newman asked.

"He will need one million dollars," Rosato said without hesitation.

"That sum has already been authorized by Frontline. It will be delivered tomorrow, assuming you can have Guteman out of jail to receive it. It's not a problem. Anything else, Mr. Rosato?"

"Just have your people deliver the money to my office in the Dayton Towers at four o'clock tomorrow afternoon. It's been a pleasure. Perhaps I can be of help to you in the future on other legal matters that come up from time to time here in Dayton," Rosato offered.

"As I understand it, you're a very resourceful and efficient lawyer, Mr. Rosato. You've been of great service to us. We'll be in touch."

Jim Rosato sat back in his high-backed, black-leather chair. He watched the snow swirl to the ground, the flakes translucent against the streetlights below. He'd tell Dave Guteman tomorrow morning the one million dollar settlement had taken hours to negotiate. He would take fifty thousand dollars of the million for his afternoon of work. It seemed only fair.

Monday—4:30 P.M.
Frontline Enterprises, Chicago, Illinois.

Marshall Conn sat at the head of the marble and teak conference table as Frank Newton turned off his cell phone. Frank dressed in the finest suits and shoes, as did Conn, though Conn's outfit was augmented by expensive jewelry: diamond rings, gold and diamond cufflinks, and gold bracelets. Conn thought it made his middle-aged, paunchy body not so noticeable.

"That was Guteman's attorney, a guy by the name of Rosato," Newton said nonchalantly.

"What did he want?" Conn asked.

"He wants a million cash delivered to his office tomorrow."

Conn chuckled. "It's amazing," he said, "that a guy can screw up as badly as Guteman did and then believe he should be rewarded for it. What an idiot. He allows himself to be taped setting up the bitch who was supposed to take the fall. We don't need him. Lane takes over again in a few days. He can replace Guteman. Guteman is a liability."

"The message I just got from this guy Rosato is we either pay the money or his client will roll over on us. Next thing we know, we'll be in federal court and Guteman will be in witness protection. It's my advice we stay with the plan we decided on this afternoon."

"I agree," Conn said. "Let's trust our people in Dayton on this. They've made us a lot of money. Call our guy and make sure he gets a bug in that lawyer's office—Maine, or whatever his name is. No more fuckups!"

CHAPTER 21

Tuesday, February 6—3:30 A.M.
Montgomery County Jail

The sheriff's special treatment of Dave Guteman in giving him his own pod made it easy. He was alone and asleep in his bunk when they came deftly, quietly. When the footsteps were upon him, he awakened, though still groggy. The noose made of torn bedding was around his throat before he could fight. It was pulled tightly by the strongest, while the two others held him. He could not scream; the crushing power paralyzed his larynx. They picked him up and fastened the other end of the bedding over an open door. He hung there, his pants soaked in urine and filled with feces. Dave Guteman had hanged himself in disgrace.

Tuesday—8:00 A.M.
Dayton Towers Parking Garage

It had been a difficult drive into work from Oakwood for Jim Rosato that morning. The swirling snow had left drifts. As he passed by the jail, he noticed a hearse at the sally port. He thought nothing of it. His card key opened the gate to the underground lot beneath his building. He moved slowly down the incline into the darkness of the garage to the parking places his firm had rented for the three years they had been in Dayton's most exclusive office building. The garage was only half full this morning because of the weather. His brother's car was not yet there.

245

Jim began steeling himself for the rigors of the day. He had an hour to review the law on contempt before the Guteman hearing. The press would be all over it.

Rosato grabbed his briefcase with his right hand; he opened the door with his left. As he swung his feet onto the cold pavement, he could hear footsteps and see the lower part of a torso emerge from behind the SUV parked next to the Rosato Brothers' parking spaces. Before he could stand, the gun, with its silencer, coughed. The bullet struck Rosato in the left temple. He slumped back in his car, a quarter of the back of his head blown off. The blood ran rapidly down the back of his camelhair coat and pooled on the rich leather. The gloved and stocking-capped shooter placed a note on the twitching body.

This is what happens to lying fucking scumbag lawyers who don't get you off after they take your money and promise they will. S.

The shooter hid the gun under his overcoat and walked calmly, but resolutely, out of the garage and disappeared into the mass of office workers scurrying to their jobs.

Tuesday—9:00 A.M.
Montgomery District County Court

At nine-fifteen in the morning, the usually punctual Judge John Hodge took the bench. His visage was ashen. Jim Brodan, Alec Hunter and Stephanie Marshall entered the courtroom moving purposefully down the aisle. They had just been informed of Guteman's hanging.

"Calling the matter of David Guteman," Judge Hodge said. "This matter comes forthwith to determine if Mr. Guteman will purge himself of contempt of this court. The record should reflect that Mr. Guteman does not appear. Yesterday, Attorney-at-Law James Rosato entered his appearance on this matter and agreed to be here to represent Mr. Guteman today. Mr. Rosato also does not appear.

"The following facts have come to the Court's attention and are regrettably dispositive of the matter." The always articulate John Hodge found himself stammering. "Sometime during the night, Mr. Guteman apparently committed suicide while confined in jail." There were a few gasps in the gallery. Hodge took a deep breath. "Therefore, I find that Mr. Guteman, in view of his death, is no longer in contempt of this court, and the citation is dismissed." Tears came to his eyes. Neither Jack nor anyone in the court had ever witnessed a judge tearing up while on the bench. "There is one other matter," he said as he wiped his eyes with tissues. "My office has just received a call from the law firm of Rosato and Rosato. Mr. James Rosato was shot to death in his car about an hour ago—apparently by a disgruntled client. The rest of the court's docket will be vacated. Court is adjourned."

Judge Hodge left the courtroom with his bailiff and court reporter. When the courtroom had cleared, the reporters approached Alec Hunter and Stephanie Marshall. As best they could, Alex and Stephanie explained what they knew.

They were as perplexed as anyone else. "Sure," they responded to the questions, "we will be doing a complete investigation on both deaths—no, there is no evidence at this time that the deaths are at all related—sure, it looks highly suspicious since the deaths occurred within hours of one another, but until someone can show the connection, our office will be considering the matter as two unrelated tragedies—preliminary finding is that Detective Guteman's death was a suicide, and Rosato's a homicide—yes, extraordinary means were taken to insure Detective Guteman's safety; in fact, he had an entire pod to himself—no, there is no apparent motive for Rosato's death, but the fact that he was a criminal lawyer automatically put him at risk."

Jack and Marci Maine heard about the two deaths but tried not to think about them. They could live scared to death or try to work around it. The Jackson trial was in two months. There was a lot of work to be done. Although Jack had won the Conley case, no new cases had come in. A settlement for Chris' false arrest case was distant. They needed an infusion of cash.

CHAPTER 22

Over the next several weeks Joe put out an extraordinary effort to find K. Blaine. The Pentagon was of no help; it stonewalled him. So he claimed he was with Farm Auto Insurance and tracked down every Blaine in the United States through motor vehicle records. There were several K. Blaines, but they were all the wrong age—either eighteen or eighty, and sometimes the wrong sex. There were K. Blaines in Washington, New York, and Delaware, but none of them claimed to have ever served in the Armed Forces.

March 12
Jack Maine and Associates

"Two things we need to talk about today, Joe," Jack said as he and Marci walked into the conference room. Joe had spread hundreds of pages of documents over the elongated table. A king-sized Starbucks' cup had left a baseball-sized ring on the pile to Joe's right. The pouches under Joe's eyes had progressed to bags since he had begun working on the Jackson case. His salt and pepper hair was now more salt than pepper.

"Only two? Ain't shit. Been here since six this morning."

"And?"

"Ain't got much to show for it. I woke up in a sweat at four this morning. I keep having the same dream. It always ends with me strapped down with a needle in my arm. I couldn't sleep, so I came down here."

"Sympathy dreams, Joe. You're into this. What's all this stuff?"

"CIA documents I got through the Freedom of Information Act. Did you ever see so much bullshit? Dudes in the CIA must own stock in magic markers. Every other line is blacked-out."

"Anything about Avery?" Marci asked.

"Nothing specific. There are no names. Just references to Army "positions and assets." The CIA had a lot going on in 'Nam. I just can't tell shit about it. Either still classified or blacked-out."

"Can you tell who the supervisor of the project was?"

"One name keeps coming up. A Dr. Hiram Storselle. I called the CIA at Langley and asked for him."

"And?"

"Been dead for twenty years. I told them I was doing a story for Ebony about the use of marijuana and LSD in mind control, and I wanted to talk to the man who replaced Dr. Storselle. Some secretary referred me to a Dr. James McGinty. I left two voice mails for the son-of-a-bitch. He didn't return them. Then the same secretary called me back and said she was incorrect in referring me to McGinty. He was not in charge of that department. When I asked who was, she said that information was classified."

"Let's follow up on McGinty," Marci said. "Just a hunch—female intuition. They're giving you the runaround. Give me the number at Langley; if you had been a white woman, you would have gotten somewhere, Joe. Does that name come up elsewhere in the documents?"

"No, Storselle died in 1980 and the documents are only being declassified before then."

Joe wrote down the number on a sticky pad while Marci grabbed a *New York Times* article Joe had found titled MIND CONTROL SUBJECT'S ESTATE SETTLES CASE WITH GOVERNMENT. She scanned it quickly while Joe and Jack sipped coffee. "This ought to get their attention. Get this. 'G.I. Montgomery McDowell, who had been given repeated doses of LSD in CIA experiments, suffered a paranoid flashback and jumped out the window. His wife settled the wrongful death action for two and a half million dollars.'" Marci dialed the number as she looked for the author of the article. "Dr. McGinty, please. This is Jan Beckett from the *New York Times*. It's imperative I speak with Dr. McGinty immediately. I'm following up on the Montgomery McDowell story with another story about CIA mind-control experiments. The story is coming out in tomorrow's paper about Dr. McGinty's being in charge, if you will, of such projects. We would like Dr. McGinty's reaction." There was pause as Marci took a sip of her coffee. "She's seeing if Dr. McGinty is in," she whispered to the two men.

An austere voice came on the other end of the line. "This is Dr. McGinty."

"Doctor, Jan Beckett from the *New York Times*. We're running a follow-up story on the Montgomery McDowell case and your involvement in it as the director of CIA mind-control programs. As you know, the case was settled for two and a half million."

"It was actually something less than that, but with attorney fees, that would probably be an accurate amount."

"The thrust of tomorrow's article is that you were responsible for the CIA activities that ultimately resulted in McDowell's death, and that you are currently overseeing such projects for the government."

"Now, just wait a minute, Ms. Beckett. If you come out with such a story, I'll be on the phone with my lawyers in five minutes. I'll sue you and the *Times* for such reckless disregard for the truth."

"What is the truth, Doctor?"

"Hiram Storselle was in charge of these projects. He oversaw the work that was done with McDowell and all the mind-control work done in the 1960s and 1970s. After Storselle's died in 1980, I just monitored those projects for the CIA that were no longer active."

"How many such projects were there?"

"That is classified information."

"Are there currently any such projects being conducted?"

"Classified information."

"You're not being very helpful, Doctor."

"It's not my job to be helpful. It's my job to protect and preserve the Constitution of the United States."

"Sounds quite presidential."

"That is the President's mandate, and everyone who works here adheres to it."

"I see. Perhaps we should change the story. Would it be correct to say that you were not in charge of the McDowell case, but that you are currently in charge of all the records for the experiments conducted under Dr. Storselle?"

"Yes. That's correct."

"And those experiments are classified?"

"Except for those documents already released pursuant to the Freedom of Information Act."

"And how about the case of Avery Jackson in Ohio—the judge who killed the sheriff in cold blood? Our sources tell us he was one of Dr. Storselle's subjects."

"I can neither confirm nor deny any of that."

"I think we'll hold on the story, Dr. McGinty."

"That would be a good idea, unless you want a defamation case looking you squarely in the eyes."

"Thank you, Doctor, you have been quite helpful," Marci said officiously as she hung up. She took another drink of coffee and broke into a smile. "Amazing what you can get out of people when you act like you have power. McGinty's the guy. He admitted he kept all the records for the experiments in the 1960s and 1970s. He would neither confirm nor deny whether Avery was a subject in these experiments, but I could tell I hit home just by the tone of his voice. It was such a terse denial."

"Piece uh cake now. I'll call the Department of Motor Vehicles in Virginia and D.C. and get his home address. I can get him served by tomorrow," Joe said.

"Okay, let's talk about the prosecution's other witnesses. Hunter has endorsed Dr. Procheska and a Dr. Horde from Harvard. We know what kind of whore Procheska is. Never met a district attorney he didn't like."

"Or whose ass he didn't kiss," Joe said.

"Exactly. I want you to talk to all the attorneys in town who ever did a criminal case with him; scour the public defender files; go to the state hospital. I don't care about the expense. Everything is on credit from now on anyway. Find every sanity case Procheska has ever done, pull the court file, get the hospital records. We need to be able to show his bias."

"What about Horde? The son-of-a-bitch must be dirty if Hunter's using him."

"Has to be. Same procedure as Procheska. Find out every case he's ever testified in. Order his transcripts. Money is no object. Look him up on the Internet, get all his publications, his record at Harvard, that sort of thing. Find out what organizations he belongs to, who he has testified for in the past. Has he ever been sued for malpractice? He's from Boston. Check the court records there. And look carefully through all this CIA stuff. I'll bet you'll find him somewhere in the pile. He might be disguised, but he'll be in there somewhere as a CIA shrink."

"Trying to kill me?"

"Better you than Avery."

"Hear ya. What's the other thing?"

"Seems that a car is following me, a tan sedan."

"Want me to have it taken care of?"

"I don't want you getting into trouble. Just keep an eye out for me. Don't know if they're local talent or Chicago boys."

"Will do."

"We'll leave you to your work, Joe," Marci said.

"Hey, Marci, you did good with McGinty. I gotta hand it to you."

"Coming from you, Joe, that's quite a compliment. Women generally can get information from men easier than men can."

"I guess," Joe said as Jack and Marci walked out of the conference room into Jack's office.

"You'll be careful?" Marci asked as she moved over to give Jack a hug.

"Certainly. You, too."

"Do you think I'm at risk?"

"Difficult to say. Guteman had no compunction about trying to destroy Chris. Male or female—I don't think it makes much difference. That's why I got you a gun."

"And money is no object, Counselor?"

"What I really meant is that if we lose this case, we won't have any money." They hugged again, then a couple of kisses.

"Interesting how the threat of annihilation brings us closer together," Marci whispered.

Monday—March 15
Jack Maine and Associates

"Isn't Terry Singleton the name of the guy Joe is supposed to be looking for on the streets—the guy who worked with Van Hazeltree?" Marci asked as she entered Jack's office. Jack was scouring a book on insanity defenses. He didn't want to be bothered with a trivia question. The Jackson trial was only one month away.

"I can't remember," Jack said dismissively.

"Jack, you're treating me like a piece of furniture. Listen to me. I think this is the guy."

Jack looked up. "What did you say the guy's name was?"

"Terry Singleton."

Jack thought for a second and smiled. "Come to think of it, I believe it is. Joe says he's been looking all over the place for him. Every time he thinks he's located him, Singleton disappears."

"You have an appointment in thirty minutes with a man by the name of Terry Singleton. He called about an hour ago and said he had to see you this morning."

"What kind of case does he have?"

"He said it was a drug case."

"That would make sense."

"Hopefully, he's got some cash."

"Where do we stand?"

"We don't. We're dead."

"Bring him in when he gets here," Jack said.

A very large, well-built, black man was sitting in the waiting room when

Marci returned to her desk from Jack's office. He was dressed in a long, leather coat, black pants and a black, turtleneck sweater.

"Mr. Singleton?" Marci asked.

"That would be me," he said coolly.

"Mr. Maine will be with you in a minute. You are a few minutes early. Can I get you something to drink—coffee or soda?"

"Dr. Pepper would be good."

"Why don't you let me take your coat."

"No, I'll keep it," Singleton said as he took off his coat and held it in a hand the size of a meat hook. Marci could see he had a huge chest and arms. Gold's Gym. Marci went back to Jack's office. On the way, she grabbed a Dr. Pepper out of the kitchen refrigerator. "Better watch what you say to Mr. Singleton, Jack. He looks like he could crush each of us like grapes."

"Now we know why Van used him for muscle," Jack said. "Show him in. Let's see what he brings to the table."

Marci returned quickly with Mr. Singleton. "Jack Maine," Jack said as he reached out to give Mr. Singleton a handshake.

"Terry Singleton," Terry responded, his handshake limp and clammy.

"What's on your mind, Terry? Do you mind if I call you Terry? We run a very informal office here."

"That's fine, bro. I'll just call you bro."

"What can I do for you, Terry?"

"I been readin' in the paper where you got that Conley girl off a while back."

"Yes."

"What I liked about that is you fucked up that asshole Guteman."

"Do you know . . . did you know Detective Guteman?"

"Oh, I knew him. He was dirty. He didn't commit suicide. They had him killed."

"How do you know that?" Jack asked, his interest beginning to grow.

"I may be able to tell you sometime. Right now, bro, I got a problem of my own."

"What's that?"

"I was busted with five keys of coke a couple of nights ago."

"How did that happen?"

"One of my dudes picked the shit up at the airport. He brought it to my crib in two suitcases. The cops came charging in, pushed my face and his into the floor, cuffed us and brought us downtown."

"Did the cops have a warrant?"

"Hell no!."

"Did you have the suitcases open when the cops came in?"

"I had just opened one of them and was testing the stuff to see how pure the shit was."

"Could be bad news."

"That's what I figured. That's why I'm here. My usual lawyer is Jim Rosato, but they killed him."

"Who killed him?"

"The syndicate. At least, that's the word on the street."

"We heard it was a disgruntled client," Jack said.

"That's bullshit. Jim didn't have any pissed-off clients—at least none connected with the organization. He took care of them. It cost them a lot, but when you paid him, everything was cool."

"Really?"

"Oh, yeah, man. He had everything greased."

"Tell me about it," Jack said.

"Maybe sometime," Singleton said coolly. "All I want to know is whether you have the same connections as Rosato. Me and the brothers are figurin' you do 'cause of the way you won that Conley case."

"Just good solid investigation and lawyering, Terry. Nothing more—nothing less. I know the law on search and seizure. If you're going to win your case, you'll need a lawyer who can convince a judge that your constitutional rights were violated when the police came busting into your house without a warrant."

"Let's just say I drop twenty-five grand on you today. How much of that would go to the cops, the DAs and the judge to take care of the case?"

"Terry, we don't pay anyone off. We don't have to. We win our cases with our wits. It's like this, you attempt to succeed in your business with your street knowledge. We succeed as lawyers with our knowledge of the law."

"I like the way you talk, bro. Rosato never talked like that. I'm up for a change. I'd like you to represent me and my man, Horace, who was also busted."

"I'd be glad to do that." Jack smiled. "But we don't pay off judges or sheriffs. What's more, we don't take retainers that are stolen money or are derived from illegal activities such as the sale of drugs."

"That, bro, is hard to believe. Rosato always told us it would be thirty thousand this and thirty thousand that 'to take care of matters,' and he never questioned where any of the money for his fees came from."

"That was Rosato, and he's dead. We don't do it. You'll have to assure me that any money you might give me is not derived from illegal activities."

"No problem, bro. I'm just borrowing the money from my rich uncle. I'll have to pay him back with my job at McDonalds," Singleton said with a big smile.

"How do you know Rosato's fee was going to payoffs? Maybe Rosato just wanted you to believe he was paying someone off when he was really just pocketing the money? Maybe he was just playing you and your buddies for suckers that he could bleed dry."

"Shit, bro; Dayton's a wired city. It's in the middle of the country where I-70 and I-75 meet. The amount of drugs that pass through here in a day would blow your freaking mind, Jack. To do business here, you need protection. The mob has put a lot of money into this place to keep it greased."

"Did you work for Van Hazeltree?"

"Yeah."

"My investigator, Joe Betts, has been trying to get hold of you for weeks on another case."

Singleton just looked at Jack, the wheels inside his head obviously turning. His eyes dropped and he sank in his chair. "I know that a big nigger been looking for me. I figured he was with the cops or something."

"No, he works for me. We're doing an investigation on the Avery Jackson case and we thought you might be able to help us with Van's connection to the case."

"Van gave me my start. I owe him everything I have. I wouldn't be wearin' these kinds of threads if it weren't for Van. You know, they had him killed, too."

"Who had him killed?"

"Guteman and the head pig."

"Who's the head pig?"

"The head pig is Mr. Hugh Lane."

"How do you know that?"

"Van knew it."

"Why was Van killed?"

"Because Van got pissed off and went to the new dude who was elected sheriff and blew the whistle on Lane and Guteman."

"How do you know all that?"

"Because Van told me before they killed him. The dude, Lane, been runnin' a crooked sheriff's office for years. He was paid big money by the syndicate in Miami and Chicago to grease everything up here for the drug business. All the drugs from Colombia that come up through Miami are shipped right up Interstate-75 to Detroit and Canada. The west-to-east traffic is the same. It comes right through I-70 from California to the east coast. This is where it's happenin', man. Lane is a crooked son-of-a-bitch. He's been paid so much motherfuckin' money over the years to protect these dudes in Chicago and all of us that sell the shit for them. It's ridiculous. Guteman was just Hugh Lane's white nigger to help keep things greased. Guteman fixed so many cases for Van it would make your head swim. Guteman even stole a couple of keys from the Evidence Room. Case dismissed. Evidence lost. Motherfucker gave the dope right back to Van and we sold it."

"How do you know that?" Jack asked.

"Because I was the only one Van confided in. If you ask me to repeat this, I'll deny it."

"Don't worry about it, Terry," Jack said. "Everything you say to me is privileged. I can't repeat it to anyone unless you give me permission. Besides, it's also hearsay."

"Ain't nobody supposed to know this stuff. If Lane or the Chicago syndicate believes you know it, they'll have you killed just like they did Rosato. Motherfucker knew too much of their business for his own good. They had to kill him. That hit was definitely professional—their style."

"How come the protection broke down? Why were you busted if you were supposed to be protected by all this syndicate money?"

"Cuz Lane lost the election, then the shit started hap'nin'. Motherfuckin' Boy Scout got in there—Sheriff Hardacre. The word is the mob tried to buy him, but couldn't. Guteman pulled the rug out from under Van. To him, the syndicate had cut off the money. Van's protection was gone. No more money—no more protection—no more drugs. Van would have to get another supplier. Guteman and Lane both threatened Van—said if Van ever got a big mouth, he'd be killed. Hell, they were planning to kill him all along."

"So, how did the killing of Burt Porter, the lawyer, come down?"

"Van told me the afternoon before he killed Porter that either Van killed the dude or they'd kill him. Van said Guteman had a taped conversation between Van and Porter where Van told Porter the syndicate had set up Jackson to kill Hardacre. They promised to cut Van back into the business if he would whack Porter and keep his mouth shut."

"How do you know that?"

"Because Van told me the afternoon before he was killed."

"So, that wasn't a drive-by shooting?"

"Fuck no. There ain't nothin' random in this business. There ain't no street-nigger, dope dealers in Dayton bigger than Van. He was the shit, man. Ain't no little street punks could kill him. It had to come from high up."

"When you say high up, who do you mean?" Jack asked.

"That came right from Lane and the boys in Chicago. You can bet on it."

"How do you know?"

"I just know how Van's organization worked."

"Do you think Jim Brodan, the DA, is involved?"

"Could be, man. He was the DA on some of Van's shit."

"What do you know about the Jackson case?"

"Not shit. All I know is Van went to Sheriff Hardacre and blew the whistle on Guteman and Lane. Hardacre was going to look into it and see what to do. Van told Hardacre he might need some sort of protection. Hardacre said they should go to the Feds—the DEA or the FBI—and get Van into a snitch program or witness protection program so he wouldn't be killed. Next thing I know, Hardacre is killed by the crazy, motherfuckin', nigger judge."

"And the next thing after that is Van is killed by Guteman and his boys. Is that about the size of it?" Jack asked.

"Yeah, bro, that's the way it came down. I'm sorry about your friend, the lawyer, Porter. He had to go. He knew too much. And the way it looks to me, bro, you know way too much. I wouldn't bet diddly shit on your life right now or the life of that pretty blonde in the other room—the one gave me the Dr. Pepper. She probably knows too much, too."

Jack sat in his high-backed chair, trying to conceal his fear. Now he needed to be concerned about Marci. She didn't ask for this. He did. He realized his gun would be of little use to him in the face of professional killers. His gut told him that what Singleton was saying was valid. "You came here to find out if I would represent you," Jack said.

"Yeah, I probably said more than I should have, but I don't give a shit. I don't work with those motherfuckers anymore—they be my competitors now; I got a new supply line. The problem is I don't have any protection anymore, and that's why I'm here. I figured you know who the crooked judge or politician is and could grease things up for me on this case."

"I can't do it, Terry. What I can do is try to get the dope charge suppressed because it was taken in violation of your constitutional rights. If you don't want me to represent you, I suggest you hire Jim Rosato's brother, Jeff. He might be more helpful to you."

"Nah, I never liked the white, honky motherfucker. Whenever I walked into his office, he'd look at me like I was shit. Jim never did that. Cocksucker Jeff got a lot of his money out of the dope business and the Chicago mob and then still acted like his shit didn't stink when it came time to talking to us. I wish they'd killed him instead of Jim. Jim fucked up; he musta said something to piss them off or got to know too much about their business. They had to kill the motherfucker, just like they killed Van and Porter."

"You've been a big help, Terry," Jack said. "I'm sorry about Van."

"Yeah, well, shit happens in this business. I'm going to stash a pile of cash and then get out. I think I'll move down to Florida. But I gotta beat this motherfuckin' rap or I ain't going nowhere." Singleton looked at Jack for a few seconds. He reached into his pocket and peeled off a large wad of one hundred dollar bills. "I like your style, bro. I want you to represent me and Horace. Here's twenty-K. I'll bring the rest by tomorrow."

"If I represent you, you cannot be dealing drugs nor can you pay me with the proceeds from drug transactions. So, if I represent you, you're going to have to find another way to support yourself. You might have to go back to school or find a trade. You'll have to become another kind of businessman. You can find a lot of lawyers in town who will take that money without any questions. I won't."

"Bro," Singleton said as he reached into his other pocket. He brought out another wad of hundreds. "Here's five-K more. I knew you'd want more than twenty thousand up front."

"I'm serious, Terry."

"You are one crazy, honky motherfucker. I'm making over a million dollars a year and you want me to go get a GED. Bullshit."

"If you're convicted on this case, you're going to prison. Getting busted with that much dope is a sure ticket," Jack said.

"I'll take that chance. I think I'll shop around some. I might be back," Singleton said as he scooped the two piles of hundreds off Jack's desk.

"Come back when you get your job at McDonald's or your MBA, whichever comes first." Jack smiled.

As Singleton left Jack's office, he handed Marci the empty Dr. Pepper can. "Your man is one crazy motherfucker," he said to Marci. She smiled at him as he put on his leather coat with bulging pockets. She could see the larger wad of cash sticking out of the left pocket.

Marci went into Jack's office. "How much did you turn down?" she asked.

"Only twenty-five thousand cash."

She looked at him incredulously. "Jack, we've taken in less than we've spent since we started two months ago, and so far you've turned down twenty-five thousand dollars! We're broke. *Broke*. Do you get it?"

"I just wouldn't have felt right about taking that money. I could just see all the crack addicts whose money Singleton had in his pocket. Then I could see their crack-addicted babies. If I take the money, I become part of the problem, not the solution. He'll find someone else who'll take it—if he lives that long," Jack said. "We'll get our chance. I can feel it," Jack said as he thought, *If I live that long*. "Let me buy you a cup of coffee."

As they were sitting and sipping their coffee in the building's snack bar, Jack said, "Let's get Joe's wiretap buddy over here to sweep this place for bugs again."

"What did Singleton say? Are we in danger again?"

"Not really."

"Jack, I can tell when you're withholding the truth from me. Now, come clean."

"Singleton says that a drug syndicate ordered Sheriff Hardacre, Burt, Hazeltree and Rosato's killings because they all knew too much. He claims Hugh Lane and Guteman were the point men here for the syndicate, and that Guteman was killed because he'd become a liability. He just speculates that we might be in danger, too. He's got nothing to base it on."

"Isn't there someone we can go to for protection? You've always had a working relationship with Alec Hunter. Maybe we ought to go to him and put our cards on the table."

"I've never liked Hunter. He's a show-boater."

"But he's basically honest, isn't he?"

"I have no reason to believe he's crooked. He runs a decent office. If I approached Hunter about it, he would just view it as an attempt to get some sort of favorable treatment on the Jackson case. No, if we look for help anywhere, it'll be from the Feds. The problem I have is I don't know who to trust."

Marci punched a number on her cell phone and made arrangements for Joe to bring his wiretap expert, Lou, over to the office at the end of the day. "Let's go back up and wait for Joe and his friend. You owe me a good dinner out tonight, Jack," Marci said, "I'm tired of cooking."

"You're right. It's a good thing we have credit cards because I'm letting the cash flow out of the office by the thousands." Jack took Marci's hand and squeezed it as he smiled at her lovingly. They chatted in the coffee shop until it was time for them to meet Joe and Lou.

Lou went over the office with his equipment. It took him all of two minutes to find a bug under Jack's desk and one in a table lamp. "Are these what you're looking for?" asked Lou.

"Can you trace the source?" Jack asked while his heart raced.

"I'll try. Give me some time on that."

"Joe, let's go to dinner. Marci and I have some things to tell you," Jack said.

"By the way, Joe, you don't have to look for Terry Singleton anymore. I spent the afternoon with him. I let him and twenty-five thousand dollars go out the door."

As Jack and Marci were driving home after dinner that night, Jack kept an eye on the sedan that followed them. He reached down. "Just to be on the safe side, I'm going to get you a gun," Jack said as he felt under the seat to see if his was there protecting them. It was.

"And," Jack said, "we better get hold of Terry Singleton to tell him his life might be in danger."

CHAPTER 23

The weeks after Terry Singleton's visit were anxious ones at Jack Maine and Associates, as they always are before any first-degree murder trial. This was different though. Their financial crisis was as real as the obvious threat to their lives. Yolanda was now on full-time, along with her salary. She handled a few DUI's. She and Jack tried a little domestic violence case. They had taken a juvenile case on in Columbus. A Mrs. Losavio had brought in a five thousand dollar retainer for her son, who had committed a burglary by picking a lock. She claimed that was all the cash her ex-husband could come up with. Those cases brought in enough to pay her and Joe's salary and the rent, but Jack and Marci were working for nothing. They were now paying the minimum, monthly charge on their credit cards as they continued to live on hope and credit with no assurance things would improve.

Joe ground away at his investigation. His operative in Washington, D.C., finally got a subpoena *duces tecum* on Dr. McGinty as he arrived home after work one night, but there was no assurance he'd show up for trial without being forced to by the Court with the threat of jail. Jack was certain they'd stonewall, claiming separation of powers—the judiciary can't make the executive branch bow to their whim. Yolanda and Jack researched the issue thoroughly for trial.

Jack talked with Dr. Offen frequently on the phone. Marcus agreed to testify without the final payment on his expert-witness retainer if Jack would just pay his coach airfare. Marcus thought the case was too important to allow money to stand in the way of the truth about Avery Jackson.

Then there was the problem of Terry Singleton and the bugs. Who had overheard his conversation with Jack? All attempts to reach him had failed.

And then there was the tan sedan that followed them so often. It had Illinois plates, so Joe tracked its registration down to Pinnacle Resources, a dummy corporation owned by Frontline Enterprises. The two goons in the car, who were indeed very much alive, remained nameless.

THE TRIAL
Monday, April 12—8:00 A.M.
Montgomery County District Court, Judge Hodge's Division

On this Monday morning, the gray skies had cleared and the moderate warmth and spring showers of April had replaced the damp cold of winter. There was hope this time of year; the ice had melted off the banks of the Miami River a month ago, and the buds were green in the branches of the oak, maple and elm trees that lined it. They were a harbinger for the bustling life of summer that was to come.

The feelings of the jurors who came to the courthouse that morning were not as hopeful as the spring. In fact, many of them felt downright hostile. The farmers didn't want to be there because this was the time of year for planting crops. The independent business people didn't want to be inconvenienced by a long trial that would take them away from the businesses that paid their bills. It was only the people who worked for institutions that would pay their salaries while they were off who could afford to serve on such a jury—as well as retired people who were on a fixed income and housewives without young children. Usually, a trial doesn't demand a substantial array of jurors, but the State of Ohio v. Jackson was not the usual trial. Never before had there been such a large pool summoned in Montgomery County.

Alec Hunter and Hank Dorsey arrived together. Jim Brodan had been removed from the team after the Conley debacle. He wasn't happy, but this was no time for hurt feelings. Dr. Alice Wolcott, a psychologist who specialized in jury selection accompanied them. Hunter's office had paid Dr. Wolcott a ten thousand dollar consulting fee. Their strategy was simple: select a jury that was poorly educated and had little knowledge or appreciation for the mind or mental illness.

Hunter was regal as he passed the hundred or so jurors milling in the hall outside the courtroom. It was these moments that Hunter lived for. He had exposure to dozens of voters and to millions more through the media. He had bought two new suits and a variety of silk ties just for this ocassion. The two men entered a courtroom packed with reporters, artists and other interested spectators.

Minutes passed before Jack Maine and Yolanda Crone wheeled boxes of files and videotapes into the courtroom. For Yolanda, this was the biggest moment of her life. It was for Jack, too, truth be known. He'd already spent a bundle on Gilmour and Offen. There was no money left for a jury-selection expert. He and Yolanda would just have to go with their common sense. Their strategy was to pick the most intelligent, psychologically sophisticated jury possible. They wanted highly-educated people who had taken advantage of mental health services themselves in the past or had family members who had.

Two deputies escorted Avery Jackson into the courtroom. Today, he would wear his dark suit. The gallery quieted as the killer entered.

"All rise," the bailiff said. "Court is now in session. The Honorable John Hodge presiding." Judge Hodge took his seat in his high-backed judge's chair. This would be his first death penalty case. Judge Hodge asked that the first fifty jurors be brought into the courtroom and seated together in the last four pews. He then asked that from those fifty, twelve be selected at random and seated in the jury box. When that was done, Judge Hodge called the case.

"This is State of Ohio v. Avery Jackson. The defendant appears along with Counsel, Mr. Maine and Ms. Crone, who are seated at the far table." Jack made an effort to look each juror in the eye. Of the twelve potential jurors in the box, nearly all of them avoided his eyes. He felt a sickness in his stomach.

"The State is represented by Alec Hunter and Henry Dorsey, who are seated immediately in front of you," Hodge announced. Hunter and Dorsey each smiled at the jurors. Most of them returned the smiles. Jack's stomach felt even sicker.

"We are about to begin jury selection in this matter," Hodge said. "Let the record reflect the array of jurors is in the courtroom with twelve seated in the jury box. The charge against the defendant is Murder in the First Degree. The State is alleging that the defendant, Avery Jackson, with malice aforethought and premeditation, knowingly and intentionally took the life of another person, Gene Hardacre. The State is also alleging that Mr. Jackson killed a law enforcement officer, and that he did so while lying in wait. This is a case where the possible penalty is death.

"The defendant, Mr. Avery Jackson, is clothed with the presumption of innocence. As he sits before you here today, he is innocent of the charges I have just read. It is the burden of the district attorney to prove this case beyond a reasonable doubt. Mr. Jackson's attorneys are claiming he was legally insane at the time Mr. Hardacre was killed. It is the burden of Mr. Hunter here to prove to you beyond a reasonable doubt that he was sane. This trial might last as long as two weeks and, if chosen to sit on the final panel, you will be sequestered. That means you will be leaving your families and staying at a hotel at state expense until the conclusion of deliberations. Are there any potential jurors who could not serve because it would inconvenience them?"

Of the fifty jurors in the room, at least twenty raised their hands. Judge Hodge excused most of them finding that their service in an extended trial would be an undue hardship on their businesses or families. After they had taken their leave, he requested that the other fifty jurors in the hall come into the courtroom. He similarly advised them of the charges and that it would be at least a two-week commitment. Half of the room asked to leave because of hardship, and Judge Hodge excused them. There were roughly fifty jurors left, including the twelve in the box. "Very well. I'm going to turn the panel over to the attorneys for voir dire examination."

Jury selection is a cat-and-mouse game where both the district attorney and the defense attorney attempt to pick people who will think favorably about their respective presentations of the case. They do so through a process of questioning called voir dire examination, which is a series of questions that require the jurors to "speak the truth" about themselves. The questions are geared to uncover biases and presumptions about life within the panel of potential jurors.

The voir dire examination of the prospective panel lasted two days. Hank Dorsey asked simple questions. "Do you think you can be fair? If we meet our burden of proving this case beyond a reasonable doubt, will you be able to find the defendant guilty and sentence him to death if you think that is the appropriate punishment?" His goal was to let the jurors know this was really a simple case and they were on the same team—the team of justice.

Jack asked questions that probed who the jurors were. "What is your job like? What do you like about it? Tell me about your family. Tell me about your education. Do you believe in the existence of mental illness? Do you believe that amnesia could be a symptom of a mental illness? Do you believe it is possible to do something and not remember doing it while sleepwalking? Do you believe in the phenomenon of multiple personalities? Have you ever had a family member who was mentally ill? Did you ever have a family member who suffered serious trauma and as a result couldn't remember doing something? Did you or anyone in your family fight in Vietnam? Would you be able to sentence a man to death who suffered from a multiple personality disorder? What do you think of the Central Intelligence Agency? Do you understand their role? If evidence were presented that the CIA engaged in mind-control/ brainwashing experiments, would you be able to listen to it and weigh such evidence?"

This was Jack and Yolanda's opportunity to allow the jury to connect with them. Jurors need to feel that defense attorney's are flesh and blood human beings just like them. If a bond can be created between attorneys and jurors, then a subliminal bond is created between the jurors and the defendant. They can see him or her as human also. Jack did the first day of voir dire, Yolanda the second.

Wednesday—April 15

"I told you I was screwed," said the note that Avery passed to Jack and Yolanda when it became clear there would be no African-Americans on the panel. After more than two days of questioning and challenging jurors, there were six men and six women left—three factory workers, four homemakers, a nurse, a golf pro, an engineer, a businesswoman and a used-car salesman. Hunter and Dorsey, over Jack's objection, had used their optional challenges to excuse all the blacks.

At the end of the process, Hodge announced, "We need at least an alternate juror in case someone can't finish his or her obligation."

"I agree," Alec said.

"Bailiff, please call another juror," Hodge ordered.

"Number twenty-seven."

Number twenty-seven, a tall, forty-year-old black man, stood and walked to the jury box. The black man's name was Calvin Stevens. He had served in Special Forces, fought in Desert Storm, was college educated and had an undergraduate degree in psychology. He was now involved in a computer software business in marketing. He was well-spoken and successful. Hunter examined him for thirty minutes, trying to establish a way to create the appearance of bias or opposition to the death penalty. He was unable to do so. Hunter passed him for cause. Jack passed him for cause after asking him only two questions. Calvin Stevens was the first alternate. He had no power unless another juror was excused.

Judge Hodge swore in the twelve jurors and one alternate.

"Ladies and gentlemen of the jury: the bailiff will bring you back here tomorrow morning at eight-thirty. Do not discuss the case with anyone, or among yourselves. From now on, you will be housed at one of Dayton's finest hotels until the conclusion of this case. Counsel, be prepared to give your opening statements first thing in the morning."

After the jurors filed out of the room, Hodge said, with a sense of triumph and relief, "Court is in recess."

"Don't worry about it, Alec," Dorsey whispered to Hunter, "Calvin Stevens is too little, too late."

"Bet on it," Alec said.

Thursday, April 16—9:00 A.M.
Montgomery County Court

"Mr. Hunter, are you ready to make your opening statement?"

"I am, Your Honor." Alec strode confidently to the podium. The new panel was like a class of eager new students. Alec and Hank had decided that Alec would do the opening statement and Hank would do most of the direct and cross-examinations. They hadn't decided yet who would close.

"Ladies and gentleman of the jury: you've just sat through three days of tedious jury selection. The State of Ohio has placed its faith in you as jurors to carry out a very serious task. You are to decide if this man, Avery Jackson, killed the sheriff of Montgomery County, and whether he did so knowingly, intentionally and with premeditation and malice aforethought.

"As he sits here today, Mr. Jackson is presumed innocent. It is our job to prove to you beyond a reasonable doubt that this presumption is not valid, and he is guilty. We believe by the end of our presentation of the evidence, you will find we have done just that. You will hear from two witnesses to the shooting. There were many more—approximately one hundred and fifty. To present all of them would be unduly repetitive and a misuse of your precious time. You will see the actual killing on videotape, and you will see that the defendant is the killer.

"You will hear testimony that Mr. Jackson is a lawyer, has been a judge and was, until recently, a professor at Sinclair University. Do not be fooled by his titles. Only confine yourselves to the evidence presented to you.

"The defense is going to present some mental-health experts who will testify that Mr. Jackson was insane at the time Sheriff Hardacre was killed. We will present our own mental-health experts who will say he was not. It will be up to you to decide, after you have heard the evidence, whether he was sane or insane at the time of the murder. We are confident we will prove to you beyond a reasonable doubt that he was sane."

Hunter attempted successfully to pierce the eyes of the jurors as he was speaking. He was their elected official, there to protect them. He ended with, "We thank you for giving up part of your life to perform the important task before you."

"Mr. Maine, are you ready to give your opening statement?" Hodge asked.

"Your Honor, we will reserve opening statement," Jack said. Jack and Yolanda had talked about waiving opening statement as a matter of strategy. They would probably not be challenging any material facts presented by the district attorney. They would wait until after the DA had presented his evidence, and then decide if they would give an opening statement.

"The defense has elected to reserve opening statement," Hodge said to the jury. "That is their right. They will have the right to present such a statement before they begin putting on their case, if they elect to put on a case. You are to draw no presumption or conclusion if they do not make an opening statement. The burden here is upon the district attorney to prove their case against Mr. Jackson to you beyond a reasonable doubt. Mr. District Attorney, you may proceed."

"The State calls Mr. Aubrey Shell."

The courtroom door was opened by the bailiff and in came Aubrey Shell in a tan suit, white shirt and tie. Aubrey was sworn in and took his seat in the witness box. Hank Dorsey rose and walked to the podium. This would be the first time for the jury to get a feel for Dorsey.

"Please state your name, sir," he said.

"Aubrey Shell."

"Mr. Shell, how are you employed?"

"I'm involved in the real estate business."

"Are you involved in Rotary Club?"

"Yes, I am."

"In what capacity?"

"I am the President of the Downtown Rotary Club of Dayton."

"And were you serving in that capacity on January fifteenth of this year?"

"Yes."

"Where did the Rotary Club meet on that day?"

"It met at the Renaissance Hotel in downtown Dayton."

"How many people were there?"

"In excess of one hundred."

"What was the occasion?"

"It was our first meeting after the holidays."

"Who was the guest speaker at the meeting?"

"Sheriff Gene Hardacre. He'd just been elected, and we thought the people would want to meet him."

"What happened at that meeting?"

"I introduced Sheriff Hardacre. He walked to the podium to begin speaking. He spoke for maybe five minutes when Avery Jackson—sitting over there," Aubrey pointed at Avery, "walked up to him and shot him in the head."

"Let the record reflect that the witness has identified the defendant, Avery Jackson," Dorsey said.

"It will so reflect," Hodge ordered.

"How long have you known Avery Jackson?"

"About five years. He was a member of the club when he took the bench and continued to be a member after he left the bench and went over to the

266

college to become a professor."

"Did you recognize him when he came into the room?"

"I didn't see him when he came into the room. I saw him as he got up close to the podium. I didn't think anything of it. He was a member. We all knew him."

"Did you hear Sheriff Hardacre say anything to Mr. Jackson before he was shot?"

"Yes, he said Avery's name—like 'Avery, what are you doing?'"

"What did the defendant say?"

"Nothing."

"Did you notice whether Sheriff Hardacre made any gestures to the defendant?"

"Yes, Sheriff Hardacre put up his hand up to shield his head before Mr. Jackson pulled the trigger."

"What happened then?"

"Sheriff Hardacre fell to the floor. Everyone stood still for a couple of seconds. Mr. Jackson dropped his gun. I jumped on his back. Judge Duncan also jumped on him. We wrestled him to the floor. Judge Kessler picked up the murder weapon. The police were there within minutes. He was arrested and taken away."

"Did you notice the condition of Sheriff Hardacre?"

"He was lying on the floor in a pool of blood. Part of the back of his head was missing. He was breathing for a short time and then . . . then . . . died." He fidgeted with his tie. He took some water and drank it.

"Thank you, Mr. Shell," Dorsey said. "Mr. Maine will probably have some questions for you."

Jack walked slowly to the podium. "Mr. Shell, from what you have just said, I take it that Mr. Jackson said nothing during this entire incident?"

"That is correct. He said nothing."

"You have known Mr. Jackson for a considerable time?"

"That's correct."

"You mentioned he was on the bench. Does that mean he was once a judge?"

"Yes, everyone knew him as Judge Jackson. Even after leaving the bench, people still referred to him as Judge Jackson, until he shot Sheriff Hardacre."

"You thought nothing of him approaching the podium?"

"No, I thought nothing of it."

"What was he wearing?"

"A tan coat, brown pants, an overcoat."

"When did you first notice the gun?"

"He didn't pull the gun until he was nearly in front of the sheriff."

"He pulled it quite slowly and methodically, did he not?"

"Yes."

"And he said nothing when the sheriff attempted to protect himself?"

"That's true."

"And when the sheriff put up his hand, Avery did nothing to acknowledge him?"

"What do you mean by acknowledge?"

"I mean, he didn't move to one side or the other in order to shoot around his hand."

"That's true. In fact, Mr. Jackson shot right through part of his hand. I could see it bleeding as Hardacre lay on the floor."

"And after the shooting, isn't it true that Mr. Jackson dropped the gun on the floor at his feet?"

"That's true. He didn't throw the gun or run. He didn't move a muscle or make a peep, even after we jumped him."

"He didn't resist in any way, did he?"

"No, he didn't."

"Mr. Shell, it sounds to me like Mr. Jackson moved somewhat like a robot. Would that be true?"

"That's probably a good description."

"What did you do after the sheriff's office took him away?"

"I stood around and talked with the other Rotarians about it. We were all shocked."

"Isn't it true that many of them said Avery had to be crazy?"

"Objection, Your Honor, hearsay without a source and insufficient foundation," Dorsey said as he shot to his feet.

"Sustained. You may rephrase the question, Mr. Maine," Judge Hodge said.

"Mr. Shell, do you remember saying to anyone afterward that in your opinion, Judge Jackson was crazy?"

"Yes, I did say that."

"Did you believe that when you said it?"

"Objection," Hank Dorsey said, "Mr. Shell is not an expert in mental health issues."

"Your Honor, the law is clear with regard to lay people being allowed to give opinions about the mental status of people they know. The fact they're not trained in the field goes to the weight the jury gives such evidence."

"I agree, Mr. Maine," Hodge said. "Objection overruled. You may answer, Mr. Shell."

"I thought he was crazy, and most of the people there did, too."

"Objection as to what the other people thought."

"Sustained," Hodge said, "the jury will disregard what the other people allegedly thought," Hodge said.

"Thank you, Mr. Shell, no further questions," Jack said.

"Re-direct, Mr. Dorsey?" Judge Hodge asked.

"Yes, Your Honor. Mr. Shell, you have no idea what the legal definition of insanity is, do you?"

"That's true."

"No further questions."

"Call your next witness, Mr. Dorsey," Hodge said.

"The State calls Presiding Judge Carl Kessler."

Judge Kessler was sworn in and testified on direct examination just as he had done at the preliminary hearing. He stated clearly that Avery Jackson was the shooter. He also described picking up the gun and turning it over to the deputy sheriff. During a short cross-examination nearly identical to that of Aubrey Shell's, Jack again asked, "Isn't it true that Mr. Jackson looked as though he were sleepwalking when he shot Sheriff Hardacre?"

"I didn't see him well enough to tell you what he looked like."

Jack went back to counsel table and brought out the preliminary hearing transcript.

"Judge Kessler, you testified at the preliminary hearing for this matter as follows: 'Certainly, it was as if he were sleepwalking afterward. I just couldn't tell exactly what he was like beforehand. It all happened so suddenly.' Would you agree that was your testimony?"

"Yes, Mr. Maine," said Kessler who was not used to being confronted and corrected by attorneys.

"Was your recollection of events at the preliminary hearing incorrect or are you incorrect today?"

"My recollection, Counsel, at the preliminary hearing was correct," Kessler said.

"Are you saying then that Mr. Jackson did appear to be sleepwalking after he shot Sheriff Hardacre?"

"Yes, in retrospect, that is true. He did look somewhat like he was in shock, or some sort of trance afterward."

"Thank you, Judge."

Jack went back to counsel table. "I'll take any small victory," he whispered to Yolanda.

"Any re-direct, Mr. Dorsey?" Judge Hodge asked.

"Did you find it unusual for the defendant to be in shock at that time?"

"No, I didn't," Judge Kessler answered promptly. "It seemed to me that anyone who had just killed another person would be in shock. That would be a normal reaction."

"Re-cross, Mr. Maine?"

"None."

"I have no further questions of Judge Kessler," Dorsey said.

"You're excused, Judge," Judge Hodge said to his colleague.

As Kessler made his way from the witness box out of the courtroom, Hank Dorsey called his next witness. "Dan Cantrell."

The bailiff opened the door. In walked a thirty-year-old man in a sport coat and tie. He was sworn in and seated himself in the witness box.

"State your name, sir."

"Dan Cantrell."

"How are you employed, sir?"

"I am a cameraman for Channel 4 News."

"Were you so employed on January fifteenth?"

"Yes, I was."

"Did you have occasion to be working at the Renaissance Hotel at approximately noon?"

"Yes, I was there videotaping a speech by Sheriff Hardacre at the Rotary Club for the evening news."

Dorsey wheeled a sixty-inch, high-density plasma television/VCR unit from the corner of the courtroom to an area between the witness box and the jury. From that position, both the witness and the jury had a clear view of it. Dorsey popped in a VHS cassette. "I show you, Mr. Cantrell, what has been marked as State's Exhibit One." The screen of the television lit up. On it was Aubrey Shell speaking from a podium that had Renaissance inscribed on it. He was fidgeting with his tie and introducing Sheriff Gene Hardacre. Dorsey pressed the PAUSE button on the remote. The picture froze. "Do you recognize this tape?"

"Yes, it's the recording I made of Hardacre's speech at the Renaissance."

"Does this tape accurately depict what happened on that afternoon?" Dorsey asked.

"It does."

"I ask that State's Exhibit One be introduced into evidence."

"Any objection, Mr. Maine?"

"Yes, Your Honor," Jack said. "May counsel approach the bench?"

When all four lawyers got to the bench, Hodge asked, "Mr. Maine, what is the basis of your objection?"

"Your Honor," Jack said outside the presence of the jury, "the shock value of the tape and its gruesomeness will unduly prejudice this jury."

"The tape is real and accurately shows what happened," Dorsey argued. "The State will be unduly prejudiced if the jury is unable to see the actual killing."

"I would ask that the court review the tape in chambers before it rules on its admissibility," Jack said.

"The court will take a brief recess. The witness and the jury will remain seated."

When Hodge came back into the courtroom ten minutes later, he was ready to rule. "It will be admitted," he said. The defense team shrugged; they'd known the chances of it being excluded were slim.

"Will you describe for the jury what happened next?" Dorsey asked as he pressed PLAY.

"I was taping the introduction and the speech, as you can see here . . ." The tape continued to roll as the jury watched carefully. It was the same tape they had seen many times on the local and national news.

"How far away from Sheriff Hardacre were you when you were shooting— or perhaps filming is a better word?"

"I would say approximately twenty feet. I tried to get a wide enough angle-shot so you could see his entire body behind the podium. As you can see here, a figure comes up to him, he raises his hand, mutters something and then—"

"Stop! No!" Avery screamed from the counsel's table. It was the first time he had seen the tape. Jack grabbed his shoulders as Avery rose in his chair as if to run to the television and stop himself from doing what was already a *fait accompli.*

Dorsey pressed PAUSE.

"Mr. Maine, would you please contain your client?" Hodge admonished him.

Yolanda gently reached for, and held, Avery's hand as he shook and shivered.

"Certainly, Your Honor," replied Jack.

"Will the witness please proceed?"

Dorsey pressed PLAY.

"As you can see, Mr. Hardacre is right here," Cantrell said. Dorsey pressed PAUSE. The jury looked carefully at the frozen frame for a number of seconds. Dorsey pressed PLAY. "Now, he's shot by the man standing over there."

Dorsey paused the video at two-second intervals. The public had not seen this part of the tape that was now being intermittently frozen before them. There was the loud popping sound of a gun being fired. One could plainly see the front of Gene Hardacre's head being pierced and his skull and brains blown away from the back of his head. A loud gasp and shriek came from the front row of the gallery.

Betty Hardacre had sat composed through every day of jury selection and now the trial. She could no longer contain herself at the sight of what happened to her beloved husband. She began to cry uncontrollably, then wail, as grieving people do who have lost loved ones. She thought she could handle it. She couldn't. Neither could some of the jurors. The men sat ashen-faced. The women cried along with Mrs. Hardacre. Avery was the shooter. There was no mistaking it. It was the most cold-blooded act that any of them had ever seen in their lives.

Avery was shaking at counsel table.

"We'll take the noon recess at this time, Counsel. The bailiff will take the jury to lunch." As the jury was composing itself, Hodge gave his admonition. "Ladies and gentlemen of the jury, try to enjoy your lunch. The State is paying for it. Please, however, do not discuss the case with anyone or among yourselves. If there is any such conversation, you're asked to bring it to my attention. You are excused."

When the jury finished filing out, Judge Hodge said somberly, "Court is in recess. Be back here this afternoon at one-thirty."

Betty Hardacre stared at the monster who had killed her husband. She was still trying to assimilate what had happened to her life and the gaping hole Avery had left in it. She looked with equal disdain at the two lawyers who defended him.

"We're meeting Marci and Joe for lunch," Jack said to Yolanda. She had little appetite. This was Yolanda's first felony, jury trial. What before she could only envision, she'd now begun to feel.

They walked slowly from the courtroom. Reporters tried to corner them in the hall to get their reaction to the morning's testimony. Jack and Yolanda met their questions with "No comment." Other media surrounded Hunter and Dorsey. Hunter was in the driver's seat. He was steadfast with his mantra that when the evidence was heard, justice would be done.

Thursday—12 noon
The King's Table

Joe and Marci were already seated and having drinks when Yolanda and Jack walked into the Table. One interesting thing about being a trial lawyer— you can anticipate how badly you're going to get your brains beaten in, but when it actually happens, it's much worse.

Jack moved into the booth next to Marci. She kissed him lightly on the cheek as he sat down. She always knew when it hadn't gone well just by looking at him.

"How did it go?" Joe asked.

"It went well, until Betty Hardacre melted down," Jack said. "Her pain is forever etched in their souls, and Avery is the son-of-a-bitch who caused it."

"That bad, *huh?*" Marci asked.

"That bad." Yolanda exclaimed. "I don't believe I can eat anything. I don't see how that jury will be able to either. I saw the shooting ten times before today, but I wasn't ready for Betty Hardacre's reaction, or Avery's, for that matter."

"So much for the presumption of innocence," Jack said. "There isn't one juror on that panel who wouldn't vote to convict Avery right now and execute him tomorrow if they could. It's just the way the tape went down. We did everything we could on cross-examination of the other witnesses, but the tape killed us. The obliteration of Gene Hardacre's skull, in connection with Betty Hardacre's wailing, might be too big a burden for us to overcome. There is just no way we could prevent it. The jury has just one night to recover before we put on our case. I guess it could have been worse. The Hardacre's kids could have been there."

"If the jury had the rest of their lives to recover," Yolanda said, "it might not be enough. They aren't going to want to listen to a word of our case after today."

"That jury is not going to give a damn about insanity and a bunch of psychiatrists that talk another language," Jack said. "We've got only one chance, and that's to prove that Hugh Lane is the real killer. Joe, you better be able to prove Lane did this. What do you have?"

"I found Marvella Dixon. I'm meeting with her this afternoon," Joe said.

"You better get something else," Jack said, "or the trial is over. We'll all be out of a job. We'll be the laughing stock of Dayton. Make sure you get a subpoena served on Hugh Lane to be in court on Monday and all next week. I don't know how we're going to use him, but somehow I just think he ought to be there."

Thursday Afternoon
Judge John Hodge's Courtroom

The afternoon session was bland compared to the morning session. Jack waived cross examination of Dan Cantrell. To even mention that tape again would be double suicide. Dorsey went methodically about his business. The medical examiner testified that the cause of death was a gunshot wound to the head. The fingerprint expert, Al Knudsen, testified that Avery Jackson's prints were on the gun. The ballistics expert testified that the gun was a .38-caliber, was purchased some ten years ago at a gun shop in Dayton by Avery Jackson, and was registered to Avery Jackson. He also testified that the bullet was so fragmented it was impossible to determine if it came from that gun. Jack had attempted to stipulate to the truth of all of those facts, but Dorsey refused to accept the stipulation. Instead, he put all three witnesses on the stand to establish that evidence. Those facts, coming from the mouths of real people, were far more vivid in the minds of the jurors than any agreement to facts being read into the record would have been. Jack elected to cross-examine Mr. Knudsen.

"Mr. Knudsen, you testified that Mr. Jackson's prints were on the gun."

"That's correct."

"Were there any other latent prints on the gun?"

"Yes, come to think of it, there were."

"How many different latent prints were on the gun, and where were they located?"

"There were two other sets of prints. We found Judge Kessler's prints on the stock. We asked him to give us his prints as exemplars. We figured they'd probably be there because he picked up the weapon after the shooting."

"And the other set of prints—where were they located?"

"There was a thumb print located at the very bottom of the barrel where it meets the cylinder."

"Were you able to identify that latent print?"

"No, we ran a search of our data banks and were unable to come up with any matches from anyone we had in the criminal pool."

"Did you happen to match the latent print against a pool of prints from law enforcement personnel?"

"No, Counsel, we didn't."

"Just one more thing. I would bet that, except for the handle, the gun looked as though it had been wiped clean. Would that be a correct statement?"

Knudsen looked at Jack and smiled. "You're the first person who has asked me that question, Counsel. That's true. Under magnification, it was clear the weapon had been wiped down, probably with a soft cloth."

"Thank you, Mr. Knudsen," Jack said as he seated himself.

With that, Hank Dorsey rose and proclaimed, "The People rest."

"Very well," Judge Hodge said, "we'll adjourn for the day. The jurors are reminded not to discuss this case with anyone. You will be sequestered tonight at the Hilton. If anyone should approach you on this matter and want to talk about it, you're to contact the bailiff immediately."

After the jury left, Jack made his obligatory motion to dismiss on the grounds that the State had not shown a prima facie case of the guilt of the defendant. It was summarily denied. There would be a lot of work to do before tomorrow. Jack and Yolanda would be working very late. The first day of trial could not have gone worse.

CHAPTER 24

I'm not going to court today," Avery said.

"Of course, you're going to court today," Yolanda said. "This is your trial."

"I'm going to waive my appearance. You and Jack can't make me go."

"That's true, but I'm quite sure he would want you there. Your children got out of college today and are going to be there."

"Did you arrange that? It's the last thing I want," Avery said. "I don't want them to hear how crazy their dad is. I don't want them to know their dad is a killer." Avery's eyes glazed over, then big tears began to fall. "I'm so thankful they were not there yesterday. I never really believed I killed Hardacre until yesterday. I still can't feel myself doing it, but I saw it. I know I did it."

Yolanda just looked at him, her mind spinning. "The deputy sheriff is going to bring you over," she said. "You'll have to waive your appearance on the record. It might be for the best today. It may be too big a shock for you to hear what the doctors say. Jack and I already know what happened to you, and your kids will know after today. I promise you, they'll be more accepting of you after they hear what happened to you in Vietnam."

"I'm dreaming about my committing more murders," Avery said. I think they're more than dreams. They are too real." Yolanda looked at him and said nothing. Her silence confirmed his worst fears.

Friday—9:00 A.M.
Montgomery County District Court

There were even more members of the media crammed into Judge Hodge's court that day. Betty Hardacre's grief, and Avery's attempt to stop the tape, got primetime billing not only on the local news, but also on the national news.

Jack was sitting at counsel table when Yolanda walked in. He looked up at her with a smile and said, "We're doing two things today—waiving Avery's appearance and giving an opening statement."

"Avery is not coming anyway," Yolanda said. "He's a wreck. He doesn't want to be here when Dr. Gilmour says he's insane. He'd prefer his children not hear it either."

Jack looked into the gallery and there were Aaron and Rebecca Jackson. He smiled at them. They reciprocated. He could only imagine what this was like for them. He tried to put himself in their shoes, but he couldn't imagine what it would have been like as a kid if his own dad had been on trial for his life. Unfathomable.

The deputy brought Avery into the courtroom. Nearly all eyes were on the cold-blooded killer, except those of Aaron and Rebecca who were looking at the man from whom they came, and whom they loved. Avery scoured the gallery with his eyes and found them. He smiled.

"All rise," the bailiff called out. A grim-faced Judge Hodge made his appearance. He called the case and brought the jury back into the courtroom. When they were seated, he went ahead. "Mr. Maine, call your first witness."

"Your Honor, we have two requests," Jack said. "The first is that Mr. Jackson be allowed to waive his appearance today. He is not feeling up to being here after having seen the shooting of Sheriff Hardacre for the first time yesterday. Furthermore, he does not feel he is able to hear psychiatric information about himself, none of which has yet been shared with him. The doctors believe it is not in his best interest to hear their testimony at this time, as it might further disorganize him mentally."

"Objection," Dorsey said as he rose to his feet. "Mr. Maine is offering psychiatric testimony himself here in front of the jury, and that is improper."

"I'm sure that you, Mr. Maine, will be able to offer evidence of what you have just asserted?" Hodge asked.

"Of course, Your Honor," Jack assured him.

"Mr. Jackson, is it true you wish to waive your appearance here today?"

"Yes, Your Honor," Avery said, "I don't want to hear any of the psychiatric testimony about me."

"As you know, Mr. Jackson, you have a right to be at every stage of the proceeding. Do you wish to waive that right?"

"I do, Your Honor," Avery said.

"Very well, then," Judge Hodge said, "you're excused. If you at any time wish to come back, tell your lawyers and we'll make the arrangements."

Avery rose and was escorted out the door of the courtroom by the deputy.

"What is your second request, Mr. Maine?" Hodge asked.

"The second request is that we be able to exercise our previously reserved right to give an opening statement," Jack said. "As you'll recall, we reserved our right to make such a statement."

"Certainly, Mr. Maine. You may proceed," Hodge said.

As Jack rose and strode to the podium, the butterflies were whipping away in his stomach. He had to stop yesterday's hemorrhaging. He hoped he could gain some sympathy for Avery from the jury when he explained why Avery wished to waive his appearance. No such sympathy was forthcoming. The butterflies got even more frantic when no juror would look at him as he addressed them. As he scanned the panel, finally one juror, Calvin Stevens, looked at him. Calvin Stevens, the only black man in the box, only an alternate. It made no difference to Jack, for a pair of eyes was what he needed to get started—any eyes to which to attach and relate.

"You've already seen dramatic evidence of Mr. Jackson blowing the back of Sheriff Hardacre's head off. You saw Mr. Jackson shoot out of his chair yesterday and try to stop himself from pulling the trigger. He did that because prior to that very moment, he did not know he had killed Sheriff Hardacre. He is not here today because of his shock in seeing himself do that. You may ask how that could be. You are all so upset about what you saw yesterday that you cannot look at me today." All thirteen of the panel looked at him. "I can understand that," Jack said, "because Avery Jackson is equally upset. The evidence is going to show that although the gun went off in the hand of Avery Jackson, he was not the person who pulled the trigger." Six of the jurors looked away. "You may ask, 'How could that be?'" The six jurors again looked at him. Calvin Stevens went so far as to nod his head, begging Jack to answer the question. "The real trigger man was not even in the Renaissance Hotel on January fifteenth. He was elsewhere. Avery Jackson was just his weapon. We know who the real trigger man is, and by the end of this trial, you will, too."

Jack knew he was taking a big chance by making these claims; he didn't know if he could prove them. It was a game of poker. He was bluffing. He hoped his bluff wasn't called. "Avery Jackson had no idea he was the gun on January fifteenth or that he had been a gun for others for many years—ever since he was programmed to be a killer during the Vietnam War. He is, and has been, a puppet for our government, the U.S. Army and the CIA. He is a decorated war-hero. Unfortunately, he is still a puppet for the man who holds the key—a key this man can turn any time. The terrible thing for Avery is he has no recollection of the shooting of Gene Hardacre. This is not the first man Avery Jackson has killed. He has killed many others. He has no recollection of them, either. They, too, were killed at the instruction of others. This is the first person he has killed since he left Vietnam.

"The evidence will show that Avery Jackson was an unwitting subject in mind-control experiments during the war, was programmed during these horrific experiments to be a killer, is still programmed to be a killer and was used as a killer by a ruthless man with a ruthless agenda. He is unable to resist this programming; it is hardwired into him like the circuits are hardwired into a television." All eyes except Stevens' turned away. They were having none of it.

"I will say no more at this time. The evidence will speak for itself. Just keep in mind that after this evidence is presented, it will be Mr. Hunter's duty to disprove Mr. Jackson insanity beyond a reasonable doubt. Mr. Jackson is still clothed with the presumption of innocence. This is a man who truly did not know right from wrong at the time he shot Sheriff Hardacre, nor was he able to appreciate the wrongfulness of his act—he wasn't even aware of it. Thank you, ladies and gentlemen of the jury. Listen carefully to the expert testimony; it is crucial."

As Jack returned to counsel table, there was an exodus of reporters from the courtroom. Although what he'd said wasn't evidence, the media was going to treat it as if it were. They were pulling out their cell phones and laptops. This was a theory of defense too fantastic to ignore, too impossible to believe. This exceeded the evidence proposed in John Hinckley's case. There, the jury found him insane when he shot President Reagan to impress Jodie Foster. This lawyer, Jack Maine, was now taking the defense to a new place. Few juries had bought an insanity defense since Hinckley. Would they buy this one? It wasn't likely, according to the media.

Hank Dorsey wrote on the legal pad as Maine was speaking and pushed it in front of Alec Hunter. It said *Bullshit*. He and Hunter knew generally where Maine was going from the brief reports of the doctors and videos that the court rules required be submitted to them. This, however, was more grandiose than Dorsey had ever imagined. Hunter sat speechless.

"You handle the cross-examination of their experts, Hank," Hunter said.

Jack sat down at counsel table with Yolanda. Yolanda rose. She would do the direct examination of the doctors. "The defense will call Dr. Phil Gilmour."

Phil Gilmour walked to the witness box. He looked professorial in his corduroy sport coat, tan pants, reading glasses and neatly-trimmed van dyke. Judge Hodge swore him to tell the truth.

"State your name, sir," Yolanda said.

"My name is Dr. Philip Reginald Gilmour."

"How are you employed?"

"I am a licensed forensic psychiatrist."

"Tell us about your education, Dr. Gilmour."

"I have an undergraduate degree from Ohio State University and a doctorate in medicine from the same institution. I—"

"Your Honor, we would stipulate to Dr. Gilmour's qualifications," Dorsey said.

"So stipulated, Your Honor," Yolanda said.

"Very well, Counsel," Judge Hodge said, "Dr. Gilmour will be offered as an expert in the field of forensic psychiatry."

"Dr. Gilmour, did you have occasion to do an evaluation of one Avery Jackson in connection with this case?" Yolanda asked.

"I did."

"How many times did you see him?"

"On four separate occasions totaling approximately twelve hours."

"What did your evaluation consist of?"

"A clinical interview, participation in a hypnotic regression of Mr. Jackson, as well as a session where scopolamine, a strong sedative, was used as a truth serum."

"What were your findings?"

"Your Honor," Dorsey said, "I am requesting a hearing outside the presence of the jury."

"Very well," Judge Hodge said, "the bailiff will escort the jury to the anteroom."

When the jury was leaving, Jack whispered to Yolanda. "Here it comes. You researched the law; you handle it, Yolanda."

When the jury had left, Dorsey began, "Your Honor, we hadn't anticipated this testimony would go here. The law is fairly settled that information taken from a person while hypnotized, or under the influence of scopolamine, is not reliable, and is therefore inadmissible. We object to Dr. Gilmour's testimony if it's based on information obtained when the defendant was under hypnosis or scopolamine."

"Your Honor," Yolanda said, "we're offering the material taken under the influence of hypnosis and scopolamine for the purposes of rendering a psychiatric diagnosis—not to prove the truth of the material taken during the evaluation. Mr. Jackson is amnestic for the actual shooting and for much of his Vietnam War experience. We found it necessary to use hypnosis in order to find out what happened to him in Vietnam, how he was programmed to kill there and how he killed here."

"Mr. Dorsey?" Judge Hodge asked. "Do you have a response?"

"Some very bold statements were made during Mr. Maine's opening statements. We believe the defense is going to try to use psychiatric testimony to prove the identity of some phantom killer other than the defendant. They will use it to confuse the issues and create a smokescreen with unreliable evidence."

"The court is ready to rule," Judge Hodge said. "At this point, I agree with the district attorney. I will only allow the information gained while the defendant was under the influence of hypnosis and scopolamine for purposes of diagnosis. Any material gained from the evaluation that is being offered to prove the identity of another killer will not be allowed."

They were done. If they couldn't deliver with the independent proof of the mind control, and Hugh Lane being the real triggerman, the trial would be over very quickly. Avery would be a condemned man, and Jack would never get any business in this town.

"Bailiff," Judge Hodge said, "bring the jury back in and let's proceed."

When all the jurors and alternates were seated, Yolanda began her questioning of Dr. Gilmour.

"Dr. Gilmour, what did your evaluation reveal?"

"It showed that Avery Jackson is a very smart man who grew up in a family where his father was an alcoholic and abused his mother, him and his sisters. His mother was controlling and used him as a substitute for a father who was not emotionally available to her. Because of his intellectual gifts, he achieved dramatically, participated in track, made National Honor Society, graduated from Wright State University while running track and working. He went to law school at the University of Toledo, passed the bar and was drafted into the war in Vietnam. He remembers his basic training up until the point where he was ordered to have a psychiatric evaluation by a doctor there who wore black, horn-rimmed glasses and a white coat. He remembers having a Coke, and then seeing a needle. This doctor was very important because subsequent evaluation under the influence of hypnosis and truth serum showed the doctor to be a Dr. Breyfogle, who was probably involved with the CIA."

"Objection," Dorsey yelled. "This material is hearsay and unreliable. It is inadmissible under the ruling the court made just minutes ago. We ask it be stricken from the record and that Ms. Crone be admonished."

"Sustained," Hodge ruled. "The court will instruct the jury to disregard the last statement with regard to the doctor's name and involvement. Ms. Crone, you're to steer clear of any of the material elicited under the influence of hypnosis or otherwise."

"Dr. Gilmour," Yolanda said, "continue without discussing the name of the doctor, or his involvement with any organization."

"That will be difficult. Mr. Jackson remembered very little of his war experience. He remembers being in a firefight, but is very sketchy about the rest of it. He remembers a strange conversation with the same doctor upon

280

exiting the service where he informed the doctor he had little memory of the last twelve months, but that he felt depression, anxiety and confusion. The doctor inexplicably informed him he should not be concerned about these symptoms because many of the men had them. He made no referrals for psychiatric services after Mr. Jackson's exit. This is a very strange occurrence because competent psychiatrists would recognize these symptoms as consistent with a post-traumatic disorder."

"Do you believe that was a correct diagnosis when he left the service?"

"It was insufficient. He had a post-traumatic disorder from his childhood when he entered the service. When he left the service, the disorder was much more pronounced. He had become a multiple personality, having developed an altered personality by the name of Periscope that was programmed to kill. Avery has no conscious knowledge of this personality within him. We were unable to gain access to it by any method other than scopolamine. As far as we could tell from the inductions—"

"Objection, Your Honor, this is prohibited material," Dorsey said.

"I agree. You are not allowed to go further with regard to what the inductions showed, Doctor Gilmour," Hodge ordered.

"Proceed, Dr. Gilmour, without getting into what the inductions showed," Yolanda said.

"When Avery got out of the service, he was carrying a personality he wasn't aware of. It's my opinion this personality could only be accessed by certain people. All of our attempts to access it were fruitless. We were able, however, to get Avery to discuss the existence of it while he was under scopolamine."

"Objection, Your Honor," Dorsey yelled again, obviously upset with the repeated attempts by the defense to get prohibited material into evidence.

"Sustained," Hodge ordered.

"Proceed with your findings concerning Mr. Jackson's diagnosis and his activities after the war," Yolanda instructed him.

"Mr. Jackson left the war and was decorated as a hero. He doesn't know why. This is indicative that he was a highly dissociative personality, a confused, anxious individual, for want of a better word, upon reentering society. He practiced law both as a defense attorney and then as a judge. In recent years, he was a professor at Sinclair University."

"What, if anything, does he remember about January fifteenth?" Yolanda asked.

"He remembers teaching his Evidence class that morning and the smell of coffee similar to that he had in Vietnam. He remembers nothing of the shooting. He only remembers being detained afterward by the deputy sheriffs when they took him to jail."

"Would you explain to the jury how this could happen?"

"I believe his altered personality, the one programmed to kill, whose name is Periscope, took over and shot Sheriff Hardacre. Avery had no control over the killer within him."

"Who had control over Periscope?"

"In my opinion, the doctor with the horn-rimmed glasses, perhaps his commanding officer in Vietnam, and a man by the name of—"

"Objection!" Dorsey flew out of his chair. "This is the very material that has been ruled inadmissible by the court. May counsel approach the bench?"

"Certainly," Hodge said.

When all four attorneys got to the bench, Dorsey began, "Your Honor, I'm going to move for a mistrial at this time with a determination by the Court that jeopardy has not attached. There have been repeated abuses of the Court's order concerning the admissibility of this type of evidence."

"Denied as to the mistrial, sustained as to the material, Mr. Dorsey," Hodge said. "In my opinion, you haven't been prejudiced one bit to this point. If defense counsel has a way of validating the material gained under hypnosis and truth serum with independent, credible, real evidence, the Court will be inclined to hear more of this material. It sounds as if it could be quite relevant. At this point, however, the material is still inadmissible."

When they returned to counsel table, Yolanda began, "Dr. Gilmour, have you reached an opinion as to whether Avery Jackson is faking or malingering this condition?"

"Yes, I have. He is neither faking his amnesia nor his psychiatric condition. In fact, he doesn't even know about it. He is not aware he has another personality that is a killer, nor has he heard it from us. He has never presented that personality to us except when I attempted to give him a shot of scopolamine. He had obviously been programmed to resist any such attempts from people like me to uncover him."

"What happened when you attempted to give him a shot?"

"He tried to kill me by strangling me. It took three people to get him off me. After it happened, Avery had no recollection of it."

Jack looked at the jury. Each of them was looking at Gilmour intently.

"In your opinion, Dr. Gilmour, is the altered personality, Periscope, who attempted to kill you, the same Periscope who killed Sheriff Hardacre?"

"It is."

"And is such behavior typical of someone who is faking a mental illness?"

"No, malingerers are really fairly rare, and a competent, forensic psychiatrist can spot them quickly. They fake a psychiatric condition but don't attempt to kill the examiner. Instead, they attempt to ingratiate themselves to the examiner while presenting a plethora of psychological symptoms."

"In other words, they suck up to you while they try to sound crazy?"

"That's correct."

"Are you familiar with the legal definition of insanity, Doctor?" Yolanda asked.

"Yes, it is having a mental illness which prevents one from knowing right from wrong, or appreciating the wrongfulness of his acts."

"In your opinion, what was Avery Jackson's mental condition at the time he committed this act?"

"He was insane," Gilmour said.

"No further questions," Yolanda said. As she walked back to counsel table, she could see Aaron and Rebecca Jackson sitting with Marci. She could only wonder what they were thinking now. Their dad was a programmed killer during their entire lifetime and they never knew it. Yolanda wondered if they could believe it. Then she looked at Betty Hardacre, who today had brought her two kids, Ashley and Derrick, disgust written plainly on their faces. They avoided her look; she was the scumbag who was trying to get their father's killer off.

"Cross-examination, Mr. Dorsey?" Hodge asked.

Hank Dorsey got to his feet and approached the podium. "Dr. Gilmour, there are a lot of people in this society who have a post-traumatic stress disorder, aren't there?"

"Yes," Gilmour said.

"And there are a lot of Vietnam War vets with a post-traumatic stress disorder, aren't there?"

"Yes."

"Most people with this disorder are not killers, isn't that correct?"

"Yes, that's correct."

"I was looking at all the cases you've handled in Montgomery County, Doctor. Isn't it true this is the first person you have diagnosed with multiple personalities?"

"Yes, that is true."

"It's true, is it not, that you have never treated a multiple personality before, much less diagnosed it?"

"That's true."

"This is your first?"

"That is true."

"That means that you have treated as many multiples as Judge Hodge, me, all the jurors, the gallery, and Mr. Maine combined. A total of zero."

Gilmour said nothing.

"Please answer, Dr. Gilmour," Hodge said.

"Yes, zero," Gilmour said.

"Isn't it also true that you have never done a hypnotic induction before?"

"Yes."

"Isn't it also true that you have never done a scopolamine induction or truth serum induction before?"

"Yes."

"Isn't it true that people can get past events all confused or inaccurate when hypnotized?"

"That can happen. They can also be very accurate."

"We really don't know which it is here, do we?"

"I believe he was for real."

"Isn't it true that to your knowledge, scopolamine has never been used before in the history of forensic psychiatry?"

"To my knowledge, information gained from someone under the influence of scopolamine has never been declared to be admissible in a court of law."

"Let's assume for a moment that your diagnosis of multiple personality disorder is correct. Isn't it true that most multiple personalities are not murderers?"

"I would suspect that it is true, but I have no data on it."

"Most soldiers coming out of Vietnam did not become multiple personalities, did they, Dr. Gilmour?"

"I haven't seen data on that, but I would suspect that is true, too."

"Isn't multiple personality a very rare diagnosis?"

"Relatively."

"You say that the defendant attacked you?"

"Yes."

"Isn't that evidence of his dangerousness and criminality?"

"Yes, if he is activated."

"Now, Dr. Gilmour, you have testified that the defendant didn't know right from wrong when he killed Sheriff Hardacre?"

"That's correct."

"You have also said that you did not have access to Periscope, the alter personality?"

"We saw him. In fact, he tried to kill me. But he would never let us talk to him at length"

"And Periscope is the killer, correct?"

"Correct."

"If you never had real access to Periscope, you then can't know that he didn't know right from wrong when he killed the sheriff. Isn't that true, Doctor?"

"That's true. It's just my belief that he didn't know," Gilmour said.

"No further questions," Dorsey said. Hank thought he'd quit while he was ahead. When he got back to counsel table, Alec smiled at him. In Hunter's opinion, Gilmour's destruction had been complete.

"Re-direct?"

"No, Your Honor," Yolanda said.

"Call your next witness, Counsel," Hodge said.

"Your Honor, our next witness will not be here until this afternoon. Perhaps we could recess for lunch now?" Yolanda asked.

"A fine idea, Counsel," Hodge said. The jury was instructed not to discuss the case and the bailiff took them to lunch. "Court is in recess until one-thirty."

Friday—12 noon
The King's Table

When Jack and Yolanda emerged from the courthouse to a bright day, they could smell spring in the air. It was a respite from the room where Avery's life hung in the balance. Jack had a risky trial strategy. It depended on a number of things coming together. It would be the biggest chance he ever took with another's life. Perhaps the vibrancy of spring allowed him to feel he could survive professionally, even if his plan failed.

They ordered quickly when they got to the restaurant.

Marci joined them and sat next to Jack.

"I'm thinking we should rest after lunch," Jack announced after Bobbi had taken their orders. Marci and Yolanda looked at Jack like he was crazy. Joe Betts arrived before they could challenge him.

"Did you find Marvella Dixon?" Jack asked.

"Yeah. She loves Avery. She'd marry him tomorrow if she could," Joe said.

Yolanda's jealous blush was a tip off to how attached to Avery she'd become. Marci had sensed for several weeks that something was going on between them chemistry-wise. She had told Jack. He didn't believe it until he saw Yolanda's blush.

"I got a subpoena on her for next week," Joe said.

"Good, fill me in on what she'll be testifying to on the walk back to court," Jack said. "When is Hugh Lane going to be there?"

"This afternoon," Joe said.

"Good, I want you to buy him a cup of coffee. I'll explain to you what I have in mind," Jack said. "Do we have the CIA lined up?"

"Dr. McGinty doesn't call me to let me know his schedule."

"If he's not, I'll ask for a warrant and a mistrial. Marci," Jack said, "please get hold of Dr. Offen and tell him that we will be needing him on Monday."

"Why, if you're going to rest?" Marci asked.

"Yeah, why?" Yolanda asked.

"I just know Hunter. He's such an egomaniac. He won't be able to resist the temptation to put his experts on the stand now that he's got them all lined up. He's like Richard Nixon and Watergate. Nixon had the election won but resorted to dirty tricks. Hunter, too, has the case won, but he's so full of himself he'll resort to overkill. He'll want to put on his experts just for the media. They'll rip our evaluation apart, saying that multiple personality disorder does not exist. They'll claim the government or the CIA never involved itself in the creation of multiple personalities. They'll claim Avery is a faker. Hunter will want the jury to hear that, so they'll give Avery the death penalty. That will open the door for us when we get a chance at rebuttal. Otherwise, we have no chance. Hodge won't let us use the tapes to prove anything but diagnosis."

"And what if we rest, and then Hunter rests?" Yolanda asked.

"Then Avery will get convicted and we'll go to the death penalty phase. I'll turn in my law license after he's convicted, and then we're all out of a job. Now, let's enjoy our lunch."

The only one at the table who had an appetite was Jack.

Friday—1:30 P.M.
Montgomery County District Court

"Call your next witness, Mr. Maine," Judge Hodge said.

"Your Honor, the defense rests."

Hunter and Dorsey looked at each other incredulously. This was not possible. Maine had put on hardly any evidence at all to support an insanity defense. They had anticipated much more. Maine had three months to prepare for trial, and then he does a job like this?

"Very well, Counsel," Judge Hodge said, trying to hide his own shock. "Very well, then, we have heard an opinion that Mr. Jackson was insane at the time of the killing of Sheriff Hardacre. The burden of proof will now shift to the State of Ohio to disprove insanity beyond a reasonable doubt. Mr. Hunter, you have the option of producing evidence or not."

"Your Honor," Alec Hunter said as he rose to his feet, "we had anticipated that the defense case would take longer. I am requesting a short recess at this time. Dr. Procheska can be here within thirty minutes. He is on call."

"Court will be in recess until two-fifteen this afternoon," Hodge said before taking his leave to chambers.

As he slumped down in his judge's chair, Hodge thought of the issues this raised for him. If Jackson were convicted, there would certainly be a round of appeals alleging incompetent defense counsel. At this point, he felt they had some merit. Certainly, Maine could have offered another witness on Jackson's mental status. The record would look terrible—a first-degree murder/death penalty case where the defense only called one witness. If Hunter elected to rest, the attorneys would be arguing the case this afternoon, and it would be in the hands of the jury by four o'clock with the likelihood of a guilty verdict returned by five. Could this be? By Monday, he might have to determine whether or not to sentence Avery Jackson to death.

Hunter and Dorsey left the courtroom. They avoided all reporters as they ducked into a small conference room away from the mass of media, all of whom were trying to grasp what had just happened.

Before Hunter even sat down, Dorsey began, "I think we should rest. I think we've won the case. No one on that jury is going to believe Gilmour. He sounded like a flake. He admitted he never even diagnosed or treated a multiple personality before. Periscope is a bad joke. We can kill them during closing argument."

"I'm worried about the wetback on the jury," Hunter said. "I think she's just trying to find a reason to believe Jackson. The colored people will try to find a way to stick together on this. I think Gilmour gave her one. I do not want a hung jury; there is too much at stake. I think we should go ahead with our two experts. How can they hurt us?"

"Maine may argue we opened the door to more expert testimony. We know that Maine has this psychologist from Denver lined up," Dorsey said. "He's the guy who refused to talk with us about the case."

"I don't think we have to be worried about him," Alec said. "He's in trouble with the licensing board back there. All the psychiatrists got together and filed a complaint against him alleging he's a quack and incompetent. If Maine puts him on, we'll crush him."

"The people elected you," Hank said. "You decide how you want to run the case. I think we've already won it, but if you think we need to do more, we'll do more."

"I think," Alec said, "the People of Ohio have the right to hear who Avery Jackson really is—a fake and a fraud. If we don't put on more evidence, we'll get killed in the press if somehow the jury finds Jackson insane or decides not to execute him. The press headlines will read, 'Killer Found Insane—DA Pleads No Contest.' I would never survive the next election. You remember how I got this job when Pete Cassidy Rose was found insane. The press buried old Dave Morgan. I can't take the chance of that happening to me. Let's put on our

287

shrinks and crush Avery Jackson. When the jury hears what a lying nigger—excuse my French—he is, they'll be more likely to sentence him to death, which is exactly what he deserves."

"You're the boss," Dorsey said. "I gotta say, though, I don't think there's any sense in using a driver when the next hole only calls for an eight iron."

"I'd rather the ball fly over the green than be short," Hunter said. "The hole is all carry and there's a huge canyon in front of the green. It's like number eight at Pebble Beach. If you don't hit it far enough, you're dead. We're going for it."

CHAPTER 25

"Mr. Hunter, do you wish to proceed?" Judge Hodge asked Alec when court resumed.

Marci's heart hadn't beaten this hard since she was trapped in the basement of the group home with Detective Guteman. Yolanda felt like she was going to throw up the small lunch she had just eaten.

Hunter stood up slowly, fidgeted with his tie for what seemed like an eternity and then said, "The People call Dr. Irwin Procheska."

Marci and Yolanda could suddenly breathe again. Avery had a chance to continue living.

Jack nudged Yolanda's arm and whispered to her, "What did I tell you? A narcissist generally takes the bait." His cool exterior belied both his jubilation and the strident, inner voice that reminded him his career could just as easily have been sentenced to death, along with Avery, had Hunter rested.

Dr. Procheska was escorted to the witness stand. In his sixties, he, like Hunter, looked imperious in his dress and demeanor. He wore an expensive charcoal suit with matching tie, fashionable dark shoes and a shirt starched even stiffer than Hunter's.

"Please state your name, sir," Alec said.

"Dr. Irwin Procheska."

"How are you employed?"

289

"I'm a psychiatrist."

"How long have you worked in that capacity?"

"Forty years."

"Tell us about your education."

"I'm a Board Certified Forensic Psychiatrist—"

Jack got to his feet. "We'll stipulate to Dr. Procheska's credentials. He's testified in this court for the district attorney's office many times."

"Mr. Hunter, do you so stipulate?" Judge Hodge asked.

"I do, Your Honor," Alec said. "Now, Dr. Procheska, did you have occasion to do a forensic evaluation of one Avery Jackson in connection with this case?"

"Yes."

"And what did it consist of?"

"I read Dr. Offen and Dr. Gilmour's evaluation. I also interviewed the defendant for approximately three hours in jail, and I read the police reports of the shooting."

"What did you find out?" Alec asked.

"This is a man who had a rather difficult childhood but was able to go to law school and do well. He became a lawyer and a judge. It is my opinion he developed a grandiose, artificial self that has allowed him to operate far above his capacities. Underneath, he is a psychopath or antisocial personality. He has had criminal tendencies his entire life and finally acted them out in one horrific crime. He has fooled many people and perhaps gotten privileges that others would not have gotten. He has used these privileges, and others, to his advantage in rising to considerable prominence. Basically though, he's a fraud and a fake who cares little for others. He mistreated his wife and is now estranged from her. He engaged in some substance abuse and made questionable decisions while on the bench. With Mr. Jackson, it was only a matter of time until something like this happened to him."

"Have you determined a diagnosis for him?"

"Yes, I have."

"What is that diagnosis?"

"He has an antisocial personality disorder, or in other words, he's a psychopath," said Procheska assuredly. "He can kill without conscience."

"There has been testimony that he suffers from post-traumatic stress disorder. Do you agree with that?" Hunter asked.

"No," answered Procheska. "He didn't appear particularly anxious to me. He spoke some of bad dreams, but in my opinion, he was faking those symptoms. I saw no evidence of a post-traumatic condition when I interviewed him."

"There has been testimony that he suffers from multiple personality disorder and has another personality by the name of Periscope who is a programmed killer. Did you see any evidence of that?"

"No. I asked him about having an altered personality, and he denied the existence of one. I saw no evidence of it. There was certainly none present when I interviewed him."

"There has been talk that he left Vietnam as a multiple personality. Did you see any evidence of that?"

"No. He could tell me of no instances in his life after the military when he lost control of himself or lost consciousness. Multiple personalities frequently lose time, wind up in strange places and don't understand how they got there. That phenomenon is called a fugue state. Jackson claims no fugue states." Procheska could not resist the opportunity to lecture the jury.

"There has been mention that somehow the defendant was programmed by the CIA during the war. Did you find any data to support that?" Hunter asked.

Jack nearly leaped out of his chair to run a victory lap. Hunter had now opened the door to the testimony that Dorsey had successfully kept out of evidence when Dr. Gilmour testified.

"No, Mr. Jackson is not aware of any involvement with the CIA. There is no evidence the CIA was conducting any mind-control projects with the Army in Vietnam. I believe this a flight-of-fancy by my colleague, Dr. Gilmour."

"Dr. Procheska," Hunter asked as he brought his direct testimony to a crescendo, "do you have an opinion as to whether the defendant was suffering from a mental illness that prevented him from knowing right from wrong, or appreciating the wrongfulness of his act when he shot Sheriff Hardacre?"

"Yes, I do," said Procheska.

"And what is that opinion?"

"Mr. Jackson is a psychopath who was well aware of what he was doing, and that it was wrong when he shot Sheriff Hardacre." Procheska emphasized each word as he spoke as if trying to burn them into the mind of the jury.

"I have no further questions of this witness. Cross-examination, Counsel?" Hunter asked of Jack.

Jack rose slowly with his legal pad. Procheska had given the jury the ammunition it needed to convict. "Dr. Procheska, you frequently testify as an expert in criminal cases, don't you?" Jack asked.

"Yes."

"And how many times have you been qualified as an expert?"

"During the course of my career, over a hundred times."

"How many insanity trials have you testified in?" Jack asked.

"Approximately ten."

"Do you recall the names of the defendants in those trials?"

"Some of them."

"Do you recall the diagnosis for each defendant?"

"For some of them."

"Do you recall whether you found the defendant sane or insane?"

"In some of them, I do."

"Dr. Procheska, do you recall if you testified for Mr. Hunter, or for the defense, the hundred or so times you testified?"

"I don't recall, but I'd say that the majority of the time I testify for the prosecution."

"Dr. Procheska, I show you what has been marked as Defense Exhibit One. Is this a copy of your résumé?"

"It is."

"And you have listed here all of the cases you have been qualified as an expert?"

"That's correct."

"Would it surprise you that I had my investigator look up all those cases, and that in every one of them you testified for the district attorney?"

"That may be accurate," Dr. Procheska said, unruffled, "I just don't recall."

"Dr. Procheska, let's take a look at all the insanity cases on which you've done evaluations. There is Miller, DePasquale, Antieto, Jarvis, Cantron, Haskins, Hardacre, Carson, Anthony, Xeno. Do those names ring a bell, Doctor?"

Procheska realized he was trapped. No attorney had ever been so diligent to look up all of his testimony.

"Do you realize that in every one of those cases, you testified for Mr. Hunter and found that the defendant was a malingering, antisocial personality disorder, and a psychopath, and was sane?" Jack asked.

"That's because, Counsel, so many defendants like your client, Mr. Jackson, are just that," Gilmour said. Procheska was a professional; he knew how to stick the knife in.

"Let's take a look at this, Doctor," Jack said. "Define for the jury an antisocial personality disorder."

"It's a mental illness within a person that is manifested by a disregard for the law and social customs and the safety of others. Clearly, by this act of shooting the sheriff, your client has shown contempt for the law and safety of others."

"Aren't you forgetting some other elements, Doctor? According to the *Diagnostic and Statistical Manual of Mental Disorders*—the DSM—there must be a history of conduct disorder or antisocial acts prior to the age of fifteen, repeated lying, and fights, that sort of thing, to qualify the person as being psychopathic. You are aware, aren't you, that Mr. Jackson has no history of lying, fighting, or committing crimes prior to the age of fifteen?"

"I'm not aware of that, sir. His record looks like that, but these people are such good liars and con men, they can fake their way through school. Mr.

Jackson may have committed many crimes prior to the age of fifteen."

"These types of people are unstable, aren't they?"

"Generally."

"Would you say that unstable people can graduate from high school and college with honors, as well as matriculate in law school, pass the bar, marry and raise a family, become a judge and a law professor without first being exposed as a liar and malicious psychopath?"

"There is no telling what the psychopath can get away with. Look at Ted Bundy. He was in law school before he was exposed."

"Let's take a look at the Xeno case. Do you remember that case?"

"I do."

"The report here says that Mr. Xeno had no criminal record, a history of being severely abused as a child and had become psychotic when he was seventeen. He also had hallucinations about people reaching in and taking thoughts out of his head, as well as being repeatedly stabbed. When he assaulted a man at the age of twenty-four, you found him to be a malingerer and anti-social personality disorder, although he was acutely psychotic at the time."

"That's correct, Counsel. I felt he was lying about his history of child abuse and faking the hallucinations. There are many people who are the victims of child abuse who don't become psychotic and even more who don't need to fake psychosis."

"Were you aware that when Mr. Xeno got to the state hospital, he was diagnosed by four other mental health professionals as psychotic?"

"I am aware of that. I disagree with them. He conned them."

"Are you aware he committed suicide a week after he arrived there?"

The room became very quiet. Procheska didn't answer.

"Dr. Procheska, were you aware of that?"

"No, but it is not unusual for psychopaths to commit suicide when they're arrested."

"How much are you being paid for this testimony today, Dr. Procheska?"

"My usual fee."

"How much is that?"

"Five hundred dollars an hour."

"And you've testified for the State approximately one hundred times in your career, is that correct?"

"Yes."

"Tell me, Doctor, how many hours does it take to do a forensic, psychiatric evaluation?"

"With testimony, approximately ten hours," said Procheska.

"Thus, your fee will be five thousand dollars on this case?"

"That's correct."

"Doing the math, then, Doctor, you've made a half million dollars working for Mr. Hunter over the years?"

"I don't work for Mr. Hunter. I practice my science and am paid accordingly."

"Your science seems to agree with the needs of Mr. Hunter's office and the flow of the money, Doctor," observed Jack.

"Objection, Counsel is testifying," Dorsey said. "I'd ask that it be stricken from the record."

"Sustained. The jury will disregard what Mr. Maine just said."

"Would it be correct to say that you have been paid at least half a million dollars by Mr. Hunter's office over the years?"

"Probably much more than that. I don't testify in every case," Procheska admitted.

"Was five hundred an hour how much you were also paid on the Xeno case?"

"It may have been four hundred. My rates have gone up."

"You have never diagnosed or treated a multiple personality disorder, have you?"

"That's correct."

"You have testified that Mr. Jackson claimed not to be one during your evaluation of him?"

"That's correct."

"Isn't it true that most multiples don't generally know about the existence of the other personalities?"

"That's true."

"How then could you expect Mr. Jackson to be aware of his altered personality when you interviewed him?"

"Quite frankly, I don't believe in the diagnosis, period. It is a convenient way for criminals and other people to gain sympathy for themselves. Psychologists and psychiatrists create the disorder in these criminals when they respond to a fake personality that is presented by the defendant. In my opinion, that is how this phony Periscope was started. He is a figment of the defense psychiatrist's imagination."

"You are aware of the fact that the disorder is in the DSM?"

"Yes, but that doesn't mean it exists."

"The DSM is accepted by the bulk of mental health professionals as the defining treatise of mental disease, is it not, Dr. Procheska?"

"Yes."

"You have also testified that there is no validity to CIA involvement in mind-control experiments in the military."

"That's correct."

"Have you heard of the MKULTRA and ARTICHOKE Projects?"

"No, I haven't."

"You have never used hypnosis as a technique by which to diagnose or treat a patient, have you?"

"That's correct. And I would never use it in a forensic situation because people may give very inaccurate information when in a trance state."

"You also have never done a sodium amytal or scopolamine induction, have you, Doctor?"

"No, I know of no one who has, except your doctors on this case."

"Thank, you, Doctor, you have indeed been enlightening. Move for admission of Defendant's Exhibit One."

"No objection," Dorsey said.

"Very well, Defendant's One will be admitted. Re-direct, Mr. Dorsey?"

"Yes, Your Honor," Hank said as he rose from his chair. Without approaching the podium, he had one question. "Has our office ever advised you what result we would like on a particular case?"

"No. I always call them as I see them."

Dorsey sat down.

"Re-cross, Mr. Maine?" Judge Hodge asked.

"No, Your Honor."

As Dr. Procheska stepped down, Jack looked at the jury. They sat rather impassively. His worst fear was that Procheska's testimony confirmed what they already believed—that Avery was a cold-blooded, murdering psychopath they could easily sentence to death. They looked comfortable.

"Call your next witness, Mr. Dorsey," Hodge ordered.

"Dr. Marvin Horde," Dorsey announced to the courtroom.

The bailiff escorted a seventy-year-old, balding man with glasses to the witness box. He wore a light-colored suit, was paunchy and homely. He took the witness stand and was sworn to tell the truth. After stating his name, Dorsey began his direct examination of Dr. Horde.

"Tell me about your education."

Jack rose to his feet. "Your Honor, we stipulate to Dr. Horde's expertise in psychiatry and hypnosis and mind control."

"Your Honor," Dorsey said, "we do not accept that stipulation. We want the jury to hear all of Dr. Horde's qualifications."

"Very well, proceed, Mr. Dorsey," Hodge said.

"Dr. Horde, tell the jury about your education," Dorsey reiterated.

"I have a bachelor's degree from Harvard and a medical degree from Cornell Medical School. I did a residency in psychiatry at Cornell. I am a Board Certified Psychiatrist. I am currently a teaching professor in psychiatry at Harvard Medical School."

"How long have you practiced psychiatry?"

"Forty years."

"Have you authored articles that have been published?"

"Yes, I have authored approximately one hundred and fifty articles in the field of psychiatry—most specifically related to hypnosis. I have done much of the original work in the field of psychiatry concerning hypnosis."

"Do you belong to any professional organizations?"

"Certainly, I'm a member of the American Medical Association and have been the president of the American Society of Clinical Hypnosis. Furthermore, I am on the Board of Directors of the Created Memory Society."

"Have you been qualified as an expert witness before?"

"Many times."

"In what sort of cases?"

"Mostly in cases where people are claiming to have memories of past events or of altered, multiple personalities."

"Your Honor, I would offer Dr. Horde as an expert in the field of Psychiatry, most specifically in the area of hypnosis, multiple personality and false memories," Dorsey said.

"No objection," Jack said

"Dr. Horde is so qualified," Hodge ordered.

"Dr. Horde, did you have occasion to do a psychiatric evaluation on one Avery Jackson?" Dorsey asked.

"I did one at the Montgomery County Jail about a month ago."

"What did the evaluation entail?"

"It consisted of a clinical interview, review of the tape of the shooting, the police reports, and the reports of Doctor's Offen, Gilmour and Procheska."

"How much time did you spend on this evaluation?"

"Approximately twelve hours."

"What did you find out?"

"I found that Mr. Jackson was a very intelligent, articulate man who claimed amnesia for killing Sheriff Hardacre. I attempted to hypnotize him to take him back to the shooting. Although seemingly hypnotizable, he claimed no memory of the event. He told me that information was 'off limits' when I attempted to probe there. While the defendant was apparently hypnotized, I explored for the existence of another personality that could have been responsible for the killing. He claimed that information was 'off limits,' too."

"What is your opinion with regard to the assertion that Mr. Jackson has another personality that was programmed to kill the sheriff?" Dorsey asked.

"I believe," Dr. Horde said in a very officious voice, as if God were speaking, "that he attempted to fake a trance by fluttering his eyes and twitching his fingers. I further believe he is faking amnesia with regard to the shooting, or denying the reality of it. As far as the existence of another personality, he shut down when I probed into that. I see no evidence he has had any amnesia for other events in his adult life like a person with multiple personalities would. Therefore, it is my conclusion that such an altered personality does not exist, as is claimed by the defense."

"Do you have a diagnosis for Mr. Jackson?"

"Yes," Dr. Horde said, "I believe him to be a faker or malinger in order to escape responsibility for this crime. I believe him to be the cleverest psychopath and one of the most insidiously-evil characters I have seen in my forty years of practice."

Marci was watching the jury carefully as she sat next to Avery's two children. They had heard that Avery Jackson was as bad as Jack the Ripper, John Wayne Gacy and Ted Bundy. She held Rebecca's hand as Horde stuck a knife through her father's heart. Rebecca and Aaron both knew that Horde had completely mischaracterized their father. The jury did not. All they knew about Avery was that he was a black man who had been thrown off the bench for possibly taking a bribe that allowed a rapist off the hook. And, of course, they knew he was a killer. Their collective brows furrowed as Horde told them that Avery Jackson was even worse than they had suspected. It would now be very easy for them to put this man to death.

"Dr. Horde, there was testimony by Dr. Gilmour that the defendant attacked him prior to his attempting to give the defendant an injection of scopolamine. What do you believe the significance of that to be?" Dorsey asked.

"I believe it to be grandstanding. It's an example of the viciousness and cunning that accompanies psychopathic personalities."

"Do you have an opinion as to whether Mr. Jackson knew right from wrong at the time he committed this crime?"

"Yes, I have such an opinion."

"What is that opinion?"

"This man not only knew what he was doing, he planned it carefully in order to garner national media attention. He did so to compensate for the loss of self-esteem he suffered when he was voted off the bench. He is a seriously narcissistic, disturbed psychopath desperately needing to bring attention to himself because of deficits in his childhood."

"Thank you, Dr. Horde," Dorsey said as if he were thanking Horde for ridding the world of all its vermin.

"Cross-examination, Mr. Maine?" Hodge asked.

"Yes, Your Honor. Dr. Horde, how much are you being paid for your testimony here today?"

"Thirty thousand dollars," Horde said. There were a couple of gasps in the courtroom.

"Mr. Hunter's office is not paying the bill, is it, Dr. Horde?"

"That's correct."

"Objection," Dorsey said. "Who pays Dr. Horde's fee is irrelevant. It is expensive to bring the world's most accomplished expert on debunking multiple personality disorder before the court, but it is not important who pays him."

"Your Honor, the source of the payment is most relevant. It goes to the witness' bias."

"I agree," Hodge said. "Proceed."

"Who is paying your bill, today?"

"The Created Memory Society."

"You are on the board of that society, are you not?"

"Yes, along with numerous other prominent psychiatrists and psychologists."

"Now, the goal of that organization is to take people who remember things as adults, such as being sexually molested when they were children, and debunk their assertions."

"That is not what we do, Counsel. We evaluate these people and try to find out if their assertions are valid. Then, we testify for or against them."

"Name one case in which you testified that their recovered memory was valid."

Horde hesitated. "There are none at this time. In every case I evaluated, the recovered memory had always been false or the product of a therapist implanting the memory."

"How many of these cases have you done?"

"Dozens."

"Do you believe that people who have been severely traumatized can later remember instances of trauma that occurred to them?"

"It is a possibility."

"What I'm hearing, Dr. Horde, is that you're especially concerned that therapists create memories of trauma that really don't exist?"

"That is correct. Research has shown that psychotherapy can have an iatrogenic effect on people and create conditions that did not exist before the therapy."

"By iatrogenic, you mean that the therapist creates the disorder?"

"That's correct."

"Now, you have been especially vocal in asserting that the phenomenon of multiple personality disorder does not exist. Would that be a correct statement?"

"It is my position that it is far over-diagnosed and many times created by therapists."

"Have you ever seen a valid case where multiple personalities truly existed?"

"No, not really."

"Isn't it true that you have testified for numerous district attorneys around the country in serious homicide cases that the defendant didn't really have the disorder?"

"That is correct."

"You have never testified that the disorder was real, have you?"

"That would be correct."

"And you testified in the Ross Carlson double homicide in Colorado that Mr. Carlson was a faker and a malingerer?"

"I did."

"And you testified in the Hillside Strangler case that the defendant was a faker, isn't that correct?"

"That's correct."

"Multiple personality is a rare diagnosis, Doctor?"

"That's correct."

"Multiple personalities can be created in a laboratory or clinical setting, can't they, Doctor?"

"That is highly doubtful."

"Dr. Horde, you have created multiple personalities in a laboratory setting for the CIA, haven't you?"

Horde just looked at Jack. "I can't answer that question."

"Why not, Doctor?"

"It's a matter of national security, and I don't have to answer it."

Jack took out a document with blacked-out names. At the top of it was PROJECT MOULTRIE—CENTRAL INTELLIGENCE AGENCY. "I show you what has been marked as Defendant's Exhibit Two, Dr. Horde; I will read it to you." Jack began reading a document that described in detail electroshock treatment of an unwitting subject. Massive doses of electroshock were given to a woman with the express intention of eliminating part of her personality and replacing it with another personality. "Dr. Horde, you're the doctor in this experiment with your name blocked out here, aren't you?"

"Objection, Your Honor," Dorsey said. He somehow had to protect his witness. He knew nothing of this material.

"On what grounds, Counsel?"

"National security . . . relevancy," Dorsey said, fumbling in the dark.

"National security? How could it be national security? This CIA material was released last year through the Freedom of Information Act," Jack exclaimed.

"Overruled," Hodge said without hesitation. "Dr. Horde, you're to answer the question."

"I can't, Your Honor," Horde said.

"There may be another way, Your Honor," Jack said, "if the Court will allow me some leeway."

"Proceed, Mr. Maine," Hodge ordered.

"Doctor, you remember being a part of this experiment, don't you?"

"I don't recall. This was done nearly thirty years ago."

"I show you what has been marked as Defense Exhibit Three." Jack showed him a document relating to a man who had been unwittingly subjected to scopolamine and LSD, put in solitary confinement, and subjected to other abuses with the express intent of creating a personality that, when cued, would transmit information overseas to military personnel. The subject remembered nothing of the mind-control techniques or the transmission of messages that had in fact been delivered.

"Dr. Horde, this was your experiment also, was it not?"

"I don't recall."

"Is your memory bad at times now, Dr. Horde?"

"Counsel, those are very old experiments."

"How long have you worked for the CIA?"

"I can't answer that."

"Why not?"

"Because it's a matter of national security."

"You know, Dr. Horde, I have the right to demand that you answer the question."

"I am sworn to secrecy on these matters, Counsel."

"By whom?"

"I can't answer that question."

"Let's talk about the Created Memory Society. They have paid your thirty thousand dollar fee today?"

"That's correct." Horde was now beginning to swallow frequently. Sweat was breaking out on his brow. He didn't want to go where Maine was taking him. He had not anticipated this. In all of the times he had testified he had never been exposed like this.

"Who funds the Created Memory Society?"

"I don't know."

"Doctor, you're chairman of the board of the society and you're telling us you don't know where the money is coming from?"

"We have various benefactors."

"Who is the largest benefactor?"

"The Rittenhouse Foundation."

"Who funds the Rittenhouse Foundation?"

"I don't really know."

"Dr. Horde, isn't it true that the Central Intelligence Agency funds the Rittenhouse Foundation?"

"I don't really know, Counsel."

"I want you, Dr. Horde, to deny under oath the first thing I say here that is untrue."

"Objection," Hank Dorsey said. Dorsey knew his witness was in trouble. He had to protect him, but he didn't want it to appear in front of the jury as if he were trying to keep the truth from them. He was walking a fine line. "This is improper cross-examination," Dorsey finished lamely.

"I'm going to allow it, Mr. Dorsey," Judge Hodge said. "Mr. Maine is within his rights to demand the answers to the questions that Dr. Horde has refused to answer. Perhaps your witness, Mr. Dorsey, can avoid contempt of court by simply failing to deny allegations."

"Here are the allegations, Doctor," Jack said. "If any of them are untrue, simply deny them. The CIA has been involved in mind-control experiments for years."

Horde was mute.

"Let the record reflect that Dr. Horde has admitted the allegation by his silence," Jack said.

Dorsey offered no objection, furious with Alec for his lame-brained decision to put on more experts when they'd had the case won.

"You have participated in those experiments for years where there has been the deliberate creation of multiple personalities or 'Manchurian Candidates.'"

Horde again sat mute.

"Let the record reflect an admission, Your Honor," Jack said.

"It will so reflect," Hodge said.

"Finally, the Created Memory Society has been set up by the CIA as a disinformation organization to confuse the public and the courts about multiple personalities as well as recovered memories."

Horde said nothing. Everyone knew that his failure to deny was an admission.

"Now, Dr. Horde, you once treated a poet by the name of Anne Faxon, didn't you?"

"That's confidential."

"Ann Faxon is dead, isn't she?"

"Yes."

"Her estate sued you for malpractice and you settled the case?" Few people knew of the Faxon case. "Dr. Horde, you're aware that this material is not confidential because she is now dead?"

"I suppose that's correct."

"Dr. Horde, isn't it true that Anne Faxon was a multiple personality disordered woman you misdiagnosed, and she subsequently committed suicide?"

"She did commit suicide, but she was not a multiple personality."

"But you settled the case after the allegations of failing to properly diagnose her as a multiple personality?"

"That's correct."

"Dr. Horde, when you hypnotized Mr. Jackson, he said material was unavailable to you, is that correct?"

"Yes."

"He said the sky, or the moon, 'was dark' for that information, didn't he?"

"I believe so," Horde muttered.

"Don't those sound like the sort of code words used in mind-control experiments by the CIA?"

"I don't know."

"Why didn't you go further with your evaluation when Mr. Jackson said the material was unavailable?"

"Because to go further would have yielded false information. Scopolamine induction is not deemed an acceptable procedure by the courts or the medical profession."

"Dr. Horde, deny this if it is untrue: scopolamine was frequently used by the CIA in its creation of multiple personalities to carry out government missions."

Horde said nothing. Again, an admission of the truth.

Jack thought a moment and said, "No further questions."

When Jack got back to counsel table, Yolanda whispered to him, "I can only hope that I live to see the day I can do a cross-examination that well."

He smiled at her. He had Joe to thank for much of it. There is nothing like a good investigator to get the goods on someone.

"Re-direct, Mr. Dorsey?" Judge Hodge asked.

Hank Dorsey stood at counsel table knowing he must rehabilitate Horde. "Dr. Horde, is your diagnosis of Mr. Jackson still the same?"

"Yes."

"And what is it?"

"He is one of the cleverest psychopathic deceivers and liars I have ever evaluated."

"Is your opinion on his sanity still the same?"

"It is. In my opinion, he is well aware of the difference between right and wrong and knew that difference on the date he killed Sheriff Hardacre."

"Thank you, Doctor Horde. No further questions."

"Re-cross, Counsel?" Hodge asked.

"Just one last question. Do you expect us to believe you know the difference between right and wrong, Doctor, given the unethical mind-control experiments you took part in?" Jack asked.

"Objection!" Dorsey screamed.

"I'll withdraw the question," Jack said.

Hopefully, the jury realized that Dr. Horde had just been stripped naked and flogged in front of them. When he walked from the courtroom, the arrogance he had exhibited at the beginning of his testimony had visibly dissipated and was replaced by the vulnerability of an old man whose secrets and motives were now apparent.

Still, Jack wasn't sure that was good enough. Avery Jackson was still a killer, and the tapes spoke for themselves. The wailing of Gene Hardacre's widow spoke much more loudly than the two charlatan psychiatrists that Hunter had put on the stand. As far as Jack was concerned, he was still losing this trial in which death was the inevitable penalty.

"Please call your next witness, Mr. Dorsey," Judge Hodge said.

"The State rests on the issue of sanity, Your Honor," Dorsey said, sighing deeply within.

"Very well, the court will be in recess until Monday morning. The jury is admonished not to discuss the case with anyone. I believe we have planned suitable entertainment for the jury this weekend and hope this is not an undue hardship on you and your families. We thank you for your service."

As the jurors filed slowly out of the courtroom, they appeared perplexed by the day's testimony. Once they were safely outside, Judge Hodge announced, "Court is in recess," and he quickly left the room.

CHAPTER 26

The jurors had filed into their seats, with one missing: Harold Warren—used car salesman, high-school educated, fast talker. Judge Hodge had been informed when he arrived in his chambers that Mr. Warren had been taken from the Hilton to the hospital by ambulance Sunday evening around nine o'clock. His appendix had burst. He was in serious condition and needed hospitalization. He was currently on IV antibiotics and morphine. Surgery and bed rest were required.

"Mr. Stevens," Judge Hodge said, "you have been chosen by the attorneys to be the first alternate juror in this case. Illness has, by necessity, eliminated Mr. Warren. I am requesting you assume his place in the jury box and to be a part of all deliberations in reaching a just result in this matter."

Calvin Stevens was now the one black man on the jury. Avery Jackson was not there to appreciate it because his appearance was still waived. Hunter and Dorsey necessarily appeared magnanimous, but the addition of Stevens to the jury was now a fly in the ointment. As far as Hunter was concerned, it made little difference. Dorsey wasn't so sure.

"Mr. Maine, does the defense have any rebuttal witnesses?" Judge Hodge asked.

"We do, Your Honor. The defense calls Dr. James McGinty."

Hunter looked incredulously at Hank Dorsey, who shrugged his shoulders.

They'd been looking for a fastball in the person of Dr. Offen and were being thrown a change-up. Who the hell was this guy? Too many things had gone wrong on Friday. Now this.

Alec shot to his feet. "Your Honor, the State objects. May counsel approach the bench?" Alec didn't want the jury to hear the basis for his objection for fear they would believe he was trying to keep something from them.

"Certainly," Hodge said.

When the four lawyers got to the bench, Hunter said, "Your Honor, we were given no notice that Dr. McGinty would be a witness in this proceeding. We have no idea who Dr. James McGinty *is*. We object to him as a witness as well as any other witnesses we were not given notice of. Mr. Maine is trying to sandbag us."

"Mr. Maine, did you fail to give Mr. Hunter notice of these witnesses?" Hodge asked.

"Your Honor, I had no intention of calling this witness except in rebuttal. The State has put on two experts who have claimed that Mr. Jackson is a faker and a fraud and not an unwitting victim of mind-control programming by the United States government. Dr. McGinty should be able to shed some light on these claims. As the court and Mr. Hunter are well aware, I cannot anticipate the prosecution's evidence and am not required to give notice of rebuttal witnesses."

"Mr. Hunter?" Judge Hodge asked.

"Your Honor, this is a game of fair play. Mr. Maine has withheld critical witnesses from us," Hunter said.

"I have withheld nothing. The testimony of both of your experts opened the door to evidence of mind-control experiments and CIA involvement. Mr. Jackson has the right to challenge that evidence. To refuse him the right to do so would constitute a violation of his constitutional rights."

"The court will allow the testimony. Lets bring the jury in."

When Jack and Yolanda turned to go back to counsel table, there was Dr. McGinty, dressed in a suit and accompanied by a distinguished-looking, middle-aged man in a three-piece suit clutching a briefcase. He was a lawyer, but not local. A young man, probably a law clerk, was wheeling in a large cardboard box full of files. McGinty was under subpoena to appear and produce all CIA files related to Avery Jackson; there were obviously a lot of them. Jack had seen none of them. The lawyer was there to see that he never would.

"J. Alexander Bronfman, Jr., Your Honor, appearing on behalf of Dr. McGinty and the United States of America. I am an Assistant United States Attorney from Washington D.C."

Hodge loved it. Now the Feds. It could only mean a high-handed move—a usurpation of his jurisdiction. "And what can we do for you, Mr. Bronfman?"

he asked.

"Dr. McGinty has been served with a subpoena *duces tecum*—"

Hunter interrupted him. He didn't want the jury to hear this. "Your Honor, perhaps the jury should be excused again while Mr. Bronfman addresses the court."

Hodge agreed and excused the jury to the deliberation room.

"Now, Mr. Bronfman, proceed," Hodge said.

"Dr. McGinty has been served with a subpoena *duces tecum* to produce all records related to Mr. Jackson's connection to the Central Intelligence Agency. He has also been ordered to be here to give testimony. The United States of America is objecting to these records being used for any purpose and to Dr. McGinty giving any testimony about anything."

"On what grounds?" Hodge asked.

"National security."

The press was listening intently. It was now obvious the CIA was involved with Avery Jackson. This story was taking on aspects of a John le Carre novel.

"I have here a written motion," Bronfman said, "to quash the subpoena in this court as well as a writ of prohibition issued by Judge Wilbur Grice of the U.S. District Court mandating that these proceedings be halted pending a hearing as to whether the interests of the United States of America with regard to its national security supersede the interests of the defendant in this case."

"Counsel," Judge Hodge said," are you telling me that it doesn't make any difference what I do here, Judge Grice is going to decide if this man is going to testify in my court about Central Intelligence Agency operations and the defendant's involvement in them?"

"That's the bottom line," Bronfman said. "May I have permission to approach the bench, Your Honor?" Bronfman asked.

"Certainly." Hodge said.

As Bronfman approached the bench, he said, "I am serving the Court with a writ prohibiting it from allowing testimony by Dr. James McGinty concerning Mr. Jackson's involvement with the Central Intelligence Agency." He handed the writ to Judge Hodge.

As Hodge read the document, his cheeks flushed. This was the same issue that had plagued America since the Constitution was enacted in 1776. The Civil War was fought over it. It was whether the power of the United States was supreme over that of the individual states.

"Mr. Hunter, what is your position on this issue?" Hodge asked.

"We would join with the United States Attorney in his motion to quash." Hunter had to keep this evidence out; and, he'd be damned how it looked, he'd ride the Feds' coattails.

"Mr. Maine?" Hodge asked.

"Your Honor, we insist on access to these files and demand Dr. McGinty's testimony. My client is on trial for his life. The mind-control activities of the Central Intelligence Agency in the '50s, '60s and '70s have already been declassified. How can the federal interests supersede the interests of my client when they have already declassified much of this material?"

"The court will take a recess, at which time it will conduct an in-camera review of the files to determine their relevancy to the proceedings. If not relevant, Judge Grice will not even need to hear the matter on the issue of national security, and we will proceed immediately without Dr. McGinty. Doctor, please wheel those files into my chambers. If you wish to sit with me while I review them, you may. This court is in recess."

As the media left to call and e-mail the developments to their employers, Joe Betts came into the courtroom. He quickly surveyed it and saw Hugh Lane sitting inconspicuously in a corner. "Sheriff Lane, I'm Joe Betts." Joe extended his right hand to Lane.

Lane didn't move, he just stared at Joe with contempt. "I remember you," he said. "You're the guy who served this subpoena on me. Do you realize what a pain in the ass it is for me to be here? I have a mountain of work to catch up on at the office. What the hell does the defense want with me on this case?"

"Why don't we go down to the coffee shop during this recess and I'll fill you in on what we need. Then, we'll let you go today," Joe said. "Let me buy you a cup of coffee."

Lane stood up. He was still obviously upset. "Fine," he said as they began to walk toward the coffee shop. He made sure to walk ahead of Betts. He certainly didn't want to show him any respect.

"You like your coffee black?" Joe asked.

"With cream and sugar," Lane said.

Joe returned to a corner table with two cups of coffee. After he sat, Joe said, "Sheriff Lane, I'll get to the point. We need to know what your relationship with Avery Jackson was. We understand that you two fought together in Vietnam and that you were social friends after you both returned to Dayton."

"That's true."

"Can you think of any reason why Avery would want Hardacre dead?"

"Avery didn't like Republicans." Lane laughed. "Other than that, I can't think of a reason."

"Seriously, Sheriff, can you tell the jury what he was like in Vietnam?"

"Betts, this isn't the sort of stuff you can use in your defense. Stop bullshitting me."

Joe thought quickly. He needed to come up with a quick, credible lie. "We thought we could use you if we lost the trial on the first-degree murder charge and then had to proceed to the death penalty phase, you'd be a good witness for Avery's heroism. He was a good soldier, wasn't he?"

"Very good. He carried out numerous top secret missions for our outfit. He was fearless."

"See? You'd be perfect, the sheriff and all, saying that kind of sh—stuff."

"I don't know what Hunter would think about it."

"I understand. Avery thought you could be helpful if it came to saving his life."

"I'll do what I can."

"Have you been over to see Avery since he was arrested?"

"No, I haven't. How's he doing?"

"Oh, as well as can be expected, under the circumstances. Let's get back upstairs and see if the judge has looked over the CIA stuff. What do you think of that?" Joe asked as they finished their coffee. "Here, let me get that," Joe said referring to Lane's coffee cup.

Lane thought nothing of it. "I think it's a bunch of defense bullshit. Maine is just trying to create a smokescreen."

"Could be, but that's what good defense attorneys are for, Sheriff. Go ahead without me. I just remembered I got an errand to run. We won't need you back here until Wednesday morning for your testimony."

As Lane was entering the courtroom, the bailiff was saying, "All rise, this Court is again in session."

Judge Hodge took the bench. He announced the appearances and moved quickly to his ruling. "The Court has examined the documents under subpoena in the presence of Dr. James McGinty of the Central Intelligence Agency. The Court finds that the documents are most relevant. The motion to quash the subpoena is denied. Furthermore, the Court shall be in recess until one-thirty. It's ten-fifteen now. I will give the U.S. District Court until one-thirty to hear this matter. If not heard by then, we will go ahead with Dr. McGinty's testimony this afternoon."

"Your Honor," Bronfman complained, "I'm not sure Judge Grice can hear this matter that expeditiously."

"Mr. Bronfman, Judge Grice used to sit on the bench in this very courtroom. He understands that I have a capital murder case in trial with a sequestered jury. I'm sure he will accommodate me. It's been a pleasure having you appear in my court," Hodge said, the judicial way for a judge to tell a lawyer to go fuck himself. "Court is in recess."

There was an exodus of media and court personnel from the State District Courthouse across the street to the U.S. District Courthouse. Everyone was interested in what Judge Wilbur Grice would do with the national security issue.

As soon as he left the bench, Hodge called Judge Grice's chambers to speak to him. Grice was on the bench for a civil trial. He took a recess to take Hodge's call. Hodge warned him of the horde that was about to descend on his courtroom. Grice agreed to hear the matter immediately. As they talked, the reporters came through Grice's courtroom door and seated themselves. The show was about to begin.

Grice quickly took the bench amidst the usual federal court ceremony. The attorneys identified themselves. Judge Grice began. "This matter comes on for hearing at the request of the United States of America. It seems the government believes that its agent, a Dr. James McGinty of the Central Intelligence Agency, should not have to testify on behalf of the defendant, Mr. Avery Jackson, in his capital murder trial. I have been informed that Judge Hodge of the District Court has already ruled the documents in question are material and relevant to the defense of this case. It is up to the government to prove to me that its interests of national security exceed the interests of the individual, Avery Jackson, who is on trial for his life. Mr. Bronfman, will you please explain to me why you don't want Dr. McGinty to testify?"

Bronfman stood. "Put simply, Your Honor, the United States of America began covert experimentation with mind-control techniques using various subjects in the 1950s in order to compete with the Russians, Koreans and Chinese. This experimentation continued into the '60s and '70s. Numerous experiments were also instituted during the Vietnamese War. These experiments were critical to our war effort. Recently, some of the materials describing this experimentation were declassified."

"What does that have to do with Mr. Jackson's case?" Judge Grice asked.

"Mr. Jackson was an important subject during the Vietnamese conflict," Bronfman said. "The psychological protocol that was used on him needs to remain confidential."

"Why is that, Counsel?"

"Because certain subjects were a template for mind-control techniques that are still being used in the military and elsewhere around the world by the Central Intelligence Agency. To reveal them would be to interfere with national security."

"Why is that, Counsel? It seems to me that you could go on doing whatever it is you did so long as you don't reveal the personnel who are currently doing it and where it's being done."

"The doctor and military personnel who did the mind-control work on certain subjects may still be alive and subject to exposure when they were promised anonymity. Furthermore, our techniques could be copied and replicated by other countries."

"Are they alive?"

"We believe the psychiatrist and one of the military personnel are alive."

"Was Mr. Jackson an unwitting subject to this experimentation?"

"I am not at liberty to disclose that information, Your Honor."

Grice's face became red. "Why not?"

"I have been ordered by the Director of the Central Intelligence Agency not to disclose that information."

"Mr. Bronfman, let me tell you this. I will order the Director of the Central Intelligence Agency to be here tomorrow if I want that information. If he will not answer the question, I will order the President of the United States to answer the question. If they will not disclose that information, I will hold them in contempt. What is upsetting me, Counsel, is that you set an emergency hearing and then aren't forthcoming with me."

"Holding the Director or President in contempt would raise issues of executive privilege and separation of powers, Your Honor," Bronfman said. "I *am* attempting to be as honest as I can while representing my client, the United States of America."

"Your Honor, if I may?" Jack offered.

"Go ahead, Mr. Maine. This is the second time you've appeared on this case where a substantial federal question has been raised, isn't it?"

"Yes, Your Honor. The shenanigans in this case would astound you. I suspect the government's resistance has to do with civil liability issues. It would seem to me that all the unwitting victims of the government's mind-control experiments are likely to be owed reparation by the United States. In Mr. Jackson's case, the damages could be substantial—he was made to kill someone and faces the death penalty for it."

"That is untrue, Your Honor," Hunter said. "We have already had two outstanding psychiatrists testify that is false, that Mr. Jackson is faking it all."

"Thank you, Mr. Hunter," Grice said, "but we aren't here right now to litigate Mr. Jackson's psychological condition. We are here to determine if Dr. McGinty's subpoena should be quashed because the security of the United States of America demands it."

Hunter sat back down.

"*Would* potential civil liability be the reason you will not disclose the nature of Mr. Jackson's participation in these experiments?" Grice asked Bronfman.

"I cannot answer that question by order of the Director of the Central Intelligence Agency, Your Honor."

"Is it true, Mr. Bronfman, that many of these documents from the '50s, '60s and '70s have been declassified?"

"That is true."

"Why hasn't Jackson's been declassified?"

"I am not at liberty to discuss Mr. Jackson's file any further."

"I suppose we can assume he was involved, or you wouldn't be here with a box of records, Counsel."

"I am not at liberty to admit or deny that, Your Honor."

"Mr. Bronfman, Mr. Jackson is on trial for his life. There has been a finding by Judge Hodge that your records are relevant. Are you telling me that Mr. Jackson's life is less important than whether the public knows the identity of an unethical doctor and the ways the government manipulates the minds of certain subjects?"

"It's the government's position that its interests in protecting itself and its citizens outweigh Mr. Jackson's individual interests, yes," Bronfman said.

"Isn't Mr. Jackson a citizen? Isn't he a decorated war hero?"

"Yes, Your Honor."

Grice sat back in his chair, shook his head, frowned. "This court is ready to rule," he said as he took a deep breath. "I find that the government's interests are largely pecuniary and self-serving, and that there will be little or no damage to national security should Dr. McGinty's records be made public. I find that, in fact, many of the records concerning these sorts of activities by the Central Intelligence Agency have already been declassified and released pursuant to the Freedom of Information Act, and that fact militates against these documents being critical to national security. Furthermore, I find that this is an attempt by the government to diminish the sanctity of an individual citizen so as to protect itself from embarrassment and civil liability. Mr. Jackson's records, as well as Dr. McGinty's testimony, will be made available to Mr. Maine in representing Mr. Jackson. The writ to quash Dr. McGinty's subpoena on the grounds of national security is denied. Court is in recess." Judge Grice left the bench.

Hunter was stunned.

Jack offered to make the records available to Hunter and Dorsey over the lunch hour. Lunch consisted of Jack and Yolanda poring over files, and then sharing them with Hunter and Dorsey. The attorneys silently took notes while chewing their sandwiches.

Monday—1:30 P.M.
Montgomery County District Court

"You may recall Dr. McGinty to the stand, Mr. Maine," Hodge said upon the jury returning after the noon recess.

McGinty took the stand and was sworn in.

"State your name, please," Jack requested.

"James McGinty."

"How are you employed?"

"I am a Division Chief in the Central Intelligence of the United States of America."

"What is your educational level?"

"I have a Ph.D. in psychology."

"Then, you should be referred to as Dr. McGinty?"

"That's correct."

"Are you familiar with the case of one Avery Jackson?"

"Yes, I am."

"How are you familiar with it?"

"I have been assigned to oversee various programs involving the Company."

"By the Company, you mean the CIA?"

"That's correct."

"When did these projects begin?"

"They began in the late '40s when the CIA was called the Office of Strategic Services, the OSS. They have continued into the '50s, '60s and '70s."

"How were you made aware of the Jackson case?"

"Through our sources." It was plain that McGinty intended to give as little information as he possibly could, while still complying with Grice's ruling that he testify.

"What relationship does Mr. Jackson have to the CIA?"

"I am not at liberty to disclose that information."

"Why not?"

"Because those are my orders," McGinty said, obviously now ready to forget Grice.

"Your Honor, I would ask for an order requiring Dr. McGinty to answer."

"Dr. McGinty, you're ordered to answer."

McGinty sat silent, expressionless.

"Dr. McGinty, you will answer this question or I will hold you in contempt of court and lock you up until you do testify. The last person I locked up for contempt of court died during the night in the county jail."

McGinty swallowed hard. He took a deep breath and began. "I have been overseeing the mind control project for a number of years because of its success. It took on special significance when Mr. Jackson apparently killed the sheriff of this county. I was ordered to find out whether our conditioning of Mr. Jackson might in some way be related to the killing."

"What have you found out?"

"It is not clear whether it is related."

"When you say conditioning, what do you mean?"

"I have been ordered by the Director of the Central Intelligence Agency not to disclose any of that material," McGinty said.

"Mr. Maine, can you assure me," Hodge asked, "that you will be presenting expert testimony as to Mr. Jackson's conditioning by the CIA and how that conditioning has affected his mental state?"

"Yes. Dr. Offen flies into town tonight. He will be ready to testify to the nature of the conditioning and its affects on Mr. Jackson's mental state. Dr. Gilmour has already laid a sufficient foundation that Mr. Jackson's Army experience created a psychological abnormality within Mr. Jackson."

"I agree, Counsel," Hodge said. "Dr. McGinty, you are ordered to answer."

"Tell us more about Mr. Jackson's conditioning," Jack repeated.

McGinty swallowed hard. "Again, Your Honor, I am not at liberty to go further."

"Mr. Maine, please repeat the question for Dr. McGinty," Hodge ordered.

"When you say conditioning, what do you mean?" repeated Jack.

"Your Honor," McGinty said, "I will *not* answer the question. I feel that if I disclose this information, I am being disloyal to my country."

Bronfman, who was sitting at counsel table with Hunter and Dorsey, rose to his feet. "Your Honor," he said, "I believe—"

Hodge interrupted. "I believe, Mr. Bronfman, that your client is being disloyal to his country if he does *not* answer the question. You are to advise him that he is in contempt of this court, and I am instructing the deputy sheriff to take him into custody forthwith. Deputy, put handcuffs on Dr. McGinty and take him to jail."

The deputy, who was sitting in a chair behind counsel table, hesitated. He had never been ordered to take a government man into custody before. He rose and walked slowly toward the witness box. When he got there, he pulled out his handcuffs. He snapped a cuff on McGinty's right hand. As he began to put the cuff on the left hand, McGinty began haltingly, "As part of a CIA and Army joint project . . . approved by the President of United States during wartime, certain military personnel . . . were chosen—"

"Deputy," Hodge interrupted, "it looks as though Dr. McGinty has had a change of heart. Remove the cuffs, and Mr. Bronfman, you may sit down. Doctor, you may proceed."

"Well, *uh*, as I was saying, certain men were chosen to be subjects in tests the CIA was conducting. They were subjected to various sorts of mind-control techniques that would program them to kill the enemies of the United States."

"Was Mr. Jackson one of these subjects?" Jack asked.

"Yes, he was. He was perhaps the most successful of all the subjects."

"What do you mean by successful?"

"He survived very rigorous programming involving augmented trauma, carried out his orders with great efficiency, and then went on to lead a relatively normal life until this point without having any recollection of what he had done."

"Why was he chosen?"

"He was chosen because of his psychological strength and intelligence. Our psychiatrist determined that he had entered the service with a post-traumatic stress condition as the result of being abused as a child. Psychological testing revealed that he would be vulnerable to extreme trauma and would dissociate in its wake. Yet, he had considerable intelligence and mental capacity to survive and function well, in spite of it. Our psychiatrists felt he was constructed in such a way that we could split him in half and create a personality within him that could execute commands and then have no recollection of the command or his execution of it."

"Was Mr. Jackson aware he had been chosen for such a project?"

"No."

"He was what you would call an unwitting subject, is that correct?"

"Yes, he was unwitting," answered McGinty deadpan, knowing full well he had probably subjected the United States of America to at least one civil liability claim.

"The psychiatrist's name was Breyfogle, wasn't it, Dr. McGinty?" Jack remembered the name Avery had seen on the doctor's white coat while he was hypnotized and under the influence of scopolamine.

"The name of the psychiatrist was cut from the materials I gave you, Mr. Maine. I am not at liberty to disclose his name," McGinty said.

"Your Honor," Jack said, "the name of the psychiatrist is relevant because Mr. Jackson was able to remember it while hypnotized and under the influence of scopolamine, the truth serum. If Mr. Jackson's recollection of the name is correct, then it goes to his credibility and the credibility of his entire evaluation, which Mr. Hunter's experts have so vigorously attacked."

"Answer the question, Dr. McGinty," Judge Hodge ordered.

"Yes, Mr. Maine, the name of the CIA psychiatrist was Arthur Breyfogle."

Jack felt the wind in his sails. "Would you tell the jury the nature of the conditioning and augmented trauma, as you call it, that Mr. Jackson endured?"

Hunter rose to his feet. "Your Honor, I'm going to object at this time. The reports indicate that this material is very graphic and its probative value is far exceeded by its prejudicial effect. It will be too much for the jury to bear."

"Mr. Maine?" Hodge asked, "do you have a response?"

"Mr. Hunter had no qualms about showing the jury Sheriff Hardacre's gory murder. When the jury hears about the nature of the violence and trauma

Mr. Jackson endured, it will be able to understand how Mr. Jackson could inflict such trauma on Mr. Hardacre."

Jack looked at Betty Hardacre, who was still sitting in the same place she had been since the beginning of the trial. Her face had softened. Maybe she would be getting an answer to her question, "Why?"

"What's good for the goose is good for the gander, Mr. Hunter. I'll allow the testimony," Hodge said. "Dr. McGinty, please answer the question."

"Mr. Jackson was given injections of scopolamine initially while in basic training. The drug is intended to take away one's personality strength and his ability to defend himself. It opens the subject's personality wide without any defenses. In this state, Mr. Jackson was very forcefully told he would be developing another part of himself that no one knew about, and that part would be called Periscope. Periscope would only respond to three people. No one else had the key to Periscope except those three people. The words 'the moon is full' would be the code that would give those three people access to Periscope. When Mr. Jackson got to Vietnam, he was subjected to more intense conditioning."

"Describe it to us, Dr. McGinty," Jack demanded.

"He was given a shot of scopolamine, and then watched the termination of various Vietnamese men and women who'd been ID'd as war criminals. The code words 'the moon is full' were used before the order was given to kill the subjects in front of Mr. Jackson. He was then told he would have no memory of the events, but that Periscope would. At the end of these conditioning sessions, he was told 'the moon was dark and the sky was dark' and that he would remember nothing that happened when he came out of the scopolamine induction."

"In how many sessions did he witness people being terminated . . . as you call it, Doctor?"

"Several."

"Describe them, please."

"Your Honor," Hunter said, "again I renew my objection on the grounds of relevance."

"Overruled, Counsel. The witness will answer."

"As I said, he was placed under the influence of scopolamine, the code words were used to unlock him and the Vietnamese were terminated," McGinty said.

"Dr. McGinty, what you're saying is that someone was executed in front of Mr. Jackson and he had no psychological defenses or ego strength, as you call it, to protect himself while he was under the influence of scopolamine," Jack said.

"That's correct," McGinty said. "The people who were executed were war criminals."

"So, what Mr. Jackson had to do to defend himself was to store the shock and trauma of the killings he witnessed in the personality the CIA created for him that was named Periscope?"

"That's essentially correct."

"Isn't this what little children do who are subjected to extreme trauma?"

"Exactly. They create other parts of themselves to store the trauma. Sometimes they create other personalities to store the trauma."

"That is called dissociation, is it not?"

"That's correct."

"Was it the goal of the CIA to make Mr. Jackson dissociative?"

"No, we knew he was dissociative when he came into the service. The goal was to increase his level of dissociation."

"A dissociative disorder is a condition where one remains, for want of a better word, 'spaced out' and unable to remember or feel certain things about his life because they're so frightening and painful, is it not, Doctor?"

"That's correct."

"So, essentially what you're saying is that it was the CIA's goal to create a mental disorder within a person for government purposes?"

"I've never really thought of it that way."

"Were you successful in doing so with Mr. Jackson?"

"Yes."

"How do you know?"

"Because the CIA and Army were able to terminate people in his presence, and he had no memory of it."

"Who was killed in front of him?"

"The records indicated that a man, a woman and a thirteen-year-old boy were killed in his presence."

"Did the CIA train him to kill people?"

"Yes."

"When was the CIA confident he was ready to kill?"

"When Dr. Breyfogle was certain that Periscope had been fully developed as a functioning entity within the subject."

"When you say 'subject,' Doctor, you're referring to Mr. Jackson, are you not?"

"Yes."

"When Periscope was fully developed within Mr. Jackson, what happened next?"

"He was ordered to execute a Vietnamese war criminal."

"And the war criminal he was ordered to kill was a child, was it not?"

"An adolescent."

"Did he do so?"

"Yes."

There were sighs in the gallery.

"Explain how the killing happened, Doctor."

"The records reflect that one of the three people who held the key to Mr. Jackson entered the passwords 'the moon is full,' and Jackson switched to Periscope. He was then ordered to kill a Vietnamese person who was placed in front of him."

"Did he kill the person as ordered without being under the influence of scopolamine?"

"He did."

There were gasps in the gallery. Betty Hardacre began to cry, as did Rebecca Jackson. Aaron sat numb.

"Did he have any recollection of it afterward?" Jack asked.

"One of his trainers said 'the moon is dark, the sky is dark,' and after being given that order, he could remember nothing of the event."

"Was that the sort of result the CIA and Army were looking for from Jackson?"

"It was."

"How did the Army use Jackson in Vietnam after he was programmed to kill?"

Bronfman rose. "Your Honor, that is classified material. We object."

"Mr. Maine?"

"We don't want the specific name of anyone executed. We're just interested in whether he was functioning as a programmed killer, a Manchurian Candidate, if you will."

"Please answer the question, Doctor," Hodge ordered, "without disclosing the specific identity of those assassinated by Mr. Jackson."

"He carried out a number of executions of Vietcong soldiers and politicians unfavorable to American interests, as well as South Vietnamese military we considered dilatory and unresponsive."

"Was he involved in any traditional sorts of skirmishes while in Vietnam?"

"Apparently, he was. He was inadvertently caught in an unexpected firefight. The Army and CIA considered him to be so valuable and important an asset they kept him out of all encounters with the Vietcong after that."

"Essentially, you just wanted to use him as a programmed murderer, an assassin?"

"It was war, Counsel," McGinty said.

"Was he examined by Dr. Breyfogle when he exited the service?"

317

"Yes, Dr. Breyfogle examined him, and found he had no memory of either his conditioning or his missions."

"He did express to Dr. Breyfogle that he felt anxious and depressed, did he not?"

"Yes, the records reflect that."

"Did Dr. Breyfogle give him a referral to seek help?"

"No."

"Why not? Wouldn't that be the normal recommendation by a competent psychiatrist?"

"Yes, but our mission was to keep Jackson's capabilities and assets hidden."

"Did you have occasion to follow Mr. Jackson after he left the service?"

"Yes, the Company was aware that he had become a lawyer and judge and subsequently a professor."

"Why did you track him afterward?"

"We tracked him in order to determine if creating another personality would hinder his adjustment back into society after his release from the military," McGinty said. "The CIA has used Mr. Jackson as an example of a successful military mission where the psyche of the subject was not destroyed."

"Do you think you might have to reconsider or revisit your perception in light of what this sort of trauma has done to Mr. Jackson?"

"Perhaps," McGinty admitted.

"Now, Doctor, you've told us that Dr. Arthur Brefogle was one of the three people who had access to Mr. Jackson's killer personality, Periscope."

"That's correct."

"Who were the other two?" Jack's heart was beating hard. He knew all of the marbles were on the table. Hugh Lane was in the back of the courtroom.

"The first one was a Lieutenant Doerning," McGinty said. "He was Jackson's commanding officer in 'Nam. He died of cancer years ago. The second one was a Kranefeld Blaine."

"Do you know where Blaine is today?"

"No, we've lost track of him."

"It was Blaine who executed those Vietnamese people used to train Avery Jackson, was it not?"

"Yes."

"And it was Blaine who was responsible for sending Sergeant Jackson out on most of his killing missions, was it not?"

"It was Blaine as well as Doerning."

"Dr. McGinty," Jack asked, "we've heard testimony from Dr. Marvin Horde in this matter. Is he one of the psychiatrists who worked for the CIA over the years designing these mind-control and multiple personality experiments?"

McGinty became noticeably agitated. "I am not at liberty to discuss our current personnel."

"On what grounds?" Judge Hodge asked.

"Psychiatrists go into the CIA with the expectation their identities will be kept secret. Some have a top secret, security clearance," McGinty said.

"Your Honor, this goes to Dr. Horde's credibility, a State witness. It isn't right that Mr. Hunter can offer Dr. Horde as a witness and then limit my examination of his credibility. There is no privilege in the law that protects the identity of a CIA psychiatrist with a top secret clearance."

"Mr. Dorsey or Mr. Bronfman," Judge Hodge asked, "do you have a position on this?"

"Certainly, Your Honor," Bronfman said immediately, "national security demands that people who perform important secret missions for the United States of America and rely on their identities being kept secret should not have that reliance disturbed."

"I concur," Dorsey said.

Jack interjected, "When those CIA witnesses are offered in a murder trial where a man's life is at stake, that evidence, if relevant, should be made available to the jury. To hold otherwise, would be a due process violation. This evidence clearly goes to Dr. Horde's credibility."

"The witness will answer the question," Hodge ordered.

"Yes, Dr. Marvin Horde has worked in the past with the Company on mind-control experiments where multiple personalities were created," McGinty answered fully.

"Thank you for your honesty, Dr. McGinty. Are you familiar with the Created Memory Society?"

"Yes," McGinty answered hesitantly.

"Dr. Horde testified that its largest benefactor was the Rittenhouse Foundation. Is the Rittenhouse Foundation funded by the Central Intelligence Agency?"

"The CIA is a benefactor of the Rittenhouse Foundation."

"Thank, you, Dr. McGinty," Jack said. "No further questions."

As Jack turned, he could see Hugh Lane leave the courtroom. Jack's real defense was walking out the door. It made no difference they had proved that Avery was a programmed killer. Avery would not find justice unless he could show that Hugh Lane had wound Avery up and turned him loose to kill. It was that simple.

"Cross-exam, Mr.Dorsey?"

"Dr. McGinty, have you ever practiced as a psychologist?" Dorsey asked.

"Only two years. Then, I went into government service."

"Why did you leave practice?"

319

"I found I didn't like it."

"Did you make any of the notes concerning the defendant's stay in the service?"

"They were made primarily by Dr. Breyfogle."

"Do you know if he made them contemporaneously with his treatment of the defendant?"

"No, but that would be the customary procedure."

"Where is Dr. Breyfogle today?"

"He is in a nursing home and suffers from Alzheimer's. He has no recollection of Avery Jackson or his work with the CIA. His Alzheimer's is advanced."

"Isn't it true, Doctor," Dorsey asked, "that you and the CIA have been unable to make a connection between Avery Jackson's military training and/or programming and his killing Sheriff Hardacre?"

"That's correct. We have made no connection whatsoever."

"Would it be a correct statement to say that only someone with Avery Jackson's 'key' could set him off?"

"That would be true. Unless, of course, he just decided to kill the sheriff of his own volition."

"Doctor, in your opinion, would it be possible for Avery Jackson, as opposed to this so-called Periscope, to have undergone the conditioning he did and still be a ruthless psychopath?"

"In my opinion, he could be both. That is to say, the literature reflects that ruthless psychopaths can also be multiple personalities," McGinty said.

"Then you're saying that Avery could have killed Sheriff Hardacre, and Periscope may never have come out?"

"That's possible."

"Now, if it were Avery who did the killing, isn't it true that he probably knew right from wrong when he did the killing?"

"Objection," Jack said, springing to his feet. "This calls for a conclusion to be drawn by a person who has never even met Avery Jackson."

"I'm going to allow it," Hodge said. "You may answer the question."

"That's probably true," McGinty said.

"And if, on the other hand, it were Periscope who did the killing, isn't it true that Periscope might have also been aware that killing was wrong, but he elected to kill anyway?" Dorsey asked.

"That's possible."

"Thanks, Dr. McGinty, no further questions."

"Mr. Maine, any re-direct before we take the evening recess?" Judge Hodge asked.

"Yes, Your Honor. Dr. McGinty, you testified that Mr. Jackson was picked by the CIA and the military for this top secret mission because he had a strong enough personality and was well-organized enough to withstand this sort of programming and still carry on fairly normally?"

"That's correct."

"Psychopaths who lack a conscience would not be included in the group of subjects suitable for this project, would they, Dr. McGinty? In other words, if Dr. Breyfogle had believed Avery Jackson was a psychopath with no conscience, he never would have been chosen for this sort of training, would he?"

"That's probably true."

"No further questions, Your Honor."

It was the end of the day. Hodge admonished the jury members not to discuss the matter—a nearly impossible request considering this fantastic testimony. They were dismissed to dinner and their hotel.

"Yolanda, please get Joe on his cell phone. We need him to meet us at the King's Table for dinner."

The afternoon session had enraged the Jackson children. Their father should never have been taken from them. Maybe he would have gotten along better with their mother had this other personality that none of them knew about never been created. Maybe their family would still be intact. At any rate, the CIA had perhaps irreparably messed up their father, their family, and them. It was unforgivable.

CHAPTER 27

Tuesday, April 20—9:00 A.M.
Montgomery County District Court

National interest in CIA mind-control experiments was white-hot. The President of the United States' Press Secretary had given an early morning briefing in the White House denying the President had any knowledge about such techniques, but guaranteeing a full investigation. He offered the caveat, however, that war is an extraordinary event, perhaps justifying the techniques used by prior administrations. The White House promised reparation to those who had "served their country in this manner without having committed heinous acts after they left the service." Later that morning, the Created Memory Society issued a press release denying any funding from the CIA, repudiating any possible conflicts of interest and stood by their position that their mission was based on firm, scientific data. They threatened legal action if they should be defamed in any way.

Media interest in the courtroom was intense as Dr. Offen took the stand. He was sworn in and qualified as an expert in the field of psychology, trauma and multiple personality syndrome. He described the evaluations he and Dr. Gilmour had done, including his psychological testing of Avery Jackson. He talked at length about Avery's childhood, his dreams and nightmares. He explained how the nightmares were related to Avery's abusive childhood and to the mind-control programming the CIA used on him. He told the jury about Avery's recurrent dream about the man with the white coat, black, horn-rimmed glasses and hypodermic needle, and the fright that it sent through Avery. He explained to the jury that man was Dr. Breyfogle. He explained that the dreams about people getting their heads blown off, and the blood running down the floor into a spout, and then a barrel, were his psyche's re-enactments of Gargoyle's executions. Offen then spoke at length about his experiences in using hypnosis with subjects who had been severely traumatized.

"Dr. Offen," Jack asked, "did you hypnotize Avery Jackson?"

"Yes, I did."

"And did you videotape a hypnosis session with him?"

"Yes, I did."

Jack turned on the TV-VCR unit to the point where Offen was doing Avery's hypnotic induction. *"Flower, flower, flower . . ."* Offen chanted.

Hunter looked at Dorsey. Horde and Procheska had assured him these tapes were a farce. According to them both, the tapes would show that Offen was a charlatan employing means of magic as opposed to science. They had not counted on McGinty's corroborating testimony. Now, Dorsey and Hunter would have to make the best of a bad situation.

"Does this tape accurately depict your hypnotic induction and regression of Mr. Jackson?" Jack asked Offen.

"It does."

"Your Honor, we would ask the court to admit the tape and allow the jury to see it in its entirety," Jack requested.

Judge Hodge had already viewed the tape-in camera at both Maine and Hunter's requests.

"Any objection, Mr. Hunter?"

"Yes, Your Honor," Alec said. "The contents of the tapes are hearsay and are full of scientifically-unreliable materials."

"Mr. Maine, what is your position?"

"Well, the district attorney opened the door to these tapes during Doctors Horde and Procheska's testimony when both claimed that Mr. Jackson was a faker, and that Dr. Gilmour's claim of CIA programming was a farce. Now we have testimony from the CIA that corroborates the content of these tapes. I am asking the Court to allow the tapes to be seen by the jury at the very least as the basis for Dr. Offen's forthcoming opinions, as well as to prove the truth of the contents of the tapes."

"Mr. Hunter," Hodge said, "is there any material difference between the contents of these tapes and Dr. McGinty's testimony?"

"Yes, Your Honor," Hunter said. "I'm sure there is, but I'm at a loss for specifics at this time."

"We will show the contents of these tapes to be valid in their entirety with further testimony," Jack offered.

"The court will allow the tapes to seen by the jury," Hodge ordered. "They are at least relevant as the basis for Dr. Offen and Dr. Gilmour's opinions."

Jack played the entire hypnotic regression for the jury. None of them had ever seen such a thing. Offen stopped the tape and offered bits of explanation for what he was doing and what Avery was recreating from the past. The notion that one could take a person back to a particular event thirty-five years before and have him remember it with the particularity of an event that occurred minutes ago, was fascinating. But was it believable? When Avery was brought back from his trance and couldn't remember what had just happened, it seemed unworldly, unnatural, perhaps faked, as Horde and Procheska had claimed.

"Is it strange for someone to come out of a hypnotic regression like this and remember nothing of it?" Jack asked.

"With the level of trauma used—execution of other human beings—I do not find it at all unusual," Offen replied.

Jack continued to run the tape. The next thing on it was the attempt by Dr. Gilmour to give Avery an injection. Avery's violent reaction reminded them he was a very dangerous man. No right-minded citizen would allow such a man on the street. He was a killer.

"What is the significance of this attack by Mr. Jackson, Dr. Offen?"

"It shows he was ordered by one of his programmers that no one was to access him by the use of scopolamine. He was programmed to fight to the death to prevent that from happening. It is my hunch that one of the programmers planted this order after the hypnotic induction and before we attempted to use scopolamine."

"In your opinion, who was the person?"

"It had to be a person who has the key to Mr. Jackson's system. In other words, the person had to be familiar to Mr. Jackson as one of the programmers, and also know the key words 'the moon is full.'"

Jack continued to roll the video of the scopolamine induction. "What is the significance of this portion of the tape?"

"This shows that Mr. Jackson had indeed formed another personality, and only three people had access to it. The name of the personality was, and still is, Periscope. We know this is true because Dr. McGinty confirmed it. The only person who would have access to it would be 'Mr. Blaine,' since the other two programmers are gone."

"Did you find it unusual, or evidence of faking, that Mr. Jackson had no memory of what he'd talked about while under the influence of scopolamine?"

"Not at all. In fact, that's exactly what you would expect. That's why scopolamine was used for delivering babies years ago, so the mother under its influence wouldn't have any memory of the pain of child birth. And, as you heard from Dr. McGinty, scopolamine was used for the same reason with the CIA's subjects. They were forced to watch acts of violence under its influence and then remembered none of it."

Jack rolled the tape through the portion where Avery was unable to explain what had happened on the day he killed Sheriff Hardacre. "What is the significance of this?"

"It shows how exhausted Mr. Jackson was from the prior day's induction. More important, however, it shows how tightly Mr. Jackson's system was locked down by his programmers. In my opinion, it was locked down even more tightly by someone before we attempted to do the final regression," Dr. Offen said.

"Did your evaluation reveal who that might be?"

"Yes."

Jack's heart began beating harder again. He wasn't sure what the reaction in the courtroom was going to be to his next question. "Who was it?"

"Our investigation revealed that Dayton's Sheriff Hugh Lane was the only visitor Avery Jackson had."

Jack could hear the reporters shuffling their notepads. The jurors, who looked as if they were falling asleep, suddenly were wide awake.

"Objection, Your Honor," Hunter said, "insufficient foundation."

"Sustained. Would you like to lay more of a foundation, Mr. Maine?" Hodge asked.

"Dr. Offen, how did you get this information?" Jack asked.

"We were informed by the on-duty sheriff, Deputy Callahan, that Hugh Lane had visited Mr. Jackson prior to our last session with him."

"Objection, hearsay," Hunter said. "We ask this be stricken and the jury be instructed to ignore it."

"Your Honor, Dr. Offen is allowed to talk about his investigation. He is offering this visit by Sheriff Lane as perhaps the reason Mr. Jackson was unable to recall, even under the influence of scopolamine, his shooting of Sheriff Hardacre. We will show, along with other evidence, that Sheriff Lane was his only visitor."

"Overruled," Hodge said, "providing you can present other evidence of Sheriff Lane's involvement."

"Dr. Offen, if Sheriff Lane were the person who had shut down Periscope, how would he do it?" Jack asked.

"He would go to Mr. Jackson, open him by uttering the key to his system, 'the moon is full,' and then threaten to kill him, just as the Vietnamese people were executed in front of him."

"Did Avery Jackson have any recollection of a visit the prior night from Sheriff Lane?"

"No, he didn't."

"Is that significant?"

"Yes, highly significant. It tells me that Mr. Jackson was programmed by Mr. Lane to not remember the meeting. It further means that Sheriff Lane is a person who has access to Mr. Jackson's psyche."

Jack could hear pens scratching across paper in the gallery.

"Dr. Offen, do you have an opinion as to whether Mr. Jackson was sane at the time he killed Sheriff Hardacre?"

"Yes. I believe he was legally insane at the time of the shooting because he wasn't aware of Periscope and had no control over him. He could not know right from wrong or appreciate the wrongfulness of his act."

"Dr. Offen, you have recommended that we not allow Mr. Jackson to see any of these tapes, or hear any of this testimony, is that correct?"

"Yes."

"Why have you made such a recommendation?"

"Because he would be devastated if he saw what happened to him, how he was programmed, and that he had killed innocent people. He might be unable to recover from it."

"Thank you, Doctor Offen. I'm sure Mr. Dorsey has some questions for you."

Hank Dorsey stood up slowly and walked to the podium. Nearly half of his planned cross-examination of Dr. Offen had been gutted when Dr. McGinty validated what Offen and Gilmour were claiming. Besides, Hank was still furious with Hunter. Had they rested after Gilmour's testimony, as Hank had suggested, neither McGinty nor Offen would have even made it to the witness stand.

"Dr. Offen, you live and practice in Denver, Colorado. Is that correct?" Dorsey asked.

"Yes."

"And you testify around the country on cases involving so-called multiple personalities?"

"Correct."

"And, you always testify for the defense, isn't that correct?"

"That has been the case because I have yet to see a district attorney claiming a murderer was a multiple." There were snickers in the courtroom.

"Your Honor, I would ask you to instruct the witness not to editorialize," Dorsey requested.

"The witness will answer the questions only," Hodge ordered.

"Dr. Offen, isn't it true that the Board of Psychologist Examiners in Colorado currently has a complaint pending against you in which it is alleges that you do not follow strict, forensic practice in your evaluations?"

"There is currently such a complaint filed by psychiatrists in Colorado who object to my using hypnosis and scopolamine regressions with patients."

"And that could affect your ability to practice psychology?"

"I suppose, if it's proven there's any truth to it. I see it as an attempt by envious colleagues to discredit me."

"Isn't it true that the diagnosis of multiple personality is made far too often when it is really a very rare psychological condition?" Dorsey asked.

"Untrue. Its existence has been known for years, and that it's probably the most closely studied mental illness in the world. I know of no other mental illness that is created clinically and experimentally by the United States of America and other governments for intelligence purposes."

Dorsey knew Offen was killing him. He needed to go to places where he could score points.

"Dr. Offen, you testified that the defendant's recall while hypnotized was valid because he could identify Dr. Breyfogle while in a trance?"

"That's correct."

"And you believe his recall while under the influence of scopolamine to be accurate also?"

"I believe it to be accurate."

"Now, Dr. Offen, you never really had access to Periscope, did you?"

"That's untrue. He, in fact, told me to get fuc—uh, screwed—and spit in my face. We also contacted him some other times. Our primary contact with him was through a third personality, a sort of historian I named Avescope, who was able to see and hear Periscope. You were able to see and hear Avescope on the tape."

"You are not able to offer an opinion as to whether Periscope knew right from wrong at the time of the killing?"

"Yes, I can."

Dorsey knew not to ask what that opinion was. He went to the next question. "Dr. Offen, isn't it true that you were unable to establish any link between the defendant's experience in Vietnam and his killing of Sheriff Hardacre?" Dorsey had honed in on the fundamental flaw in the defense case.

"That is essentially true."

"No further questions."

"Re-direct, Mr. Maine?" Hodge asked.

"Yes, Your Honor. Dr. Offen, you stated that you had an opinion as to whether Periscope knew right from wrong at the time of the killing."

"That's correct."

"What is that opinion?"

"Periscope is not a separate person. He is merely a place in Avery Jackson's mind where the fright and terror of the CIA conditioning was stored and the unlocking and locking words and orders encoded. Mr. Jackson had no conscious control over this part of himself. It was Mr. Jackson who didn't know right from wrong when he shot Sheriff Hardacre."

"Thank you, Doctor."

"Re-cross?" Hodge asked.

"You have never really tested this so called Periscope, much less questioned him, about whether he understood the difference between right and wrong or knew whether it was wrong to kill Sheriff Hardacre, have you," Dorsey asked.

"No," Offen replied.

"In fact, your most intimate interactions with Periscope involved his strangling Dr. Gilmour, cursing at you and spitting in your face."

Offen squirmed in his chair and then muttered, "That's essentially correct."

"And, when he was strangling Dr. Gilmour, don't you believe he—Periscope—intended to kill him?"

"Yes."

"How can you then represent to this jury that he didn't intend to kill Sheriff Hardacre?"

"I can only represent that Mr. Jackson didn't know right from wrong when he killed him."

"But you can't represent that Periscope didn't know what he was doing was wrong?"

"I can only conjecture."

"No further questions," Dorsey announced.

Hunter scribbled on a legal pad. *That was brilliant. You saved the case, Hank!* Hank Dorsey was not so sure.

"It is now five o'clock. We will take the evening recess," Judge Hodge said, "and resume testimony at nine o'clock tomorrow morning. The jury is admonished not to discuss the case with anyone. Have a good dinner."

The jury was dismissed and filed out of the room. Each looked tired. They had seen and heard things they had never dreamed of in their lives. Avery Jackson looked different in their eyes. He, too, appeared to be a victim. That notion created uneasiness within them. Tomorrow, each of them hoped something would happen in the trial to make things simple again for them.

After Jack and Yolanda took Dr. Offen to the airport, they were then to meet Joe and Marci for dinner. Dr. Offen would catch the seven o'clock flight to Chicago, and then go on to Denver.

"It was easy for me today, except the cross-examination about the mental intent of Periscope and whether he knew right from wrong," Marcus said. "It's the first time I've ever had a CIA agent validate my findings on a case. When you get a verdict, let me know. It was a great case to work on and I thank you for the opportunity." He grabbed his suitcase out of the backseat. Jack and Yolanda shook his hand, and he headed into the airport. They knew he had given them a rare adventure into the human psyche that they never expected to have again in their lifetimes.

Their trip back to the restaurant was slow. The rush-hour traffic was murder in the drizzling rain that had fallen the entire day. Jack noticed the tan sedan with two men following him. He reached under the seat to make sure his gun was there. It was.

When they got to the restaurant, Marci had a clipping from the morning *Dayton Daily News*. She handed it to Jack. Its headline read: DRUG PUSHER FOUND SHOT TO DEATH.

"What's this about?" Jack asked.

"Read it," Marci said.

Terry Singleton, recently indicted for Possession of Dangerous Drugs for Sale, was found dead behind the wheel of his car. He had been shot in the back of the head at close range. Police are looking for a late model, tan sedan that was seen leaving the scene at about the time of the shooting. An autopsy is being performed by the Montgomery County Coroner.

CHAPTER 28

Wednesday, April 21—9:00 A.M.
Montgomery County District Court

This was the last day of trial. Jack and Yolanda would divide up the direct-examination of remaining witnesses. Jack would do the closing argument. They had coal pits burning in their stomachs as they sat in the courtroom waiting for the judge to arrive. They had not been able to establish the crucial connection between the CIA programming and Avery's killing Sheriff Hardacre. Their mission was clear. The path it would take was still largely unknown.

The media attention was still at saturation level. The interest in Sheriff Lane and his possible involvement had grown. Who more than he would have a motive to kill Sheriff Hardacre? It was now surprising to the media that these questions hadn't been asked earlier.

Jack had informed Judge Hodge that Avery was no longer waiving his appearance. Yolanda had gone to the jail early in the morning to get Avery ready. When he was brought into the courtroom, the antipathy that had previously been directed at him by nearly everyone had dissipated. For the first time, Betty Hardacre was able to look at him. Marci had made sure Aaron and Rebecca were there. They could understand their father better now, and he didn't have to feel so guilty when looking at them.

"Would the defense call its next witness, please?" Judge Hodge ordered after the jury was seated.

"The defense calls Marvella Dixon," Yolanda said. "Please state your name," she said after Marvella had been sworn in.

"Marvella Dixon."

"How are you employed?"

"I'm not," she said nervously. "I'm a student at Sinclair University."

"What is your age?"

"I'm twenty-one years old," Marvella said, her heartbeat slowing with the routine questions.

"If you need water or anything," Yolanda said, "there is a canister next to you." Marvella nodded. "Are you familiar with Professor Avery Jackson?"

"Yes, I am."

"Where is he seated in the courtroom?"

"He's the gentleman seated at that table."

"How do you know Professor Jackson?"

"He was my Evidence and Criminal Justice professor at Sinclair University. I'm a Criminal Justice major studying in the police academy where he taught."

"Did you have occasion to see Professor Jackson on January fifteenth of this year?"

"I did. I was in his eight o'clock Evidence class."

"Do you remember what the topic was that day?"

"The hearsay rule. Everyone in the class had difficulty with it."

"Don't worry," interjected Judge Hodge with a big smile, "we've had trouble with it here in this trial, too. It will get worse for you." The jury chuckled. Hodge had a nice way of relieving tension.

"When the class ended, what did you do?"

"I talked to Professor Jackson about hearsay. He was complimentary of my ability to understand it, which really felt good." Marvella blushed.

"What happened next?"

"He said he was going to get a cup of coffee and prepared to leave the classroom. He picked up his books and put them in his briefcase. He grabbed his overcoat. It was really cold that day—below zero."

"What happened then?"

"I went to the cafeteria to get a cup of coffee and Professor Jackson was seated in the corner of the room. He was drinking coffee and reading the paper. Sheriff Lane joined him and they sat together and talked for a while. Then the two of them got up and left."

There was whispering and shuffling of paper throughout the courtroom.

"How do you know it was Sheriff Lane?"

"Because Sheriff Lane had visited my Evidence class earlier in the semester and taught one of our Criminal Justice classes."

"What happened then?"

"I finished my coffee and went to my car. In the parking lot I saw Professor Jackson sitting in a car with Sheriff Lane."

"What type of car was it?"

"It was a dark-green, Jeep Cherokee. It was not Professor Jackson's car. He drives a Toyota."

"I have no further questions," Yolanda said. "Your witness, Counsel."

Dorsey stood. "You seem quite enamored of Professor Jackson. You speak of him in reverent tones."

"Objection," Yolanda interjected. "Is Mr. Dorsey testifying, or is the witness?"

"I'm sure there is a question in there somewhere, isn't there, Mr. Dorsey?" Judge Hodge asked.

"Ms. Dixon, are you married or single?" Dorsey asked.

"I'm single."

"Would you say that you're infatuated with the defendant, Mr. Jackson?"

"He's a brilliant man and a good man. Other than that, I have no particular feelings for him."

"No further questions, Your Honor."

"Any re-direct, Ms. Crone?" Hodge asked.

"No, Judge. We call Joe Betts to the stand," Yolanda said.

Joe walked briskly down the aisle. He was dressed in a suit that fit forty pounds ago. As he took the stand, Joe reached to his collar like a man about to choke. Joe was sworn in, took his seat and identified himself.

"How are you employed?" Yolanda asked.

"I am an investigator for Jack Maine and Associates, and I also do part-time investigations for other lawyers."

"How long have you worked in that capacity?"

"Fifteen years."

"Have you ever been convicted of a felony?" Yolanda asked, knowing it was better to get Joe's manslaughter conviction in the open before the DA brought it up.

"Yes. I was convicted of manslaughter twenty years ago."

"Mr. Betts, did you have an occasion to do an investigation in the case involving Mr. Avery Jackson?"

"Yes, I did."

"Describe it."

"I took Sheriff Hugh Lane for coffee," Joe said.

"What did you do with the coffee cup?"

"I kept it and took it to Alfred Knudsen, the fingerprint expert."

"I show you what has been marked as Defendant's Exhibit Two, do you recognize it?"

"It's the Styrofoam cup Hugh Lane handled and drank coffee from. It has my initials on it."

"Move to admit Defendant's Two," Yolanda said.

"Mr. Hunter," Hodge asked.

"No objection."

"What else did you do?" Yolanda asked.

"Yesterday, I went to the county jail and looked at the log of visitors."

"Did Avery Jackson have any visitors at the jail during the period of his incarceration?"

"Other than his lawyers, psychiatrists and Dr. Offen, he had none. No, that's not true. His ex-wife came to see him once, right after he was arrested. Also, his two kids, Aaron and Becky, have been there a few times."

"You are sure there were no other names in the logs?"

"Objection, Your Honor," Hunter said, "this is irrelevant, immaterial and hearsay."

"It is actually quite relevant," Yolanda argued. "We'll tie it up soon. As for hearsay, it would certainly be a business-records exception to the hearsay rule."

"I'm going to allow it," Hodge ordered, "on the condition you tie it up."

"There were no other names on the log books," Joe assured her.

"No further questions," Yolanda said.

"No questions," Dorsey said.

Joe lumbered off the stand. As he walked down the aisle of the courtroom, he loosened his tie and remembered he had promised to call Hugh Lane when they were ready for his testimony. He made the call when he was outside the door.

"We call Deputy Thomas Callahan," Yolanda announced.

Deputy Callahan had no idea why he had been subpoenaed. He was dressed in his sheriff's uniform as he took the stand. He'd had to leave his shift in order to accommodate the subpoena ordering him to testify. He was sworn in as a witness.

"Deputy Callahan, how are you employed?" Yolanda asked.

"I am a shift commander at the Montgomery County Jail."

"Who is your boss?"

"He is currently Sheriff Hugh Lane."

"Do you know Avery Jackson?"

"Certainly. He's seated over there." Callahan pointed to Avery.

"Did you have occasion to see Sheriff Lane visiting with Mr. Jackson at the county jail?"

"Yes, I did."

"Do you remember when?"

"No. I would have no way of remembering."

"Let me refresh your memory, Deputy. Do you remember seeing him there the night before the Super Bowl?" Yolanda asked.

"Oh . . . yeah . . . Sheriff Lane visited him then. Sheriff Lane told me that he and Jackson had fought in 'Nam together. He just spent a few minutes with him."

Yolanda and Jack could hear the whispering and the scratching of pens and pencils.

"Was Mr. Lane the sheriff at that time?"

"No, he was a civilian then. He came on board again later."

"Did you have occasion to see Sheriff Lane at another time with Mr. Jackson?"

"I believe I saw them talking in the Contact Visitation Room a day or two before the visit I just described."

"Is it unusual for visitors to talk with inmates without signing the log at the front desk?"

"It is against the rules."

"Would it surprise you to hear that Sheriff Lane had not signed in?"

"Not really. No one ever really considered Sheriff Lane to be a visitor. He'd run the jail for years and was about to be in charge again. I hope I'm not getting him in trouble here. You know, he's my boss. I just saw him a few minutes ago over at the jail."

"All we're seeking here is the truth. Thanks, Deputy. No further questions."

"Cross-exam, Mr. Dorsey?"

"I have just one question," Hank said as he stood to address Callahan. "You thought nothing of the fact that Hugh Lane was at the jail talking to the defendant, right?"

"At the time, it didn't seem unusual."

"Thank you, Deputy," Hank said.

"You may call your next witness, Ms. Crone," Hodge said.

"Alfred Knudsen," Yolanda called. Mr. Knudsen approached the witness stand.

"Mr. Knudsen," Judge Hodge said, "you have testified before in this proceeding. You are still under oath."

"Yes, Your Honor," Knudsen said.

Dorsey was fuming inside. Now, they were getting their own witnesses thrown at them on rebuttal.

"Your Honor," Yolanda said, "the jury has already heard Mr. Knudsen's qualifications as a fingerprint expert when he testified as the State's witness. The defense is now offering him as its witness in that same capacity."

"Very well," Hodge said, "any objections, Mr. Dorsey?"

"None," Dorsey said.

"Mr. Knudsen, I show you what has been marked as Defense Exhibit Two. Would you identify it please?"

"Certainly, it's a Styrofoam cup. It has my markings on it at the bottom."

"How did you come in contact with it?"

"A Mr. Joe Betts brought it to me. He informed me that it would have latent prints on it that he wanted compared to the latent prints found on the murder weapon—I'm talking about the prints that were unidentified."

"Did you examine the cup for prints?"

"Yes, there were two sets of prints on it. I removed both sets and compared them to those of Mr. Betts and those taken off the murder weapon."

"What did you find out?"

"There was a match between the prints on the cup and those on the gun at the top of the barrel."

"Were Joe Betts' prints on the barrel?"

"No, it was the other set—those of Sheriff Lane. There were eight points of comparison."

A smoking gun! Reporters whispered out loud. Some leaped up to make calls. As the reporters reached the corridor outside the courtroom, Hugh Lane was approaching its door. They quickly turned to hurry back to their seats.

"Court will be in order!" Hodge banged his gavel down. "Any further commotion and I will clear the courtroom. Any cross-examination, Mr. Dorsey?"

"No, Your Honor," Dorsey said. He couldn't imagine what would happen next.

"Can't you impeach him on points of comparison on the prints?" Alec whispered to Dorsey.

Had court not been in session, Dorsey would have exploded and slugged him. "We are not going to start impeaching our own witnesses."

"We need to figure out how Lane's prints got on that gun," Alec replied, belatedly realizing the stupidity of the remark.

"Defense moves for the admission of Defendant's Exhibit Two," Jack said.

Jack and Yolanda could see the discord at counsel table. So could the jury.

"No objection," Dorsey said.

"Defense Two will be admitted."

"The defense calls Sheriff Hugh Lane."

"Bailiff, please escort Mr. Lane into the courtroom," Hodge ordered.

Sheriff Lane strode to the witness stand. He had been elected many times on the basis of the confidence he instilled when he walked and talked. He was sworn in and announced his name. "I am Hugh Lane, Sheriff of Montgomery County, Ohio."

Avery was getting agitated now. The reporters didn't know who to look at.

"Sheriff Lane, drawing your attention to January fifteenth of this year, where were you at approximately nine o'clock that morning?"

"I don't recall, Counsel."

"I'm asking the court for permission to cross-examine Sheriff Lane as a hostile witness," Jack said "Objection," Hunter said. "There is no indication whatsoever that Mr. Lane is presently adverse."

Hodge gave Hunter short shrift. "Overruled."

Lane was startled. He had been told he would be needed as a character witness for Avery Jackson. Now, he was being cross-examined as a hostile witness. He had heard from a reporter that his name had come up in the trial, but that it was of little consequence. He could feel sweat popping out on his forehead. His underarms started to drip. What did this son-of-a-bitch Maine know?

"Sheriff Lane, January fifteenth was the day Sheriff Hardacre was murdered. Now, can you tell the jury where you were that morning at about nine a.m.?"

"I believe I was at home."

"You saw Avery Jackson that morning, did you not?"

"I don't believe so."

"We've just heard from a witness that you had coffee with Avery Jackson in the coffee shop at Sinclair University that morning. Would that be correct?"

"I believe the witness is mistaken."

"You are a friend of Avery Jackson's, are you not?"

"Yes, we're friends."

"Didn't he help you with your campaign against Sheriff Hardacre?"

"Yes, he did."

"Where did you first meet?"

"Objection, Your Honor," Hunter interjected. "This is irrelevant. It's nothing more than a fishing expedition." Hunter had taken over the examination of witnesses. Dorsey would have nothing to do with Lane. The trial was now Hunter's.

"Your Honor," Jack argued, "the primary reason for the testimony we have offered today is that the State of Ohio is claiming there is no relationship between what the CIA did to Mr. Jackson in Vietnam and his killing Sheriff Hardacre. We believe Mr. Lane can establish that link. It is certainly relevant for the purposes of our insanity defense."

"I'll allow it," Hodge ordered.

Lane now got the picture. He was in danger. His instinct was to fight, but he had no gun. It would be a war of wits. He needed to survive. Even if he survived Maine's questions, he was skeptical about eluding the syndicate. He knew the score.

"Mr. Lane," Jack asked, "where did you meet Mr. Jackson?"

"We met on the bus on our way to basic training for the service."

"What year?"

"Nineteen sixty-nine."

"You fought in Vietnam together?"

"Yes."

"Mr. Jackson was the subject of CIA mind-control experiments in Vietnam. You were part of those also, were you not?"

Lane laughed. "Heavens no."

"Do you know anything about such experiments in your unit?"

"No."

"What is your full name, Sheriff?" Jack asked.

"Hugh Lane."

"What is your middle name?"

"I have no middle name."

"What is your date of birth?"

"March 2, 1947."

"We've heard testimony that there was a member of your unit by the name of Kranefeld Blaine. Did you know Kranefeld Blaine?"

"Yes, he was in our unit. We called him Krane."

"Mr. Lane, are not you and Krane Blaine the same person?"

"Not the last time I checked." Lane laughed again, feigning nonchalance.

"Mr. Lane, your fingerprints were on the murder weapon. How do you explain that?"

"That's easy, Counsel. Mr. Jackson once let me handle his .38 when I was at his house on a social occasion. I believe we took it out for target practice."

Jack needed to reload. He should have never asked him a "how" question he could slip out of. Jack took a moment. "Sheriff Lane, we've heard testimony from one of your own officers, Dan Callahan, that you visited with Mr. Jackson in jail on two occasions. Is that correct?"

"Yes, that's correct."

"You didn't sign the jail register as a visitor, did you, sir?"

"That's a possibility. I ran that jail for nearly two decades. Everyone knows me. I was probably socializing and forgot to sign it."

Everything Jack threw at Lane was getting knocked down with a reasonable explanation. He was sure that Lane was perjuring himself, but there was no way to prove it. Jack knew he was losing face in front of the jury. The trial now hung in the balance. Jack walked over to Avery and took his arm gently. He walked Avery directly in front of Hugh Lane, no more than ten feet away. He could feel Avery begin to tremble.

"Mr. Lane, please repeat the following words exactly as I say them while looking Mr. Jackson directly in the face."

Hunter jumped to his feet. "Your Honor, I object! This is highly unusual."

"This is a demonstration, Your Honor, and it is a valid form of evidence," Jack said.

"Go ahead, Mr. Maine," Hodge said.

"Mr. Lane, please say the following to Mr. Jackson: 'The moon is full.'"

Lane could feel his chest tighten. "'The moon is full,' he muttered quietly, trying to avoid eye contact with Avery.

Avery did not respond.

"Mr. Lane," Jack said, "please say the words with conviction *and* with full eye contact."

The jury and gallery were watching with rapt attention.

"The moon is full," Lane said while he looked at Avery.

Avery shook visibly. His eyes glazed over.

"Now, Mr. Lane," Jack said, "Say the following words: 'Periscope, you're ordered to take that gun and blow Judge Hodge's brains out.'"

"I don't have to do this. I won't do it," Lane said.

"On what grounds, Mr. Lane?" Judge Hodge asked.

"I'm not going to order a man to blow a judge's brains out. My job is law enforcement and maintaining the peace—not fomenting violence," Lane said.

"Your Honor," Jack said, "it is crucial to our case that Sheriff Lane utter these words. We believe he is one of Mr. Jackson's programmers. He already admitted having fought with him in Vietnam, so he was in the same place at the same time."

"Sheriff Lane," Hodge said, "I am ordering you to repeat the words that Mr. Maine tells you to repeat—just so long as there are no bullets in the chamber of that gun."

Jack rechecked the gun. It was empty. "I can assure the court there are none."

"Mr. Lane, you're instructed to cooperate with Mr. Maine," Hodge ordered.

Lane hesitated. "I won't," he finally said.

"Your Honor," Jack said, "this is not testimonial evidence I'm asking for. It's like a blood sample, fingerprints, or DNA. The Fifth Amendment privilege against self-incrimination only applies to testimony. He has to give us a sample of his voice. He can't take the Fifth."

"I agree, Mr. Maine. Sheriff, you're ordered to repeat the words Mr. Maine has requested," Hodge said.

Lane shifted his feet. What would he do now? How would he stay alive? He wouldn't do what Guteman had done. To play hardball and risk contempt would be his death. The syndicate would kill him tonight in jail. If he played along, he could still walk out of the courtroom a free man.

"Say the following words, Sheriff," Jack said, "'the moon is full.' Then say 'Periscope, you're to pick up that gun over there on the table and blow out Judge Hodge's brains.'"

Perspiration dripped from Lane's underarms into his uniform; a wet moon-shaped crescent grew under each arm. He reached for the canister of water, poured himself a cup of it and took a sip.

"We're waiting, Sheriff," Jack said.

In a monotone, while avoiding eye contact, he repeated the words. Avery's eyes rolled to the top of his head. Periscope emerged. Like a sleepwalker, he moved two steps to the right. He picked up the gun that had already been marked as State's Exhibit One. He then walked to his left to a point directly in front of Judge Hodge. He pulled the trigger. The gun made the sound of a hammer falling on an empty cylinder: CLICK. There were gasps throughout the courtroom. Betty Hardacre began to shriek. Aaron and Rebecca cried. The Hardacre children cried. As they were crying, Avery kept pulling the trigger. He squeezed off one non-existent round after another. He had not finished his task as ordered. Periscope kept pulling the trigger, one CLICK per second. Lane had to stop it.

"The moon is dark," he blurted desperately.

Avery put the gun down and stood in front of the judge. Jack led him back to counsel table. He looked exhausted. This time, the fatal mistake looked to be Lane's.

"Mr. Lane, you have not witnessed the tapes of Mr. Jackson's psychological evaluation, have you?"

"No, I haven't."

"Nor have you heard their content?"

"That's true, Mr. Maine."

"How did you know that the only way to stop Mr. Jackson was to tell him 'the moon is dark'?"

"Because I was sitting in court the other day when a doctor said those were the words that would deactivate Mr. Jackson."

In his years as a trial lawyer, he had never seen such a clever liar, and Jack had seen many. "Who told you that?" Jack asked.

"I witnessed some of Dr. Offen's testimony the other day."

"And, from that testimony, you expect us to believe that you learned to deactivate Mr. Jackson as facilely as you did here?"

"When you're a squadron commander in Vietnam and are responsible for keeping a whole group of men alive, you learn pretty damn fast."

This guy is good—very good, thought Jack. He had more moves than Houdini. "Are you telling us that you never used those words with Mr. Jackson in Vietnam when you used them so perfectly here?"

"That's precisely what I'm telling you, Counsel."

"Why, then, did you leave 'the sky is dark' out of your command?"

"I don't know what you mean, Counsel."

"You know what I mean, Sheriff," Jack said with an edge in his voice. "Only you would know that the command 'the moon is dark' would be enough to stop Mr. Jackson without also mentioning the sky being dark, isn't that correct?"

"I don't know what you mean," Lane shot back.

"I think you do, Sheriff," Jack retorted confidently.

"Objection, argumentative," Hunter said sharply, trying to stop the bleeding.

"Sustained," Hodge ruled.

Jack went back to counsel table to look at his notes. As he did so, the courtroom door swung open and Joe Betts came through it with some papers in his hand. He handed them to Jack. They spoke briefly. Joe had a grin on his face. Jack was deadly serious. He turned again toward the witness as Joe seated himself next to Avery.

"Mr. Lane, your mother's name was Cornelia, was it not?" Jack asked.

"That's correct."

"And your father's name was Harold?"

"That's correct."

"You have already testified that you were born on March 2, 1947, is that correct?"

"Yes."

Jack moved over to the court reporter's table and asked her to mark two documents as Defendant's Exhibits Three and Four. Jack held the first document in his right hand. "I show you what has been marked as Defendant's Exhibit Three, Mr. Lane. Do you recognize it?"

Jack showed it to Lane. Lane refused to answer.

"Let me read it to you, then. Maybe that will refresh your memory. At the top it says, Certificate of Live Birth, Montgomery County, Ohio, March 2, 1947, born to Cornelia and Harold Blaine, a boy named Kranefeld Hubert Blaine. This is your birth certificate, is it not?"

"I don't know."

"You have never seen your own birth certificate, Mr. Lane?"

Lane sat mute.

"When did you change your name to Hugh Lane?"

Everyone waited expectantly for his answer while Lane shifted in his chair and looked around the room.

"Please answer the question, Sheriff," Hodge ordered.

Lane sat mute.

"Perhaps this will refresh your memory. I show you what has been marked Defendant's Exhibit Four," Jack said as he handed Lane the document. "Can you identify it?"

"No," Lane said.

"That's strange. It has your signature right here, doesn't it?"

Lane looked at the document. "I'm not sure," Lane said.

"It's a Petition to Change Name," Jack noted. "It's dated June 15, 1974. It was filed in the Montgomery County Court. The Petitioner was Kranefeld Hubert Blaine and he changed his name to Hugh Lane. That petitioner was you, was it not, Sheriff?"

"I refuse to answer the question."

"I am ordering you to answer the question, Sheriff," Hodge said.

"I'm taking the Fifth, Your Honor."

"Very well," Hodge said, "that is your prerogative. The jury is instructed that the witness has refused to answer the question because he feels to answer it may incriminate him. That is his constitutional right."

The noise in the courtroom was such that Hodge had to pound his gavel. The jury had seen the Sheriff of Montgomery County take the Fifth. He was guilty of something.

"Sheriff Blaine," Jack said, "you programmed Avery Jackson in Vietnam, didn't you?"

"It's Lane, and I take the Fifth."

"You programmed him to kill Sheriff Hardacre, didn't you?"

"Fifth," Lane said.

"Why did you kill Sheriff Hardacre?"

"I didn't, your client did."

"Upon your orders, Sheriff. Isn't that correct?"

"I take the Fifth."

"Sheriff Lane, isn't it true that you're part of an organized crime ring that imports drugs into and through Dayton, and you needed to kill Sheriff Hardacre to keep the ring intact?"

There were more whispers and gasps throughout the courtroom.

"I take the Fifth."

"Move for the admission of Defendant's Exhibits Three and Four, and I have no further questions," Jack announced.

Alec Hunter stood up, slump-shouldered. "No objection. We have no questions, Your Honor. The State of Ohio does not endorse either perjury or criminal behavior."

"The defense rests," Jack announced as Lane sat in the witness box.

"The prosecution rests," Hunter said.

Hugh Lane started to get up. "Please wait right there, Sheriff," Hodge ordered. "I am releasing the jury for lunch at this time. Everyone is ordered to be back here at one-thirty for closing arguments. Do not discuss the case among yourselves or with anyone else," Hodge admonished them again. When the jury had left the courtroom, Judge Hodge said, "Mr. Hunter, you're the district attorney. I am instructing you to decide what charges should be brought against Sheriff Lane. Are you requesting that he be arrested at this time?"

"That would be my request, Your Honor," Hunter mumbled, barely able to stay in the courtroom.

"Court is in recess until one-thirty. Counsel will be ready for closing arguments at that time."

CHAPTER 29

Wednesday, April 21—12 noon

Hank Dorsey refused to further argue a case he saw as without merit. He believed Avery Jackson had been victimized and Lane was behind it. On the way back to the office, Dorsey tried to convince Alec that a plea bargain should be offered to Jackson in order that he not be exposed to a possible life sentence or the death penalty. He informed Alec that if he persisted in going for the death penalty, he would resign. They parted angrily. Alec believed he could still pull out a conviction—maybe not a death sentence, but at least a conviction.

When he got back to the office, Alec sat in his chair trying to marshal his thoughts for the afternoon. He had pulled several files on the Jackson case when Stephanie entered talking on her cell phone. "I can't give a statement to you now," she said to the caller. "The office will have no official position on this until the end of the Jackson trial." She pressed the button to terminate the call. "The media is driving me nuts, Alec. Are you going to go to lunch?" she asked.

"Sorry, I can't do it. I have to do closing argument on the Jackson case."

"I thought Hank was going to close."

"He was, but the case blew up today. I'm going to need you to do some major repairs with the media. Hugh Lane screwed the thing up today worse than Guteman did on the Conley case. He might be behind Hardacre's murder. I want you to deny that we had any knowledge of his culpability."

"So, that's why every reporter in town has called me within the last fifteen

343

minutes. They're all asking how we're going to charge Lane. I had no idea what they were talking about. I told them I would have a statement for them once we talked about the matter," Stephanie said as she put her cell phone down on the corner of his desk to dig her eyeglasses out of her suit pocket.

"Just keep putting them off. I haven't decided what I'll do about Lane. When I do, I'll let you know and you can hold a press conference."

"I know the routine," she said.

"I'll give you a rain check for lunch," offered Alec. "How about tomorrow, after this is over—at the Hilton?" They had not been there for their afternoon trysts for two weeks because of the Jackson trial.

"Fine," Stephanie said as she adjusted her glasses. "There are a number of things we need to talk about. I'll order lunch for us." The moment she agreed, she felt a twinge of anxiety. The thought that that might not be the best place to meet flitted through her mind.

"I need it," Alec said. "I'll be exhausted after this trial. I think I can still pull it out with a strong closing."

"Good," Stephanie said. "I'll leave you to your work."

She turned to walk out of the office, forgetting to pick up her cell phone, which sat next to Alec's stack of files on the Jackson case. She would go across the street to Wendy's for lunch.

She'd been thinking about a lot of things over the two weeks since she'd last been with Alec. She was convinced she needed to break it off. She would wait until after the trial to tell him tomorrow at the Hilton; no sense upsetting him now. She wanted a real relationship—authenticity. Yes, she would tell him tomorrow. She just hoped she didn't lose her job, but she knew she could survive if she did. She just wasn't sure how fragile Alec was under his veil. She hoped he'd be able to take it in stride—he still had a wife at home, maybe he could salvage his relationship with her.

Two blocks away at the office of Maine and Associates, Jack had barricaded himself in his office with a sandwich and a bag of potato chips while he gathered himself for closing argument. Marci was shielding him from all calls. *CBS News* tried unsuccessfully to get an interview with him over lunch.

Defense cases are rarely lost on closing argument, but they're occasionally won. No one will ever forget Johnny Cochran's mantra when closing in the OJ Simpson trial, "If it doesn't fit, you must acquit." Jack didn't know if such an inspiration would come to him. Maybe he was fresh out of rabbits to pull out of his hat. He had only a few minutes to enjoy his unmasking of Hugh Lane. He now had to distill the testimony the jury had seen and heard over the last week into something meaningful. Adrenaline kept him pumped.

Wednesday—1:30 P.M.
Montgomery County District Court

Jack and Marci walked together the three blocks to the courthouse from the office. They said little; Jack's mind was in a whirlwind. When they got to the door, she kissed him. "Good luck, Counselor," she whispered. He gripped her hand, kissed her again and made his way to the courtroom. She sat with Aaron and Rebecca. Even if Avery were convicted, they had the assurance of knowing what had happened to their father. They smiled at him when he was brought in. He smiled back. As Jack suspected, Avery had no recollection of attempting to shoot the judge that morning.

Hank Dorsey was seated at counsel table when Alec Hunter joined him. There was no eye contact or conversation between them—only iciness. Betty Hardacre and her two children were seated in the first row behind Hunter. While the situation had become clearer to Rebecca and Aaron Jackson as the trial progressed, Ashley and Derrick Hardacre's beliefs had become more confused. They were not sure that Avery Jackson should be convicted of their father's death. Hugh Lane was the real shooter. But why? Was it simply because their father had beaten him in the election? There had to be more to it than that, didn't there?

Judge Hodge assumed the bench and ordered the jury brought into the courtroom. "I hope you all had an enjoyable lunch," he said. "We have concluded the testimony. The lawyers will now present their arguments to you. I will then tell you the law you need to apply in reaching your decision. After that, you will retire to the jury room for deliberations. Mr. Hunter, you may proceed," Hodge said.

Alec moved slowly from counsel table to the podium in front of the jury box. The yellow, legal pad he carried was filled with notes and scribbles. He placed it on the podium and looked for a juror with whom to make eye contact. Immediately in front of him was Bill Botelho, the aeronautical engineer. He was bright and very conservative. As the senior white male with the most education, he was destined to be the jury foreman. If Hunter could connect with him, perhaps he could sway the rest of the jurors. When Alec looked at Botelho, he accepted his eyes as well as the eyes of other jurors. Alec Hunter was still in control.

"It is our job," Alec started, "the job the State of Ohio, to prove to you beyond a reasonable doubt that the defendant, Mr. Avery Jackson, killed Sheriff Gene Hardacre and that he did it with premeditation—he intended to do it. We have done that with Rotary Club President Aubrey Shell's, and the Presiding Judge of this county, Carl Kessler's, testimony. We have done it with graphic videotape showing Mr. Jackson killing Sheriff Hardacre.

"This is really a very simple case. The defense has tried to complicate and confuse it by tricking you into believing there is a reasonable doubt as to the defendant's sanity. They've put on evidence—bizarre, psychological evidence that is not to be believed by any right-thinking and intelligent human being. They have brought the CIA and U.S. Government into this. So what? That doesn't detract from the fact that Avery Jackson is a cold-blooded killer. Our experts have told you just exactly what he is—the most cold-blooded, psychopathic killer they have seen.

"What the defense has done is create the illusion that this murder was masterminded by the sheriff of this county. There is one fatal flaw in their theory. They have not been able to show one single, solitary piece of evidence as to why Sheriff Lane would want to kill Sheriff Gene Hardacre, and why he would use a friend of his to do so—not one piece of evidence. Avery Jackson and Hugh Lane are friends. Avery Jackson helped Hugh Lane on his campaign. The defense has shown that Sheriff Lane fought in Vietnam with Mr. Jackson, that he changed his name, and that his fingerprint was on the murder weapon along with the defendant's. I say to you, so what? It was a gun Lane and Jackson had fired together as friends. They have shown that Lane visited his friend, Avery Jackson, in jail without noting his visit. So what? It had been Sheriff Lane's jail for twenty years. They claim Sheriff Lane had a cup of coffee with Mr. Jackson. So what?

"That is what they have proven. Don't let this smokescreen fool you. You are too intelligent. This case has little to do with Hugh Lane. Our office will deal with Hugh Lane later if we find he has acted illegally. This case is about Avery Jackson, a psychopathic overachiever who became a judge and then lost it. It was Avery Jackson who pulled the trigger of this gun—not Hugh Lane.

"Now, you can feel sorry for Avery Jackson all you want. He had a rough time as a kid. All of us have had rough times. That does not make one insane, He may have had a rough time in the service. That does not make him insane and certainly did not give him the right to take the life of another human being. You may or may not believe this bologna about multiple personalities. The defendant might be programmed. That did not give him the right to take the life of our number one law enforcement officer. Don't be led astray by the smokescreens that are being put in front of you. This man is guilty, and we have proved it beyond a reasonable doubt. Insanity for this man is just a cop-out that you, as responsible citizens, cannot allow.

"Now, Mr. Maine will get an opportunity to talk with you, and then I'll be able to have the final word with you."

"Thank you Mr. Hunter," Judge Hodge said. "Mr. Maine, you may proceed."

Jack looked for Calvin Stevens, the lone black-man. He was confident he could make eye contact with him. Calvin looked him in the eye; so did other jurors. He needed every connection with the jury he could get.

"Mr. Hunter speaks of smokescreens. He speaks of Mr. Lane not having a motive to kill Sheriff Hardacre. What Mr. Hunter needs to acknowledge is that through this entire proceeding, he has presented no motive whatsoever for Mr. Jackson killing Sheriff Hardacre—none. It is Mr. Hunter's burden to prove this case beyond a reasonable doubt, and to disprove insanity beyond a reasonable doubt. It is not our burden to prove anything. What Mr. Hunter has done is prove that Mr. Jackson shot Sheriff Hardacre, and that is all. He has not shown premeditation, intent or knowledge on the part of Mr. Jackson as to what he was doing when he fired the bullet that killed Sheriff Hardacre. He has not disproved insanity beyond a reasonable doubt. Instead, we have proved who the real triggerman was—Mr. Hugh Lane. We have done so with hard evidence. We have not used hired guns like Dr. Horde and Dr. Procheska. Dr. Horde was so dishonest that he discounted the very psychological condition within Mr. Jackson that he had been creating for years with the CIA. In fact, the CIA paid for Dr. Horde's testimony here.

"We have proved with competent psychiatrists and psychologists, including a CIA psychologist, Dr. McGinty, that Mr. Jackson was programmed to be a killer in the Army, and that his condition had never been treated afterward. We have proved that Mr. Jackson had no knowledge of what he'd done to Sheriff Hardacre, and that a killer by the code name of Periscope had been programmed into him by the CIA without his knowledge. We know that Hugh Lane, or Kranefeld Blaine, as he was known in the service, was one of his programmers, and that Kranefield Blaine, or Hugh Lane, if you prefer, had coffee with Mr. Jackson the morning of the shooting. Lane's reason for the coffee was to turn Periscope on to kill Gene Hardacre. He told Mr. Jackson the 'moon was full' and to go to the hotel and kill the sheriff. That is what happened, though as yet we don't know why—Mr. Lane took the Fifth Amendment when it came to explaining that to us. We know that Mr. Lane handled the murder weapon and that he probably gave it to Mr. Jackson that morning while they were seated in Lane's Jeep Cherokee. We know that Mr. Lane met with Mr. Jackson in jail and tried to sabotage the psychological evaluation, and did so. We know that Mr. Jackson had no recollection of those meetings, or the killing.

"Mr. Hunter says this is a common sense case. It is a common sense case, but not the way he claims. He is asking you to disregard the facts here and play on your mistrust of the insanity defense. The common sense of this case is that a law professor does not go and kill the sheriff in front of a hundred and fifty people. The common sense of this case is that Mr. Lane used Mr. Jackson because Mr. Lane knew he was a human, loaded weapon that Lane could discharge at any time by chanting the code words, and then giving an order to kill. Was there one of you who doubted what happened in here when Mr. Lane ordered Mr. Jackson to shoot Judge Hodge with those code words? Was there any doubt in your minds who the real culprit was when Mr. Lane ordered Mr. Jackson to stop shooting Judge Hodge by uttering 'the moon is dark'? He slipped up there. That mistake was fatal to Mr. Hunter's case, and to Mr. Lane.

"The common sense here is that Hugh Lane used Avery Jackson as an unwitting weapon to kill Sheriff Hardacre. We can't prove why. All we know is that Sheriff Blaine—I mean Lane—took the Fifth when I asked why.

"Now, let's look at one final thing—the insanity defense. If you should find Mr. Jackson not guilty by reason of insanity, he would go to the state hospital. He would not be released to the streets. You, as jurors, don't need to worry about that, or concern yourselves with it. He may spend the rest of his life there. If you find him guilty of first-degree murder, he will go to prison for life, or be executed.

"The law should punish only those who have knowledge of their crimes. It should not punish those like Mr. Jackson, who didn't know what he was doing, or know right from wrong, when he was doing it.

"The best way for you to look at Mr. Jackson when he killed Sheriff Hardacre is as a sleepwalker. He is like you or one of your children when he or she sleepwalks. Do you or your children remember what you did when you were sleepwalking? Of course not. If you or your children had hurt someone while sleepwalking, would you believe justice was done if you or your child went to jail for life or was put to death? Mr. Jackson was sleepwalking through this killing, just as he was sleepwalking when he killed in Vietnam for the political and military expediency of the United States of America. Mr. Jackson was sleepwalking when he pulled the trigger on Judge Hodge. He had no recollection whatsoever of it. This is a man who didn't know right from wrong, or know what he did *when he was doing it*. The law only holds people responsible for acts they're aware of and know are wrong. It is your duty, therefore, to find Mr. Jackson not guilty by reason of insanity.

"The person who is responsible for this crime is Hugh Lane. You tell Mr. Hunter that it's his job to prosecute Hugh Lane, the real culprit. The only way you can do this is by finding Mr. Jackson not guilty by reason of insanity. That will give Mr. Hunter the message that you, as representatives of the people, demand that justice be done here.

"Thank you, ladies and gentlemen. Now, Mr. Hunter has the final word with you. His burden is so great that he gets two chances to talk to you."

Alec rose and walked to the podium. He knew that Maine had made a powerful argument.

"Things in this country have become far too soft. It is up to you as jurors to stop this nonsense and epidemic of crime that is afflicting us. We have an obvious murderer in the person of Avery Jackson coming before you and saying he didn't know right from wrong when he pulled the trigger of this gun"—he picked up the gun on the evidence table—"and slaughtered Sheriff Hardacre. That is what John Hinckley said when he shot President Reagan. He got away with it. Are you going to let this man," he pointed at Jackson, "Avery Jackson, get away with the murder of Sheriff Hardacre?"

"Think about it. Do you realize how crazy you have to be to not know right from wrong? You have to be like a wild beast, an animal. Do you think Avery Jackson, an intelligent man, a lawyer and college professor, doesn't know right from wrong? He is a con artist, a faker, coming before you trying to deceive you, as he has tried to deceive the mental health people on this case." Hunter looked to the jury. "You don't have doctorates like they did, but you have common sense and the power to stop the insanity of this case. The insanity in this case is not within the defendant. No. The insanity is that Avery Jackson could present such an outlandish defense like this and believe he could fool you as jurors. That is insanity. Don't let it happen. Do your job as citizens and stop this landslide of crime. When you get back to the jury room, use your common sense and do the right thing for Dayton and for the widow of Gene Hardacre. Find the defendant guilty of first-degree murder. Thank you."

Hunter returned to his seat. He and Dorsey made no eye contact.

When Judge Hodge finished reading the law to the jurors, he said, "Now, ladies and gentlemen of the jury, you're finally free to discuss this case among yourselves. In fact, that is your job. When you reach a verdict, knock on the door and the bailiff will bring you into court. If you should have questions, address them to the bailiff who will bring them to my attention."

The trial was over. Jack and Yolanda knew they could say and do nothing more. They were spent. Avery hugged both of them and was taken back to the jail. Yolanda, Aaron and Rebecca would go to the jail to visit Avery. Jack and Marci would go to the office to begin the torturous wait of jury deliberation. The entire defense team included Aaron and Rebecca in their dinner plans later on that evening. Jack would put the tab on his credit card. He and Marci would worry about their financial condition later.

Wednesday—3:30 P.M.
Jury Deliberation Room

The jurors had been supplied with coffee and a mid-afternoon snack of chocolate-chip and macadamia-nut cookies. They ate while picking their jury foreman. Alec Hunter had been correct—Bill Botelho was elected by an eleven-to-one vote. Calvin Stephens was the one dissenter. He wished to be foreman, but had no support. Botelho had been nominated by Vanessa Parker, a society woman from Oakwood. The women agreed with the nomination, as did the younger men. It was a father-thing, and Botelho was white. It just seemed like Botelho should be the leader of the group.

Botelho's first act as foreman was to ask for a straw vote.

"I've never been on a jury before," Bill said, "but I've done a lot of board meetings. What I propose is that we take a vote immediately to see how everyone stands on this. There are three possible votes you can put on your ballot—guilty, not guilty, not guilty by reason of insanity, what the lawyers call NGRI. Write your name and vote on a piece of paper and pass them to me."

Each of the twelve quickly filled out their ballot and passed it to him. He wrote the results on a piece of paper. "There are seven votes for guilty, one not Guilty, and four NGRI. It looks like we have quite a bit of work to do. I propose we go around the table and express our viewpoints. I'll begin." He took a sip of coffee and the final bite of his chocolate-chip cookie. "For me, this is an easy decision. I agree with the district attorney. This insanity stuff is a way of throwing us off course. Jackson is a very smart man. When a smart man kills someone else, he knows what he's doing and intends to do it; it's that simple. I don't give a damn about what the psychiatrists said, or what the CIA guy said about what happened to Jackson. I'm sick and tired of criminals getting off on this insanity stuff. People have to take responsibility for what they do."

The three assembly-line workers all agreed with Botelho. Hansen, DuQuesne and Dubinski each had the concern that Jackson had far more privileges than they did. If this had happened to them, they would all have been convicted and the key thrown away, or "fry," as they put it. Why should they give a break to this lawyer and professor? He was no better than they were. The golf pro, Dunlop, was concerned about letting Jackson go to the state hospital and then the possibility of him being out on the street again soon. He had heard that the doctors at the state hospital did nothing. They would just shoot a little Thorazine or Mellaril in Jackson's ass. It was a revolving door, and Jackson could be on the street again to kill. He thought Jackson ought to go to prison for life. That way the public would be protected. Sheila Parker and Heather Southern agreed with Dunlop, an attractive man who had a popular, weekly golf instruction program on television. They were not about to challenge him. Each of them remembered Betty Hardacre's pain. They could only imagine how it would be for them if their husbands, whom they loved and who supported them, were suddenly killed.

Each of the seven who thought Avery was guilty expressed the feeling that an elected official like Hugh Lane could not possibly have done this murder.

They needed to support and protect their law enforcement people since they were the ones that served and protected them. They resented the fact that a psychologist from Denver would come to Dayton and try to interfere with the law enforcement structure by accusing Sheriff Lane of this. They also didn't believe the CIA would be involved in this sort of activity. What's more, if they were, it didn't give Jackson the right to kill anybody. Alec Hunter had been in office for years, and they needed to believe in him and support him.

The five other jurors listened while the majority spoke. Botelho then asked the first of the NGRI-leaners, April Nunn, an emergency room nurse, to state her position. She talked to them about the effects of acute trauma. She saw it every day. She saw how it terrorized patients, put them into shock and changed their lives. She talked about Patty Hearst and Elizabeth Smart and made the point that people can be brainwashed when they're subjected to overwhelming fright and trauma. She felt great sympathy for Avery Jackson and what he had witnessed. She could only imagine how such mind-control treatment had affected and injured him. Justine French, who had been molested as a child and had just recalled her victimization, was appalled by Hunter and his doctors' insensitivity. For Horde to come in and try to caste doubt on the validity of recovered memories told her that Hunter's entire case was a fraud. She made it clear that it would be a cold day in hell before she would change her position. She was prepared to hold out forever. Arlene Gallegos believed that Jackson had been mistreated in the service. She could only wonder if Avery had been chosen to be a guinea pig because he was black. She pointed out the mistreatment of her brother in the service, the abuse she had suffered as a child and how it had affected her later. Sure, it didn't cause her to commit crimes, but she hadn't endured what Avery Jackson had either. She and Betty Daily were sure Sheriff Lane was dirty. They wouldn't forget how Avery had responded to his commands. They were sure Lane had set Avery up to kill the sheriff. When Lane had commanded him to stop shooting the judge by uttering "the moon is dark," they knew that Lane was the man. Both felt Jackson was insane at the time of the shooting.

Calvin Stevens listened intently as the others spoke. Then he began. "I think Mr. Jackson is not guilty, and that as jurors we must keep our eyes on the ball. The DA has to prove this case beyond a reasonable doubt. I don't think he proved Mr. Jackson knew what he was doing. Not only is he legally insane, but also not guilty. They haven't showed any premeditation by Jackson, or guilty knowledge of the crime. It stands to reason that Lane had a reason to kill Hardacre, not Jackson—Hardacre had just beaten Lane in an election. When the defense attorney, Mr. Maine, compared Jackson's situation to that of a sleepwalker, that made the most sense to me. If you, Mr. Botelho, slugged someone while sleepwalking, would you be guilty of a crime?"

Botelho thought for a moment. "Of course not. But that assumes I was sleepwalking and not faking sleepwalking. I think Jackson was faking. That's what the two psychiatrists said."

"You know," Stevens said, "I could accept your position if there was any *evidence* he was faking. He had no reason to fake anything. He had no reason, at least that we were shown, to kill the sheriff. We know the CIA set Jackson up, we know he was programmed to kill, we know that Lane knew the program, and was a killer himself. He killed those Vietnamese in front of Jackson. He did it without conscience. It only makes sense that Lane could kill Hardacre without conscience. We don't know why, though I've got a guess. Lane had to get rid of him for some reason and had Jackson kill him. Lane's cold-blooded enough to use a friend to do it. The only real psychopath in this case is not Jackson, but Lane. He is one cold son-of-a-bitch. Mr. Botelho and the rest of you, doesn't it mean something to you that Lane took the Fifth?"

None of them could answer.

"In my opinion," Stevens said, "the DA's case was over when Lane took the Fifth. I'm not sending anyone to prison for life when a member of law enforcement takes the Fifth for any reason. I'm with Justine, I will not give in on this if I must sit here for a year. Does anyone disagree with what I'm saying?"

"Yeah, I disagree," Harold Dubinski said. "You're letting the color of your skin influence your vote. You and Jackson are black. You're going to protect a brother, that's the bottom line."

"No, Harold, the bottom line is that you won't listen to the evidence because you're white, and you aren't going to let this nigger go when he killed a white man. You, and the rest of you, don't care what the evidence shows, or how dirty the cops are on this case, you need to preserve the white aristocracy. You can have a sheriff who's a cold-blooded killer and you don't care. And you don't care that the government destroyed Avery Jackson's mind—it was all right to do that to a nigger as far as you're concerned."

Dubinski was on his feet, fists clenched, ready to throw a punch at Stevens.

Stevens just sat there. "People get furious like this, Harold, when they know the person who confronts them is right. I've hit a nerve and you know it. Now, sit down and get your white, racist head out of your ass."

Dubinski started again at Stevens. Dunlop got up and stood in his way. Dubinski backed off.

"I don't think it necessary to talk that way," April Southern said to Calvin.

"It's real," Calvin Stevens replied. "You can go to your country club, play bridge and forget about the fact that our government has done this to another human being. Now, you want to doubly punish him by convicting him of a crime when the dirty, white sheriff of this county wound him up and set him off like a spinning top. And, you know why he did it?" asked Stevens rhetorically.

"Because he could. He's that evil and shameless, and you don't want to acknowledge that the real criminal here is your white sheriff and the people who are protecting him."

"This whole experience is too bizarre to think about," Vanessa Parker said, trying to intervene as the voice of reason before fighting actually broke out. "I believe we need to sleep on it and begin deliberations in the morning when we've all settled down."

"I agree," Botelho said. "I'm just going to have a hard time bringing myself to finding someone not guilty by reason of insanity when he killed someone. I don't care what anyone says. It's just not right."

"Here, here," Will Duquesne and Scott Hansen said.

"I just won't do it," Dubiniski added, "and I don't give a damn what the law is on this insanity shit, what Avery Jackson did was commit murder."

Botelho went to the door and knocked. The bailiff opened the door. "Do you have a verdict already?" he asked.

"Far from it," Botelho said. "We need to go to dinner and then think about this overnight. Things are getting pretty hot in here, and I think we need a break."

"I'll tell the judge," said the bailiff.

CHAPTER 30

Thursday, April 22—9:00 A.M.
Jury Deliberation Room

When the jury returned the next morning to deliberate, Bill Botelho suggested they take another vote. This time April Southern and Vanessa Parker had each changed their votes to NGRI. Calvin Stevens still believed Jackson was not guilty. Dubinski, Botelho, Duquesne, Dunlop and Hansen were holding out for guilty.

They began deliberations again in earnest. By noon, Dunlop had agreed to NGRI. Calvin Stevens realized there was no chance of getting anyone to join him in finding Avery not guilty. He had to agree that Avery did have a mental illness. The vote was now eight-to-four for NGRI. The jurors were taken to lunch by the bailiff. They all hoped they'd have a verdict by the end of the day.

Calvin Stevens had already angered the other white men on the jury who wanted to convict Jackson. He further agitated them after lunch when he said calmly, "We will be here all year unless the white men on this jury re-examine themselves, and their lives, in terms of racial prejudice, beliefs about human vulnerability and mental illness. A couple of guys here have alcoholics in their families, and they're claiming there is no mental illness in their families. You're also in denial about what a criminal Hugh Lane is. It'll be a tall order for you white boys to get real about anything."

"Are you calling us racists?" Dubinski yelled, ready to fight again.

"We're all racists. I'm a racist because I don't trust white people. My dog doesn't trust them either. And I bet your dog doesn't trust black people. Arlene

354

Gallegos is a racist because she obviously doesn't trust white people. Look what the white boys did to her brother in the service." Arlene said nothing, though she agreed with him. "I know you're racists. Bill, Harold, Will, Scott, are you trying to tell me that you trust black people as much as white folks, because if you are, you're full of it right up to your blue and brown eyes."

They said nothing. They knew they didn't trust black people as much as whites.

"Black is just different," Harold said.

"That's right," Calvin said, "and white is different for me. Brown, like Arlene, is different for both of us. It's our job as human beings to own up to it and deal with the inherent mistrust we feel instead of pretending that we aren't racist. We're all racist. O.J. Simpson got off because the jury was made up of a bunch of racists who didn't trust white people. Let's see that we don't do a miscarriage of justice here, like was done there. That's the only way we're going to really deal with the problems between us. Here we have a black man who has been really screwed by white people. The kicker is that these white people used the black man to kill one of their own, a white man. Think about it. Lane's playing you guys for suckers."

None of them said anything. The room was quiet. Botelho suggested another vote. They all agreed to vote again. This time it was ten-to-two for NGRI. Botelho and Dubinski were still holding out. They continued their deliberations. A resolution was looking hopeless.

Thursday—12 noon
The Hilton Hotel, Room 911

As usual, Stephanie arrived at the Hilton first. She knew this would be the last time she would be using the name of Dr. Claryce Fordyke. Part of her was hopeful about her future because she would be extricating herself from the cave of secrecy and deception that was her life since she began her affair with Alec. The other part was very anxious because of her uncertainty about his reaction. There had always been some vital part missing in him, and she didn't trust what that part might be like if he found it.

Her job could also be at stake. She could have gone to Dorsey with the problem she'd discovered, but he hadn't come to work this morning. But . . . maybe Alec would have an explanation.

The problem surfaced yesterday afternoon while Alec was in court giving his closing argument. Stephanie had returned to Alec's office to retrieve the cell phone she'd left on the stack of Jackson files on Alec's desk. As she picked up the phone, the label on the top file caught her attention: *GRAND JURY— HARDACRE.*

She'd looked at its contents only because she knew that Sheriff Hardacre had never been connected with any grand jury investigation.

If he couldn't explain it, she'd have to resign from the office. If he could, she would be relieved. It would be their last lunch together. Perhaps they could celebrate their time together. She would tell him that she was dating another man. It would be all right, she told herself.

When she got to the room, she ordered two luncheon steaks with salads, rolls and butter. Alec had told her he wanted a very dry Martini to celebrate the end of the trial. It arrived along with the food. There was a knock at twelve-thirty. She thought it would be Alec, but it was room service with lunch. She pulled out forty dollars and told the waiter to keep the change. She turned on the television to CNN. There was a story about the Jackson case, the arrest of Sheriff Lane and CIA mind-control projects. That morning people from *Larry King Live, The O'Reilly Factor, Dateline NBC* and *60 Minutes* had called her. She would discuss the media opportunities with Alec. She was sure he would want to be on these shows if he won the trial. There was another knock at the door. It was twelve-forty. She opened it. Alec stood there in one of his best suits. If there was a verdict today, he had to be ready, and he was, physically, but his usual cool, suave demeanor had been replaced by an ashen look. His eyes were distant and fixed. The thought occurred to her he looked like Avery Jackson when he shot Sheriff Hardacre—distant.

"Come in, Alec. What's wrong?"

Alec righted himself. He always seemed to be able to bring out the façade of control in the face of disaster. "Nothing I can't handle. It looks like you're ready to eat," Alec said. "I had something else in mind." He walked over to her and kissed her on the lips and put his tongue in her mouth. She didn't respond. He embraced her and pulled her slowly toward the bed. "I thought we could take care of this business before lunch," he whispered to her. He began to unzip his fly. "I haven't been in your mouth for two weeks, and I am dying for it." He pulled her down on the bed and began pushing her head toward his already hard penis.

It made her angry. She pulled abruptly away. "Our lunch is getting cold, Alec. We have some other things to talk about first." She had promised herself she would not have sex with him this time—he needed to tell her about the file, and she needed to tell him she was breaking off the affair. Sex certainly would be inappropriate. She got off the bed. "Please come over here and eat. I ordered you a Martini." She grabbed the drink and handed it to Alec as he lay on the bed, his penis shrinking, going flaccid.

He put it back in pants but left his zipper open. He guessed he could wait until after lunch. That he was pissed-off was obvious. He sat up and downed half of his Martini with one gulp. There was something urgent, primitive and animal-like about him today. She had not experienced it before. It scared her.

She had second thoughts about confronting him now, but decided to go for it anyway. If she backed down now, she would hate herself. She reached into her briefcase and brought out the file. She opened it. "Alec, I left my cell phone in your office yesterday. I noticed this file when I went back to retrieve it. I could not help but read it."

"What is it?" Alec asked, obviously not remembering the file or its contents.

"It's a record of a meeting you had with Sheriff Hardacre on January tenth."

The look of annoyance was replaced by the ashen, distant look he had only minutes ago. Then his face flamed red. He jettisoned off the bed and grabbed the file from her. "How dare you go through my desk!"

"I was hoping," she said, afraid of him now, "you could explain it to me. It's in your handwriting."

"It's not your business and has nothing to do with the Jackson case."

"Who said anything about the Jackson case, Alec? It says that Sheriff Gene Hardacre came to you on January tenth and informed you that he had uncovered widespread corruption within the sheriff's office and wanted you to convene a grand jury investigation . . . that Sheriff Hardacre had been approached by an informant by the name of Ovanul Hazeltree about organized crime and corruption within the Sheriff's Department, and that Hugh Lane and Guteman were involved."

Hunter said nothing. He was trying to marshal his thoughts.

"Alec, isn't that the dope dealer who killed Burt Porter?" she asked.

Hunter said nothing. He stared at Stephanie, his mind spinning, his eyes wild.

When she looked at him, she knew. "Why didn't you convene the grand jury, Alec?"

Hunter said nothing.

"You are involved in all of this, aren't you, Alec?"

He didn't answer.

"If you weren't, you would have told me about Hardacre's request to convene the grand jury. You just hid it all. The next thing we know, Gene Hardacre is dead, and then Guteman is dead. You even had something to do with setting up Avery Jackson, didn't you?"

Alec stared at Stephanie with cold, hard eyes. "Of course, I had something to do with it," he said with contempt. "Hardacre had to be killed. He was ready to take down a bunch of very powerful people—mobbed-up people out of Chicago and Miami. They needed him killed. I just decided to make the most of the situation by being the one to prosecute his killer. Why the hell do you think we had an in-service on January fifteenth on jury selection?"

"You tell me, Alec."

"Because I didn't want anyone from our office at Rotary Club that day. I didn't want any witnesses to the killing from our office. Otherwise, I might not be able to prosecute Jackson. Witnesses from our office would create a conflict of interest. I knew for a couple of days the killing would happen. Hell, I helped plan it. The problem I have now is much greater. Lane rolled over on me with the Feds yesterday afternoon. He had them on the phone two hours after Hodge forced me to take him into custody. The DEA wants to meet with me this afternoon. They asked me to have a lawyer present. I'll either roll over for them or I'm going to prison. If I roll over, the syndicate will kill me just like they did Jim Rosato. I have nowhere to turn."

"Rosato's part of this?"

"Hell, yes. He knew too much. So did Guteman. They hanged Guteman in the jail. That was no suicide. The best deal I'm going to get out of this is a new ID in a witness-protection program. I could go down for life . . . maybe even get the death penalty," Alec said with a distant calm that belied his desperation.

"When you told me you'd been consulting with outside, business interests for awhile, it really meant you were taking money from organized crime along with Guteman and Lane, didn't it?" She knew now she was no longer safe. She, too, knew too much.

"I have millions stashed away from protecting the syndicate, Lane and Guteman. We fixed cases. They were going to finance me when I ran for the Senate. Jackson's case was the way for me to get out of here, out from under their control and into the Senate."

"If they had financed that, Alec, they would have owned you even more."

"We've got to get out of here."

"*We* . . .?"

"We're going to walk out of here, go straight to my car and fly to Nassau. I've got a lot of the money hidden there. It's our money now," Alec said.

"Alec, please tell me you didn't have anything to do with Gene Hardacre's death," Stephanie pleaded, willing to be fooled.

"Of course, I did. After Hardacre came to me, we decided we had no choice but to kill him; the only question was how. Lane had the answer with this mind-control hocus-pocus. The syndicate in Chicago loved it. The Manchurian Candidate thing looked perfect. I wanted it because I saw it as a way to get out of the DA's office. I wanted more from my career. It's my life. I no longer want to deal with murderers and scumbags every day."

"Alec, listen to yourself. Can't you see you're one of them?"

Hunter's eyes rolled in his head. "I'm not one of them!" he shot back.

Stephanie just looked at him, knowing she was dealing with a crazy person. He was dangerous—a threatened, trapped animal.

"Let's go," Alec ordered her. His eyes were strange—primitive.

"Alec, I can't go anywhere. I can't just leave my daughter."

He shot off the bed. "We're walking out of here, Stephanie. When you get to Nassau, you'll love it," he said in a low, cold, demanding voice so as not to draw attention to the room. He grabbed Stephanie hard by the left arm. She saw white. When he pinched her like that—controlling her—it ignited all the pent-up rage she had for Alec and her ex-husband, who had controlled her, used and discarded her. She got up from the table and slapped him so hard with her right hand that it sounded like a small firecracker exploding.

His mother had done that to him when he was a boy. He had always been humiliated by it, but could never hit her back as much as he had wanted to. He had hated her for it. He saw red, then white. The blood rushed to his cheek. "You stupid bitch." He took both hands and began to strangle her. The table went over, plates, silverware, steaks and salads flying against the wall and onto the floor. She attempted to knee him in the groin. She scored only a partial hit. It only served to enrage him more. He maintained his hold on her. He pushed her over. "I'll kill you, bitch, I'll kill you," he kept whispering in a voice that said he meant it.

Her eyes began rolling up in her head. She could get no oxygen. She felt herself starting to lose consciousness. She grasped frantically for anything on the floor with which to hit him. She found a steak knife. She grasped it blade first, cutting her hand on the serrated edge. She was able to switch it around and swung it with all her force into the side of his face.

He screamed. "Now you're dead, bitch," he muttered as the blood flowed down his cheek. He tried to grab her arm and missed. She had one more chance. She swung again with all her power and caught him with a slash on the left side of his neck. The blood spurted out in massive amounts with each beat of his heart, propelled to the wall with each throb. He fell on top of her. The hot blood spurted onto her face and into her blonde hair. His breathing quickened. He was gurgling as the blood ran into his cut trachea. She had cut his jugular vein and windpipe. He was suffocating. He gasped for breath like the dying animal he was. She was finally able to get him off her.

She righted herself in shock, breathing rapidly. She leaned against the wall. His breathing became more frantic, the gurgling deeper . . . then it slowed. Within a minute, it stopped. His eyes remained open, staring at her; he still terrified her. She felt her neck; it was dripping with blood. She could feel the burning red of scratch marks on it. She sat there a minute. Her purse was on the floor. She reached in it, found her cell phone and called 911.

CHAPTER 31

The bustling around the court was intense. The details of Alec Hunter's death were sought like pieces of precious gold and diamonds. Hank Dorsey had promised a press conference after the hearing in Judge Hodge's court. Only the prosecution, defense, Judge Hodge and the families knew the purpose of the hearing. At counsel table sat Hank Dorsey and Stephanie Marshall for the district attorney. Jack and Yolanda appeared with Avery Jackson for the defense. Avery's family, as well as Gene Hardacre's, and the media were present.

When the jury was seated Judge Hodge said, "Mr. Foreman, has the jury reached a verdict?"

Bill Botelho rose, "No, Your Honor," he said. "We are hopelessly deadlocked."

"Very well, then, you've been deliberating for three days. I'm going to declare a mistrial. You may remain seated, or take your leave now with the thanks of the court for the civic duty you have performed on a very difficult case." Not one juror left.

"Mr. Dorsey, do we have a disposition in this case?" Judge Hodge asked.

"Yes, we do, Your Honor," Hank said.

The jurors looked at one another. There was a plea bargain. They had nearly come to blows, and now the matter was being resolved this easily? Why couldn't this have been done sooner? The jury and gallery were hanging on every word.

"The People would add an additional count of negligent assault, a class three misdemeanor carrying up to one year in jail. If the defendant will enter a no contest plea to that charge, the People will move to dismiss Count One, Murder in the First Degree with Specifications for Death Penalty," Hank Dorsey said. "Additionally, Your Honor, the People will agree to a jail sentence of a hundred and four days, the period of time Mr. Jackson has already done in the Montgomery County Jail. Furthermore, the defendant will be on probation for two years with a condition that he undergo psychotherapy with a mental health professional experienced in treating trauma. Finally, we agree that Mr. Jackson is pleading to an offense that does not constitute moral turpitude and that this offense should have no effect on his ability to practice law. Ms. Marshall and I agree to appear before the Ethics Committee of the Bar to see that his license is not affected."

"Mr. Maine, is that your understanding of the plea bargain?"

"It is, Your Honor," Jack said. "As the court is aware, Mr. Jackson has no recollection of the events that brought him to court. He is therefore entering a no-contest plea."

"How then, Mr. Jackson, do you plead to the charge of negligent assault?"

"No contest, Your Honor," Avery said.

"Very well, sir. The plea is accepted. You need to report to the Probation Department and seek mental health treatment for the psychological damage that has been done to you. I wish to apologize to you for the People of Ohio for what has been done to you, sir. I hope you can find peace. You are free to go. Court is in recess." Hodge left the bench.

There was a crush of media around counsel table. Avery answered the mundane questions: no, he wasn't sure what he would do; he hoped he could get his job back; maybe he could practice law again; he would have to evaluate things.

Stephanie Marshall had no comment about her ordeal with Alec Hunter. Hank Dorsey said that no charges would be filed against her. A determination was made that she had acted in self-defense. Stephanie would be taking a leave of absence from the office to evaluate her options. She felt the need to be in court today. She had told the police and Dorsey of Alec's complicity in the killing of Gene Hardacre, as well as the murders of Burt Porter, Guteman, Hazeltree and Rosato. It was a healing thing for her. Yes, Sheriff Lane would be prosecuted to the fullest extent of the law. However, he now was in the custody of the federal authorities, whose jurisdiction was paramount over the state's.

Hank Dorsey would just say the interest of justice demanded this disposition. He had to be careful about apologies. Although he wouldn't breathe a word to the press, he knew his office as well as the sheriff's office, had liability for what they had done to Avery Jackson. He had already contacted their insurance carrier and asked them to contact Jack Maine to reach a quiet settlement.

After the media left, Betty, Ashley and Derrick Hardacre approached Avery. Betty shook his hand. They hugged each other and both cried, saying they were sorry. Ashley and Derrick Hardacre shook Avery's hand. What was a bitter split two weeks ago was now a healing rapprochement. Rebecca and Aaron Jackson shook hands with Ashley and Derrick Hardacre. Hatred and division had turned to understanding and alliance. Rebecca and Aaron hugged their dad. They had him back and never wanted to lose him again.

EPILOGUE

Friday— 6:00 P.M.
The Kings Table Restaurant

Jack, Marci and Joe sat in their booth at the King's Table. Champagne was on the house. They were waiting for Yolanda to join them. When she arrived, she was hand-in-hand with Avery Jackson. They drank, toasted one another and ordered.

"Looks like you two are an item," Marci said to Yolanda.

"We've been an item for awhile now—as much of an item as we could be when half of us was in the county jail. I think Avery will need a place to stay tonight. I've offered him my place." Yolanda winked.

"There are still two questions none of us knows the answer to," Jack said.

"What are they?" Avery asked.

"How did Lane get your gun and why didn't you remember that Hugh Lane's name in the service was K. Blaine?"

"I don't know. I hope to figure that out in my treatment."

"The sky is dark for that information, Avery?" Jack asked with a grin on his face.

"I guess you could say that. He conned me somehow. The question I have for you is how I'm going to be able to pay for all this, Jack?"

"Well, you have civil suits against Montgomery County and the United States of America that I'd be interested in taking on."

"Sure. I figured I'd be spending the rest of my life in prison or a mental hospital," Avery said.

Marci took a sip of champagne, smiled and said, "An adjuster for Professional Risk Management called today. They want to meet with Jack concerning what they referred to as 'the quiet settlement' of all claims against the county. A lawyer also called us from the U.S. Treasury Department discussing claims that may be asserted against the Central Intelligence Agency. He asked that we be discreet. And, there was a call just before we came over here from Betty Hardacre talking about a wrongful death suit on behalf of her and her children."

Everyone smiled and then toasted each other.

"It looks like Jack Maine and Associates might last for awhile," Yolanda said. "I really didn't want to return to the public defender's office."

"Me either," Jack said.

"And I didn't want to go back to selling cosmetics. Maybe we can pay our credit card bill now," Marci said.

"The question I have," Marci asked, "is who was Hardin Long?"

"Don't know. Probably never know," Joe said.

"He's like Bob Woodward's Deep Throat-a person who changed the course of history," Jack added. "Maybe we'll find out someday."

The TV on the bar across from Jack's table switched from a Cincinnati Reds' game to the news. "Look," Marci said, "there's that phony group home and pictures of Lane and Hunter."

They all looked at the TV.

The newscaster began with the lead story. "In another bizarre twist on the Avery Jackson murder case, a local group home for children, Experiences in Growth, was shut down by the Drug Enforcement Administration as part of a money-laundering scheme for organized crime. Also arrested in connection with it were alleged organized crime figures, Marshall Conn and Frank Newton, in Chicago." The screen shifted to Conn and Newton being led out of their offices to a police car. "They are being charged under the RICO Act prohibiting racketeering and organized crime. They are alleged to be responsible for the deaths of Sheriff Gene Hardacre and prominent attorneys, Burt Porter and James Rosato. Also alleged to have been involved in the drugs, money laundering and murder scheme, were long-time District Attorney Alec Hunter and Montgomery County Sheriff Hugh Lane. Lane is apparently cooperating with authorities and is being held in the county jail. Hunter was killed Friday in self-defense by former lover and District Attorney Stephanie Marshall."

"Bastards got what was coming to them," Joe added as he flipped a bug on the table in front of them. "We found another one today in the office under the desk. Let's just hope it's the last."

Jack patted under his arm to see if his gun was there. It was.

AFTERWORD

Documents recently released pursuant to the Freedom of Information Act have revealed that in the 1950s, as a response to the political pressures of the Cold War, the United States, through the CIA, developed top secret, mind-control projects. They were called ARTICHOKE and BLUEBIRD, and the subjects they used had no idea they were being exploited; they were unaware of their participation. In subsequent years, additional mind-control projects were instituted called MKULTRA and MKSEARCH. The goal of these projects was to create programmed robots to carry out military and spy missions with no recollection of what they had done.

Ironically, *The Manchurian Candidate,* starring Frank Sinatra, was up for an Oscar at the same time the government was moving at full speed to create multiple-personalitied test subjects. In 2004, a remake of *The Manchurian Candidate*, starring Denzel Washington and Meryl Streep, was released. Again, the public thought the whole concept was too fantastic to be believed and purely fictional. It wasn't. Unfortunately, the remake never emphasized that it had a basis in fact.

The released CIA documents reveal the CIA used LSD, scopolamine, sodium amytal, hypnosis, sensory deprivation, electro-convulsive shock therapy and brain electrode implants to create dissociative conditions. The top psychiatrists and psychologists in America were given security clearance to implement these techniques. They did so in violation of their ethical responsibilities under the Hippocratic Oath, and their duty to do no harm.

The characters and content of *Proof Evident* are wholly fictional. The concepts, however, are not. There are likely still Manchurian Candidates among us as the result of these projects, and we have no reason to think that our government is not still creating them.